CATHY

Titles available in this series

Yannis
Anna
Giovanni
Joseph
Christabelle
Saffron
Manolis
Cathy

CATHY

Beryl Darby

ISBN 978-0-9554278-7-9

Printed and bound in Great Britain by
MPG Books Group, Bodmin and King's Lynn

First published in the UK in 2011 by

JACH Publishing
92 Upper North Street, Brighton, East Sussex, England BN1 3FJ

website: www.beryldarbybooks.com

For Philip (Jack) who loved
to tell make believe
stories to his children.

Author's Note

All the characters in this novel are entirely fictitious. Any resemblance to actual persons, living or dead, is entirely coincidental.

The previous book about Manolis the fisherman, who first appeared in *Yannis*, related what happened to him during the Second World War, when the Germans and Italians occupied Greece, and takes his story up to 1953.

Although *Manolis* was the seventh book to be published in the continuing saga, it does not actually follow *Saffron* in the overall timescale. It was written really at the insistence of many readers who wanted to know more about Manolis and his activities. This book, *Cathy*, is the sequel to *Manolis*.

1944 – 1946

Basil landed at Southampton when the ship bringing him from Crete docked. He had spent most of the voyage in the cabin he shared with three other men, his face turned to the wall, not sharing in their company. Now he wandered bemused down the gangplank and looked around. What was he supposed to do?

'Over there, mate.' The man indicated with a jerk of his thumb and Basil walked slowly towards the building.

Once inside he completed the formalities and was directed to the Red Cross room. There a cup of tea was placed before him and he sat staring at it morosely.

'You haven't drunk your tea.' A young woman stopped by the table.

'It's cold,' muttered Basil.

'I'll fetch you another.'

Before he could refuse the offer, she had taken the cup and made her way to the counter, picking up a freshly poured beverage and returned to Basil.

'There you are. That one is nice and hot.'

'I don't want it.'

'We haven't any coffee.'

Basil shrugged.

'Is there something you would like that I can get you?'

Basil shook his head.

The woman slid into the seat opposite him. 'Are you waiting for someone to meet you?'

'No.'

'Where are you planning to go?'

Basil raised his eyes for the first time. 'Wales, I suppose.'

'You have relatives there?'

'Maybe.'

'Drink your tea, then I'll show you where you can get a rail pass for your journey.'

'A pass? Don't I have to pay?'

The woman shook her head. 'Returning combatants are given a free rail pass to travel to their home town. Many of them wouldn't have any money and we can only accommodate the truly homeless here. Even then, we try to find them somewhere to live as soon as possible. We couldn't cope with the numbers otherwise.'

Basil finally picked up his cup and took a sip. It was a long time since he had drunk a cup of tea and he was not at all sure if he liked the taste. He pushed the cup away.

'Show me where I have to go.'

He followed the volunteer across the room and he added himself to the queue of men waiting patiently.

'You shouldn't be too long. They'll give you directions to the station. There'll probably be a bus going there soon. Have you got your luggage?'

'I haven't any luggage.'

'Nothing?'

Basil shook his head and the volunteer frowned again. 'Maybe I should take you to the Red Cross supplies before you get your pass. They can kit you out with the basics.'

Basil stood in line waiting to be given a razor, comb, toothbrush, toothpaste, face flannel, a small piece of soap and a thin towel and a bag in which to place the items. To his surprise three one pound notes were placed in his hand along with a temporary ration book.

'What's this for?' he asked.

'Everyone is given a small amount. Enough to cover a bed for a week. You'll need to hand over your ration book wherever you stay. Sign there.' The man pointed to the place on the paper and Basil dutifully signed his name.

To Rebecca's surprise, two weeks later Basil walked into the Red Cross Centre again. He sat down at an empty table and seemed uncertain what he should do next.

'I'll go,' she said to her companion at the counter and poured a fresh cup of tea.

Rebecca sat down opposite Basil and passed the cup to him. 'Hello. I am right, aren't I? You were here a couple of weeks ago, weren't you?'

Basil looked at her. She was vaguely familiar. He nodded.

'My name's Rebecca. Would it help to talk?'

Basil hesitated. He had not held a conversation with anyone for a considerable length of time. He had talked to the solicitor when he had found out his aunt had died and he had inherited her house and a sizeable amount of money. He had talked again with the estate agent as he arranged to have the house placed on the market. He had then returned to the Red Cross Centre as he did not know where else he could turn for help.

'What about?' he asked finally.

'Whatever you wish. English people always discuss the weather.'

'It's damp.'

'And you are used to somewhere warmer?'

'Not always. We nearly froze in the mountains.'

'What were you doing there?'

'Whatever was needed.'

Rebecca was not going to find out anything more about this strange man by asking questions about his activities during the war.

'What do you plan to do now you've returned?'

Basil shrugged. 'I don't know.'

'What work did you do before the war?'

'I trained as a teacher.'

'You're fortunate. You can always go back to that. Teachers are always needed.'

'I don't like teaching and children don't like me.'

'So what else could you do?'

Basil shrugged again and did not answer.

'Have you always been so morose? If you smiled you could find the children you taught did like you.'

'I have nothing to smile about.'

Rebecca rose to her feet. 'I lost my father to cancer three years ago and my older brother is a prisoner of war in Japan. Our house was bombed and my mother and younger brother were found dead in the rubble. My fiancé was in the air force and didn't return after a mission. I have nothing to smile about either, but I try not to inflict my unhappiness on others.'

She walked away, feeling close to tears, leaving Basil alone, staring at his cup of tepid tea. He pushed it to one side, slopping it onto the table and walked out of the building. Rebecca looked after him in annoyance. If he ever returned she would not make any effort to help him a second time.

Basil booked into a small hotel and dutifully handed over his ration book. What was he going to do? He had used all his savings before leaving Crete. The money he had inherited and the eventual sale of his aunt's house would not be enough to enable him to live without working for the remainder of his life. That reminded him that he should advise the estate agent who was handling the sale of his aunt's house of his address. He would not want to miss a sale because he could not be found. He sighed. That would mean he had to purchase some writing paper and envelopes, then find a post office. He could do that tomorrow.

He considered his options. He certainly did not want to return to teaching again, farming in England was totally different from

Greece, and there would be no call for archaeology for some considerable time. His only accomplishment was speaking fluent Greek and he doubted there would be any need for that in the foreseeable future. He had walked past the Labour Exchange and he had no intention of joining the queue of despondent men standing outside. Tomorrow he would have to buy a newspaper and see if any work was being advertised that he would be capable of doing.

He sat in the communal lounge at the hotel and switched on the radio. It had seemed so important to hear the news a few months ago, now he felt disassociated from whatever else was happening in the world. Fighting was still taking place in Burma, the Philippines and Malaysia. The Japanese were refusing to surrender. What was it the girl had said; her brother was a prisoner of war with the Japanese? He had seen the treatment meted out to the Cretans and allied troops who had been unfortunate enough to be captured by the Germans, but it was rumoured that the Japanese were merciless. Basil's conscience stirred. He would have to return to the Red Cross building tomorrow and apologise to her.

Basil looked around. He could not see the volunteer anywhere. He wandered over to where a man appeared to be in charge of the tea counter. He held out a cup to Basil.

Basil shook his head. 'Is Rebecca around?'

'Not today. She only comes in on Wednesday afternoons.'

Basil stood there. If he had to wait a week before seeing her he knew he would change his mind about apologising.

'Half day at the shop,' he explained when Basil showed no sign of moving.

'Where does she work?'

'Edwards. Newsagent down the road.'

Basil nodded and made for the door.

'Never heard the word "thank you",' he heard the man grumble to his back.

Basil walked down the road until he saw the dimly lit shop. He walked inside and thumbed through the newspapers on sale, finally selecting one that appeared to have some jobs advertised. He walked over to the counter, the pennies in his hand.

'Is Rebecca around, please?'

''Oo wants ter know?'

'I do.' Basil glared at the man. 'I won't keep her from her work for more than a moment.'

The shopkeeper glared back, but dropped his eyes first. 'Becca,' he shouted. 'Yer wanted.'

'I've just put the potatoes on to boil,' Rebecca called back.

'Someone ter see yer.'

Rebecca's face lit up for a moment in the hope that it was her brother; then she just looked puzzled when she saw Basil standing there.

'I came to apologise,' he said quietly. 'I forget other people have suffered as much as I have.'

He turned to go, the newspaper tucked beneath his arm.

''Ere, you 'aven't paid fer that.'

Basil turned back and handed the man the coins.

'Just a minute.' Rebecca walked over to Basil's side of the counter. 'I shall be at the Red Cross Centre on Wednesday afternoon if you want a cup of tea.'

Basil nodded and walked out of the shop.

Basil scanned the newspaper. There were very few jobs advertised and those that were seemed to be asking for bricklayers, roofers or plasterers. He sighed. He had to do something. He realised that part of his melancholy stemmed from boredom. He needed to occupy his mind. It seemed he would have no alternative but to apply for a teaching position and hope he was able to enjoy the work a little more this time.

He cursed with frustration that he had not bought the notepaper and envelopes. That would mean going out again. He looked longingly at his sheepskin jerkin. The strange looks he had received whilst wearing it with his baggy black trousers and long boots made him reluctant to wear it. He shrugged himself into the thin, second hand coat he had purchased for a few shillings from the Red Cross depot and left the hotel. The raw wind made him shiver and something damp and cold was stinging his face. He realised he must find out how he could get hold of some clothing coupons and buy himself some warmer clothing to wear.

It was nearly dinnertime, and as he walked down the street, he saw the various shops placing their signs on the door advising their customers they would be closed for an hour. He quickened his pace, hoping the newsagent would still be open.

Rebecca was putting the sign in place as he arrived. 'Just in time,' she smiled, inwardly feeling aggrieved. She had been looking forward to the shepherd's pie she had made that morning, now it would probably have to be reheated, and it never tasted as good then. 'What can I get for you?'

'Some notepaper and envelopes, please.'

Rebecca nodded and reached into a drawer below the counter. 'Applying for jobs?' she asked.

'No. I need to tell the estate agent where I'm staying.'

Rebecca raised her eyebrows. 'Are you buying a property?'

'No. How much do I owe you?'

'A shilling.'

Basil felt in his pocket and drew out ten pence. He pushed it back again and opened his wallet, taking out a crisp, white five pound note.

Rebecca's eyes opened wide. 'I can't change that. I've never even seen one before!'

'Where can I get some change?'

'I don't know. You'd probably need to go to the bank. They're down on the High Street.'

Basil nodded. 'I'll come back when you're open again.'

'There's no need for that. Give me the ten pence. I'll put two pence in the till to make it right and you can call in again tomorrow to pay me back.'

'I'd rather come back later. I don't like owing money.'

Rebecca smiled at him. 'I trust you. Besides, it's horrible out there now. They say it might snow tonight.'

Basil looked out through the shop window. 'That reminds me; I wanted to ask where I could get some clothing coupons.'

'You'll have to go to the Town Hall. They'll be closed for dinner now.' Rebecca hesitated. 'Why don't you stay here and have a bit of dinner with me? You could go to the Town Hall and Bank on your way home. Save you going out a second time.'

Basil looked at her in surprise. 'What about your boss?'

'He's not my boss. I'm just staying here whilst things get sorted out. He's an old friend of my father and he said I could have a room for free if I cooked his meals and took a turn in the shop.'

'He won't be very pleased if I eat his dinner.'

'He's already eaten. He's gone off to the pub for an hour. He likes to have a pint with his friends.'

'So I shall be eating yours?'

Rebecca shook her head. 'There's plenty for two. Come into the back room and take your coat off.'

Basil felt his resistance leaving him. He had been chilled to the marrow during his brief walk. It reminded him of the days he had spent in the mountains. There he had been forced to shelter in a cave with only a small fire to sit beside and a blanket to wrap around himself, suffering the same as the other men.

'If you're sure?'

'Come on through.' Rebecca opened the door to the back room. 'Take your coat off and have a seat by the fire. I'll not be a minute.'

Basil stood before the small, miserable, fire and rubbed his cold hands together. He now debated the wisdom of accepting the invitation. When the shop owner returned he could object strongly to the girl entertaining a man whilst he was out.

Rebecca opened a precious tin of marrowfat peas to

supplement the portions of cabbage and carrots she had saved for herself. She divided the shepherd's pie on to separate plates, selecting one that had only a small chip for Basil, and added the vegetables, collected a second set of mismatched cutlery from the drawer and carried everything to the table.

'Come and sit down. You start whilst I stoke that fire up a bit.' She busied herself with the poker, making the embers glow and placed a lump of coal on top of them.

Basil waited until she was seated also, then picked up his fork and allowed himself to take a mouthful. 'You're a good cook,' he remarked.

'Thank you.' Rebecca accepted the compliment. They ate in silence, Rebecca racking her brains to find a topic of conversation. It was Basil who spoke first as he swallowed the last of his peas.

'How long are you staying here?' he asked.

Rebecca shrugged. 'Mr Edwards has said I could stay until things get sorted out.'

'What things?'

'My mother hadn't made a will. That means that now she's dead everything goes to my older brother. He's in a prison camp somewhere and we don't know if he'll come back.' Rebecca's eyes misted over and her lip trembled. 'Until we hear for certain,' she swallowed, avoiding the word "dead", 'I can't touch anything.'

'Have you always worked in a shop?'

Rebecca shook her head. 'My father was a postman and I decided I'd like to work in a post office. I hadn't been training long when war broke out and I left to join the WAAF's – Women's Auxiliary Air Force,' she explained as she saw Basil frown. 'After the bombing I was given some compassionate leave. I have to return after Christmas.'

'Will you go back to the post office after the war?'

'I doubt there'll be a place for me. I hadn't finished my training and probation. All the men who return will be looking for work and I'm sure they'll be given priority over me.'

'What will you do then?'

Rebecca shrugged. 'I don't know. If Sam comes back I may have to look after him until he gets back on his feet.'

'Sam?'

'My older brother.'

'Wouldn't Mr Edwards keep you on?'

Rebecca shook her head. 'The shop isn't really busy enough for two people. Besides, his son will be demobbed eventually, then he'll need my room back and Barry can give him a hand in the shop.' She collected up their plates and walked into the kitchen, depositing them beside the sink and returning with two small bowls of stewed apple.

'I'm sorry there's not very much,' she apologised.

Basil pushed his bowl towards her. 'I don't like apple,' he lied. 'You have it.'

'Are you sure? Had I known this morning you were coming for dinner I could have made something different.'

'It was kind of you to ask me to stay.'

'What are you planning to do for Christmas?'

Basil looked at her puzzled. 'I haven't thought about it.'

'It's only four days away. Come and have dinner with us. It won't be very exciting. We'll listen to the King's speech; then I might go for a walk when I've washed up. You don't want to spend it alone.'

'I'm sure Mr Edwards wouldn't want me around.'

Rebecca pulled a face. 'Mr Edwards is not the best of company. He'll probably just go to sleep in his chair. He does most evenings when he's listened to the news. Then he turns the radio off. I'd like to listen to some of the music they play, but he says it's rubbish and not worth wasting the battery.'

'You don't have a radio of your own in your room?'

'I told you, our house was flattened. There was nothing to be salvaged.' Rebecca sighed. 'If only it had happened during the day. Mum would have been at work and Davey would have been at Tech. He wanted to be a draughtsman.'

‘What work did your Mum do?’

‘Cleaning at the Town Hall. It was all she could get after Dad died.’ Rebecca looked at the clock on the mantelshelf. ‘I’d better get washed up. Another fifteen minutes and I’ll have to open the shop again.’

Basil followed her into the kitchen and picked up a cloth. ‘I’ll dry for you.’

Rebecca flashed him a quick smile. ‘You don’t have to. I just like to have it done by the time Mr Edwards comes back.’

‘What do you do with yourself when you’re not cooking or looking after the shop?’

‘I read or go for a walk. Bit of washing and mending. What about you? What do you do when you’re not writing letters?’

Basil frowned. ‘Writing letters?’

‘You bought some notepaper and envelopes. I presume you are going to write some letters.’

‘Only one. I have to let the estate agent know where I’m staying.’

‘Are you buying somewhere to live?’

‘No. I’m selling my aunt’s house in Wales.’

‘Don’t you want to live there?’

Basil shook his head. ‘Unless I want to go down the mines there’s very little work in Wales.’

‘Have you seen any jobs advertised that would suit you?’

‘Not yet.’ Basil replaced the tea towel. ‘I should go before Mr Edwards comes back. I won’t forget I owe you two pence.’ He walked back into the living room and picked up his damp overcoat, forcing his arms back into the sleeves. ‘Thank you for dinner.’

‘You will come for dinner on Christmas Day, won’t you?’

‘I’ll think about it.’

‘Let me know tomorrow. I’ve managed to order a joint from the butcher and I can get a few extra vegetables.’ Rebecca unlocked the shop door and turned the sign to indicate that it was once more open for trade.

'What was 'e doin' 'ere?'

'Buying some notepaper.' Rebecca remembered she had not placed the two pennies in the till. 'You don't mind, do you, Mr Edwards, but I've invited him to come for Christmas dinner.'

'Why? You sweet on 'im?' He glanced at her keenly.

'No,' Rebecca shook her head. 'He just seems so lonely and unhappy.'

''E could go ter the Red Cross Centre.'

'Would you want to go there for Christmas Day?'

Mr Edwards looked at her sourly. 'You're doin' the cookin'; just make sure there's enough.'

Basil gave one of his rare smiles. 'That was very good, Rebecca. I appreciate you asking me to share your dinner with me, Mr Edwards.'

'You can smoke if you like.' Mr Edwards took out his packet and offered one to Basil.

Basil shook his head. 'I had to give up some years ago and never saw much point in starting again. Thanks all the same.'

'I've just got time to wash up before the King's speech,' smiled Rebecca. 'I'll do that then bring you both a cup of tea.'

Basil rose. 'I'll dry up for you.'

'There's no need. I've already done the saucepans, so it won't take long.'

'If you're sure?'

Rebecca nodded and picked up the plates. 'You could take the cloth off and fold it up for me.'

By the time Mr Edwards had smoked two cigarettes Rebecca had returned with a pot of tea. 'Put the radio on, Becca. It's just abaht time.'

Rebecca obeyed and they sat in silence listening to the King's speech, followed by another from Montgomery.

'Yer can turn that orf now,' ordered Mr Edwards. 'Nuthin' else on werf list'nin' to.'

'Well,' said Rebecca brightly. 'They both sounded positive that the war would be over soon.'

Mr Edwards snorted. 'What do they know abaht it? They're not out there. They're sittin' sumwhere warm an' comf'table. Bet they 'ad more for their lunch than we did.'

'Montgomery has been in Egypt fighting,' protested Rebecca.

''Is idea of fightin' would be ter sit be'ind a desk an' tell uvvers ter risk their lives.' Mr Edwards took another cigarette from his packet. 'Aren't I right?' He turned and looked at Basil.

Basil shrugged. 'I don't know. I wasn't in the army.'

'What was yer in?'

'It was a different organisation.'

Mr Edwards looked at him suspiciously. ''Aven't yer bin fightin' fer yer country?'

Basil sighed deeply. 'Yes.'

Rebecca looked anxiously at the two men; the situation had suddenly become tense. 'Shall we go for a quick walk, Basil? It's quite bright out.'

'If you want. I won't be a moment.' Basil left the room and walked into the shop, returning with a parcel in each hand. He handed a bag to Mr Edwards. 'I understand from Rebecca that you enjoy a pint. I hope I've chosen the right brand.'

Mr Edwards pulled a bottle from the bag and looked at the label. He nodded. 'I like that one. Thanks.'

'Rebecca, this is for you.' Basil handed her a box with a carrying handle and her eyes widened in surprise.

'Whatever is it?'

'Open it up. Don't damage the box. You'll need it.'

Carefully Rebecca removed the flaps of the box to reveal a radio with a carrying handle. She pulled it out with a delighted smile on her face. 'Oh, Basil! Is it really for me? I haven't anything for you.'

Basil shrugged. 'I don't expect anything. I remembered our conversation the other day and thought it could come in useful.'

Rebecca frowned. 'It must have been terribly expensive. I can't accept anything that cost so much.'

'It wasn't that much. Make sure you keep the box; then you'll have something to carry it in when you go back to the WAAFs.'

'Are you sure, Basil?'

'I wouldn't have bought it if I hadn't wanted to give it to you.'

Rebecca blushed, she felt rebuked. 'Thank you. I really do appreciate it. It was very kind of you.' She placed it on the table and turned it on. Bing Crosby was singing and she looked at Basil with laughter in her eyes when she saw the look on Mr Edwards's face. 'I shall enjoy it so much,' she said.

'I 'ope yer not thinkin' of playin' that darn 'ere. If yer want ter listen ter rubbish it'll 'ave ter be in yer room, turned darn quiet, like.'

'I promise I'll not disturb you.' Rebecca turned the radio off. 'I'll take it upstairs with me now and get my coat.'

Mr Edwards turned to Basil as Rebecca left the room. 'Wot yer give 'er sumthin' expensive like that fer? You sweet on 'er?'

Basil shook his head. 'I happened to know that she would like one and I could afford it.'

'Mister Moneybags,' grumbled Mr Edwards beneath his breath.

Basil ignored him and took his coat from the hook behind the door. 'Have a good afternoon, Mr Edwards. I'll make sure Rebecca's home before it's dark.'

Basil and Rebecca walked along the pavement towards the park, their hands pushed deep into the pockets of their coats against the cold.

'How do you usually spend Christmas?' asked Rebecca.

'Differently.'

'Tell me.'

'Why? Why are you always asking me what I did and where I was?'

Rebecca bit her lip. 'You need to talk. You're so obviously unhappy. It could help you to come to terms with whatever has happened. When my fiancé died I sat up all night and talked to a girlfriend in the WAAF. I went through all his good and bad points, everything we had done together and planned to do in the future. It didn't change the facts, but it helped me to come to terms with the inevitable.'

'Talking cannot bring them back.'

'Of course not. I couldn't wish my father back unless he was well. Suppose my mother and brother had survived, but been hopelessly crippled, mentally or physically? I wouldn't want that.' Rebecca's voice dropped lower. 'I would rather know that Sam was dead than imagine him being tortured day after day.'

'I should never have left them.' Basil's voice was anguished.

'Tell me,' urged Rebecca. 'You can tell me whatever you want. You don't have to be embarrassed. You can walk away and never see me again.'

Basil stood silently for so long that Rebecca was convinced he was not going to answer her. Finally he took a deep breath.

'I lived in Crete. I agreed to deliver a radio to the resistance. One thing led to another and we ended up down the coast from Preveli. The Germans destroyed my friend's boat. We took to the mountains and spent our time fighting with the andartes, locals who had formed guerrilla units. When the war finished I returned to my farm.' Basil's voice broke. 'My wife and child had been shot and their bodies burnt.'

A tear ran down Rebecca's cheek. 'How awful for you.'

Basil looked at Rebecca, his mouth set in a grim line. 'So now you know why I'm bitter and unhappy. If I had stayed on the farm I could have saved them.'

Rebecca shook her head. 'I'm sure you could have done nothing to prevent it. You would probably have been forced to watch. That would have been truly terrible.'

Basil did not appear to hear her. 'He was four years old, a baby.'

Rebecca brushed away her tears with her gloved hand. 'Is that why you came back to England?'

'I couldn't stay there. Too many memories.'

'Think of the good memories. Your wife would want you to remember the happy times you had together.'

'I stayed away too long. In the four years I spent with the andartes I only visited occasionally. I thought they would be safe in the village.' Basil shook his head. 'I should have known better.'

'How could you know what was happening if you were miles away?'

'I saw what the Germans did elsewhere. I should have taken them into the mountains with me.'

'You cannot blame yourself. Suppose you had stayed with them all the time, then, one day you had to go somewhere on business, and that was the day the Germans chose to go to your village? You could not have prevented what was inevitable.'

'I saved others, but let those I loved the most be killed.' Basil spoke bitterly.

'Who did you save?'

'Various people. You don't want to know about them. They're not important.'

'I'm sure they were all very important to someone.'

Basil shrugged. 'We ought to start walking back. I told Mr Edwards I would make sure you were home before dark.'

Rebecca placed her gloved hand on the lapel of Basil's coat. 'I don't know how to help you. I just hope you feel a little more – settled.' She searched for the right word. 'Thank you for telling me.'

Basil turned into the road leading to the newsagent. He had left Rebecca at the door on Christmas Day and not thanked Mr Edwards for his hospitality, now he must remedy his lapse of good manners.

'Morning, Mr Edwards. I just called by to say thank you for letting me join you for Christmas dinner.'

Mr Edwards looked at him, a cigarette drooping from his lips. 'If that's an excuse to see Becca yer just in time.'

Basil frowned. 'What do you mean?'

'She's orf. Back ter the WAAFs. Didn' she tell yer she was orf terday?'

'I'd like to say goodbye, if it's no trouble.'

Mr Edwards opened the door that led to the living room. 'Becca, yer chap's 'ere to see yer.'

Basil could hear Rebecca's footsteps as she hurried down the stairs and appeared at the doorway in her uniform.

'You look very smart,' he observed. 'I called to thank Mr Edwards for having me here on Christmas Day and he told me you're leaving today.'

'I have to catch the ten thirty train.'

Basil nodded. 'I hope you have a good journey. It was nice knowing you.' He turned on his heel and left the shop leaving Rebecca looking after him, a puzzled expression on her face.

She finished packing her small suitcase and placed the wireless Basil had given her into the carrying box. She wanted to leave in plenty of time to walk to the station and hoped she would be able to get a seat. Rebecca looked around the room to make sure she had not left anything behind, picked up here case and wireless and walked down the stairs to the shop.

'Thank you very much Mr Edwards. I appreciate that you let me stay here.'

Mr Edwards shrugged. 'Yer've bin a bit of 'elp ter me.'

Rebecca looked out of the shop window and could see Basil standing across the road waiting for her. 'I'll be off, then.'

Mr Edwards shook his head. ''E's bin waitin' a while. 'E's too old fer yer, Becca.'

Rebecca's face flamed. 'He's just a friend. He'll probably have moved on by the time I return and I'll never see him again.'

'I'll carry that for you.'

Rebecca blushed. 'There's really no need. It isn't heavy.'

Basil ignored her remark and took it from her. It was indeed very light and he held out his other hand for the wireless.

'I can manage,' Rebecca assured him.

'I've bothered to meet you. The least you can do is let me carry your luggage.'

Rebecca blushed and handed over the box. 'It was kind of you. I wasn't expecting to see you again.'

'How long will you be away?'

'Oh, months, then provided the war is over I can leave if I want to and return to civilian life.'

'Will you?'

'I've not made any decisions yet. I'll need to know if my brother's returning home.'

The station, being no more than ten minutes walk away, they had arrived with time to spare, the train having been delayed by fifteen minutes.

Rebecca sighed.

'I might have guessed it would be late.'

'I'll see if there's anywhere we can get a cup of tea.'

Rebecca followed him across the concourse to the drab cafeteria where they found the premises closed.

'I'll just go to the waiting room. It will be warmer in there than out on the platform. Thank you for carrying my case.'

'I'll wait with you.'

'There's no need.'

Basil shrugged. 'I've nothing else to do.'

'Are you going to continue to live at the hotel?'

'Once I've found some work I'll look for some convenient lodgings. I thought I'd ask Mr Edwards if he'd let your room to me for a few weeks. If he refuses I'll have to look around for lodgings elsewhere.'

Rebecca bit at her lip. 'I'm not sure he likes you very much.'

'I don't particularly like him, but I need a roof over my head.

Even when I'm working I can't afford to live in bed and breakfast indefinitely and pay for my meals out all the time.'

'If he's not willing to have you stay he might know someone who has a room and needs a bit of extra. It's worth asking.' Rebecca looked at the station clock. 'Maybe I ought to get onto the platform. They said fifteen minutes delay, but you can never be sure and I'd like to get a seat if I can.'

Basil picked her case up again. 'I'll get a platform ticket.'

'I can manage. Nothing's heavy.'

'It will be easier if you get on and find a seat and I bring your luggage to you.'

'I'm in uniform. The other service personnel who are travelling are usually pretty helpful.'

Basil ignored her protestations as he placed a coin into the machine and pulled out the ticket giving him permission to go onto the platform. He took the wireless from her hand. 'You go ahead and find a seat somewhere. I'll find you.'

Rebecca began to open doors and look into the carriages that were already filled with service personnel returning to duty after their leave until she finally saw a space between two air force men. She signalled to Basil and he climbed aboard, placing her case and the wireless in the rack above her head.

He held out his hand. 'Goodbye, Rebecca. It's been a pleasure meeting you.'

Rebecca took his hand. 'Thank you, Basil. I hope you sort out somewhere satisfactory to live.'

Basil nodded briefly and returned to the platform. He raised his hand and walked rapidly away from the train.

Mr Edwards looked at him suspiciously and shook his head. 'I don't let rooms. I only let Becca stay 'cos I was a friend of 'er farver. 'Sides I'll need the room fer when my Barry comes 'ome.'

Basil nodded. 'I understand. Would you know of anyone who does let?'

'Mrs Spicer might be willin'. She's a widder now. Needs as much as she can get. She 'as a daughter ter feed an' clothe, not ter mention a big 'ouse. Bit orf more than they could chew there, I should think.'

'Where does she live?'

'Turn left at the bottom of the road. Abaht five 'ouses along. The big 'un wiv a garden in front.'

'Thank you. I'll ask her.' Basil left the newsagents without making a purchase and Mr Edwards glowered after him. The extra money would have been useful, but he had no desire to have the man around under his feet all day.

Mrs Spicer looked Basil up and down suspiciously. He looked a bit down at heel, but many people did. At least he spoke well, had addressed her as madam and hoped it was not an inconvenient time to call.

'I've only got the attic left. My other rooms are occupied,' she said smugly.

'The attic would be fine. I only need a bed.'

'It's twelve and six a week in advance. That includes your laundry and one bath a week.'

'Suppose I had more than one bath?'

'Then you'd have to pay extra.'

Basil nodded. 'What about food?'

'If you want me to include you in the evening meal that's an extra ten bob. If you want a Sunday lunch that's extra as well. You'll have to give me your ration book. We don't do so bad as we all club together.'

'How many people do you have living here?'

'You'll make us up to seven.'

Basil looked at the small house. 'Is there enough space?'

Mrs Spicer nodded. 'I've two married couples and my girl has a bed in my room. That leaves the attic that you can have.'

Basil stood there and calculated rapidly. It would be cheaper than staying in the bed and breakfast hotel and having to buy all his meals out. 'May I have a look at the room, please?'

Mrs Spicer led the way up two flights of stairs and opened the door that led into the attic. The ceiling sloped and it was only possible for Basil to stand upright in the centre of the room. The single bed looked clean, there was a rug beside it and beneath a small window was a table and chair.

'Is there anywhere to put my clothes?'

Mrs Spicer scowled at him. 'I thought you said you only wanted a bed.'

'A box would do. Anything.'

'Does that mean you're taking it?'

Basil nodded. 'I'd like the evening meal also.'

'A week in advance.'

Basil pulled out his wallet and extracted a note, then fumbled in his pocket for some change, finally finding half a crown.

Mrs Spicer pushed the money into her apron pocket. 'When do you want to move in?'

'Would tomorrow be convenient?'

'You'll owe me for three extra days. I usually run from Sunday to Saturday.'

'That is no problem to me, if it's no inconvenience to you.' Basil put his hand into his pocket again and withdrew some more silver, examined it and returned it to his pocket. 'I shall have to give you another note.'

'I've no change.'

'Just deduct the difference from next week's rent,' smiled Basil.

'I could use it to buy the chest of drawers in the second hand furniture shop,' suggested Mrs Spicer. 'I can't afford it otherwise.'

'As you please. If you want to go along there now I could probably help you to bring it back and carry it up the stairs.'

'You'd have to do that yourself. It's as much as I can do to carry the shopping. Bad back.' She touched the small of her back and gave a wry smile.

'I'm sure I could manage. If you would just come with me and show me the one you have in mind.' Basil felt impatience overtaking him. The woman should have provided somewhere for him to put his clothes, he should not have to be buying it, collecting it and carrying it up two flights of stairs.

Basil sat with the newspaper open on the table before him. He had ringed various advertisements that said they were looking for staff. He went through them a second time and crossed out anything that mentioned a skilled worker or said experience was necessary. He finally whittled it down to a delivery boy, a milkman or a road sweeper. He was probably too old to be considered as a delivery boy and he did not want to be a road sweeper except as a last resort. Carefully he tore out the small piece of newspaper with the address of the dairy, picked up his coat and walked down the two flights of stairs to the front door.

The usual smell of boiled cabbage assaulted his nostrils and he made a guess at the evening meal Mrs Jackson would prepare. A mince and onion pie, mashed potato, cabbage and carrots. She was not a bad cook, but the meals were predictable and plain. Basil would certainly not complain. He knew what it was like to be desperately hungry and to eat whatever you could find. He appreciated having a full stomach when he went to bed.

He walked briskly along the road to the dairy, despite the bright sunshine there was a chill wind and he wished he had worn his sheepskin beneath his coat. He hoped he would not find a queue of men all hoping to fill the position when he arrived.

To his delight there was only one other man in the small room where he was told to wait. He smiled apprehensively at him and took his seat. Within a short while a door opened and a man with one arm emerged, a despondent look on his face.

'Next.'

The man who had arrived before Basil rose to his feet and as he did so he began to cough. It shook his whole body and he had to wait until the spasm had passed and get his breath back before he could approach the office. Basil heard the man cough again, the sound travelling through the door.

Basil sat immobile as he had trained himself to do when in the mountains on lookout. He fixed his eyes on the door and hardly blinked until he heard it open. The man wandered out, a handkerchief before his mouth and slammed the door behind him.

The door opened again. 'Next.'

Basil rose to his feet and walked across his hand extended. 'Good morning. My name is Basil Hurst and I've come to apply for the position you have advertised.'

His hand was ignored as a weary looking man eyed him up and down. 'Do you have any disabilities?'

'None.'

'Are you fit and well?'

'I believe so.'

'Are you a good time keeper; able to rise early?'

'Yes, sir.'

'Why do you want to be a milkman?'

'I need some work,' replied Basil honestly.

'What did you do during the war?'

Basil hesitated. 'I was a translator. More than that I cannot say.'

'Before the war?'

'A teacher.'

Basil bent the truth, missing out the years he had spent in Greece.

'Why haven't you gone back to teaching?'

'After my years out of the profession I would have to retrain. I didn't like teaching very much so I didn't want to make the effort.'

'Do you plan to be a milkman for the rest of your life?'

Basil shrugged. 'I couldn't say. I had originally planned to be a teacher until I was old enough to draw a pension.'

The manager sighed. The only decent applicant and it was unlikely he would stay with them for very long. 'Very well. You've got the job. Go over to the depot and Jerry will show you how to drive a milk float. You'll be expected to load up when you arrive at six in the morning and your route will be the same each day. Remove the empties from the float when you return, leave your cap and apron and don't forget to check out. On a Friday you'll collect the money from the customers and wait until it has been counted and certified as correct by the office. Any questions?'

'How much am I paid each week? What time can I expect to finish and do I have a day off?'

'The time you finish depends how quickly you complete your round. Most men are away by two thirty. You have every other Sunday off and the pay is four pounds six shillings a week. If there are any shortfalls in the money from the customers it is deducted from your wages the following week.' The weary looking manager sighed. 'Anything else?'

'When do I start?'

'Tomorrow.'

'Thank you.' Basil rose and once again held out his hand which was ignored.

Basil found the work as a milkman boring and monotonous. He had learnt the round quickly and the customers' orders did not vary. He had soon memorised which days he had to call at the different houses for their money and make a note in his receipt book of the amount paid. Once back at the depot he listed his receipts and counted the change in his pouch, only on rare occasions being a penny or two short.

He was not happy living in the cramped quarters at Mrs Spicer's. He was pleased that he was out of the house early and did not have to fight for a turn in the bathroom each morning, but he disliked being squashed around the table in the dining room for his meals. The black line that had been painted around the bath to show the occupant how much water was allowed annoyed him. He only bothered to take one bath a week so he should have been able to use more than the thirteen centimetres of water he was allowed on that occasion. When he broached the subject with Mrs Spicer she shook her head.

'Government regulations. Up to you whether you bath once or twice a week.'

'Who would know if I was using twice as much for one bath?'

'I would. The tank would either run dry or the water would be cold when anyone else wanted a wash. If that becomes the case I'll know who to blame and you'll be given notice to quit.' She glared at him from behind her pebble glasses, her hands on her hips, daring Basil to defy her and he turned away defeated.

The German forces surrendered at the beginning of May and the whole country breathed a sigh of relief. Now their loved ones could come home and life could get back to normal. Basil marvelled at their naivety. Did they not realise that nothing would ever be the same again for those who had lost a loved one during the war? There was still a shortage of housing due to the bombing raids and extended families were living together, placing additional stress on them as they tried to rebuild their relationships. Little work was available for the returning men, the women having taken many of their traditional jobs whilst they were away and were now reluctant to leave them. They had discovered a modicum of independence from their men folk and relished having their own money in their pocket and not having to ask for every penny.

Food, clothes and petrol were still rationed, and prices for the commodities that were available were rising rapidly. The Black Market, that had flourished during the war years, continued to have eager customers, despite the government exacting harsh penalties on those who were discovered participating.

Basil inspected his wardrobe. He had two pairs of trousers he had hardly worn, still feeling more comfortable in the black, baggy Greek ones that he tucked inside his long boots, despite the looks he encountered. His shirts were clean, but each one needed a button or two. He would walk over to the main shopping area and call at the haberdashers.

He took his place behind a woman who was looking at lace trimmings and waited. An assistant approached him.

'Can I help you?'

'Hello, Rebecca. What are you doing here?'

'Working, but we're not allowed to talk to the customers,' replied Rebecca quietly. 'What can I get for you, sir?'

'Shirt buttons, please.'

Rebecca pulled out the drawer with small compartments holding buttons of various sizes. 'How many would you like?'

'Six please.'

'And needles and cotton? Do you need those?'

Basil smiled. 'Trust a woman to think of that. Yes please.'

Rebecca placed the buttons in a screw of paper and added a reel of white cotton and packet of needles.

'How much do I owe you?'

'Nine pence, please.'

'Thank you. What time do you close?'

'Five thirty.'

Basil picked up his purchases and walked out of the shop, leaving Rebecca looking after him in surprise.

Basil stood on the corner a short distance away from the haberdasher's door and watched as the employees left. Rebecca was one of the last and he walked towards her.

'It's good to see you again. Have you time for a cup of tea?'

Rebecca looked at her watch. 'Just about. I must be home by six thirty. Mrs Pearce has the supper on the table at that time.'

Basil raised his eyebrows.

'She has two little boys. She needs to get them to bed afterwards.'

'You haven't gone back to Mr Edwards to live, then?'

Rebecca shook her head. 'I thought it better to find somewhere else. I'd only have to look for new lodgings when Barry comes home.'

'He's not back yet, then?'

'According to Mr Edwards he's somewhere in the Med: A 'mopping up' operation they're calling it. Going round the islands to make sure there aren't any Germans still hiding out over there.'

Basil opened the shop door for Rebecca to enter and the woman behind the counter frowned. 'I close at six.'

'That's quite all right. We would just like a pot of tea, please. Would you like a rock cake, Rebecca?'

'No thanks. If I don't eat my supper Mrs Pearce will think there's something wrong with her cooking.'

'Is there?'

'What? Something wrong with it? No, I can't complain about that.'

'You don't like the lodgings, though?'

'My room is fine. It's the family. Mr Pearce has only just come back and they seem to spend all their time arguing at the top of their voices and the children are a nuisance.'

'Don't you like children?'

'I do, but not when they spend all their time whining and crying for attention. Where are you living and what are you doing?'

'Don't their parents play with them?'

'They're too busy shouting at each other.'

'How sad. Are you looking for somewhere else?'

'It's difficult. As more men come home the women don't want a stranger living in their house. I'm hoping that when the insurance is finally sorted out I can rent a small flat.'

'Why don't you think about buying one?'

'Buying one!' Rebecca opened her eyes wide. 'I doubt if the insurance money would cover that! A flat would cost money and then there's all the furniture you need.'

'Now is the time to buy,' Basil urged her. 'Once normality returns property prices will probably rise.'

'I'll have to see how much the insurance eventually pays out. If you think this is the right time why don't you buy a somewhere of your own?'

'I'm looking around,' replied Basil vaguely. 'There's no point in buying just for the sake of it. I have to be sure it's what I want.'

'And what do you want?'

Basil shrugged. 'I shall know when I find it.'

Rebecca looked at her watch. 'I ought to make a move. Mrs Pearce will have the supper ready at six thirty and she doesn't like it if I'm late.'

'Are you often late?'

Rebecca shook her head. 'Only once. We were kept an extra hour at work. One of the tills was short and we all had to stay whilst they checked them again.'

'Was the difference found?' asked Basil as he helped her on with her jacket and she picked up her cotton gloves.

'Yes, the cashier had made a mistake in his addition.'

'Thank you,' called Basil as he opened the shop door and held it for Rebecca. The woman gave a thin smile as they left and turned the sign to 'closed'. She had made an unexpected five pence.

1946 – 1947

Basil took his place in the post office queue, his book and his two pounds in his hand. He was a little later than usual. For the first time the cashier had found a discrepancy of three pence in Basil's accounts. He had to wait whilst the money was checked against the receipts again and was just about to hand over a coin to rectify the error when the cashier had found a three pence piece caught in the seam of the leather bag. Basil had scowled at him and received his wage packet with barely a thank you.

He pushed his book and the money beneath the grill of the counter and looked up to see Rebecca smiling at him.

'What are you doing here?' he asked.

'They agreed to take me back into the post office. They're giving me some more training and I'm on probation again, of course. What are you doing?'

'Are you going to stand there gossiping all day?' a voice came from behind Basil and he felt someone poke his back.

'Thank you, miss.' Basil picked up his book and turned to the customer waiting behind him. '*So* sorry to have kept you waiting.'

The woman smiled. 'No problem, dearie.' She indicated with her thumb. ''E was the one 'oo reckoned 'e 'ad a train ter catch.'

Rebecca was surprised to see Basil waiting for her when she left the post office for the day. Since their chance meeting months ago at the haberdashers she had seen no sign of him. They walked along the road in silence and Rebecca wondered why Basil had bothered to meet her.

'Are you still working as a milkman?' she asked eventually.

'I'm looking for something better. Have you heard anything about your brother?'

Rebecca nodded. 'He won't be coming back.'

'I'm very sorry to hear that.'

'Apparently he died within three months of being captured. Dysentery.' Rebecca ran a finger beneath her eye to wipe away a tear. 'I'm glad my mother didn't know.'

'I'm sorry to hear that, but maybe he was one of the lucky ones. Some of them suffered for years.' Basil reached across the table and touched her hand.

She nodded sombrely. 'I try to console myself with that thought.'

'Have you managed to sort out the house insurance and other problems now?'

Rebecca sighed. 'She'd let the insurance on the house lapse after Dad died.'

'So you won't receive anything?'

'Mum left thirty pounds in her savings account. I shall get a bit of compensation from the government. That won't go far. They're promising to provide low cost housing for families who were bombed out, but as I'm single I'm at the bottom of the list.' She spoke glumly but smiled brightly. 'I was so pleased when they accepted me back into the post office. At least I enjoy the work.'

'I'm pleased for you. Are you still in the same lodgings?'

Rebecca pulled a face. 'I don't really have a choice. Now so many men have returned people don't want to share their homes with strangers. What about you?'

'Yes,' sighed Basil. 'I'm still in the attic and sharing the bathroom. I mustn't complain. I could be far worse off.' They reached the end of the main road. 'Which way do you go?' asked Basil.

'I'm a few roads down,' Rebecca waved her hand in the direction of the residential area.

Basil held out his hand. 'It's been good to see you again.'

Rebecca shook his hand and he turned and began to walk rapidly back towards the post office. Rebecca gazed after him, puzzled. Why had he bothered to meet her and then not walked all the way back to her lodgings with her? She felt vaguely aggrieved. He was a strange, lonely man, but not her responsibility.

Basil walked along to Mr Edward's shop for his usual newspaper and was surprised to find the sign said closed and a blind had been drawn down. He checked his watch. It was mid afternoon, a time when it should have been open. Basil clicked his tongue in annoyance. He would either have to retrace his steps almost back to the dairy to purchase a newspaper or leave his quest until the following day. He shrugged. He had nothing else to do. He might just as well walk the extra distance. If he took it slowly it could take up half an hour. He could find a sheltered spot in the park and sit there and read it, maybe complete the crossword, and make a list of any work or lodgings that seemed interesting when he was back in his attic.

There was nothing in the newspaper either in the way of work or lodgings that looked suitable to him and having completed the crossword he laid back on the grass and tried to relax. What did he want to do with the remainder of his life? He needed an occupation that stimulated him mentally and tired him physically. Nothing came to mind and he realised how lonely and isolated he had become. He offered little to the conversation that took place during the evening meal, he did not visit the local pub and had not joined any of the working men's clubs in the area so he only had himself to blame for being friendless.

It had been so easy in Greece. Wherever he had gone he had made friends with the local people, been invited to their homes and spent evenings in the taverna playing dice or backgammon whilst gossiping, and, of course, there had been Katerina. He felt the hot tears prick at the back of his eyes as he thought of her and his small son.

He sat up, blinking his eyes rapidly. What would people think if they saw a man sitting in the park crying? He should be thankful that he had a roof over his head, a job of work to do and some money in the bank. He felt in his pocket. He had a considerable amount of change in there and he knew he had a ten shilling note in his wallet. That would be more than enough to replenish his stock of toothpaste and shaving cream. He would buy them when he had finished work tomorrow. Walking to the chemist would give him something to do in the afternoon.

When Basil left for work the following morning the sun already felt warm despite the early hour. He removed his jacket and completed his deliveries in his shirt sleeves, rolling them back down and replacing his jacket before he returned to the depot. Once there he removed his jacket again and unloaded as quickly as possible. The empty bottles, many of them unrinsed, had begun to smell. He hung up his cap and apron, washed his hands and picked up his jacket. As he exited the washroom he looked up in surprise. The sun had disappeared and the temperature had dropped considerably. He shivered and pushed his arms into his jacket, obviously a sea mist had come in, no doubt caused by the earlier excessive warmth.

The chill air seemed to be penetrating his bones and he changed his mind about visiting the chemist. He plunged his hands as far into his jacket pockets as possible and hunched his shoulders as he walked along. He would buy his newspaper from Mr Edwards if he was open; if he was still closed he would go without.

The shop door opened at his touch, the bell jangling stridently. Mr Edwards looked up, hardly seeming to recognise his regular customer.

'Afternoon, Mr Edwards. Shame about the weather. It was such a beautiful morning.'

Mr Edwards shrugged and Basil handed him the coins for the newspaper.

'Yer'll 'ave ter get yer newspapers elsewhere in a couple of weeks.'

Basil looked at him in surprise. 'Aren't you stocking them any more?'

'I'm closin' darn.'

'Closing?'

'You 'eard. Closin'. My Barry's not coming back so there's no point me stayin' 'ere.'

'You mean...?'

'That's right. Went darn on the ship.'

'I'm very sorry, Mr Edwards.'

'Shouldn't never 'ave still bin out there. War's bin over best part of a year. Should 'ave come 'ome an bin safe.'

'What do you plan to do?'

'Goin' ter me sister in Bournemuff. Bit a company, like.'

'What are you going to do with the shop?'

'Sell up. It was goin' ter be fer Barry when I went. No point in keepin' it now.'

'What will you be asking for it?'

'Why? You in'trested in buying?'

'I could be. At the right price. I'll call in and speak to you tomorrow.'

Mr Edwards looked after him as he left the shop. 'Mr Moneybags,' he muttered.

Basil stood outside in the damp mist, no longer noticing the chill. Provided Mr Edwards was not asking an extortionate amount he should be able to afford to buy the shop using the money from his aunt's house. Suddenly he was anxious to return to his attic room and work out exactly how much he could afford to spend, but his conscience pricked him. He should really go to the post office and tell Rebecca.

Rebecca was surprised when she saw Basil standing outside waiting for her and greeted him with a smile.

'Hello. I haven't seen you for a while. How are you?'

Basil ignored her question. 'I thought I ought to tell you that Mr Edwards's son won't be coming home.'

'Oh, no.' Rebecca's face fell. 'How awful. Barry meant everything to him. He was so proud that he was a petty officer in the navy.'

'He's closing the shop.'

'Why close the shop? He'll still be living there; he might as well have it open.'

'He says he's moving to Bournemouth to his sister and thinking of selling.'

Rebecca stopped walking. 'I'll go round there now and tell him how sorry I am.'

'I thought you'd want to know. What's your news?'

'I've passed my probation at the post office.'

'That is good news. I'm sorry I had to spoil it for you by telling you about Mr Edwards. Good luck.'

Basil walked away down the street, leaving Rebecca looking after him with a puzzled frown. He had bothered to tell her about the newsagent's son, seemed pleased that she was going back to the post office, but obviously did not wish to spend any more time with her. Despite being a little later than usual leaving work she would still have time to visit Mr Edwards before returning to her lodgings by six thirty.

Basil walked into the newsagents when he had finished his work at the dairy and raised his eyebrows at Mr Edwards. 'Have you worked out a price?' he asked bluntly.

'Eight fifty.'

Basil glanced around the shop. 'That includes the stock?'

'That's separate.'

'How much value do you reckon you have?'

'Prob'ly baht an 'undred.'

Basil looked around at the shelves again. He thought the figure over estimated.

'And your weekly turnover?'

'Baht twenty five.'

'I'll have a word at the bank and with my solicitor and let you know.'

Basil sat at the table in his room, papers covered with figures before him. There was no way he could afford to pay nearly a thousand pounds for the shop and he was not at all sure it was worth it. He had just over eight hundred sitting on his deposit account and sixty pounds in his saving account at the post office, but now he wanted the property. He would change from being a newsagent and tobacconist and become a general store, stocking convenience items for the people in the vicinity. He was sure they would appreciate being able to buy an aspirin from him rather than have to walk to the chemist. He must also find out if there was any restriction on the goods he stocked.

He began to make a list of questions he would have to ask a solicitor and if he still felt it would be worth his while he would approach the bank and ask for a loan. If Mr Edwards knew he was to be paid in cash he might be willing to drop his price.

He made an appointment with an estate agent for when he had finished his milk round and waited whilst the man shuffled some papers around on his desk.

'It's a very nice property,' the agent assured him. 'Plenty of living space, two bedrooms. Could do with a lick of paint here and there, but nothing a man like you couldn't tackle. The furniture is included in the price.'

Basil raised his eyebrows. How did the estate agent know what he was capable of undertaking? 'I'm not concerned with the living quarters. How much does the shop take each week?

What are the rates? What's the stock worth? Are all the bills paid up to date? Are there any restrictions on what I can sell?'

'According to the figures Mr Edwards has given me the shop takes in the region of twenty five pounds a week, giving a rough profit margin of five to six pounds a week. Prices are rising all the time so your profit margin would rise accordingly. He estimates his current stock to be worth approximately a hundred pounds, mostly in cigarettes. He assures me he has no outstanding bills except the newspapers. He only pays for those he sells. The printers collect the unsold ones when they deliver each day and you don't make any profit on papers, you realise. They are just to draw customers into the shop and they usually buy their cigarettes and any other odds and ends at the same time.'

Basil nodded. 'So if I wanted to add some groceries there wouldn't be a problem?'

'You wouldn't be allowed to sell fresh meat or fish, nor could you sell postage stamps. I don't know of any other restrictions.'

'And the rates?'

'Business rates for the shop and household rates for the living quarters. They're paid monthly. Mr Edwards would expect reimbursement for the portion of the month he's already paid, of course. Add on our conveyancing fee and you're looking at a figure in the region of a thousand pounds.'

Basil shook his head. 'Too much. Offer him seven fifty, cash, all in.'

'I doubt he'd accept such a low figure.'

Basil shrugged. 'He could have the property on his hands for some months and it wouldn't be bringing him in any income at all. I'm offering him a quick sale for a cash price. I suggest you put the offer before him. I'll call in tomorrow for his answer.'

Basil looked around the shop. It was his. He had driven a hard bargain with Mr Edwards, finally agreeing on a purchase price of eight hundred pounds including the stock and the furniture. Having finally signed the papers giving him ownership he had a moment of misgiving. All he had left in the way of cash was sixty one pounds five shillings and four pence in his post office account.

He walked into the living room and looked around, noticing the cobwebs in the corner and the layer of dust on the picture rail. He carried his bag of possessions up to the largest bedroom and dumped it on the unmade bed. The mattress looked reasonably clean, but when he banged it with his fist the dust rose from it along with the smell of cigarette smoke. Mr Edwards had obviously smoked in bed. Before he made it up for the night he would need to give it a vigorous brushing. He looked in the cupboards and drawers for some bedding only to find them empty. He shrugged. He could always use his sheepskin and overcoat as covers.

Everywhere needed cleaning, but the first thing he must do was clean the shop. He wanted everything to be in readiness to enable him to open on Monday morning to catch the men who bought their cigarettes and newspapers on their way to work. He drew the blinds down over the windows and began to remove the stock from the shelves, placing it in a box on the counter. Beneath the kitchen sink he found a bucket, a couple of dirty cloths and a scrubbing brush. He should have thought and bought some scouring powder the previous day, in the meantime he would just have to make do.

Basil washed off the shelves and whilst he was waiting for them to dry he cleaned the windows, polishing them with an old newspaper from the day before. He replaced the stock on the front of the shelves as Mr Edwards had, to disguise the gaps. Basil sighed. He should have insisted on a proper stock take and not taken the man's word for the amount. He wondered if the figures the man had shown him for his weekly turnover had been true and thought it unlikely

As he scrubbed at the worn linoleum he noticed that it was threadbare and split in places, but at least it appeared to be a little cleaner. He looked at his watch, pleased to find that it was only two thirty. He would have time to brush the mattress and make a start on the kitchen before he returned to Mrs Spicer for the Sunday lunch he had persuaded her to save and reheat for him.

He was sure when he had been there with Rebecca the kitchen had not been dirty and he speculated about how much cleaning she had done whilst she stayed there. That could explain her reluctance to return and lodge with the shop keeper. He scraped at the accumulation of grease on the cooker, boiled some water and placed all the removal parts into the sink with a generous measure of soda.

Mr Edwards had left behind his crockery and cutlery, along with a miscellany of saucepans, even some odd bits of food in the larder. He inspected the items suspiciously, decided there was nothing there that would make him ill, but wished the man had left a small amount of tea. He would just have to make do with a drink of water. Once again he cursed himself for his short sightedness. He should have stocked up on some food on the Saturday, now when his shop was closed the other shops would be closed also.

As he scraped congealed and burnt food from the cooker he turned the problem over in his mind. It could be a wise move to be open when the other shops were closed. He did not need an afternoon off in the middle of the week. He could give it a trial for a month and if he found it impractical he could always revert back to the original times.

Leaving the burners from the gas cooker soaking in the water he went into the living room and drew a sheet of paper towards him. He had to be up by six thirty to receive delivery of the newspapers and return any unsold items from the previous day. It would be practical to have the shop open as soon as the newspapers had arrived, seven or at the latest seven thirty. If he closed again from ten thirty until twelve he would have time to go out and run any errands of his own or do his washing or cleaning. Opening between twelve and two thirty would mean he caught any passing trade as the women took their children to and from the local school.

A further break from two thirty until three thirty would give him the opportunity to prepare a meal, or even have a short nap if he fancied. To have the shop open again from three thirty until six would make him available once again to the women with their children and the men who finished work at five thirty. He added up the hours, pleased to find they did not exceed the forty eight that he was allowed to trade each week.

He drew a clean sheet of paper towards him and collected a cigarette packet from the shop to enable him to draw straight lines.

NEW OPENING TIMES
OPEN EVERY DAY
7.00 - 10.30
12.00 - 2.30
3.30 - 6.00
CREDIT 5/- per week

Basil felt pleased with himself. Adding the amount of credit he was willing to allow people each week was a good idea. They would be more inclined to come to him when they were down to their last few pence, and most shops restricted the amount to ten shillings. He took the notice into the shop and looked around to see where he should put it. Ideally it should be on the door, but the 'closed' notice would obscure it. He would place it in the window, propped up by a box, until he was able to go into town and purchase some glue. He would then stick it to a piece of card and hang it below the notice.

He felt disinclined to return to the onerous job of cleaning the cooker, but forced himself to complete the task. He wiped out the shelves in the larder and washed the crockery, noticing that much of it was cracked or chipped, tines on the forks were bent and the knives blunt. More things he would need to replace, but he could make do for the time being. Finally he washed the dirty, worn linoleum that covered the floor and emptied the bucket of filthy water into the outside drain.

Basil stretched his back and looked at his watch. He had half an hour before he was due to arrive at his previous lodgings and he knew he would not receive a warm welcome if he arrived early. He took another piece of paper and began to write a list of essential items he would need to purchase the following day.

Basil was pleasantly surprised on the Monday morning at the number of people who called in and purchased a newspaper or cigarettes. He guessed that the word had gone round that the shop had a new owner and the people were satisfying their curiosity. During the time that he was closed he had walked to the main shopping area, made his essential purchases and requested information from the grocer and chemist. At first they had been reluctant to give him the name and address of their wholesalers, but when Basil explained that he was the other side of the town from them and new to the business they relented.

Whilst waiting for customers in the afternoon he realised it would be more practical to telephone the wholesalers and ask them to send one of their representatives to call on him. He would have to do that the following morning and wished he had a telephone. It would necessitate a trip to the post office and he would have to draw some money from his account to replace the change he took from the till.

He sighed. He should have thought more about becoming a shop keeper and solved all these problems before he had agreed to buy the premises. He had been too busy to prepare a meal and would have to make do with scrambled egg on toast at the end of the day if he wanted to accomplish some more cleaning.

By the end of the week Basil was feeling happier. He had received visits from the wholesalers and placed orders with them for small quantities of goods that he thought he would be able to sell easily. Having paid the bill for the newspapers, he was left with seventeen pounds one shilling and two pence half penny. He paid fifteen pounds into his bank account to enable him to write cheques to pay his bills and hoped there would be enough accumulated in there to pay his rates when they fell due. It would be at least six months before he knew if he was actually making a profit from the shop and it was too late to back out of the enterprise now.

Within a month the shop looked very different from the back street premises Basil had purchased. Both the exterior and interior needed a coat of paint, the industrious cleaning he had undertaken could not disguise the dilapidation that had taken place over the years of neglect, but it was well stocked with a variety of groceries and essential commodities. Trade was gradually increasing and he breathed a sigh of relief when he did the end of month accounts, checked his bank balance and saw he had made twenty two pounds five shillings and four pence profit.

Each evening he counted up the money he had taken during the day, deducted the float he had started with, entered the amount in a ledger and sorted his bills into date order for payment. It was most gratifying on a Saturday evening when he was able to add up the total for the week and compare it with that of the previous weeks. Each week was showing a small increase in his profit. He always felt depressed when he had written cheques for the outstanding bills and saw his bank balance diminish, but buoyed himself up with the knowledge that he was solvent and the amount of stock he had was far greater than when he had first bought the premises.

He sealed the cheques inside their envelopes and walked down to the post office. He would buy a supply of stamps whilst he was there and it would save him having to spend his time waiting in the queue another time. When he finally reached the counter he looked into the friendly eyes of Rebecca.

'Hello, Basil. I haven't seen you in a long time,' she remarked. 'How are you? Are you still working as a milk man?'

Basil shook his head. 'I bought Mr Edwards's shop.'

'Really? How do you like being a shop keeper?'

'It's an improvement on being a milk man.'

The customer behind Basil cleared his throat.

'I need twenty stamps, please,' said Basil hurriedly, passed the coins across the counter and took the stamps from Rebecca before moving away. He licked seven stamps and placed them on the envelopes before dropping them into the box. He looked back towards Rebecca, but her head was bent as she dealt with an elderly woman.

Rebecca left the post office by the side door and looked to see if Basil was anywhere around waiting for her. There was no sign of him and she realised that he would still be tending the shop. If she hurried she would have time to buy a newspaper before he closed. If he seemed pleased to see her she would call in again occasionally.

She stopped outside and looked at the windows in surprise. She could see an array of goods that Mr Edwards had never stocked. Propped up against the glass was a handwritten sign and she read it curiously.

OPEN EVERY DAY
7.30 – 10.00
11.30 – 2.30
3.30 – 6.00
Credit limit 5/-

Rebecca pushed open the door and Basil emerged from the back room. He looked surprised to see her.

'What can I get for you?' he asked.

Rebecca blushed. 'I've come for a newspaper.'

Basil raised his eyebrows. There was a newsagent far closer to the post office.

Rebecca's blush deepened. 'I came to be nosy,' she admitted. 'I wanted to see if you had made any changes.'

Basil nodded. 'Quite a few.'

'I saw your opening times. They're certainly different from the other shops. When do you have a half day?'

'I don't. Why do I want a half day when all the other shops are taking theirs?'

'Won't you be in trouble for having the shop open for too many hours?'

'No. I worked it out. I'm actually open the same amount of time as I would be if I closed for a lunch hour and a half day each week.'

'But that means you don't have any time off during the week.'

Basil shrugged. 'What do I want time off for? I have nowhere to go or anyone to see. Once people have gone off to work there's very little trade in the morning so I might as well close. I'm open to catch any trade as people return for their lunch and it's the same in the afternoon. I'm open when other shops are closed.'

'You've raised the credit limit, too. Other shops only give three shillings, and you have so many other things in stock.'

'I need to attract customers. Mr Edwards was hardly covering his overheads,' Basil replied grimly. He looked at his watch. 'Do you want a cup of tea? I'm closing in five minutes.'

'Thank you.'

'Go and put the kettle on, then.' Basil jerked his head in the direction of the door to the living room.

Surprised and slightly annoyed, Rebecca walked through into the living room and into the kitchen. She lifted the kettle, pleased to find the handle was not covered in grease and filled it. She lit the gas, again noticing that the cooker was clean and lifted the teapot from the shelf, seeing it was the same one with the chipped spout that had belonged to Mr Edwards.

By the time Basil had locked up the shop and brought his till into the living room she had carried cups and the teapot through to the living room.

'I'll just wash my hands and I'll be with you.'

Rebecca looked around for a stand to place the teapot on and could not see anything suitable. She carried it back into the kitchen and took a breadboard from the cupboard. That would have to do. Basil looked at it in surprise when he returned.

'What's the breadboard for?'

'I couldn't find the stand. I didn't want to mark the table.'

Basil nodded. 'Trust a woman to think of things like that. I usually pour a cup in the kitchen. Mind you, the table is so scratched and marked it wouldn't make a lot of difference.'

'Not like Mrs Pearce's. It's always covered with a cloth, she places mats beneath the plates and the boys are always being reminded to put their knives and forks down carefully. 'I couldn't find any milk or sugar,' she said apologetically.

'I'll get it.' Basil returned with milk in a jug and a bowl of sugar. 'I can't use the larder at the moment,' he explained. 'Ants.'

'Mr Edwards always had ants in the larder. I used to keep the sugar covered, but they still managed to get in.'

'Mr Edwards was not exactly house proud.'

Rebecca smiled. 'I did the best I could whilst I was here, but he didn't seem to notice. It looks a good deal cleaner now.'

'I do my cleaning in the morning whilst the shop is closed. I don't feel like starting that in the evenings. Would you like a biscuit? I bought a tin of broken biscuits earlier in the week.'

Rebecca shook her head. 'No thanks. I have to get back for my meal. I don't want to spoil my appetite.'

'You're still lodging with the same family, then?'

Rebecca pulled a face. 'They're talking about separating. She says she's taking the boys and going back to live with her mother.'

'That's sad.'

Rebecca sighed. 'It is; Mr Pearce is obviously having a problem readjusting to family life after being away. He doesn't seem to understand that the boys are jealous that they have to share the attention from their mother with him. He expects them to behave like adults and if they make a noise he shouts at them. They start to cry and that starts a full scale row between the parents.'

'So what will you do if the family split up?'

'I'll have to look for somewhere else to lodge. I wouldn't be prepared to stay there with just him in the house.'

Basil stirred his tea thoughtfully. 'Mrs Spicer may have my room free still. I could ask her when she comes in tomorrow.'

'Would you? I'd appreciate that.'

'It's no trouble.' Basil lifted the teapot. 'Another cup?'

Rebecca shook her head. 'I must go or I shall be late. I've taken up enough of your time as it is.'

'Call in tomorrow and I'll let you know about Mrs Spicer.'

Rebecca entered the shop hopefully. If the room with Mrs Spicer was free it could be the answer to her recent prayers. She waited patiently whilst Basil served a customer with a tin of peas and some powdered egg, then stood to one side as a man entered to buy his newspaper and five cigarettes. As he left Basil jerked his head towards the living room as he had done the day before.

'Put the kettle on.'

Rebecca went through to the kitchen to comply. She opened the cupboards and found the milk and sugar for herself, taking it through to the table and returning to warm the pot. As she carried the teapot and cups into the living room she could hear Basil talking to someone and hoped he would not be too long or the tea would be stewed.

'Did you see Mrs Spicer?' she asked anxiously, once Basil had poured the tea.

Basil nodded. 'She's already let the room. Said she had five people after it as soon as she put a sign in her window.'

Rebecca sighed. 'I'll just have to keep looking around then.'

'You could come here,' suggested Basil. As soon as he said

the words he wondered why he had offered. He was not sure he wanted a lodger interrupting his solitary routine.

'Here? With you?'

'There's a spare room upstairs.'

'Wouldn't you mind having me around all the time? You're used to being alone.'

'You're out at work all day. You'd only be around in the evenings and weekends. If you found my company too obnoxious you could always spend your time in your room. You'd be no worse off, but you wouldn't hear arguments and have whining children around.'

'Do you really mean it, Basil?'

Basil nodded. He was not sure what had prompted him to offer accommodation to Rebecca initially. He had planned to use the spare bedroom to store his surplus stock.

Rebecca considered the offer. 'What would you expect in return?' she asked cautiously.

Basil shrugged. 'You'd have to keep it clean, along with the bathroom and the kitchen after you'd used them. I wouldn't want to find dirty dishes in the sink and scum round the bath or basin.' Basil reddened as he said the words, realising there was more to her question than he had realised. 'I'm not suggesting or expecting anything improper,' he assured her. 'I'll have a lock put on your bedroom door.'

'How much rent would you want?'

'I haven't thought about it.'

'How much was Mrs Spicer charging?'

'One pound two and six a week and a shilling for laundry.'

'Then I should pay you the same.'

Basil shifted uncomfortably in his chair. 'She was including meals in that. I'm not much of a cook.'

'If I moved in could I do the cooking?' asked Rebecca. 'I really enjoy cooking and I've missed being able to use the kitchen as I pleased.'

'If you cook for me as well I'll reduce your rent.'

'That wouldn't be necessary.'

'It would be only fair. I hate having to cook a meal for myself when I close the shop. I usually end up with something on toast.'

'What are you having tonight?'

'I've got some soft roes. What about you?'

'Monday will be cold meat left from the joint and mashed potato, sometimes there's a bit of beetroot to go with it, Tuesday will be shepherd's pie made from the remainder of the meat, Wednesday will be sausages, Thursday will be baked heart, Friday is always cod, Saturday I go to the cafe as she only provides a sandwich that evening.'

Basil pulled a face. 'Is it the same every week?'

Rebecca nodded. 'I think it's the predictability that I hate.'

'If you take charge of the cooking I shall expect something different every day of the month.'

'I don't know that I could promise that, but at least it wouldn't be something on toast every night.'

'You'll come then?'

Rebecca hesitated. What did she have to lose?

'Ten shillings a week and you do the cooking.'

'And the shilling for the laundry,' added Rebecca.

'Sixpence. You'll only be sending a couple of single sheets, once I've found out where I can get some.'

'Didn't Mr Edwards leave you any bedding for that room?'

'He didn't leave me any bedding!'

'So what are you sleeping in?' asked Rebecca in horror.

'Just on the mattress. It's warm enough at the moment. I'll need to get a couple of blankets by the winter or I can use my sheepskin.'

'You can't live like that!'

'Why not? I've slept rough out in the open and in a cave wrapped in a blanket before now.'

Rebecca shook her head. 'I've still got my allowance for being bombed out. I'll go along to the depot and see what I'm entitled to have.'

'You can't use your allowance on me.'

'I'd rather use it. If I leave it too long before claiming they could discontinue the scheme. I'll let you borrow some sheets and blankets from me until I need them.'

'That means you're coming here, then?'

Rebecca smiled. 'I suppose it does. I'll speak to Mrs Pearce tonight and give her a week's notice as from Saturday. Would that suit you?'

'Any time. The room's free.' Basil did not mention that he had not yet cleaned the room and would have to do so before he could expect Rebecca to occupy it.

Basil opened the spare bedroom windows and took the threadbare rug down to the small area that was called a garden, hung it over the line and attacked it vigorously with the broom, feeling a degree of satisfaction as he saw the dust rising from it. He put the curtains into the bath to soak whilst he wiped over the bed frame, wardrobe, chest of drawers and dressing table; then turned his attention to the windows and the paintwork.

He scrubbed the linoleum, once again bringing the bald and worn places to the fore, wishing he was able to purchase a piece of carpet. By the evening Basil decided the room was as clean as possible. He collected the rug from the washing line and left the curtains to be hung out the following day. He wondered, not for the first time, what had possessed him to offer the room to the girl.

1948 – 1950

Basil looked at his account ledger from the previous year. He had made a healthy profit. It was easier now some items were no longer restricted or on ration. He had invested in a large upright fridge which had enabled him to store butter, margarine and lard, and the fact that it was now pre-packed it needed no effort on his part to prepare it. The cheese he still cut in front of customers and soon became adept at estimating the size and weight. The sacks containing rice, flour, dried peas and beans needed to be weighed out, but he was able to use the new scales that were meant for weighing sweets and have bags of various quantities sitting on the shelves.

At first, when he had presented the goods ready wrapped to the customers, they had looked askance and asked him to weigh it again, sure they were being cheated. Once they realised he was dealing with them honestly they appreciated the time they saved whilst he collected their order together. He had extended his credit limit to ten shillings as prices had risen and many of his customers relied upon the agreement towards the end of the week when they were waiting for their wage packet.

Rebecca enjoyed thinking up new meals that she could prepare on a restricted budget and limited availability of fresh meat and vegetables. Each evening Basil would praise whatever she had cooked for him and usually dried the dishes after she had washed up. They would spend the remainder of the evening either listening to the radio together or reading, occasionally they would take a walk down to the seafront or a stroll in the park.

Basil no longer had to go to the post office and queue to purchase his stamps and send off his bills. Each Monday Rebecca would take them with her and bring him back the till receipt. He was able to leave all their food shopping to her, whilst he purchased all the cleaning materials and any other necessities. He began to realise just how dependent he had become on her in his life and felt guilty.

He had not increased her rent or the contribution she made to their food, despite her protests. She was earning more now, the price of everything, including rent, had risen and it was only fair that he should raise his prices accordingly.

'I appreciate all the unpaid jobs you do for me. If I raised your rent I'd have to start paying you a wage.'

'Don't be silly, Basil. I do very little.'

Basil looked at her. 'You keep the house clean, do all the cooking, help me with the accounts and sorting out those awful coupons. If I had to do it all myself the house would be a mess and I'd be living on bread and cheese.'

'And I would still be living in one room somewhere. It's like having a house of my own.'

'With a miserable old man under your feet.'

'You're not miserable and you're certainly not old, Basil.'

Basil sighed. 'You don't have to be polite or kind to me. I know I'm no fun to have around.'

Rebecca looked at him indignantly. 'I'm not being either. You're far less miserable than you were when I first knew you and you haven't any grey hairs even.'

Basil shook his head. 'You ought to be going out and enjoying yourself in your spare time, not staying in and looking after me. You'll never meet a nice young man to settle down with stuck in this back room.'

‘Who says I want one?’ Rebecca could feel the colour rising in her cheeks.

‘It’s not natural for a young girl like you.’

‘I could say it’s not natural for you not to have...’ her voice tailed off as she realised what she was about to say. She pushed her chair away from the table. ‘I think I’ll have an early night when I’ve washed up. I’ve had a busy day.’

The conversation niggled away at Rebecca as she lay in bed and tried to read. Basil was obviously tired of her presence. He wanted his house to himself again and he had been trying politely and tactfully to tell her it was time to go. She had been able to make regular savings from her wages as a post office employee since living with Basil and although she did not have enough to purchase a house or even a small flat, at least she did not have to worry about meeting increased expenses. She would speak to her colleagues the following day and see if any of them knew of a room or a cheap flat she could rent.

As usual Basil had the shop open by the time she came downstairs. She made a pot of tea and took a cup through to him in the shop before toasting two slices of bread for her breakfast. She looked in the larder. There was half a cooked rabbit from the previous day sitting there. She could pick the remainder of the flesh from the bones and make a rabbit stew for them.

‘I think I need to find somewhere else to lodge,’ said Rebecca to Mary whilst they were on their morning break.

‘Isn’t it working out?’

‘Well, I thought it was; I’ve been there nearly two years now. It’s just that last night Basil seemed to be throwing out hints that he had had enough of me being around.’

‘Have you actually asked him if he wants you to go?’

Rebecca shook her head. ‘I’ll do so after we’ve had our supper tonight. I’m sure he’ll be willing for me to stay until I have found somewhere else suitable. If you happen to hear of anywhere can you let me know?'

Mary nodded. From the little Rebecca had told her she thought they had a strange relationship. They lived like a married couple, but Rebecca was adamant that she had her own room and they were no more than friends.

'Thanks. I'll ask Brenda tomorrow. She might know somewhere.'

Dennis placed his cup in the sink, making no attempt to rinse it. 'Finally fed up with the old boy, then?'

'No, I just feel he wants me to go. To have his home back to himself.'

'Suppose you thought he was going to pop off and leave it all to you. Now you realise he's not going to you're ready to find another sucker.'

'What do you mean?'

'Well, it's obvious, isn't it? What would you see in a man his age apart from his money? You need someone young to satisfy you.'

Rebecca rinsed her cup and placed it on the shelf with deliberate calm. Her face was red and she was furious.

'I understand exactly what you are implying,' she said icily, 'I have known Mr Hurst for a number of years and when I needed somewhere to stay he offered me a room in his house. It was a business arrangement that has worked well, but it was not meant to last forever.'

'Yeah, tell that to the Marines.' Dennis walked away smiling. He loved to annoy Rebecca since she had refused his invitations to spend her evenings with him.

Basil and Rebecca ate the stew in silence, usually Basil asked after her day at the post office and Rebecca would ask if he had been busy in the shop. Rebecca picked up their empty bowls and Basil placed his hand on her wrist.

'Leave those. I want to talk to you.'

Rebecca sat back in her chair. A feeling of dread came over her. She wanted to tell him that she had stewed some pears and made some custard to go with them. The words would not come and she sat there with her eyes downcast.

Basil also seemed at a loss for words. He cleared his throat. 'Rebecca, I don't want people talking about you, besmirching your reputation. I've taken advantage of you by accepting your help. I should have realised and asked if you would consider marrying me. I've become very fond of you. I can't imagine living here without you now.'

Basil covered his face with his hands. 'Each night when I'm in bed I think of Katerina. At first the pain was so great I thought it would kill me. I wanted it to kill me. I still think of her, but the pain is less. I picture her face and it gradually becomes your face. You'll never take Katerina's place, but I love you, Rebecca. If you were to leave I would miss having you around. I would go back to being that miserable, bitter man that you took pity on in the Red Cross centre.'

Rebecca swallowed hard. This was not what she had expected to hear. 'Are you sure you want to marry *me* or do you just want a housekeeper?'

Basil looked at her sadly. 'If I just wanted a housekeeper I wouldn't have mentioned marriage. Think about it, Rebecca. If you decide to refuse me you can still stay here as long as you want.' Basil rose from the table.

'You haven't had your pudding,' said Rebecca lamely.

'Save it for tomorrow. I'm going for a walk.'

Rebecca scoured the pot she had used to make the rabbit stew. Did she want to marry Basil? Her heart did not leap and do somersaults when he walked into the room as it had when she was engaged to Charlie, but she felt safe and comfortable with him. He was trustworthy and reliable. When she had first had a problem with Dennis she had felt able to ask his advice about how she should deal with the unpleasant young man. He had not accused her of being over sensitive, told her to forget it and get on with her job. He had sat and listened to her, asking pertinent questions, until he had finally asked whether she thought she should complain to the manager or whether she felt capable of ignoring the jibes and veiled insults she was subjected to.

If she did refuse to marry Basil she wondered if she would ever have the opportunity to get married. Her friends who had lived in the area had moved away for various reasons and she no longer met up with them for an evening out. She smiled to herself. She and Basil were really like an old married couple. They were comfortable together. She returned from work, prepared their meal and then they would spend the evening listening to the wireless whilst she would sew or knit. During the summer months they would go for a walk, either down by the sea or in the park, but Basil had never asked her to go to the cinema or a local dance with him. He would take her elbow to steer her across the road, but he had never attempted to hold her hand or shown her any other sign of affection.

She sighed deeply. Getting married was a problem she needed to discuss with Basil – and he was the one person she could not approach for advice on this occasion.

1950 – 1960

A month before their wedding day Basil had finally talked to her about his earlier life. As he described some of the horrors he had witnessed, the starvation and oppression of the people Rebecca had cried with him and held his hand tightly

'Why haven't you kept in touch with your friend Manolis?'

Basil shrugged. 'What for?'

'I still write to Margaret, my friend I was in the WAAFs with. Wouldn't you like to know how he is and what he's doing now?'

'I don't know his address. He was living with his aunt when I turned up; he's probably moved on from there by now, but I would guarantee that he's still a fisherman.'

'You could go back and try to find him.'

Basil shook his head.

'I can understand your reluctance to return, but I think you should. A visit could help you to clear your mind of all the bad things.'

'One day, maybe.' Basil smiled wryly. 'I've taken a big step forward asking you to marry me. I'm not a man to rush things.'

The plain gold band on Rebecca's finger went unnoticed by the staff at the post office for over a week. Mary suddenly saw it and grabbed at Rebecca's hand.

'You're married!'

Rebecca blushed. 'Nearly two weeks now.'

'Why didn't you tell us? We'd have collected and bought something for you.'

'That's a kind thought, but there's really nothing we need.'

'What did your relatives give you? Something special?'

'We neither of us have any relatives.'

Mary frowned. 'None at all? Who acted as witnesses?'

'The couple Basil lodged with at one time came along. They're not really friends, but Basil has known them some years now and we went for a drink afterwards.'

'Preggers are you?' asked Dennis, pointing to Rebecca's stomach.

'No. I'm not like the girls you go out with.'

'You don't know what you've missed.'

Rebecca raised her eyebrows. 'In my book it was a good miss.' She smiled at the woman who had entered and now stood before her till, relieved that her colleagues could question her no further. 'How can I help you?'

Rebecca had been married for three months and she noticed the change in Basil. He smiled more, even laughed on occasions and seemed content to spend so much time with her. He would still wake in the night, shaking, moaning and covered in sweat where he had dreamt he was back in Crete. Rebecca would hold him until he had calmed down, then slip out of bed and make a cup of tea for them both, giving Basil time to compose himself. She never asked him about his nightmares; he had told her enough and she had no desire to hear details of the carnage he had witnessed.

She swung her legs over the side of the bed. Basil had been up for over an hour to receive delivery of the newspapers and open the shop. He rarely disturbed her when he rose, but somehow she was conscious of the space beside her in their bed.

Rebecca pushed her feet into her slippers and reached for her dressing gown. As she did so a momentary blackness descended before her eyes and she sank back on the bed gasping.

What was that about? She regained her feet gingerly and reached for her dressing gown. She felt perfectly all right now. Maybe she had moved a bit too fast and upset the equilibrium in her ears or had a touch of blood pressure.

She washed and dressed, made her way to the kitchen and brewed Basil his usual cup of Camp coffee, the smell making her feel quite nauseous. She toasted two slices of bread and wished she had some strawberry jam to spread on them. She wondered why she had suddenly fancied strawberry jam. She had always found it rather sweet and sickly. Having rinsed her plate and cup she picked up her bag and jacket, the sandwich she had made the night before, and exited through the shop, bidding Basil farewell.

It was no more than a ten minute walk to the post office and she always liked to arrive just before the manager opened the door. Whilst walking there she would decide what she would cook for their meal that evening. Maybe she would call at the butcher on her return home and buy some liver. They could have liver and bacon, Basil liked that. The thought of the liver suddenly made her shudder and she rapidly changed her mind. She would buy some sausages instead and they could have them with onions and mashed potato.

Rebecca turned the sausages in the pan. She felt ravenously hungry. So hungry that she couldn't wait the fifteen minutes that it would take for their meal to be ready. She cut herself a slice of bread, gave it a thin spread of butter and began to eat it as quickly as she could, hoping it would not spoil her appetite.

Whilst Basil counted the takings for the day and made his ledger up to date she washed up. It seemed to take her a long time that evening and she felt so tired. She must be going down with something, probably a cold. She remembered her moment of dizziness that morning and hoped it would be a cold and not an ear infection. A cold she could work with, but an ear infection was just too painful.

She carried a cup of tea through to the living room and sat down in the easy chair. In ten minutes the news would be on and after that there was a serial they always listened to, enjoying the way it ended each evening with an unanswered question that made them wait eagerly for the next instalment.

'Good day?' she asked Basil and he nodded.

'Not bad. We're one pound ten up on this time last week.'

'That's probably due to your hard work.'

Basil shrugged. 'Probably more due to the fact that Mrs Schofield paid her bill from last week. If she hadn't settled it by this evening I was going to refuse her any more credit.'

'I think she's genuinely struggling to make ends meet.'

'So do I, but I can't afford to let her run up large bills that she can't possibly pay off.'

Rebecca yawned. 'How would she manage then?'

'She'd just have to pay cash or go without.'

'She might go elsewhere.'

'That's a chance I'd have to take. I'll just put this away.' Basil placed most of the money into a cloth bank bag and carried it upstairs with him to place in the wardrobe. The ledger he left on the table and took the change into the shop, placing it in the till ready for the next day. He re-entered the living room and looked at Rebecca in surprise. She was fast asleep in the chair. He had never known her do such a thing before, she must have had a very tiring day and he felt guilty that he had not even offered to dry the dishes for her.

Basil listened to the news whilst Rebecca slept. He could always tell her of anything of importance that had happened in the world, but she would be annoyed if he left her to sleep through the serial.

'Rebecca, are you going to wake up? It's time for the serial.'

Rebecca opened a sleepy eye, then sat up straight. 'I must have been to sleep. Has the news finished?'

'You slept right through it.'

'Goodness! I'll listen to the serial; then I think I'll go to bed. I think I might be going down with a cold A good night's sleep could nip it in the bud.'

Rebecca had no sign of a cold the following day, but she did feel "odd". There was nothing she could really say was wrong with her. She just did not feel quite right. She would see how she felt by the beginning of the next week and if she felt no better she would go to the doctor and ask for a tonic. She was probably just over tired.

Basil watched her with concern. She had admitted to him that she was feeling very tired by the evenings and he suggested that she took some time off from the post office.

Rebecca smiled. 'If I took time off I'd probably decide to do the spring cleaning. I couldn't just sit and do nothing.' She shook her head. 'No, I'll go along to the doctor next week if I'm not feeling any better.'

'You said that last week,' Basil reminded her.

'I thought I was better, then the tiredness seemed to come back.'

'Do you want me to come with you?'

'Goodness, no. I'm not ill. I expect he'll tell me that I'm wasting his time.'

'It's rather too soon to tell, Mrs Hurst, but from what you've told me I would say you are very likely in the early stages of pregnancy. My advice is to eat if you feel hungry and go to bed when you feel tired. Don't do any heavy lifting and come back and see me in six weeks. By then we should know for certain. If you've had a period in that time and you're not feeling any better then we'll do a few tests and see if we can get to the bottom of it.'

Rebecca felt the colour drain from her face and then return with a rush. 'What shall I tell my husband?'

'That you're probably pregnant.' The doctor looked at her. She seemed an intelligent woman; what had she not understood? 'Men are usually delighted when they know their wife is expecting.'

'No, I mean, I'm not sure that...' Rebecca's words tailed off. 'Thank you, doctor.'

'Come and see me again in six weeks, remember.'

Rebecca nodded. She was so thankful that Basil had not insisted on coming with her. She walked slowly along by the park, looking through the railings at the children who were playing there. Was she really going to have a child of her own? Well, it would be Basil's child as well and she was not sure how he would feel about being a father again. She leant her head against the cool railing. It could be a false alarm. There was no need for her to confide in her husband yet. She would wait and see what the doctor said when she returned for her next appointment.

'Looking forward to becoming a grandfather, is he?' asked Dennis.

Rebecca gripped his shoulder, her fingers digging in painfully. 'I know you get a perverse pleasure from making unpleasant remarks to people. I'm used to your nasty little ways Dennis, but if you ever make any of your sly innuendos in front of my husband you'll regret it.'

Dennis flexed his shoulder. 'You need to get a sense of humour.'

Rebecca glared at him. 'You need to get a sense of respect for others. Before I leave I'm putting in an official complaint about your behaviour.'

'That won't get you anywhere.'

'It may not get me anywhere as you say, but it will give me a sense of satisfaction knowing you'll have to try to wriggle your way out of the situation.'

'And I'll back her up,' added Mary who had been listening. She took Rebecca's elbow. 'Don't let that Smart Alec upset you.

You'll not be here much longer to have to put up with him. Not like some of us,' she added, glaring at Dennis with dislike.

Basil looked at the tiny dark haired bundle that lay in Rebecca's arms. He had told her how pleased he was and reiterated that throughout her pregnancy, whilst in his heart he was dreading the event. Suppose she had a boy? How would he feel? No one could ever take little Vasilis's place in his heart. Now he gazed at his daughter and his heart swelled with love for her. She was beautiful. She was perfect. He vowed that whatever happened he would protect this child for ever, with his own life if necessary. Nothing must ever take her from him.

He kissed Rebecca's forehead. 'Thank you,' he said, 'Catherine is beautiful.'

'Catherine?' Rebecca looked at him in surprise. 'I thought we were going to call her Veronica if she was a girl.'

Basil shook his head. 'Her name is Catherine. Catherine Rebecca.'

Rebecca looked down at the tiny, red faced infant. Katerina had been the name of Basil's first wife. For a moment she wanted to scream at him and tell him to forget the Cretan woman – that she was his wife now; then she remembered how he had suffered. She forced her face into a smile.

'Catherine is a very nice name.'

Cathy leant her head back against her father's chest. 'Tell me a story, Daddy.'

'What shall I tell you?'

'The one about the pond in the garden.'

Basil smiled. 'Well, there was once a little girl who lived in a big house with a big garden. In the garden was a pond and every day the little girl, whose name just happened to be Cathy, would go down to the pond and look at all the wonderful things she could see. There were water lilies and on their pads there would be dragon flies and damsel flies, on the water would be boatmen skimming their way across. The goldfish would swim around lazily and sometimes a frog would be sitting on a stone warming himself in the sun and waiting for an unsuspecting fly. When Cathy saw the frog sitting on the stone she always knew it was going to be a special day. She would be able to make a wish and the wish would come true.'

Cathy snuggled further into her father's arm. 'And will the frog be there today?'

'I think he might. What do you think Cathy would wish for today?'

Cathy considered. 'She'd like to be made very tiny so she could sit on a lily pad and talk to a dragonfly.'

'Oh, I think that could be two wishes.'

Cathy smiled. 'Then maybe she could just talk to the dragonfly?'

'If you close your eyes tight and make the wish we'll see if the frog can arrange for a dragonfly to come and sit on her shoulder? How would that be?'

Cathy nodded eagerly and closed her eyes.

Rebecca looked over at the pair of them whilst she continued with the ironing. She enjoyed listening to the fairy stories that Basil told to Cathy. They were always happy tales, the sun would be shining and the pond life would live amicably together. The worst that could happen would be for a fly to fall into the pond, be rescued by a water beetle and have to sit on a lily pad to dry out his wings.

She cast a surreptitious eye on the clock as she folded a pillow case. Cathy would be happy to listen to the stories as long as her father was willing to tell them, but it would be time for her to go to bed in fifteen minutes. She nodded discreetly towards the mantel-piece and Basil nodded back. Rebecca was a stickler for routine.

Basil carried his daughter upstairs and placed her on her bed. He waited whilst Rebecca tucked the bed clothes around her and kissed her goodnight. He went through his usual ritual. He smoothed Cathy's hair, stroked her cheek and kissed her. He then stood at the doorway and took a long look at her serene face before returning downstairs to his wife.

Rebecca smiled at her husband. 'You really should write those stories that you tell her down and send them away. I'm sure someone would want to publish them.'

'Don't be silly. They're just for babies. Besides, who ever heard of a man writing fairy stories!'

'You could send them off in my name.'

'They would need to be typed. No one would look at them if they were hand written, particularly in my bad writing.'

'I could type them,' offered Rebecca. 'I learnt to type when I was in the WAAFs. I'd need to practice for a little while, but I'm sure it would soon come back to me.'

'We haven't got a typewriter.'

'There's a second hand shop on the corner. I've seen one in the window and it's quite cheap.'

Within a couple of weeks Rebecca was able to type a page without more than a couple of mistakes. Whilst Basil told Cathy her bedtime story she would sit and make notes. Once Cathy was in bed she would type out the notes she had made and hand them to Basil to read and alter. By the time Basil declared himself satisfied she had often typed it a dozen times.

At the end of two months there were twenty short fairy stories that Basil felt were suitable to send away to a publisher. He packaged them up and walked down to the post office with Cathy, promising to take her into the park afterwards.

'Is Mummy coming?' asked Cathy.

'Not today. She has some sewing she wants to finish. Besides, we can't stay too long as I have to go back and open the shop.'

'Mummy could open the shop.'

Basil shook his head. 'Mummy has far too many other things that she has to do. All the washing and ironing, the cleaning and cooking. She hasn't got time to open the shop as well.'

'Do all Mummy's have lots of things to do?' asked Cathy.

'Lots and lots.'

Cathy considered this information. 'I don't think I'll be a Mummy,' she announced solemnly, took her father's hand and skipped along beside him. 'Will you push me on the swings, Daddy?'

Basil opened the package that had been returned to him by the publisher. It was as he had thought. No one would want to read fairy stories. He pulled out the letter and scanned it, then read it again more slowly, a smile breaking out on his face. He handed the letter to Rebecca.

'Read that and tell me what you think,' he said.

Rebecca read the letter slowly and looked up at Basil her eyes glowing. 'That's wonderful. If you can send them ten more they'll definitely publish. That's easy. All you have to do is choose from the pile in the cupboard.'

Basil nodded. 'It seems a strange thing for a man to be writing fairy stories, but if it brings in some extra money I'm not too proud to have my name associated with them.'

Basil sorted through the collection of short stories, rejecting those that he thought were too similar to some he had already submitted. Within three weeks Rebecca had retyped them and he carried the package down to the post office, hoping that this time the publisher would accept them and not ask for any more.

It was a month before the letter came and Rebecca handed it to Basil. 'Open it up. I'm so excited.'

Basil handed it back to her. 'You open it. I'm probably being told that they've changed their mind.'

'Surely they would have returned them all if that was the case.' She ran a knife under the flap and handed it back to Basil. He drew out the sheet of paper and the enclosed cheque. It was far more than he had received for the sale of his aunt's house. He turned the cheque round so Rebecca could see the amount.

Rebecca gasped. 'That much! It's a fortune. What are you going to spend it on?'

'Half of it is yours. You did the hard work. What would you like?'

Rebecca considered. 'A new winter coat, maybe.' She had worn her current one for the past three years and it was certainly showing signs of wear. 'What about you?'

'I'm going to buy a car.'

'A car?'

Basil nodded. 'Just a small one. We can take Cathy out to the countryside on Sundays.'

'Can you drive?'

'Of course,' replied Basil confidently, not admitting he had never taken a driving test and did not possess a license.

Basil looked at the slim book, a picture of a pond with a frog sitting on a stone and a fairy hovering above, made the cover attractive. Without consulting Rebecca he had asked that a symbol should be placed on the spine. The second cheque that had arrived with the book delighted him. It was far more than he would have expected a writer to receive and the additional knowledge that he would be paid a percentage on every book that was sold was a bonus.

The book of fairy stories sold well and Basil began to think about a second one, the stories gradually becoming a little more educational as Cathy matured and began to understand how caterpillars became chrysalis and butterflies would emerge eventually or how plants took up moisture and nutrients from the earth and flourished. Cathy was full of questions, why did some trees lose all their leaves in the winter, why did some animals go to sleep when it was cold, why weren't they hungry when they were asleep?

Rebecca would listen avidly, amazed how Basil could explain complex nature so simply and turn it into a story so that a child could understand the science and biology involved. The publisher liked the stories also and Basil found he was in demand for as many as he could produce. By the time Cathy started school he had five books published in his name.

The little Morris eight Basil had bought with his first money had been exchanged for a Ford ten and each fine Sunday during the summer Rebecca would prepare a picnic and they would drive out into the countryside. During their walks Cathy would pick a collection of wild flowers and when they returned home Rebecca would show her how to press and mount them. When the primroses or blue bells flowered she was allowed to pick a whole bunch and have them in a vase on her bedroom window sill.

Basil impressed upon her that she must not touch deadly nightshade or the brightly coloured toadstools they came across, disturb a nesting bird or poke a stick down a hole to see if it was occupied. She spent an hour sitting quietly by her parent's side whilst they watched some baby blackbirds take their first flight; then became anxious that they might get lost and not remember where their nest was located. Basil reassured her and also promised to tell her a story that night before she went to bed about a lost bird.

After six months at school Cathy announced that she was no longer interested in fairy stories. 'They're for babies,' she declared. 'I'm not a baby now. I go to school.'

Rebecca raised her eyebrows at her husband and he nodded. 'I must admit I'm fed up with fairy stories also. Time for me to grow up a little bit.'

For the next two weeks Rebecca read from a book to Cathy before she went to bed, but after the first few times Cathy seemed disinterested and would look longingly at her father, his stories were much more exciting even if they were for babies. The looks were not lost on Basil and he began to think about stories that a child of six could relate to and enjoy.

'Why don't you tell her adventure stories?' suggested Rebecca.

'What do you mean?'

Rebecca laughed. 'You're the one with the imagination. Add in some more children instead of a fairy, have the good children triumphing over the bad ones. Simple things. The boy who continually steals apples from the local shop and the children teach him a lesson by putting a plasticine one there. He takes a bite and it makes him sick so he doesn't steal again. What about a boy the teacher knew was cheating at exams and he taught him a lesson by changing the exam paper at the last minute? I'll try to remember some of the tricks my brothers played on each other.'

'You think up some ideas for me and I'll see what I can do.'

'Would you like me to tell you a story tonight?' he asked Cathy.

Cathy's face lit up and then dropped. 'Not a fairy story, Daddy.'

Basil shook his head. 'No, this is about a little girl called Cathy who had a friend called Christopher and a dog called Captain. They went for a holiday at the seaside in a place called Cornwall. It wasn't like the seaside here, the beach was sandy and there were rocks that could be climbed and rock pools to be investigated.'

Cathy immediately went over and sat on her father's knee. 'What happened?'

Basil smiled and began the story of the two children and a dog. Cathy sat enthralled until Basil said that was all he was telling her that evening.

'But what happened? What did they do next?' she asked anxiously.

'They went home and had their tea, followed by a bath to get rid of all the sand and salt, and then they went to bed.'

'What about Captain?'

'He was given a bone to chew and then he went to bed also.'

'What are they going to do tomorrow?

'That you will have to wait to find out.' Basil smiled at her. 'It's time for you to go to bed now.'

Cathy gave a deep sigh. 'I won't be able to sleep unless I know what they will be doing tomorrow,' she insisted.

'Oh, dear, if my stories are going to keep you awake I'd better stop telling them to you.'

Cathy pouted, but she knew that once her father had said that was the end to his story telling for that evening he would not change his mind. 'If I promise to *try* to go to sleep will you tell me some more tomorrow?'

Basil smiled at her. 'You try very hard and I'll see if I can find out what happens to them.'

Each night Cathy settled herself on her father's lap and listened enthralled to the adventures he conjured up.

Rebecca thought of a number of scenarios that she thought Basil could use, some he rejected, but gradually ideas took shape in his head. He would tell Cathy the stories and judge their merits on her reaction. If she turned her attention to her colouring or jig-saw puzzle he knew he would have to improve the story line to keep her attention.

Some evenings she sat there enthralled and kept asking what happened next, reluctant to go to bed and having to wait for the next instalment the following day. He had found a theme that had caught her imagination. Cathy and Christopher were the central characters in each story, along with their incredibly intelligent dog, Captain.

The more Basil composed the tales the more he began to enjoy working out a simple plot that was both intriguing and also had a moral. He began to look at the clock anxiously towards the end of the afternoon, longing to close the shop and dictate his thoughts from the day to Rebecca. Cathy would sit and listen, no longer hanging on every word. She knew she would be given the story to read when her mother had finished the typing and she would be asked for her opinion.

'You ought to learn to type,' Rebecca chided Basil.

'Are you tired of doing it for me?'

'Not a bit,' she shook her head. 'I just feel you could find it more satisfying to put your thoughts down as they come to you, rather than wait for me to type them and then have to read them through.'

'I enjoy telling them to you. When I begin to put them into the spoken word I can become really involved with the characters and that's when my ideas come to me, besides Cathy isn't interested in me telling them to her any more. She's moved on to proper books.'

'Yours are proper books, Basil. I feel so proud of you when I go into a bookshop or the library and see your books on the shelves.'

'We had a new girl in our class today,' announced Cathy.

'That's nice. What's her name?'

'I don't know. It's a funny name.'

'What do you mean?'

'She's not English.'

'Where does she come from?'

Cathy shrugged. 'I don't know. Mrs Green said she had come to live in the cafe by the station.'

'Well, be nice to her. She must feel very lost and lonely in a foreign country. Make her feel welcome.'

Cathy smiled. ''Course I will, besides she's sitting next to me.'

Basil listened as his daughter chatted on to her mother about her day in school. If the shop near the station that had been empty for some time was going to be turned into a cafe he might well be able to drum up a bit of business there with them. The shop was not making the same profit as it had in the past. He had noticed that some of the larger specialist grocers were able to offer some of their goods for less than he had to pay the wholesalers and his customers were wise enough to spot the savings they were making. It was fortunate that they had a very satisfactory bank balance due to his books.

Basil walked down to the station and looked at the double fronted shop, its windows were whitewashed and he could not see what was taking place inside. He rang the bell and waited until a small dark woman opened the door.

'Yes?'

'May I come in? I believe you are new here. I'd like to introduce myself.'

A puzzled look crossed the woman's face. Still holding the door she turned and called out in Greek to her husband. Basil felt his head reel. He had not heard Greek spoken for so long. A man appeared at her shoulder, spatters of paint on his shirt.

'Can I help?'

Basil smiled and greeted him in Greek. A look of amazement passed over the couples' faces and the door was opened wide.

'Come in, you're welcome.'

Basil entered and looked around. The man was obviously busy repainting the walls.

'I can see you're busy. I'll not hold you up. I just wanted to introduce myself. I have the general store a couple of roads over. I understand you're planning to open as a cafe?'

Tassos nodded and answered in Greek. 'We thought it could be a prime position. People wanting a quick meal or cup of tea before they caught a train. Which part of Greece do you come from?'

'I don't,' smiled Basil. 'I lived out there for a few years. I didn't even realise I remembered the language until your wife called you.'

'How did you know we were planning a cafe?'

'My daughter told me. She said a new girl in her class was sitting next to her and she was living here.'

'Ah, your daughter must be Cathy. My Despina talks about her a good deal. I feel they will be friends. When we open you must all come for a meal. My wife is a good cook.'

'I'm sure she is.' Basil felt the uncertainty growing in him. He did not want to become friendly with this family. Sooner or later awkward questions would be asked of him. 'Well, I will leave you to get on. If you need anything I have the general store round the corner.'

Basil accepted the invitation for them to visit and have a meal with the cafe owners. Had he refused it would have been the height of rudeness. He insisted Cathy must accompany them as they had no one to leave her with and it would also provide an excuse to leave at an early hour in the evening.

Rebecca found the visit exhausting. Basil tried to keep the conversation in English but as the cafe owner's wife spoke very little he often had to revert to Greek and then Rebecca would not understand.

Despina and Cathy seemed able to communicate with each other well enough, Despina seizing avidly onto new words and adding them to her vocabulary.

'Will you teach me to speak Greek please, Daddy,' Cathy asked as they walked home.

Basil shook his head. 'You have no need to speak Greek. You live in England.'

'I'll ask Despina to teach me.' Cathy tossed her head impatiently. 'We'll be able to talk properly then.'

Basil smiled. 'I am sure Despina will be able to speak very good English in no time at all. It is far more helpful for you to talk to her in English.'

'Who taught you to speak Greek, Daddy?'

Basil shrugged. 'I learnt a bit when I was at University and then I just listened to people talking.'

'Then I'll listen to Despina talking and I'll learn that way.'

'That sounds like a good idea. Do you want to know what is happening in the new story I'm writing? As it's Sunday tomorrow you can stay up a little bit later tonight.'

Cathy slipped her hand into his. 'Can you tell me the story in Greek?'

'No, you crafty little monkey, I can't.'

Basil looked at his account books for the shop. He was still making a profit, but the income he received for his books was more than enough for them to live on in comparative luxury.

'I think now is the time to sell the shop,' he announced to Rebecca.

Rebecca looked at him in surprise. 'Sell? I thought you were happy being a shop keeper.'

'I used to be, but not anymore. The money isn't in it any longer. We make enough to cover our expenses and a bit over, but I make far more from my books. What is the point of working eight hours a day to make ends meet when I could work three hours a day and make enough to live comfortably?'

Rebecca looked at him dubiously. 'Where would we live?'

'We can buy a small house. Cathy will be changing schools in six months so we ought to look in an area that has a reputable school nearby.'

'Are you sure, Basil? Suppose children suddenly decide they no longer like your books. What would we do then?'

'There are two options. I have to change my stories or I go back to work as a milkman.'

'Oh, Basil, you hated being a milkman.'

Basil leaned across the table and took his wife's hand. 'I'm joking. Even if no one liked my books any more there's plenty in the bank.'

'I thought you wanted to save that for Cathy so she could go to University?'

'I'm sure there'll be enough.'

'How can you be sure?'

Slowly Basil withdrew an envelope from his pocket and handed it to Rebecca. She took out the sheet of paper and gasped.

'Do they really mean they are going to pay you that much? It's a fortune.'

'There's a condition attached. They want a new book each year for the next five years. I don't see how I would have time to work in the shop.'

Cathy was not happy. They had moved to the other side of the town and in September she was to attend a new school where she would know no one. She missed Despina and continually asked when they would be able to return to the shop. Basil had explained to her that the shop no longer belonged to them and she would have to go to a new school in September wherever she lived.

'Will Despina come to that school with me?' she asked.

'I don't know,' Basil answered honestly. 'It will depend upon which school her parents think is the best one for her.'

'Why do you think this one is best for me?'

Basil sighed. He did not wish to tell his daughter that her peers would be coming from the homes of lawyers, teachers and bankers. Many of the children in her previous school had been the offspring of road sweepers, shop assistants and factory hands, and he wanted her to mix with people who would have a broader horizon, able to see the benefits of a University education.

'Trust us,' he said. 'I promise you, Cathy, we would never, ever do anything that we did not think would benefit you. When you are grown up I think you will realise that the school we have chosen for you was the right one.'

'I don't see why I have to go to school anyway. I want to be a gardener.'

'That's fine, but to be a good gardener you will need to know the names of the plants and how to look after them. When you are old enough to you can go to Horticultural College. You could end up being the head gardener at Buckingham Palace.'

Cathy scowled. She had no desire at all to be a gardener,

working outside in the cold and rain, and had only plucked the occupation out of thin air in the hope of an adverse reaction from her father. As usual, he had an answer for everything.

Cathy sat at her desk, feeling very conscious of her new navy blue gym slip, white blouse and blue tie. Her parents had assured her she looked very smart and all the girls would be wearing the same uniform. Despite having looked surreptitiously at the other girls in the class and satisfied herself that everyone was dressed exactly the same she did not feel comfortable. At her previous school they had been able to wear whatever clothes they wished. Barbara had always worn an old red jumper with darns at the elbows, Jackie's mother had been a great knitter; whatever colour dress or skirt Jackie wore she always had a matching cardigan. Despina had always worn a black skirt with a bright coloured blouse.

Cathy sighed deeply. Despina and her family had returned to Cyprus as the cafe had never become popular. Now she knew no one, and how would she ever remember their names if they were all dressed the same?

She stood dutifully when the teacher pointed to her and asked her to tell the class her name. 'I'm Catherine, I like to be called Cathy.' Her face scarlet she sank back down into her seat.

The teacher nodded. 'I'm pleased to hear that as we have two other girls called Catherine in the class.' Miss Watson pointed to the girl at the next desk.

'I'm Marion.' She sat back down with a thud on her chair.

Cathy screwed her head round to see each girl as they stood and gave their name. The girl sitting towards the back of the room was called Janet. She would be able to remember her as she had black ringlets, quite unlike anyone else. She looked again at Marion, trying to take in every detail of the girl. If she could at least recognise her when they had their break she would be someone to talk with.

Most of the morning seemed to be taken up with the teacher handing out various exercise and text books and making them copy a time table for their weekly lessons. Cathy pulled a face as she saw that every day they would have at least forty minutes of Maths, one afternoon would be taken up completely with games lessons and another with art. She was not at all sure she was going to enjoy being at this school whatever her father said about it being the right one for her.

She joined the queue for lunch, collected her plate and looked for somewhere to sit. 'There's a space at that table,' an older girl pointed the place out. Cathy nodded, walked over and took the vacant seat.

Marion looked at her. 'Any idea what this is?' she prodded the food on her plate with her fork.

Cathy shook her head.

'Well, I guess they won't try to poison us on our first day. I'm Marion.'

'I know. You sit at the desk next to me. I'm Cathy.'

'So you do. Everyone looks the same to me. I suppose it's the uniform.'

Cathy breathed a sigh of relief. 'I thought it was just me. Do you think you're going to like this school?'

Marion shrugged. 'My sister says it's not too bad.'

'You've got a sister?'

'Two. One older and one younger. What about you?'

'I'm an only child.'

'Think yourself lucky.'

'Why?'

'My younger sister is always trying to take my things and my older one considers us both to be babies. She's only two years older than me, what makes her think she's so grown up?' Marion placed a piece of potato into her mouth.

'How old is your younger one?'

'She's nine.'

Cathy wondered if Marion was able to make conversation so easily because she had sisters, whereas she felt at a loss for words.

'If I have a new dress Lizzie wants one too. If I go out to tea she whines and complains because she isn't going to a friend that day. She's just a nuisance.'

'Don't your parents explain that you do different things as you're different people?'

Marion looked at her scathingly. 'Do your parents ever explain anything to you?'

'Always.'

'Really? Don't they just tell you what they think you want to hear?'

Cathy shook her head. 'I don't think so.'

Marion scooped up the remainder of her meat and potato onto her fork. 'That was better than it looked. Shall we see what they're giving us for pudding?'

Cathy pushed the remainder of her meal to the side of the plate and rose to join Marion in the queue for a portion of sponge pudding and custard. She felt considerably better now she had a companion.

1966 – 1971

'Cathy, we have to talk seriously about the subjects you are going to specialise in ready for your exams. Have you any idea what you would finally like to do when you leave school? Do you want to go to University?' Basil held up his hand as his daughter was about to interrupt him. 'The choice is yours. We're not going to insist you go on to University if you would prefer to do something else. We only want you to be happy. We just don't want you to make a decision now that you regret later.'

'I don't want to go to Uni.'

Basil nodded and waited.

'I know I wouldn't be able to cope with the work.'

'What do you mean?' frowned Basil.

'I'm not stupid, but nor am I particularly academic. There isn't a single subject that I really shine at. I'm what the teachers call a "good all rounder". You need to be really good at something to think of studying it further at University.'

'What would you like to do?'

Cathy blushed. 'This might sound stupid, but there's nothing that I particularly want to do. I know I have to go out to work eventually, but I don't know what work I would enjoy doing every day.'

Basil smiled at his daughter. 'There's no rush to decide. Choose whatever subjects you think you would enjoy working at most for your O Levels. When you see the grades you've been given that might help you to decide.'

Cathy smiled at him gratefully. She truly had no idea what she would like to do when she finally left school. Some of the girls, like Marion, had known for years that they wanted to become a nurse or go into teaching, but Cathy admitted she had no particular vocation or ambition.

'Have a word with the careers teacher at school. She may suggest something that appeals to you.'

Marion and Cathy sat on the grass in the park. Cathy sighed deeply. 'I wish I was like you and knew exactly what I wanted to do.'

'I've always wanted to be a nurse. Why don't you try it?'

Cathy shook her head and pulled a face. 'I really wouldn't want to have to deal with people so intimately, besides I don't like blood.'

'Isn't there anything that you like to do more than anything else?'

'Well, I suppose messing around with makeup and trying my hair out in different styles. I'd love to bleach it blonde, but I'm sure Mum and Dad would have a fit if I did such a thing.'

'Why on earth would you want to be blonde? You've got beautiful dark hair.'

'Straight as pump water! I wish I'd inherited my mother's natural waves.'

'You could always cut it and have a perm.'

'I wouldn't want it cut short. I wouldn't be able to put it up.' Cathy lifted her long, straight locks and held them up.

'You look good like that,' observed Marion. 'Why don't you wear it like that during the day?'

'Too much effort. It's easier just to run a brush through in the morning.'

Cathy thought about the conversation she had had with her friend. Maybe she would enjoy being a hairdresser. The girls who worked in the local salon always looked glamorous, their hair immaculate and their make-up and nail varnish freshly applied. She might make an appointment for a trim and ask them a few questions. If she didn't like their answers she didn't have to take the thought any further.

'Your results were good, Cathy. A pass in every subject you took.'

'Just.'

'A pass is a pass. Have your results helped you to decide on your A Level subjects?'

'I don't want to stay on at school and take A Levels.'

Basil frowned. 'Why not?'

'I've decided I want to be a hairdresser.'

'A hairdresser?' Basil raised his eyebrows in surprise.

Cathy nodded. 'So there wouldn't be much point in me staying on to do A Levels.'

'No education is wasted. You could find out you're not suited to hairdressing and then you might have to take your exams at a later date. That's never so easy.'

'You don't want me to be a hairdresser.'

'I have no objection if that's what you truly want to do. But I do want you to stay on at school and get your A Levels first. You're only sixteen, Cathy. In a couple of years you could have decided on a very different career.'

Cathy sighed. 'I knew you'd say that.'

'Is it so awful to have to stay at school?'

'I shall just feel so childish. Marion will be working and I will still be at school.'

'If the situation was the other way around would you feel Marion was childish?'

'No, of course not.'

'And I'm sure she won't think that way about you. You stay on at school and get your A Levels and then we'll help you to find a place at a recognised school of hairdressing. In time you could even open a salon of your own.'

Marion held up a pair of white shorts, trimmed with green and pink and a matching top. 'What do you think?'

'Wow! You'll look terrific in that outfit.'

'You don't think the pink is wrong with my hair, do you?'

Cathy shook her head. 'There's not enough to worry about. When are you going to wear that? Not on the beach here, surely? You're bound to get tar on it.'

'I've bought it to take to Greece with me.'

'Greece!'

'I've been saving up all year. A couple of the girls I work with are going to Rhodes and I asked if I could join them.'

Cathy felt envious. Still at school she only had her allowance and the two pounds she earned at the hairdressing salon on a Saturday for sweeping the floor and cleaning the basins. She was not earning a proper wage like Marion, but she was sure if she had asked her father for a loan he would have agreed. 'Why do you want to go there?'

'I would be happy to go anywhere. I haven't been off to the south of France every summer like you.'

Cathy's envy turned to guilt. It was true, every year since she had reached the age of twelve her parents had taken her to southern France for the whole of the holidays. Once she had asked if Marion could come with them, and despite her parents agreement and the arrangements made, Marion had contracted chickenpox. The following year Marion's mother had been ill and Marion was needed at home to help whilst she convalesced.

'What is there to do out there?'

'Well,' Marion's eyes took on an enthusiastic gleam, 'According to the guide book there's a fabulous old medieval town, beautiful beaches, plenty of places to eat and drink and the sun shines every day.' She frowned. 'I'll have to take plenty of sun cream with me. I don't want to fry.'

'You'll end up the same pink as the trim on your outfit,' Cathy smiled and was rewarded with a slap on her leg from Marion.

'I'm taking my camera, the one I had for Christmas, and plenty of film with me. As soon as I come back I'll get them developed and when you come back from France we'll have a photo evening and I'll tell you all about it.'

'I wish I was going somewhere exciting like you,' sighed Cathy. 'I know we go to a different place each year, but it's still France. Dad insists on driving down and it takes three or four days. It's nice to have a car whilst we're there, but I get terribly bored on the journey.'

'At least you can stop when you want and have a break. I shall be sitting in a 'plane for four hours or so.'

'Even that's exciting. I've never flown anywhere.'

'Nor have I.' Marion cast a surreptitious glance at her friend. 'I'm not sure if I'm looking forward to it.'

'Don't be silly. It will be part of the holiday. If it's only four hours you'll be back down before you know it.'

Marion leaned back on the grass, placing her bag beneath her head. 'Once I'm there I plan to just relax. I'm not taking any text books with me even though we shall have exams a month after I return.'

'You've never had a problem with exams. You always got high grades.'

'That was school work.' Marion frowned. 'I don't want to fail and have to do the year over again. This is important.'

Cathy pored over Marion's photographs. 'It looks wonderful. That sea is such a deep blue and the sunset, well, it looks like the photographs you see of Africa.'

'It was fantastic. I'm already saving up to go away next year.'

'Back to Rhodes?'

Marion shook her head. 'No, one of the other islands. I shall go on my own this time, though. All the other two thought about was how much they could drink and how many men they could snare for freebies. I'm not interested in that. A couple of drinks with a nice meal and then a walk around to see the Old Town at night is more to my taste. I don't want to spend the evening snogging some chap whose name I won't even remember the following day.'

'You've got a beautiful tan.'

Marion regarded her arms. 'At least I didn't go red and peel. You should have seen the state of some people over there. It must have been so painful. I limited my sun exposure. Most of the time I was on the beach I sat under an umbrella. I read the guide book in the morning and decided where I would go in the afternoon or the following day. I couldn't manage to see the whole island, but I went to Lindos one day and the site at Kameros another.

'What about the language?' asked Cathy. Despite spending five years studying French at school she still spoke the language haltingly.

'No problem. Most people I met, you know the waiters and bar tenders, they all spoke English.'

'Did you wear your shorts and top all the time?'

Marion shook her head. 'I wore it for the first couple of days, then I found a cotton skirt and blouse was cooler when you were walking in the town or on a site. I took far too many clothes. I only really needed beach wear and something decent for the evening when we went out for a meal. I even took a cardigan and a jacket with me! They stayed in the case the whole time I was there.'

Cathy nodded and flicked through the photographs again. Marion's holiday had certainly been far more interesting than her own.

'Where are you planning to go this year?' asked Cathy, seeing Marion had a collection of travel brochures beneath her arm.

'Kos, I think. It's quite close to Turkey so I could do a day trip over there and see what the country is like. I can also take trips to other islands. They say that on Nisiros you can walk down into the crater of a volcano. I'd like to do that.'

'You're still planning to travel alone?' asked Cathy tentatively, hoping Marion might invite her to accompany her.

'Yes,' Marion nodded vehemently. 'I can see and do what I want then without having to consider anyone else. Are you going to France as usual?'

'Dad hasn't mentioned it yet, but I expect so. I'm going to ask him to teach me to drive this summer. I should have learnt when I was eighteen. He might have considered giving me a car for my twenty first then.'

'Why do you want a car?'

Cathy shrugged. 'I don't particularly, but I don't know what else to ask for when it's my birthday.'

'Are you planning a big party?'

Cathy shook her head. 'No. I'm not a party person and Dad would probably curl up and die rather than go to a party. Besides, the only people I know apart from you are the other girls at the hairdressing school, and I'm not that friendly with any of them. What about you?'

'No, I said I'd rather have the money a party would cost towards paying for my holiday. Dad came up trumps and I shall be able to afford to stay for two weeks. I think he was relieved that I didn't want a big splash like Sarah had. She's talking about getting engaged and that will mean another party he has to fork out for and then her wedding. I hope she doesn't decide to get married the year Lizzie becomes twenty one or poor Dad will be in the workhouse.'

'Are you going to celebrate when you're fully qualified as a nurse?'

'Only with the other girls, I expect. When do you finish your hairdressing training?'

'Two more months. If I pass my final tests Mrs Hadley has agreed to take me on as an apprentice.'

'If you're qualified you're not an apprentice,' argued Marion.

'I shall still have an awful lot to learn. It's one thing working on dummy heads or the other girls. If things go wrong we just laugh it off, but a customer would not be very happy. You didn't see me the time I agreed to have a blonde streak put in and Naomi used the wrong strength solution and it went green. Dad nearly had a fit and it took weeks to get rid of it. Mrs Hadley has promised that once I have proved myself she'll allow me to have my photograph in the window along with the other stylists. I'll still have to work under her direction until she's confident that I really know what I'm doing, but I don't mind that.'

'Let me know when you start and I'll book in with you for my regular trim. I'll see if my Mum will come along for her weekly wash and set when her girl is on holiday. She might prefer you and come regularly.'

'Would you spread the word amongst the hospital staff? My prices will be less than any of the other girls and I'm sure my work will be just as good.'

'Of course.' Marion looked at her watch. 'I must go. I'm on nights for the next three months and I want to have a bath before supper.'

'How do you manage to stay awake?'

'You get used to it. I'll call round when I'm back on civilized day-time duties and I shall expect to hear that you're at Mrs Hadley's.' Marion picked up the brochures. 'I am awful,' she remarked. 'I'm much more excited about going to Kos than I am about qualifying as a nurse.'

Cathy looked at the photograph of herself in the hairdresser's window. It was a head and shoulders shot that her father had taken whilst they were in France and she was waiting for her meal to be served. She was pleased with it; she looked mature and glamorous. Her title was 'junior stylist' but Mrs Hadley had assured her that was only temporary. She still found that most of her day was taken up with sweeping the floor, cleaning basins and mirrors and being at the beck and call of the more senior girls, handing them rollers or perm papers, but Marion had been true to her word and insisted that Cathy had trimmed her hair. Rebecca gave up washing her own hair and visited Cathy each week, although Cathy felt guilty when she handed her the bill. If a customer came in without an appointment it usually fell to Cathy to wash their hair until a more senior assistant was available to cut or set it. Cathy began to wonder why she had spent three years training. She was doing no more now than when she had worked as a Saturday assistant.

A young man entered the salon and looked around, his eyes alighting on her. Cathy placed her broom against the wall and walked to the reception desk. They were not a men's hairdresser and she wondered whom he had come to meet.

'Can I help you?' she smiled.

'Just the girl,' he said, displaying white, even teeth. 'That is your photo outside, isn't it? Junior stylist?'

'Yes, but we don't cut men's hair.'

'Is the old thatch that much of a mess?' He ran his hand across his hair, flattening it down. 'I don't want a haircut. I want to talk to you.'

'Me? Are you offering samples of a new product? If so you need to speak to Mrs Hadley.'

'That's definitely not my line. I'm a photographer.'

'We don't pay for the window display. They're just snapshots that we have blown up so the customers know what we look like.' Cathy cast a glance behind her. Mrs Hadley had noticed that she was talking to the young man and frowned in disapproval.

'No, no. I want to take a photograph of you.'

Cathy stared at him in amazement. 'Whatever for?'

'I told you, I'm a photographer.'

'Cathy, have you got a problem?'

'No, Mrs Hadley. The gentleman just had a query.'

'You obviously can't talk now. What time do you finish work?'

'Five thirty, although it's usually nearer six by the time I've finished clearing up.'

'I'll meet you in the coffee bar at the corner. Don't let me down, will you?' He gave Cathy another of his dazzling smiles and raised his voice. 'Thank you for your help, miss.'

Cathy watched as he left the salon, giving her a broad wink as he closed the door behind him. She was still unsure exactly what he wanted, but there could be no harm in meeting him in the coffee bar to find out.

Cathy pushed open the door of the coffee bar tentatively. She tried to lull her misgivings by reminding herself that she was meeting this unknown man in a public place and she was certainly not going anywhere alone with him or accept a ride if he had a car.

Keith saw her enter and rose to his feet. 'Coffee?' he asked.

'Yes, please.' Cathy sat down in the seat opposite his and waited for him to return. He placed a cup in front of her and regained his seat.

'Look to the right,' he said.

Surprised Cathy did so.

'Now the left.'

Cathy obeyed him.

'Now straight at me.'

Keith sat back with a satisfied smile. 'As I thought, you're virtually symmetrical.'

'What do you mean?'

'Both sides of your face are almost identical. Each side of you is slightly different from the other. In some people it is very noticeable when you look at them full face. Most people talk about having a "best side" for a photograph. That means one side is more in proportion than the other. You're lucky.'

Cathy smiled and took a sip of her coffee.

'Will you let me photograph you?' asked Keith. 'You have tremendous potential.'

'Why would you want a photograph of me?' asked Cathy. 'You don't know me.'

'I'm a professional photographer. I'm always on the lookout for new talent.'

'You just want a photo?'

'No, I want you to come up to London to my studio and be properly made up. I'll take a few shots and then see if anyone is interested. You have nothing to lose.'

'London?' Cathy looked at the young man doubtfully.

'Is that a problem?'

'I'm working.'

'What about on your day off?'

'I'm not sure. I'd like to speak to my parents first.'

'Fine. I'll come along and meet them if you want. Make sure they know I'm bona fide and not planning to abduct you. Not that I'd be averse to abducting a pretty girl like you.' Keith showed his amazing white teeth to her and Cathy felt herself warming to the young man. He was far more attractive than any of the young local men whom she had accepted invitations from for a visit to the cinema or to go to the weekly dances. He dug into his pocket. 'Here's my card with my telephone number. Give me a call when you've had a word with your parents. If your answer's no I shall do my best to change your mind.'

Keith smiled at her again, rose and held out his hand. 'I'd offer you a lift home, but I didn't bring my car into town with me.'

'That's quite all right.' Cathy took his hand and was sure he held it a little longer than necessary before he released it.

She sat with her half empty cup of coffee growing cold before her, finally she shrugged. She had nothing to lose by speaking to her parents and persuading them that she should go up to London. Even if they objected she was over twenty one and could do as she pleased.

Rebecca frowned when Cathy relayed her conversation with Keith to her parents. 'I thought you were happy as a hairdresser?'

'I am, but this is an opportunity that will probably never come again. If Keith decides I'm not suitable all I've lost is the train fare. On the other hand if I turn it down without going to London I won't know what I've missed.'

'How old is this man?' asked Basil suspiciously.

'In his twenties, I would think, and gorgeous looking. He has the most amazing smile.'

'Sounds just like a con man,' remarked Basil dryly.

'I'm sure he isn't a con man. Surely he wouldn't have been willing for me to discuss it with you and given me his card with his 'phone number?'

'You really want to do this?' asked Rebecca.

'I'd like to go to London and find out exactly what he is offering. He could always decide that I don't photograph well and that will be the end of it.'

'We can't stop you going, Cathy, but will you allow us to come with you?'

Cathy looked at her parents in surprise. 'If you want, but I'm not a child, you know.'

'You are still a vulnerable young lady who is proposing to meet a young man whom she has only just met at an unknown destination. If we come with you we can take you to the address, meet this man and arrange a time to return. If we're not happy with what we find there's safety in numbers. It might not be so easy for you to walk away if you were on your own.'

Cathy nodded. She realised the sense behind her father's words. 'I'll phone him and see if we can go up on Wednesday.'

Cathy tried Keith's telephone number four times before she was able to speak to him.

'So sorry,' he apologised. 'I've been visiting the parents. Birthday and all that, you know. Are you about to give me good news?'

Cathy gave a little giggle. 'I can come up on Wednesday. My parents are coming with me.'

'Fine. I'll see if Lucy and the studio are free. No point in you coming this week if they're already booked. Give me your number and I'll call you back as soon as I know and tell you what time to arrive.'

'I'll be at work. My mother will probably pick up.'

'No problemo.'

Rebecca wrote down the address of the studio and listened carefully to the directions he gave her. Finally she interrupted him.

'I think it would be much easier to take a taxi from the station,' she said firmly. 'We don't plan to bring the car, far too difficult to park. How long should we allow?'

'Depends upon the traffic. At least half an hour. I've only hired the facilities for three hours, but two should be sufficient for the shots I've planned. It's make-up that can take an age.'

'It isn't your studio, then?'

'Not yet. When I have made my fortune I'll have my own.'

'Does Cathy need to bring anything with her?'

'Just her beautiful self. I'm looking forward to meeting her again and you, Mrs Hurst. Must dash. 'Bye.'

Rebecca repeated the conversation to Basil. 'He seems genuine. No problem with us accompanying Cathy. He'd like us to be there by eleven.'

'What was your impression of him over the 'phone?'

'He sounded pleasant enough. Admitted he did not have his own studio, but had to hire one. If he had been trying to impress he would surely have claimed that it was his.'

'He probably knew we'd find out he was lying as soon as we walked through the door. What time do we have to be there?'

'He said eleven. He's hired the studio for three hours so Cathy should be finished by two.'

Basil nodded. 'I'll see if I can make an appointment with my publisher. We'll have a late lunch; then I'll leave you two to do some shopping and meet up with you later.'

'It could be rather a nice day out,' smiled Rebecca.

'When will I be able to see my photos?' asked Cathy eagerly.

'Patience, sweetie. I need to get them developed. I shan't know until then whether their good enough for what I have in mind.'

'What's that?'

Keith tapped the side of his nose. 'Me to know and you to wait and find out. Pop back in to Lucy and she'll clean all that muck off your face. I'll go and entertain your parents for a while. They must be bored to tears.'

To Keith's surprise Cathy's parents did not appear to realise how long they had been waiting for her. Basil had a pad of paper on his knee and was writing assiduously, his wife looking over his shoulder and reading as he wrote.

He smiled and pulled up a chair opposite them. 'I do hope you haven't felt too neglected. I tend to become completely engrossed in my art and forget there are other people around.'

'I brought work with me,' replied Basil.

Keith raised his eyebrows as Basil closed the pad. 'The boss making you work on a day off? Tsk, tsk. Change of employer needed. That's the beauty of working for yourself. You can work the hours that please you. I often work all weekend; then I have time for play during the week.'

'Really? What do you consider play?'

'Cinema, exhibitions, reading. Odd night out with the boys when I know I don't have to be up early. Of course, having my work based in London is a great advantage. I'm on the spot, so to speak, for all the events that take my fancy.'

'You live in London?' asked Rebecca.

'Bunk down with mates when I want to stay over. Never short of a place to lay my head.'

'And when you don't stay over?'

'The parents welcome me back into the fold with open arms. Good way to keep the washing up to date and have some decent meals. Often have to eat on the hoof, pressure of assignments. Too many burgers and I shall lose my figure.' Keith placed a hand on his flat stomach and gave Rebecca the full benefit of his dazzling smile.

Basil looked at his watch. 'Talking of eating, how much longer will Cathy be? I'm taking the ladies for lunch and I have an appointment afterwards.'

'I'll see how things are moving along. She and Lucy are probably having a girly gossip. You know what girls are like.' Keith wagged his finger and hesitated before swinging the chair back into place. He had hoped to be included in the luncheon invitation. Basil raised his eyebrows at Rebecca and she stifled a laugh.

Ten minutes later Keith emerged with Cathy, his arm draped casually around her shoulders. 'Just one last formality. Need to complete the paper work.'

'What paperwork is that?' asked Basil suspiciously. 'You didn't mention that earlier.'

'Nothing to worry about. It's to protect Cathy. If her photos are suitable for commercial use she will receive twenty five percent of whatever is paid for them. Stops me from selling them and pocketing all the dosh.'

'How will we know if you have sold them or not?' asked Rebecca.

Keith made an exaggerated gesture of crossing his heart. 'Trust me. I'll telephone Cathy when they've been developed and I decide if she's suitable for me to tout her looks around. If they're sub-standard we'll either arrange another session or call it a day. If they're as good as I'm expecting she'll start to make her fortune. No use me saying there are no takers and you see her face smiling out from magazines and bill boards.'

'Why does she only get twenty five percent? Surely she should have more than that?'

'All in good time. Overheads have to be covered. Studio hire, make-up artist, film. All costs money, you know. Let's see how things pan out to start with.'

'Are you happy with that, Cathy?'

Cathy nodded. 'I'm sure Keith and I can always come to another arrangement later if necessary. As he says, let's see how things work out.'

'That's my girl. I wish they were all as sensible and good looking as you. Make my job considerably easier.'

'You have other girls on your books?'

Keith struck his forehead. 'I should have given you a portfolio to look through whilst you waited. You could have seen how good my work is. Here, I'll get it for you now.'

Basil shook his head. 'I'd really rather go for lunch. Sign that agreement, Cathy, and we can be off.'

Keith was very much at ease in Cathy's home. He sprawled across the settee, patting the seat for Cathy to sit beside him, before he opened his briefcase and took out a portfolio of photographs.

'Well, what do you think?' Keith held up a large photograph for their approval.

Rebecca looked at it in disbelief. 'Is that you, Cathy?'

Keith turned the photograph towards Cathy and she gasped. 'Do I really look like that?'

'You certainly do,' he smiled. 'I've made appointments with a number of magazines for next week and I guarantee they'll be falling over themselves to be the one who snares you for their front cover. I won't necessarily go for the highest bidder. It's circulation that counts. Once your potential has been exposed the offers will increase, then is the time to accept. I know my way around the business world. Trust me to get you the best deal available. Now, with your permission, I'd like to take Cathy out for lunch. I don't want to miss the opportunity of being seen around with the best looking girl in town. Where do you suggest, Cathy?'

Cathy looked at her parents anxiously after Keith had left. 'You do like him, don't you?'

'We're hardly in a position to like or dislike him. I don't feel we know him, as we've only met him a couple of times. If he's going to be a permanent fixture in your life we shall no doubt meet him again. You'll have our opinion at a future date.'

'Don't be so stuffy, Dad. If he comes down again I'll see if we can meet Marion. I'm sure she'll like him.'

Keith became a regular visitor to the house on a Saturday, he talked continuously about himself. He and Cathy had so much in common, they were both only children, they had found they enjoyed the same music, the same films, the same books, he explained. That was why they had such a good working relationship and Cathy had learnt so much from him, she really was becoming a very well-rounded person.

Basil raised his eyebrows and looked at Rebecca, who had a great desire to laugh at the pretentious young man. She certainly hoped the working relationship would not develop into anything more personal, although Cathy seemed to hang on his every word and gazed at him adoringly.

After he had left Cathy would mope around for a while, then telephone Marion to see if she was free.

'He's so alive, so vital. He brings excitement into the most mundane events.'

'I've noticed,' said Marion dryly. 'Are you serious about him?'

Cathy looked at her, her eyes shining. 'I certainly could be.'

Marion felt her heart fall. 'More to the point is he serious about you?'

'What do you think?'

Marion did not answer. She valued Cathy as a friend, but wished she could like the man she appeared to be choosing as a partner.

Basil paced across the living room floor. 'I really cannot stand that obnoxious, self-opinionated little idiot.'

'Maybe as he gets to know us all better he will seem less objectionable.'

'You mean you like him?'

'No, I can't bear him, and I can't understand why Cathy seems so besotted with him. We have to wait for her to realise that he's not as wonderful as she thinks. If we object to him now she'll only side with him and think we are being unreasonable. Maybe he'll get tired of her.'

A car drew up and hooted outside. Cathy immediately ran out to greet Keith and an animated conversation took place between them. Keith withdrew his briefcase, kissed Cathy and placed his arm possessively around her waist as she led the way into the house.

'Mum, Dad, Keith and I have a surprise for you.'

Rebecca and Basil exchanged glances. Please don't let their daughter say she planned to marry this young man whom they disliked intensely.

Cathy sat beside Keith on the settee as usual, her eyes were glowing and there was an excited flush to her cheeks. Keith withdrew a photograph and held it up for Rebecca and Basil to view.

'What do you think?' he asked.

'Excellent, as usual.' Basil could find no fault with the photographs that Keith produced of his daughter.

'Keith submitted it to Par Excellence and they want it for the next month's cover; but that's not all. They want him on their staff, resident photographer and me to work as a model.'

'Only until something better comes up,' Keith assured them.

'Better for whom? You or Cathy?' asked Basil.

'Both of us. With my talent Cathy can go to the very top of the tree.'

'Is that what you want Cathy? I thought you wanted to be a hairdresser and have your own salon eventually.'

'That's not important now.'

'It could be later, when your looks have faded or someone new takes the publics' eye.'

'Cathy has classic looks. It will be years before they fade away, if they ever do.' Keith smiled at her. 'Besides, she's going to make her fortune before she's very much older. I have great plans for her.'

Basil clenched his hands. 'What plans are they, then, Keith?'

Keith tapped the side of his nose and winked. 'Hush hush at the moment, but exciting events in the pipe line, you know.'

'No, I don't know. What I would like to know is exactly what my daughter is becoming involved in.'

'I'm not becoming involved in anything, Dad. I'm simply doing some modelling.'

'Are you? How long will it be before Keith suggests that you remove a piece of clothing and the next thing we know you're on the cover of some top shelf magazine?'

'That won't happen, Dad, will it Keith?'

'No need. Cathy has plenty of pulling power with her clothes on. Not that she doesn't look great with them off.'

Cathy blushed and muttered at Keith under her breath.

Basil looked at the young man. 'Do I understand from that remark that you have seen my daughter without her clothes on?'

Keith looked at Cathy's father mockingly. 'I go swimming regularly. Keeps me in trim. Managed to persuade Cathy to come with me a couple of times. She looks good in her swimsuit.'

Basil turned away. He felt sick. He had promised himself that he would look after and protect this child of his from all the horrors and dangers of the world and he felt he was letting her down. He had lost his son forever. He could not face ever losing his daughter, even if it meant he had to bite his tongue and appear to accept a man whose motives he did not trust.

'I've decided,' said Cathy, tilting her head defiantly. 'I'm leaving the hairdressers.'

'Whose idea is it for you to give up hairdressing? Yours or Keith's?'

'It's mutual. We talked it over. Since I qualified and have worked for Mrs Hadley I've done hardly any proper hairdressing. She still regards me as a junior and gives me all the cleaning to do. I'm really not happy there. If this opportunity with Keith had not come up I would have been looking for somewhere else to work.'

'Does this mean you're going to be travelling to London every day?' asked Rebecca.

'Probably not every day. Only when I'm needed.'

'That's going to be time consuming and tiring for you.'

Cathy shook her head. 'I have my car and I hardly ever take it out of the garage. This will be a good opportunity to use it, besides if I have to stay late I can always bunk down with Keith's friends.'

'What's your percentage now?' Basil directed the question to Cathy, but looked at Keith.

'I've put it up to thirty,' Keith announced smugly.

Basil raised his eyebrows. 'So you will still receive seventy?'

'I told you, overheads and all that. Cathy's doing well. Most of my girls are lucky if they clear twenty percent.'

'Really,' remarked Basil dryly.

Keith nodded vehemently. 'They know if they were working in their old job they'd only be taking home a fraction of the amount they earn with me. Very soon Cathy is going to be earning a fortune.'

'And you will be earning an even larger one!' replied Basil under his breath. He shrugged. 'I'm not happy about you doing this, Cathy, but if this is what you want to do we'll not stop you. When you get tired of standing in front of a camera let us know and I'll set you up in that salon you dreamed about.'

'Don't tempt her, Mr Hurst. Cathy is really going places. With me behind her she can't fail.'

Cathy enjoyed driving up to London three or four times each week. Having finished her photographic assignment she would spend the rest of the day with Keith, sometimes they would browse an exhibition but most afternoons they would return to the flat belonging to his friends and spend the afternoon in bed. The days when she was at home she would have long telephone calls with him, curled up on the settee, often not bothering to dress until mid-day. She met Marion whenever she was able and occasionally met up with one of the girls she had worked with in the salon. Nursing and hairdressing seemed very mundane to her now. She was leading a glamorous and exciting life, often meeting quite famous people.

Basil and Rebecca still disliked the young man and forced themselves to be welcoming and polite when he visited, although this had become less frequent of late. Cathy also noticed that he was spending less of his free time with her and made excuses for him. He was so busy arranging her work with the magazines and so popular amongst his peers that she could not monopolize his company as she would have liked.

It would be different when they were married. Although Keith had never mentioned marriage to her, their relationship was so good and their understanding of each other so complete that it was surely only a matter of time. She bought a copy of the latest magazine for prospective brides and her interest in it did not go unnoticed by her mother.

'You and Keith are planning to get married, then?'

Cathy shrugged. 'One day I expect, when the time is right.'

Rebecca sighed. 'I presume you mean when you're pregnant.'

'Don't be silly, Mum. Models don't get pregnant, besides, I'm on the pill.'

'You're what?'

'I take the pill to prevent me from getting pregnant. All the girls do. There's nothing wrong with that.'

Rebecca shook her head. 'I don't approve, Cathy. When I was young you waited until you were married before you shared a bed with a man.'

‘Yes, well, you didn’t have much choice, did you? Society condemned you as a “loose woman”. *Everyone* lives with their partner now.’

‘Marion doesn’t.’

‘Marion doesn’t have a partner. She has a succession of boyfriends. She says she’s waiting for the right man to come along. I think she quite fancies Keith, actually.’

Rebecca raised her eyebrows. She could not understand the attraction Keith had for her daughter and she had always considered Marion far too level headed to be taken in by such a shallow young man. He reminded her of the obnoxious Dennis she had been forced to work with at the post office. Mary had called him a Smart Alec and the name applied very aptly to Keith.

1972 – 1973

Cathy opened her eyes and closed them again quickly. Dust and grit irritated and she tried to lift a hand to brush it away. Her right hand was pinned beneath her back and he left arm had a heavy weight laying on it which completely immobilised it. Her eyes still closed she tried to think rationally. It was a well-used road. Someone was bound to travel past fairly soon and she would be found.

She could breathe, there was no pain in her chest, her arms hurt, they were probably both broken, but her legs were fine, she could feel no pain there. No pain! A warning bell rang in her head and she tried to move them. There was no response and no feeling at all. Beads of sweat stood out on her forehead. No feeling in her legs meant her spine was probably damaged.

How long had she been laying there? The longer she was denied treatment for her injuries the more serious they could become. The smell of escaping petrol was making her feel sick, along with the taste of blood in her mouth. Suppose the engine caught fire? There was no way she would be able to escape and save herself. She heard the swish of a car's tyres as they passed, then the sound of a motor in reverse and the slam of a car door.

'Hi! Anyone there?'

Cathy tried to answer. 'I'm trapped. Please...' her voice tailed away as she coughed painfully as dust and grit entered her mouth and throat.

'Hold on. I'll get some help. I'll be as quick as I can.' Footsteps crunched on the gravel and she heard the vehicle drive away.

Hot tears stung the back of her eyes and she could feel them beginning to course their way down her cheeks. Why hadn't he stayed with her? She was alone again, frightened and in pain. At least the unknown man had been a voice to comfort her. She tried telling herself he had gone to the nearest telephone and would return once he had alerted the emergency services, but each minute seemed like an hour and no one came.

Once again she tried to open her eyes and found the tears had cleared most of the grit. Cautiously she swivelled them from side to side, but could see little, unable to move her head. Panic began to overwhelm her. No one would ever come to rescue her. She would lay there and die like a trapped animal.

'Please, God, let someone come. Please,' she muttered over and over again.

The doctor looked at the concerned couple sitting across the room from him. 'It isn't good, but it could have been a lot worse. She has multiple fractures of her legs, a broken arm, dislocated shoulder, cuts and bruises. All her injuries will heal in time. She's very lucky to be alive.'

Cathy's mother twisted her damp handkerchief between her fingers. 'Can we see her?'

'You can have a quick look at her in about an hour. She'll be back from the operating theatre by then. Don't expect any response from her as she'll be heavily sedated.'

'Do you know how it happened? She was a careful driver and familiar with that road.'

'I'm sure the police will eventually be able to help you there. They're hoping to be able to take a statement from her tomorrow or the day after.'

Rebecca looked at Basil. His face was grey and he continually shook his head in disbelief.

'Is there anything else either of you would like to ask me?' The doctor sensed both the girl's parents were in shock. 'Would you like someone to telephone a friend to be with you?'

'There's no need... I suppose we ought to 'phone Keith.'

'You can,' replied Basil. 'If he hadn't persuaded her to go up and down to London all the time this would never have happened.'

'We don't know that. We must just be grateful that it was no worse. I think I'll wait until we get home before I phone him. We'll have been able to see her by then. He'll be devastated and want to know the latest news of her.'

'I'm staying here,' announced Basil.

'Mr Hurst, there really is no need. Your daughter's life is not in danger, despite her injuries. Once she has been brought round from the anaesthetic she will be sedated. She is not going to know that you are with her for at least twenty four hours. It would be more beneficial for you to go home and get some rest.'

'He's right, Basil. We can come back tomorrow and sit with her.'

'Listen to your wife, Mr Hurst. Once your daughter begins to recover she'll probably be only too pleased to have your company, at the moment she will not know that you're with her.'

'I can't leave her,' insisted Basil.

Rebecca reached out and took her husband's hand. 'I understand, Basil, but this is different. Cathy is in good hands. If we stay we'll only be in the way.'

'I assure you there will be a nurse with her constantly. If there was any cause for concern we would contact you immediately.'

'I have to stay.'

Rebecca nodded. 'Then we'll both stay. If we're in the way in her room we can sit outside.'

The doctor sighed. There was obviously no moving the man. 'I'll let you know when she returns from the theatre.'

Basil looked at the bruised and broken body of his daughter. He had never wished to look upon such sights again. A lump rose in his throat and he was unsuccessful in choking back his tears. His shoulders heaved and he buried his face in his hands as he sobbed, Rebecca holding him tightly, her tears mingling with his.

Keith entered the small room, carrying a large bouquet of red roses. He approached timidly, shuddering as he saw the plaster casts on both Cathy's legs that were held up in traction. As he stood beside her bed he took in her bruised and lacerated face, the broken arm and bandaged hand, and felt the bile rising in him. He had relied on Cathy to make his fortune for him. Now she would never stand before his camera again and enthral people with her grace and beauty.

'Cathy, Cathy, I've brought you some flowers.'

The nurse came forwards. 'Shall I find a vase?'

Keith relinquished his burden thankfully. 'I'd be very grateful.'

'Have a seat. I'll be back shortly.'

Keith sat self-consciously beside the bed, his eyes fixed on the wall. The nurse returned bearing an arrangement of roses that she placed on the windowsill.

'They'll be nice for her to look at when she wakes up.'

'How long is she going to stay asleep?'

'Probably another five minutes or so. She's still sedated. I could make you a cup of tea whilst you're waiting.'

Keith nodded eagerly. 'I'll come with you There's no point in just sitting here.'

He followed the nurse into the minute kitchenette that adjoined the room, having a great desire to squeeze her buttocks, which rose and fell seductively beneath her uniform dress.

'I don't feel I should talk in there,' he explained. 'How is she?'

'The doctor is pleased with her progress.'

'Then why is she still sedated?'

'You're in considerable pain when you break your bones, not to mention the shock. To keep a patient sedated for the first few days helps them to get over the worst.'

Keith stirred his tea. 'There's not a lot of point in visiting, then.'

'I wouldn't say that. She'll be conscious for about ten minutes before the next injection I give her takes effect. I doubt if she'll feel much like talking to you, but I'm sure she'll be pleased to know you're here with her.'

'Has she said how it happened?'

The nurse looked at him with something akin to amusement. 'Do you think you'd feel like talking about it yet if your teeth had been knocked out and you were swathed in plaster and bandages, Mr...? I'm sorry; I don't know your name.'

'Keith Masters, call me Keith.' He held out his hand. 'I'm a photographer, you know.'

'Really.'

The tone of voice told Keith she had never heard of him. He took a sip from his tea. 'I'm one of the top men in my field. I've heard it rumoured that in a few years time I'll probably be commissioned by royalty.'

'How interesting.' Again she managed to intimate that she was not in the least impressed. She took down a biscuit tin from the shelf and inspected the contents. 'Not a very inspiring assortment, I'm afraid.' She held it out to him, but Keith shook his head.

'Not for me. Have to watch the old tum, you know.' He patted his flat stomach with self satisfaction.

Rosemary raised her eyebrows and helped herself to a digestive. 'I thought it was only women who were so figure conscious.'

'Not a bit. I take a pride in my body. Regular work-outs at the gym, bit of weight lifting, not too much. I don't want to end up muscle bound.' He flexed his biceps in her face.

'No doubt carrying your ego with you is heavy going.' Rosemary slipped off the stool. 'I must check on my patient.'

Keith made no move to follow her, but took a gulp of his tea. The nurse's sarcasm had not been lost on him. He decided he did not like her; she was obviously unimpressed by him. He was not used to that sort of reaction amongst the women he met. They usually exuded admiration and squeezed his upper arm gently when he showed his muscles.

Rosemary returned. 'She's just beginning to stir. Finish your tea whilst I prepare her medication, then you'll be able to talk to her for a few minutes.'

Keith scowled. He was not used to being told what to do by a woman. He followed Rosemary back into the room and hovered by the bed until Cathy's eyes flickered open. She tried to smile and Keith recoiled from the grimace that showed her broken front teeth.

'I've brought you some roses,' he managed to say.

'Thank you.' Cathy's broken lips framed the words. 'Stay with me.'

Keith looked at his watch. 'Can't do that, old thing. I've got a busy day. Besides, you'll be asleep again in a while. I'll look in again in a day or two.' He backed away, ignoring the pleading in Cathy's eyes and waved at her from the doorway. 'Bye. See you soon.'

Rosemary inserted the needle deftly into Cathy's arm, wishing she could stick it viciously into the irritating young man who had just left.

Marion opened the door to Cathy's room and peered round with a broad smile on her face.

'Hi, there, how you doing?'

'Marion! I wasn't expecting you. I thought you'd be working.'

'I am. I've managed to wangle a transfer to your unit.'

'You mean you'll be here nursing me?'

'That's right. You don't mind, do you?'

'Mind? It's wonderful. The nurses are all lovely, but I really have nothing to talk to them about. I'm so bored between visitors.'

'You won't be with me around. Now, let's get you ready to go for your physio. Up you get, on your own. I'm not helping you.'

Cathy planted the crutches on the ground firmly and hauled

herself into an upright position. She managed two small steps and let herself sink down into the wheelchair.

'Marion, will I ever walk again?'

'Of course you will,' Marion replied firmly. 'You've just got to be patient. These things take time. Three months ago you were laying there in plaster. Not only do the breaks have to mend, but the muscles have to be strengthened. Why do you think you're off to physio every day?'

'I do want to be able to walk again.'

'There's no reason why you shouldn't.'

'I want to surprise Keith and walk over to him the next time he visits.'

'And when will that be?'

'When he has time. He's been terribly busy recently. I feel awful about the way I ruined his plans.'

'I don't know why you are worrying about his plans! You need to think about yourself.'

'You don't like Keith, do you?' Cathy was unable to turn and see the reaction to his name on Marion's face.

'It's not up to me to like him. He's your friend. We're all different, what suits one doesn't suit another. Keep your elbow in so you don't bump it on the door.'

'Why don't you like him?' persisted Cathy.

'He's not my type. I like them dark and ugly, not blonde and handsome.'

'He is good looking, isn't he? When I first saw him I could hardly believe he was a photographer and not a model. Most camera men are stooped and have squint eyes through looking into lenses all day long, but he isn't a bit like that.'

Marion smiled. She hoped their conversation would not always revolve around Keith. She turned the corner and parked the wheelchair next to the door of the physiotherapy department.

'I'll see you in an hour. Don't work too hard.' With a cheery wave of her hand Marion left and took a deep breath. She was so pleased she had persuaded the doctor to assign her as Cathy's personal nurse, but if she was going to extol the virtues of Keith continually she would have to learn to hold her tongue. She walked down the corridor to the canteen and joined her fellow nurses for a gossip over a cup of coffee during her break.

'Where are you off to for your holiday this year?' asked Seema, her dark eyes and swarthy complexion heightened by her white dress.

'I thought I'd try Corfu. I've heard the scenery is out of this world. What about you?'

Seema shook her head. 'I can't afford it. I'm saving up to go back home for a visit.'

'You should find yourself a rich patient,' remarked the porter at the end of the table. 'Don't know what's wrong with you girls. If I had to nurse some of the rich old devils you get stuck with I'd make sure they were grateful to me.'

'Rich old devils that come into National Health hospitals are also tight fisted. You're lucky if you get a box of chocolates from them.'

Margaret gave a little giggle. 'I was given a pair of fish net tights the other day and asked if I would try them on and show him if they fitted.'

'What did you do?'

'I told him I never wore tights and gave them back. Some of them seem to think that a couple of blanket baths makes them irresistible to you. What they forget is that you've seen it all before – and usually in better condition.'

Seema rolled her eyes. 'Have you seen that young man on Ward Three? Wow! He certainly has some attributes.'

Margaret frowned. 'I thought you were working on Ward Two?'

'I am, but Sheila told me and I sneaked in with some gloves for her and took a quick look.'

Marion smiled with the others. 'I'm lucky at the moment. I'm with Cathy and we've been friends since we were at school together.'

'She was a model, wasn't she? The one who rolled her car?'

Marion nodded. 'It wasn't her fault. A pony ran in front of her.'

'Lucky to get away with it.'

'They showed it on the news that night. It was a real mess.'

'So was she when she came in.'

'I remember. That chap that comes to visit her gave an interview. Talked about her being his most interesting discovery for years and how with his help she could have reached the dizzy heights.'

Marion picked up her cup. 'I'd better get back. I like to have the bed changed and everywhere tidy for when she's finished in physio. She always needs a sleep and I don't like to be moving around then, besides, I've two other rooms to keep an eye on now.'

Marion surveyed the room with satisfaction. The bed was changed and turned back ready to receive Cathy on her return. The flowers had been re-arranged, everywhere dusted and the floor mopped. She would now see how Mrs Montgomery was faring with her hip replacement and provided the old lady was not too garrulous she would have time to spend with the hysterectomy patient who was feeling more than a little sorry for herself.

Cathy leaned back in the wheelchair. She always felt so drained when she returned from physiotherapy. Her legs ached and all she wanted was to lay in her bed and sleep. The burly porter who pushed her chair with ease lifted her from it and deposited her gently on the clean sheets.

'I'll let Marion know you're back. See you tomorrow,'

'Thank you, Sean.' She smiled at him gratefully as he turned the wheelchair with one hand and held the door open with the other.

Cathy lay back against the pillows and closed her eyes, opening them again as she heard the door, expecting to see Marion, but instead Keith stood there.

'Hello,' she smiled. 'I wasn't expecting you until this evening.'

Keith advanced a short distance into the room. 'I'll be a bit busy this evening, old girl. Thought I ought to come and tell you now.'

'That was good of you.'

'I'll be busy tomorrow as well. I'm going away at the weekend.'

'Oh.' Cathy's face fell. 'Anywhere nice?'

'Just Italy for a week or so. I've been asked to do a few special shots that need a bit of the old know how.' Keith tapped the side of his nose.

Cathy nodded. 'You'll be able to tell me all about it when you get back. Who are you working with? Anyone I know?'

Keith shook his head. 'I don't think so. She's a new discovery of mine. Found her a couple of months ago and I've been bringing her on. She's pretty good, should be able to fill your place.'

'Fill my place?' Cathy felt dazed. 'How do you mean?'

'Well you have to face facts, don't you? You'll never be able to model again. You'll never be able to stand up again for any length of time, let alone walk! And your face, it would take so much make-up to hide the scars. You're just not good business for me now.'

'Keith, I'm getting better. I will be able to walk again one day,' Cathy protested desperately.

'Yes, old thing, one day, but I need business now.'

'My scars will fade.'

Keith shook his head doubtfully. 'You know what the camera is like, picks out the slightest flaw. No, forget it. We had a good run whilst it lasted, but I suggest you think of another career now. Why don't you train as a secretary? You'd be able to sit at a desk most of the time, keep the weight off your legs.'

'But, Keith,' Cathy's voice had a tremor in it. 'I don't want a new career.'

'Accept the facts, Cathy. You couldn't possibly work as a model again. You have to understand that. I need someone who can keep up with my pace. I move, remember. I could never work with a cripple.'

'I'm not a cripple. I'm having physio. They say that one day I'll walk again.' Cathy could feel the tears running down her cheeks. 'I thought you cared about me.'

'No.' Keith shook his head. 'I couldn't take on a hideous cripple. Think of my image. It wouldn't work, old thing. I'm a man who's going places and you just couldn't keep up. I'll pop in again sometime when I get back, just to see how you're progressing. Bye.'

Cathy turned her face to the wall and did not see Marion standing in the doorway or hear the hissing hatred in her voice.

'If you come back when I'm here you'll not get past this door, you conceited bastard. She's too good for a little shit like you – and once she had fully recovered she'd have worked that one out for herself.'

Keith recoiled visibly from the verbal attack and his face blanched. 'And what would you know about it?'

'I know a decent, caring man when I meet one, the same as I know a selfish, immature, arrogant snob.'

'My, my, what people the lower classes do mix with,' he sneered. 'Now let me past, you fat fool.'

Marion stood to one side, her chest heaving with indignation and the flush of fury in her cheeks. As Keith sauntered down the corridor, she shook her fist at his back before closing the door and going to the bed to try to comfort Cathy.

'You do look well. Did you have a good time?'

Marion smiled at Cathy. 'Wonderful. Corfu is everything the guide book claimed.' She looked at Cathy's white face. 'You could do with a bit of sunshine yourself.'

Cathy shrugged. 'Not much chance of that whilst I'm stuck in here.'

'I was told you were being discharged in another couple of weeks.'

Cathy looked at Marion in horror. 'They can't send me home. I can't walk.'

'They seem to think you'll get on better once you've left here. You'll still come in a couple of times a week for physio.'

'It's not possible. I couldn't manage on my own and my parents have their own life to lead. They can't be expected to look after me.'

'Your mother is turning the dining room into a bed-sit for you. You'll be able to get to the kitchen and the downstairs toilet on your own. I'm sure you'll cope far better than you envisage.'

Cathy shook her head miserably. 'I'm never going to walk again, am I? That's why they're sending me home.'

Marion sat on the end of Cathy's bed and took her hand. 'The specialists are convinced you can walk. There is no medical reason why you shouldn't. You've had physio to strengthen your muscles and your bones have mended well. It's just a question of you having the will power and making the effort.'

'It's easy for you to say.' Cathy spoke bitterly.

'I've seen people far more badly injured than you were. They had to have their limbs amputated, but they had the courage and determination to fight back and overcome their disabilities.'

Cathy shook her head. 'Keith was right when he said I was a hideous cripple. I am, and I'll never be anything else.'

Marion snorted with derision. 'He didn't know what he was talking about.'

'Yes he did. He was right when he said I wouldn't be able to keep up with him. I can never model again and he wouldn't want me dragging around slowing him down all the time.'

'If you want my opinion that young man didn't care for you anyway. He wanted to climb the ladder of success on your reputation as a top model. If he'd truly cared for you he would have stuck by you whatever happened.'

'You don't understand...' Cathy's voice tailed away.

'I understand only too well. Once he knew you weren't going to be able to model for him he had no further use for you. He wanted an excuse to be rid of you and look for someone else, so he said you'd be crippled. He has sown a seed in your mind and you're letting it grow and flourish instead of stamping it out and proving him to be the ignorant little man he really is. I don't know what it's like to be famous and have people fawn all over me, but I do know a good, loving man when I meet one and I know what a support they can be in a time of trouble. Now, I've said my piece. You think about it and make up your mind that by this time next year you'll be dancing, let alone walking.'

Marion rose from the bed and walked into the kitchenette. She was shaking with emotion and near to tears. She loved Cathy like a sister and did not want to see her spend the rest of her life in a wheelchair unnecessarily.

Cathy found the move from the hospital to her home traumatic. Her parents fussed over her and Marion called in each day when she had finished working at the hospital. Cathy insisted she was unable to walk more than two or three steps without a walking frame and if Marion tried to insist she would collapse in an ungainly heap on the floor.

'It's her state of mind, Mrs Hurst,' Marion assured the worried woman. 'Physically she is quite capable, but her mind won't accept the fact. She's not doing it deliberately to be difficult. She could stay in hospital forever and not regain her mobility. They're hoping now she's at home she will gradually become more independent.'

'What if she doesn't? We can cope now, but what about when we are too old to look after her? What happens then?'

'I'm sure you don't need to be so pessimistic. If there are no visible signs of improvement in a few months she'll be referred to the psychiatrist for more help.'

'Why don't they do that now?'

'They feel sure the move home will do the trick for her. If that stupid young man had not put the idea into her head that she would be crippled she would have made far better progress.'

Mrs Hurst shook her head. 'We never did like him, he seemed so artificial. We weren't very happy about her going up to London all the time to model. It would have been so much better if she had remained as a hairdresser and Basil had set her up in her own business.'

Marion nodded. 'I told him a few home truths when he came to the hospital the last time. I would have thought Cathy was too intelligent to be taken in by such a scheming poser. Now, if you've completed those forms I'll put them in my bag so I don't forget them. I'll be in again tomorrow. I've persuaded Cathy to give me a trim. She's the only hairdresser I've ever found who understands the way my hair curls.'

'That does look better. You're quite beautiful again.' Marion admired Cathy's rebuilt front teeth. 'It's amazing the difference teeth make to a person. Aren't you pleased? It was worth waiting for. He's done a wonderful job.'

Cathy nodded. 'I feel a bit more human again. I can at least open my mouth without feeling self-conscious.'

'How's the walking going?'

'It isn't. I'm no further forward than I was last week. My legs just won't hold me up.' Cathy spoke in a resigned tone.

Marion gazed at her sharply. 'You can do it, you know.'

Cathy shook her head. 'I don't know why I keep going to physio. It's just a waste of time.'

'If you won't walk your muscles will start wasting away and when you do decide to make the effort you'll not have the strength. Besides, you've got a nice shape back to your legs; you wouldn't want to lose that.'

'It doesn't matter to me whether my legs are a nice shape or not now. No one is going to see them.'

'What about when you go on holiday? Wouldn't you consider wearing a bathing costume?'

'Whatever for? I'd just look stupid sitting in a wheelchair with a bathing costume on.'

'I was thinking of you lying on a beach or by a pool in the sun.'

'Don't be silly.'

'You ought to think about having a holiday.'

'I could go to Bournemouth or Eastbourne. That's where all the geriatrics go, isn't it? Nice and flat for their wheelchairs.'

'I was thinking of a proper holiday, somewhere in the sun.'

'How can I?' asked Cathy scornfully. 'I need someone to help me all the time.'

'What about your parents? They could do with a rest. If you went away for a week or two it would give your Mum a break.'

'They've mentioned going to the south of France again.'

'You don't want to go there?'

'Not really, and it certainly wouldn't be a break for them.'

Marion smiled. 'Where would you go if you could choose? America? Paris?'

Cathy smiled back. 'No, I'm not interested in America and I've been to Paris with my parents. You made Rhodes sound wonderful. I'd quite like to go there one day.'

'There's a lot to see everywhere, particularly on the islands, and if you get fed up with the sites you can always lay in the sun. I love the islands; I've been to quite a few now. I can never decide which one is my favourite. Shall I bring in my photos again next week? We can look at them again and I'll try to make up my mind.'

Cathy nodded. That was all she did now – enjoy looking.

'I've sown the seeds, Mrs Hurst. I'll work on the idea again next week. It would certainly do her good to get right away and have some sunshine.'

'You're very patient with her, Marion. I do appreciate it.'

'It's nothing. You and your husband need a rest and a change as much as she does.'

'If you can get her to agree we'll pay all the expenses, you know that.'

'You don't have to pay for me, Mrs Hurst. I would be going to one of the Greek islands anyway,' Marion spoke firmly.

'That would be your holiday. If you can persuade Cathy to go you'll be working and you won't be able to do half the things you would if you were on your own.'

Marion smiled. 'I usually spend most of my time lying in the sun,' she lied.

Marion spread the brochure out before Cathy. 'I've looked into everything. Rhodes just isn't a practical place to take a wheelchair. The Old Town is very steep in places and cobbled. I don't think I could push you up and down there. Santorini is out of the question as that's even steeper. I thought about Athens, but it will be far too hot for me. All their pools seem to be up on the roof, probably pretty inaccessible. Kos seemed a good idea, it's very flat along the coast but not very much to do or see. You need to be able to take the boat trips.'

Cathy sighed. 'I suppose I'll have to accept Mum and Dad's offer to take me to France with them. You could come with us.'

Marion shook her head. 'Your wheelchair will take up most of the space in the boot. There wouldn't be room inside for me and the luggage.'

'Dad could hire a bigger car. I'm sure he wouldn't mind.'

'I've a better idea. What do you think about Crete?' Marion turned the page and placed her finger on the picture of small chalets set in their own grounds.'

'It looks nice,' admitted Cathy.

'According to the brochure it isn't very far from the airport. Individual chalets, so you don't have to worry about lifts. It's only a short distance from the beach and there's a decent sized swimming pool. I'm sure we'd be able to arrange to visit some of the sites.' Marion frowned. 'I wish I had the confidence to drive over there.'

Cathy felt apprehension rising in her. 'What's wrong with driving over there?'

'Nothing really. It's just being on the other side of the road that takes so much concentration. The local people get very impatient with the tourists in their hire cars who don't know where they're going and dawdle along holding everyone up.'

'Dad doesn't have a problem in France.'

'He's been doing it for years. I only passed my driving test a couple of years ago. Anyway, what do you think? Shall I make a booking?'

Cathy hesitated. Would she be able to cope with staying in a strange country, unable to make her needs understood unless someone spoke English? 'I'm not sure.'

'Oh, come on. It will give you an opportunity to wear some of those gorgeous clothes you have hanging in your wardrobe.'

Cathy shrugged. 'I wish you were the same size as me. I'd give them to you.'

'Then I'm glad I'm not. I'd never look as good in them as you do. You ought to wear them from time to time. You always wear the same old jeans and shirts. Just because you're sitting in this chair it doesn't mean you can't dress nicely.'

'Why do you want to go to Crete?' Basil frowned.

'Marion wants to go. She's found a hotel where they have chalets in the grounds and it would be no trouble to get my wheelchair in and out. You know what some of these big hotels are like. The lift is small and people resent having to make space for me.'

'I'm sure we could find a hotel with a room on the ground floor in France.'

'I'm sure you could, and I've loved going to France with you, but this year I want to go on holiday with Marion. I've become far too dependent upon you since my accident.'

'Why doesn't Marion come with us and we all go to France?'

'There wouldn't be room in the car for four of us, my wheelchair and extra luggage. She wants to visit Crete. It's one of the islands she's not yet been to. If she's willing to look after me it's only fair that I go where she wants,' Cathy argued reasonably.

'There are other islands and I'm sure they would have hotels with easy access to their rooms.'

'Marion's really spent a lot of time looking into it. In some places the hotel is fine, but it's at the top of a hill. I couldn't expect Marion to be continually pushing me up and down. Others haven't got a pool and I couldn't cope with the beach. My chair would sink up to the rims of the wheels and I'd be stuck. If I'm going to have to spend all my time sitting on a patio I might just as well stay here. What have you got against Crete, Dad?'

Rebecca touched her husband's arm. 'Let them go and enjoy themselves. They don't want to spend their time with a couple of old folk like us.'

Cathy beamed. 'Thanks, Mum. I'll go and phone Marion now and tell her to confirm the booking.' She wheeled herself quickly out of the lounge and into the hall. Rebecca closed the door behind her and turned to Basil.

'I understand why you would like her to go somewhere else, but Crete is a big place. You've told me so yourself. Why should anyone associate Catherine Hurst with you?'

Basil sighed. 'I know. I'm just being foolish.'

'You could tell her, Basil.'

Basil shook his head. 'We agreed. Once I'd told you that was to be the end of it. She has no need to know about the time I spent out there.'

'I'm sure she'd be very proud of you.'

'Would she?' asked Basil bitterly. 'If I hadn't been so busy running around with the andartes I would have been there to save my family.'

'Basil, you can't still blame yourself. You could have been working in the fields when the Germans marched through. The end result would have been the same.'

WEEK ONE – JUNE 1973

Marion pushed Cathy along the path from their chalet to the swimming pool. 'How are you feeling?'

'Fine. I'm not even tired. You organised everything so well, Marion.'

'It's not difficult. I appreciated not having to wait in long queues. Do you want a lounger or will you stay in your chair?'

'I'll stay in my chair. Maybe I'll have a lounger tomorrow.' Cathy shut her eyes and raised her face to the warm sunshine.

'I'm going in for a swim. Just give me a shout if you want anything.'

Cathy nodded without answering. She was torn in two. Part of her appreciated the trouble Marion had gone to in arranging the holiday in Crete and part of her was resentful that she could not enjoy herself as she would have done eighteen months ago. It hurt to see other people striding around, doing just as they pleased, taking their mobility for granted, whilst she sat like a statue in a chair. She hated to see the sympathetic looks they gave her when they thought she was not looking, or talked across her as though she was some kind of invisible obstacle.

She opened her eyes and saw Marion cleaving her way through the water strongly. Maybe if she could persuade Marion to wake her early she would try exercising her legs in the pool. She certainly would not want any onlookers to see the way she had to be hauled in and out ignominiously.

She looked at her surroundings. The pool was set back from the beach, shaded by palms set in grassy banks. The surround to the pool was paved and on the far side was a small bar where drinks or snacks could be purchased. A number of hotel guests sat on the patio beneath sun umbrellas, talking and drinking, supervising their small children who were playing close by.

'That felt really good.' A cold hand was placed on her arm and Cathy turned to see Marion standing beside her.

'Was it really that cold?'

Marion shook her head, sending silvery drops of water cascading from her hair. 'It was refreshing. It only feels cold to you because you're hot. I'll move you back into the shade. You don't want to burn.'

'I can do it.' Cathy released the brake and propelled herself back a few feet so that she was beneath the umbrella.

'Fancy a drink when I'm a bit dryer?'

'I'd love one.' Cathy waited until Marion was dry enough to slip a light dress over her costume. 'I'd like one of those lemonades with all the bits in. If they haven't got that I'll have an orange juice.'

Cathy watched as Marion walked over to the bar and had a long and laughing conversation with the bar tender, finally returning with two bottles which were frosted where they had just been removed from the fridge.

'Thanks. What was that all about?'

'Just general chat. He wanted to know where we had come from and how long we were staying, then I asked him for lemonade and he produced that clear, sparkling stuff. I told him I wanted lemonade with bits in and he didn't understand. I finally pointed to the bottle and he said "Ah, limontha", which was what I'd asked him for in the first place.'

Cathy giggled. 'Do you think he was having you on?'

'Who knows? He could have been, but I'll take an empty bottle with me the next time I go over. They've got some interesting looking sticky cakes. I might try one. How about you?'

'Later. My lunch has hardly gone down yet.'

'If you're talking about that apology for cooked cardboard we had on the plane I'm surprised mine hasn't come up! It was worse than the hospital canteen when the cook is off sick.'

'It wasn't that bad,' protested Cathy.

'I'd like to know what it was! It was like the scrapings from the plates of the last flight pushed beneath a piece of soggy pastry. Have you finished?' Marion took the empty bottle from Cathy's hand. 'Do you want your book? I'm going to have a sleep.'

Cathy watched as Marion spread out her towel in the shade of the tree and peeled off her dress. 'If I was a millionaire I'd have a house on every Greek island,' she announced.

'There'd be little point. You'd only be able to visit each one about every two years. Better to choose the island you liked most and have a house there.'

'I love them all, but at the moment this is my ideal spot.' Marion yawned hugely.

'I doubt if you'll get planning permission.'

'I'll just take root, then. Wake me in about an hour.'

Marion closed her eyes and Cathy opened her book. She hoped her friend and nurse would want to spend every day lying by the pool.

Cathy read a chapter and passed her tongue around her dry mouth. She could do with another drink. She looked down at Marion who was obviously fast asleep, then across at the bar. To reach it she would have to negotiate the slope of the bank down to the paved area around the pool and along the paving that ran beside it until she reached the main path. One false move and she would end up in the water with the wheelchair on top of her. She decided to try to attract the bar tender's attention and waved. He was deep in conversation with a bikini-clad teenager and did not glance her way. Cathy bit at her lip and glanced again at Marion who had not stirred. She waved again and still there was no response.

'Do you need some help?' A soft voice spoke at her side and she turned to look up into a pair of dark and smiling eyes.

'Would you be terribly kind and fetch me a lemonade from the bar? I've been trying to attract his attention without success.'

The man looked across and frowned. 'Certainly. It would be my pleasure. Would you care to come with me?'

'I would have gone myself if I were able to walk,' replied Cathy brusquely.

'I am sure you are no great weight for me to push. Your friend appears to be asleep so she will not miss your company.' He placed his hands on the back of the chair. 'Remove the brake and we will go.'

'She'll wonder where I am.' Cathy hesitated. Was it safe to allow a strange man to take her away in her wheelchair?

'As soon as she sits up she will be able to see you. I assure you I will be very careful how I push you.'

Still dubious, Cathy looked again at Marion's sleeping form before releasing the brake and feeling her escort take the weight of the chair to prevent it from rolling down the slope. Carefully he manoeuvred her down to the paved area.

'We will take a small detour which will make it more comfortable for you,' he announced as he pushed her towards the sea. They reached the end of the swimming pool and followed the path parallel to the beach, ending up at the corner of the bar where he pushed her across to the patio and stopped beneath a large umbrella.

'What would you like to drink?'

'Oh, just lemonade, please.'

'You will not have an ouzo or a glass of wine?'

Cathy smiled. 'It's a little early in the day for me to drink alcohol.'

'I am sure a glass of local wine will not make you inebriated. You will not mind if I have a glass?'

'Not a bit. Here, let me give you some drachmas.' Cathy delved into her handbag.

'Certainly not. I asked you to join me.' He walked across to the bar and Cathy heard a rapid interchange of Greek. Cathy's companion gathered them up their drinks and returned to their table where, with a deft flick of the wrist he removed the cap from the lemonade bottle and poured half into a glass that clinked with ice. He raised his glass of wine.

Cathy lifted hers. 'Thank you. It was so hot sitting there.'

His dark brown eyes met hers across the rim of the glass. 'You would not like to swim? It is cool in the water.'

Cathy shook her head. 'There are too many people around. Maybe another day.'

He nodded and did not ask the reason for her modesty. 'I am Vasilis.' He held out his hand.

'I'm Cathy.'

'I'm pleased to meet you, Cathy. How long are you staying here?'

'For four weeks.'

'And you arrived today,' Vasilis smiled.

'Yes, how did you know?'

'You do not have a sun tan.'

'I hope to have by the time I return.'

'Please, do not talk about returning yet. You have only just arrived. What do you plan for the weeks you are here?'

'I haven't really got any plans. I shall probably just sit by the pool and enjoy the sunshine.'

Vasilis shook his head in disbelief. 'It would be sad if you sat beside the pool the whole time. There is much more to Crete than sunshine and swimming pools.'

'It's rather difficult for me to get anywhere on a bus and I don't know if I would be able to find a taxi with a driver who was willing to take my chair and help.'

'Why not hire a car?'

Cathy shook her head. 'My friend doesn't feel confident about driving over here.'

Vasilis smiled easily. 'I am sure something could be arranged. Maybe a coach trip?'

'It would be rather a waste of time going anywhere if there were steps. Marion can't manage my chair up and down steps on her own and you couldn't expect other tourists to lag behind and help her.'

Vasilis leaned forward. 'I get the impression that you do not want to go anywhere.'

Cathy felt her face flame. 'I'd love to be able to.'

'Then do not forever put an obstacle in the path.' Vasilis smiled at her. 'Now would you like a cake? Come and have a look at them.' Without waiting for her answer, he removed the brake from the chair and propelled her across to the bar. 'This is baklava. You should try it whilst you are here. It is a traditional cake, but very sweet. There are others, or, if you prefer, there is yoghurt that you mix with honey. That is very good also.'

Cathy looked at the tempting array of tarts, gateaux and pastries. 'I'll try a baklava.'

Vasilis nodded and one was placed on a plate with a fork beside it and he handed it to her. 'It will be safer with you while I push.' He wheeled her back to the table beneath the umbrella and watched whilst she took a mouthful. 'It is good?'

'It is very good, but, as you say, very sweet.'

Vasilis sat back and looked at her. 'You have been to Crete before?'

Cathy shook her head, her mouth full of the sticky pastry.

'I feel I have seen you somewhere before.'

Cathy bent her head over her plate. 'Were you at the airport this morning?' she asked.

'No.'

'Then you cannot have seen me before.'

'It is not important.' He shrugged, but continued to gaze at her.

'I wonder if my friend is awake.' Cathy looked across to where Marion still lay.

Vasilis shook his head. 'I think not. Do you wish to wake her?'

'No. I'm quite happy sitting here.'

'That is good. I, too, am happy to sit here.' Vasilis signalled to the bar tender who hurried over with a carafe of wine and two clean glasses. 'You have tried the baklava, now you must try the wine. We will sit here and drink and talk. I should like to know much more about you, Cathy.'

'So – who is he?' asked Marion when they were alone in their chalet.

'I don't really know. His name is Vasilis.'

'And?'

'That's all I know about him. I expect he was just at a loose end this afternoon so decided to chat to me.'

'Are you seeing him again?'

Cathy looked at Marion in surprise. 'Why should I?'

'You seemed to be getting on very well this afternoon.'

'We were just talking.'

'What about?'

'Nothing much. I said how good his English was and he said he had learnt at school and listened to the television programmes from America. My father said the way to learn was to listen.'

'Did he speak Greek?'

Cathy nodded. 'I don't know how well. When I was friends with Despina he always spoke Greek to her family.'

'Where did he learn?'

'At University and he spent some time in Greece.'

'When? During the war?'

'I don't know. Whenever I tried to ask him he said he didn't want to talk about it.'

'Did he never talk about it?' Marion was consumed with curiosity.

'No, and I never pressed him. I wasn't that interested when I was a child. When I was older Mum told me he his first wife had been killed in the war. I understood then why he would never talk about it. He had obviously had a bad time and preferred to forget all about it.'

'Does that mean you have some half brothers and sisters somewhere?'

Cathy shook her head. 'I only know his first wife died. There was never any mention of any children.'

'Doesn't your mother know?'

'Probably, but I've never liked to ask her. It's a bit delicate somehow, asking your mother for details about her predecessor.'

Marion nodded sympathetically. 'It could be difficult. I don't know that I'd like it if I were in that position.' She looked at her watch. 'We ought to get a move on if you want to have a shower before dinner.'

'You go first whilst I decide what to wear.'

Marion nodded and picked up her wrap from her bed. 'I'll have to give my hair a quick wash. It feels all sticky.'

'Take as long as you like. Dinner goes on until nine.'

'I'm hungry. It's all right for you. You were stuffing yourself with cakes this afternoon.'

'I only had one,' protested Cathy as Marion disappeared into the bathroom.

Marion pushed Cathy down the tarmac path to where the dining room was situated. A flight of shallow marble steps led up to the glass doors and a marble ramp joined it at the side.

'That makes life easier,' remarked Marion. 'I did think I might have to ask for help. Do you want to have a drink in the bar before we eat?'

'No thanks. I had two glasses of wine this afternoon.'

'You could have told him you had a thirsty friend.'

'We'll go to the bar if you want. I don't mind.'

'No,' Marion shook her head. 'I was only teasing. We'll have a bottle of wine with our meal.' She pushed Cathy into the large dining room and the waiter directed them to a table by the window that stretched the full length of the room.

'I'm looking forward to breakfast,' commented Cathy. 'There should be a wonderful view across the sea.' She picked up the menu and studied it. 'I know it's written in English words but I don't know what they're talking about.'

'I can at least tell you that.' Marion ran her finger down the items. 'Dolmades are vine leaves with a stuffing of rice, sometimes they have a bit of meat in them and a lemon sauce over them. Chicken is obvious, so is pork, stifado is a kind of stew. Souvlaki is pieces of pork on a skewer and grilled. Why don't you try something different every night? That way you'll find out exactly what they all are.'

Cathy looked dubious. 'I'll stick to the chicken tonight. Maybe when I see what some of the other guests are having I'll be a bit more adventurous.'

The waiter placed a large bowl of green salad on the table and Marion began to pile her side plate. 'I think they do this deliberately. They always send the salad well in advance so they can send smaller portions of the main course.'

'You don't have to eat it now. You could wait.'

'I'm hungry. Oh, here comes your man.'

'He's not my man,' protested Cathy.

'Well he doesn't appear to be anybody else's either. He's on his own.'

Cathy refused to turn and look where Marion indicated; instead she helped herself to the salad. 'What's this?'

'Goat's cheese. If you don't like it you can pass it my way.'

Cathy took a mouthful and chewed it slowly. 'You're out of luck. I do like it.'

'Some wine, madam?'

Marion nodded. 'Two bottles of your house wine, please. One white and one red.'

Cathy looked at her in horror. 'We'll never drink two bottles.'

'I'm having stifado and you're having the chicken, so we need both red and white.'

'Couldn't we have bought a glass?'

'You could, but it's much more expensive to buy it that way. Don't worry. They'll mark the bottles with our room number and bring it out for us tomorrow or we can take it back to our chalet with us.'

They lingered over their meal, Cathy drinking far more of the wine than she had intended. She had enjoyed her chicken and tried Marion's dish of stifado. She decided she liked the rich taste and determined to have it for her meal the following day. After a final ice cream, they decided to move into the bar for coffee.

Marion settled Cathy into a corner where her wheelchair would not cause an obstruction and collected two cups of coffee and two glasses of water. She looked around and smiled in appreciation.

'This is really nice. The Greeks love bright colours and often their lounges are anything but relaxing.'

Cathy sipped her coffee and made a face. 'I don't like this – it's all sweet and gritty.'

'It's traditional Greek coffee. I thought you ought to try it. I'll get you an espresso instead.'

'Finish yours. There's no rush.'

Marion did so and rinsed her mouth with some water. She rose and went up to the bar which by now had become quite crowded and the sole bar man was serving as fast as he could. She waited her turn and it was some minutes before she carried a frothy cup back to Cathy.

'What have you found?'

'One of the tour brochures.' Cathy handed it to Marion.

'Where do you fancy going? There's Knossos, Malia, Phaestos or an evening of Greek dancing.'

Cathy shook her head. 'I'm quite content to stay here.'

'I should have taken you to Bournemouth! You must see something of the country whilst you're here.'

'You go. You don't have to spend all your time acting as nursemaid to me. It's your holiday too, remember.'

'I'll make some enquiries. You can't be the first person to have come over here dependent upon a wheelchair. Tomorrow I'll ask at the reception desk, see what they say. How do you find that coffee?'

'Much better. Oh, don't look now, here comes Vasilis.'

'I hope he's not one of those lonely men you hear about who latch on to holiday makers and you can't get rid of.'

Vasilis advanced towards the two women. 'Good evening. Did you enjoy your meal?'

'It was delicious.'

'I am pleased to hear it. Now, may I buy you a drink? An ouzo or perhaps you would prefer a whisky?'

Cathy laughed. 'I'm not a whisky drinker. I've not tried ouzo, and I've already had wine with my meal.'

'Then we will have retsina. If you do not like it you can have another glass of the local wine.' He called across to the bar tender who nodded and brought a bottle to their table, despite having other customers waiting.

Vasilis waited until he had pulled the cork; then took the bottle from him. He poured a little into a glass and passed it to Cathy.

'Smell the resin. That is why it is called retsina. Try; see if you like the flavour.'

Cathy took a cautious sip. There was definitely something different about it and she sipped again. 'It's quite nice.' She held out her glass and Vasilis filled it.

'And for you, Marion?'

'Thank you. I know I like it.'

'Ah, you have been to Greece before?'

'Many times.'

'Where have you stayed?'

Marion began to list the various islands she had visited and Vasilis encouraged her to talk about them, adding comments about some and admitting she had visited many more than him. Cathy began to feel quite left out and her eyes strayed back to the brochure. Vasilis, despite appearing to be deep in conversation with Marion, saw her glance and picked up the pamphlet.

'You have been deciding where you will visit tomorrow?'

Cathy shook her head. 'Marion is going to make some enquiries to see if it's possible, but by the pictures everywhere seems to have steps or be very steep.'

'Malia is not steep and has no steps.'

'That might be possible, then. Is there a coach that would take us?'

Vasilis nodded. 'You would have to go to the bus station in Heraklion.'

'It's out of the question then.'

'Your friend may wish to go.'

'She can. I told her earlier I didn't expect her to stay with me all the time.'

Marion frowned at Vasilis. 'We don't have to decide anything tonight. There's plenty of time for visiting.'

'Of course. Now, another glass, ladies?'

'Not for me,' replied Cathy firmly. 'I've had more than enough alcohol for one day.'

'Do you want to go back to your chalet?'

'No. I'm quite happy sitting here. I just don't want any more to drink tonight.'

The number of people at the bar had thinned and the bar man called something to Vasilis who looked at his watch before answering.

'In half an hour the bar will close,' he explained.

'Why so early?'

'Takkis has been working since midday. Also when the bar is closed people who wish to continue to drink will go to the disco and the prices are higher,' he smiled.

'That's a con,' said Marion indignantly.

'A con? What is a con?'

'A trick, a rip off.'

Vasilis shook his head. 'They can drink their fill in the bar before it closes, or spend the evening in Heraklion. We do not make them go to the disco.'

'Well I shall be going back to bed,' declared Marion firmly.

Cathy woke early; her head surprisingly clear considering she had drunk her fair share of the retsina. She levered herself into a sitting position and looked across at Marion.

'Are you awake?'

'Mmmm.'

'I know it's early, but if we got up now there might not be anyone up at the pool.'

Marion gave a deep sigh, followed by a yawn and closed her eyes again. 'Give me five minutes.'

Cathy pushed back the bed cover and lifted her legs over the side of the bed. She reached for her crutches, supporting her weight on her arms as she propelled herself into the bathroom.

As Cathy had hoped, the pool was deserted and Marion pushed her close to the handrail of the steps.

'I'll go in first, then you hold on to the rail and let yourself down into the water. It won't be difficult, the water will take your weight.'

Cathy nodded. The manoeuvre held no fear for her as she had used the pool at the hospital as part of her physiotherapy. As she began to slide her hands carefully down the rail Marion placed her arms around her waist and gave added support until the whole of her body was immersed in the water and she was able to lie on her back and float. At first she found the water cold and began to move her arms and legs vigorously, nearly submerging herself in the process, until she became used to the temperature.

Marion swam the length of the pool twice before returning to Cathy's side. 'Would you like me to give you a tow?'

Cathy shook her head. 'You enjoy yourself. I'm going to be good and do my exercises.'

She held onto the tiled lip and began to move her legs slowly in a succession of moves aimed at strengthening her muscles. It was so much more satisfying doing the exercises in the water as she could lift her legs higher and hold them up for longer. She knew Marion was watching her and worked for longer than usual before realising how chilled her arms and shoulders had become.

'Marion, can you help me out, please? I'm getting cold.'

Marion swam over to her. 'I'll go up backwards until I can sit down, then you can sit between my legs and I'll help you to move up step by step.'

Using the lip of the pool Cathy pulled herself along to the steps. Marion placed her heels on the first ledge and tried to move upwards. Each time she seemed to get a purchase her heel slipped.

'This is not so easy. The steps are nowhere near as wide as I'm used to. I'll go up and then turn and sit down.' Marion sat on the top step and reached her arms down to Cathy. There was no way she was close enough to support her weight and the step below was far too narrow for her to sit on. 'Let me try sideways.'

She turned, but there was not enough space for both girls to move up inside the handrail at the same time. 'Suppose you sat on my shoulders. Do you think you could haul yourself out then?'

'I can try.'

'Do you have a problem?'

Both girls had been so engrossed in their struggles they had not noticed Vasilis walking over the grass towards them.

'It's just a bit difficult getting out. The steps are not as wide as the ones we're used to,' explained Marion.

'One moment. I will help.' He stripped off his shirt and trousers, removed his sandals and dived gracefully into the water, swimming back to them with powerful strokes. He placed his arms beneath Cathy and she instinctively clasped her hands around his neck. Taking her full weight on one arm he pulled himself effortlessly up the steps.

Cathy could not help gasping at the strength she could feel emanating from him as he carried her across the grass to a lounger.

'You do not wish to sit in your chair. It will become wet.' He bent and deposited her gently, an arm still around her. 'Did you enjoy your swim?'

'I didn't really swim. I just did my exercises.' His face was on a level with her own and the smell of his aftershave was just discernible to her nose. She was not sure if it was the aroma or the warmth emanating from his arm that made her feel quite breathless.

'I will fetch your towel.' He strode across the grass and returned to drape the towel around her shoulders. 'You are warm now?'

'Oh, yes, thank you. I'm fine.'

He sat on the grass beside her. 'You are very early. The water is not warm yet for swimming.'

Cathy felt her face flushing. 'I didn't want people looking at me.'

'Why not? You are beautiful to look at.'

Cathy's flush deepened. 'I don't like having to be helped all the time.'

'Is it necessary – or have you just become used to being helped?'

'I can't walk,' insisted Cathy. 'I'm a cripple.'

'That is very sad. Your friend – she is also your nurse?'

'She was my nurse whilst I was in hospital. We were friends at school and she agreed to come here to look after me.'

'Does she also look after you in England?'

'I live with my parents.'

Vasilis nodded. 'That is how it should be before you marry.'

'Marry!' Cathy opened her eyes wide. 'I've no plans for getting married.'

'When the right man comes you will make plans.'

Cathy did not answer. She had thought the right man had come, only to be badly hurt and disillusioned. She gave a little shiver.

'You are still cold. I will fetch some coffee.'

Without waiting for Cathy's answer Vasilis walked over to the small bar and entered through a door at the side. The shutters were still down and she could not see him hurriedly heating the water and making three cups of steaming coffee for them. He carried them carefully over to where she was sitting and handed her a cup.

'It is very hot. Your friend would like one also? I have made for her.'

'I'm sure she would. We haven't had breakfast yet. Marion,' she called. 'Come and have some coffee.'

Marion climbed easily out of the water, shaking the drops from her hair. 'My compliments to the chef. This is a wonderful idea. I'm going back to get dressed when I've had this. Are you coming, Cathy?'

Cathy nodded. 'I really am quite cold. You were right, Vasilis, when you said it was too early in the morning for a swim.'

'In one or two hours the sun will have made it warm. Then it is better.'

'You must be cold. You haven't dried yourself.' Cathy looked at the man beside her.

'I did not bring a towel. I did not intend to swim so early.'

'Why were you here, then?' Cathy looked at him suspiciously.

'I was just walking by when I realised you had a problem.'

'Here, take mine.' Cathy pulled the towel from around her shoulders. 'I'm quite warm enough now I've had some coffee.'

Vasilis appeared to hesitate, then took the towel from her gratefully and rubbed it over his face and hair before drying his arms and torso. Cathy watched as his muscles rippled gently beneath his bronzed chest.

'Thank you.' He passed it back to her, his aftershave once more wafting before her nose. 'That does feel better.'

Marion drained her coffee cup and rose to her feet. 'I'll bring your chair over.'

'There is no need.' Vasilis was on his feet. 'Cathy is very light. I will carry her.' Without waiting for an answer he swept her into his arms from the lounger and Cathy had no choice but to place her arm around his neck. He walked to the edge of the pool and pretended to throw her in. 'You would like another swim?'

Cathy clung more tightly to him. 'Not until after breakfast. No, Vasilis,' her voice rose as he became more threatening.

'Then I will meet you in two hours and we will swim.'

'Maybe...'

'There is no 'maybe'. You promise to meet me or I throw you into the water now.'

Cathy gave a nervous giggle. 'All right, we'll meet you.'

Vasilis was waiting for them when they reached the pool, with three loungers placed beneath the trees. A family sitting on the far side of the pool hardly glanced at them as they settled themselves, Vasilis lifting Cathy gently from her chair and onto a lounger. He placed a cushion behind her head and made sure her book was within her reach. Marion stretched herself luxuriously.

'Wouldn't it be wonderful to live like this all the time?'

'Soon you would be bored and want to do something different.'

'I'm not so sure. I'd be willing to give it a go and find out.'

'You will have to find a rich Greek husband whilst you are here,' smiled Vasilis.

'Mmm.' Marion closed her eyes. 'Do you know any rich Greeks?'

'A few.'

Marion opened her eyes wide. 'Really?'

Vasilis smiled at her mockingly. 'They are elderly and probably have heart conditions.'

'Out of the question.' Marion spoke firmly. 'They have to be young, active, handsome and loaded.'

'I am reasonably young and active,' suggested Vasilis.

Marion shook her head. 'I'm looking for all four qualities in one man.'

'Then I am sorry to disappoint you. You will have to look elsewhere. I will use my brain to see if I can think of anyone who would be suitable.' He looked at Cathy quizzically. 'Do you have the same requirement?'

Cathy appeared to consider the question seriously. 'I'm even more particular than Marion. He has to be about six foot, muscular, but not muscle bound, attractive rather than handsome, kind and considerate, have a sense of humour and be able to keep me in comfort.'

Vasilis raised his eyebrows. 'I see both of you are very ambitious ladies, but I notice you neither of you speak of love.'

'I was talking of an arrangement, not a marriage.' Marion closed her eyes again.

'I see, and you, Cathy?'

'I didn't take the question seriously.'

Vasilis turned his dark eyes on her. 'You should.'

Cathy felt a flush creeping into her cheeks and tried to laugh. 'I'm on holiday. I refuse to take anything very seriously at the moment.'

Marion gave a heavy sigh. 'I meant to buy some cards from the kiosk and write them whilst I was laying here.' She sat up and pulled her skirt over her bathing costume. 'I'll have to go and get them or I'll put off sending them until it's time to go home. Do you want any, Cathy?'

'Half a dozen would be a good idea. Can I pay you later?'

Marion nodded and took up her purse. 'I won't be long.'

Cathy watched as she walked down the bank and along the gravel path towards the reception area and the kiosk.

'It can't be much fun for her to be stuck here with me.'

'She seems to be happy to lie in the sun.'

'If she were on holiday on her own she'd go into town, visit some sites, probably go to the disco in the evening. She might even meet that rich young man she was talking about.'

'There is no reason why she should not do those things. I would keep you company if you wished, or I could take both of you in my car to make visits.'

Cathy eyed Vasilis warily. 'But we hardly know you. We couldn't expect you to put yourself out for us. This is your holiday as well.'

Vasilis laughed, showing his white, even teeth. 'I am not on holiday. I work each day, but at times to please myself. This morning I will spend by the pool, this afternoon I will work. Some days I have to go to other towns on business and I could take you with me and collect you later.'

Cathy looked at him nonplussed. 'I'll speak to Marion; see how she feels, then, maybe if it would be no trouble.' She spoke doubtfully. 'I would like to see more than the swimming pool whilst I'm here and I know Marion would appreciate it.'

'Then it is settled. Tomorrow we will visit Heraklion. You must decide where you wish to see.'

'I would love to see the museum.' Cathy spoke wistfully.

'That is no problem. There is a step at the entrance, but there are attendants and there is a lift to the second floor.' As Vasilis spoke he looked at Cathy's long, slim legs. 'You have very beautiful legs.' He touched her ankle with his finger.

'You're tickling me,' she complained laughingly.

Vasilis looked at her in surprise. 'You can feel my finger?'

'Oh, yes. I have feeling in my legs, just no strength. Maybe it will come back one day.'

'I would like to see you walk, Cathy.' The way in which Vasilis said the words sent a tingle through her and made her blush as if he had said he wished to see her naked. His hand was still resting on her ankle and he was massaging her heel with his fingers. She realised how much she was enjoying the sensation, quite unlike the feel of the masseur's hard hands as they pushed and pummelled at her.

'Marion is taking a long time,' she said inconsequentially.

Vasilis shrugged. 'It is of no matter if she takes another hour.' He continued to massage Cathy's foot, his hand gradually moving up to her calf.

'Vasilis, you mustn't. We're at the swimming pool,' she protested.

'So? I am giving you a massage to help your leg.'

'You don't feel a bit like my masseur.'

'Then that is good. Maybe I will have the better effect.' Vasilis looked deep into her eyes and Cathy felt her heart turn over.

'No, that's enough,' she managed to say. 'I'm going to sleep for a while.' She closed her eyes and hoped he did not know how her heart was racing.

Vasilis withdrew his hand. 'Very well. I will not disturb you.'

Cathy wondered if she had offended him and looked at him from under lowered lids. He had moved back on his lounger and turned on his side so he could watch the swimmers in the pool. She hardly dared to move until Marion returned, a selection of postcards in her hand, and sat down beside her.

'I'm sorry I was so long. I had to wait whilst he served some locals and that included a chat. Take whichever ones you fancy. They're all the same price.' She thrust the cards into Cathy's hand. 'I'm going for a swim. It was baking standing up there.' She peeled off her dress, ran to the side of the pool and dived in.

Vasilis looked at Cathy. 'You too would like to swim.'

It was a statement, not a question and he did not wait for Cathy's answer before he scooped her up in his arms and carried her to the side of the pool. Carefully he lowered himself down the steps until they were both in the cool water. Still he did not release her and Cathy's heart was racing against his bronzed chest.

'We will swim together,' he announced, relinquishing his hold on her momentarily, whilst he turned on his back and placed a supporting arm beneath her waist. 'You will use your arms and I will use my legs,' he said with a disarming smile and Cathy had no choice but to comply.

She felt secure with his arm beneath her and parted the water firmly with her hands until they had completed three lengths. Vasilis lowered his legs and stood with the water up to his chin, turning Cathy deftly in his arms so her face was on a level with his own. He held her tightly to him, and she could feel her breasts hardening and the nipples rising as her legs drifted slowly down through the water, feeling the taught muscles of his own and the hard nub of his masculinity.

'Please, Vasilis, take me to the side,' she gasped breathlessly.

He looked at her mockingly. 'You are tired of swimming with me?'

'I ought to do my exercises,' she made the excuse lamely. Cathy held on to the lip of the pool and bent her head. She was trembling, and she was not sure if it was from suppressed passion or nerves. She wished desperately that she were able to climb out of the pool unaided and return to the lounger where she could feign sleep. Instead she had to wait until Vasilis had swum a number of lengths before he rejoined her at the side. He smiled jauntily as he flicked back his hair.

'You would like to swim again?'

'No, oh, no. I'd like to get out now.'

'Very well.' Once again his strong arms took her weight and he climbed easily up the narrow concrete steps. Instead of taking her over to the lounger, he deposited her at the side of the pool, her legs over the side and feet just in the water.

'Now, you will do some good exercises.'

To Cathy's surprise he slipped back into the water and took her feet, pressing the palms of his hands against her soles, forcing her knees to bend and lift.

'It does not hurt?' he asked solicitously and Cathy shook her head.

For half an hour Vasilis stayed with her, insisting that her legs moved up and down with the pressure of his hands, until finally sensing her weariness he placed his hands around her waist and lifted her back down into the water beside him.

'Now we will walk,' he announced.

'I can't walk, you know that.'

'You can walk in the water. I will hold you.' Vasilis turned to face her, still with his hands placed firmly on her waist.

Tentatively Cathy placed her weight on her feet and Vasilis took a step backwards. Hesitantly Cathy moved her right leg, then her left, repeating the motion until they had reached the far side. Vasilis lifted her and turned her round. 'Now we will walk back.'

Cathy complied and when they reached the side a smile creased Vasilis's face. 'That was very good. The next time we will walk across the pool two times.'

'Twice,' Cathy corrected him automatically, acutely conscious of his hands on her body. 'I ought to get out now.'

'You are cold?'

'No, just a little tired.'

'Of course.'

He lifted her easily and carried her back to the lounger. From her reclining position in his arms she was acutely aware of the throbbing artery in his neck and the way his dark hair curled attractively at the back of his ear. Having lowered her to her seat he withdrew his hands and she felt sure he had deliberately touched the edge of her breast with his thumb. The feeling had run through her like an electric shock and she dared not look up at him.

'You would like me to dry your back?' he asked.

'No!' Cathy spoke more sharply than she meant to. She held her towel tightly in front of her. 'No, I can manage, thank you.'

Vasilis picked up his own towel and rubbed his back vigorously. Cathy could not help noticing the muscles across his chest and inadvertently her gaze travelled down his body, resting on the obvious swelling between his loins. Colour flooded her face and she buried her head in her towel, hoping he had not noticed her embarrassment.

By the time Marion climbed out of the pool Cathy had regained her composure and was writing a card to her mother. 'It's difficult to know what to say on postcards,' she complained.

Marion shrugged. 'Just put weather good, food good, having a wonderful time. I do.'

'It seems bit pointless sending a message like that.'

'It's pretty pointless sending cards anyway. They usually arrive after you get home.'

'My parents will expect one regularly. When I send the next one I should have something more interesting to write on it.'

Marion raised her eyebrows. 'I'll buy some stamps later and post them up at reception.'

'I'll come up with you,' Cathy offered eagerly, not wanting to be left alone with Vasilis again that day. 'I'd like to see what else they have for sale.'

'The usual sort of tourist bits and pieces. Nothing exciting.'

'I'd still like to see,' insisted Cathy.

'I can take you up to reception,' offered Vasilis. 'Shortly I have to leave.'

'Oh, no,' Cathy spoke firmly. 'I'll wait for Marion.'

'As you please. Now, would you like something to drink or eat before I go? I can bring it over here for you.'

'I think I'd rather go and sit at a table. Is it nearly lunch time? I'm starving.'

Vasilis looked at the gold Rolex he had slipped onto his wrist. 'I will take you over and have a beer with you. When I leave you can order your food.'

'Why don't you stay and eat with us?' suggested Marion.

Vasilis shook his head. 'I have to work this afternoon. I will eat later.'

'What work do you do?' asked Marion curiously.

'Many things. Today I will be checking invoices and deliveries.'

'Oh!' Marion was obviously disappointed with his answer. She slipped her sun dress over her head and pushed her feet into her sandals. 'I'm ready. Do you want any help, Cathy?'

'Just pull me up, please.'

'I will help you.'

Before Marion could move Vasilis had Cathy in his arms and was placing her gently in her wheelchair. 'Now, what time would you like to leave tomorrow, ladies?'

'Tomorrow?' Marion looked puzzled.

'Vasilis has offered to take us in to Heraklion in his car so we can go to the museum,' explained Cathy.

'Oh, that's wonderful!' exclaimed Marion. 'I must admit I did want to go there.'

Cathy found herself lying awake that night thinking of Vasilis. Was she fooling herself that he found her attractive? She was in a wheelchair, unable to move around as she wished, yet at one point she had thought he was going to kiss her. It had taken all her will power to resist running her hand across his smooth, bronzed chest and tangling her fingers in his mat of curly black hair which grew between his nipples. It was ridiculous for her to think of him in any way other than a casual holiday acquaintance.

She turned on her side and brushed her hand down her ribs to the curve of her hips. Vasilis had done the same when they were in the swimming pool and she had enjoyed the slight caress, even if it had been accidental. She gave a deep sigh. His aroused manhood whilst he was drying his back had excited her and she covered her face with her hands as if to shut out the memory. She had not thought of any man since her accident and Keith had left her and now frustration welled up within her.

'I must stop this silliness,' she vowed. 'He probably flirts with every woman whilst he's here. He's probably married with children.' As the thought came to her she felt a pang of jealousy.

'I won't encourage him. We'll go to Heraklion with him tomorrow, but that will be an end of it. I'll just tell him I don't want to swim and wait until he's gone away.' At that idea Cathy bit her lip. If she refused Vasilis's help she would be unable to climb out of the pool, even with Marion in attendance. She turned the problem over and over in her mind. Vasilis's bronzed body continually returning to haunt her. She shook herself impatiently. She was being ridiculous and reading far more into a situation than she should.

She awoke to hear Marion moving around their room quietly.

'Sorry, did I wake you?'

Cathy shook her head. 'Not really,' she yawned. 'I didn't sleep very well.' The rumpled state of her bed bore witness to her disturbed night.

'Were you in pain?'

'No, why should I be?'

'I thought I heard you groan a couple of times.'

'I was probably snoring.' Cathy threw back her sheet and lifted her legs over the side of the bed. Gripping the arms of her chair she pulled herself upright. She forced herself to stand for a few moments until the familiar numbness made her sit hurriedly and she propelled herself into the bathroom.

'Don't take too long,' called Marion. 'We're meeting Vasilis at ten, remember, and we've not had breakfast yet.'

Cathy did not answer. How could she forget that they were meeting the attractive Cretan? She took a deep breath. Today they would both be fully clothed and there would be no excuse for him to take her in his arms, nothing would disturb her composure.

She chose her outfit carefully, a short sleeved apricot silk blouse teamed with a matching skirt and jacket. The colour enhanced her dark hair and already tanned skin. She folded the jacket across her knees. 'I'm ready.'

Marion looked at her. 'Do you think you'll need a jacket?'

'It could be chilly in the museum,' she defended her decision.

Marion took stock of herself in the mirror. Cathy could be right and her apple green sleeveless dress would not afford much warmth. She picked up her cardigan and placed it around her shoulders.

'I'll take this with me.'

Vasilis was waiting for them in the reception area when they arrived. He greeted them both and devoured them with his eyes. 'I insist upon taking you to lunch with me. You are both too beautiful to eat at a roadside taverna. I will take you where the surroundings will do justice to your beauty.'

Cathy raised her eyes and looked at the man standing before her. He looked very different from the one who had held her in his arms in the swimming pool. A pale blue shirt beneath a well-cut navy blue suit gave him the appearance of an influential business man. From his pocket he produced a tie.

'I will make myself truly respectable a little later. It is too hot to wear a tie,' he smiled. 'Shall we go?' He pushed Cathy in her chair to where a gleaming white car stood waiting for them in the morning sunshine. 'Where will you be most comfortable, Cathy? The front or the back?'

'I really don't mind.' Cathy tried to sound disinterested.

'You know you prefer the front,' frowned Marion. 'You always say you have more leg room.'

'Then the front it shall be. You will not need your jacket in the car.' Vasilis opened the door and lifted Cathy on to the seat. As he placed her inside their faces were close together and Cathy felt an almost irresistible urge to run her fingers across his lips. As he bent and tucked her skirt around her legs she felt the blood rushing to her face.

He settled Marion in the seat behind his own, folded the wheelchair and placed it in the boot before sliding into the seat beside Cathy and smiling happily at her.

'Would you like some music?'

Cathy nodded. It would save having to talk. Usually she could find plenty to say, but somehow this morning she could not think of any small talk.

Vasilis inserted the cassette and pulsating Greek music filled the car. 'Do you like Greek music?' he asked.

'I like all music,' replied Cathy.

'I too, like all music, but mostly I like the Greek love songs,' he appeared not to notice the flush that spread to Cathy's cheeks. 'They are always so sad, of love not returned, or loved ones departed.'

Cathy's flush deepened. 'I don't speak Greek so I wouldn't know.'

'You do not need to understand the language. There is a sadness to the music that tells you it is a love song.' He pushed the "fast forward" knob, then released it and the music changed. 'This is the story of a boy who falls in love with a beautiful girl in his village. She goes away to the city and marries a rich man. She returns to her village and the poor boy sees her, wealthy and out of his reach. He sings sadly of the love he will always have for her.'

Cathy listened, the words meaning nothing to her, but the music did have a poignancy about it which made her heart constrict.

As they neared Heraklion the car slowed to a crawl amongst the other traffic and Vasilis wound his window down and shouted at the driver who was trying to inch himself forwards and block their passage. The driver shouted back and continued to move, Vasilis doing the same, finally accelerating and ensuring his place in the queue at the traffic lights. He revved the engine whilst they waited and tapped impatiently on the steering wheel.

'Always there is a problem here,' he complained. 'It was better before we had the traffic lights.' He ran a finger across his forehead. 'I am too hot. Can you take my jacket from me, Cathy?' He shrugged first one arm and then the other from the sleeves and Cathy pulled it from behind him, laying it across her knees.

Vasilis wriggled his shoulders appreciatively. 'That is better, ah, now we move.'

Having passed the junction where the traffic had been forced to halt, they continued swiftly into the centre of the town and Vasilis pulled up smoothly outside the museum. A policeman whistled and waved him on. Vasilis ignored him and began to unpack the wheelchair from the boot. The policeman walked over and ordered him to move his car which was causing an obstruction.

With much gesticulation Vasilis explained that he was stopping only for a few minutes and one of his passengers could not walk. Whilst he argued, Marion alighted, carrying her cardigan and Cathy's jacket and draped them over the handles of the chair. Vasilis left her in charge and opened the passenger door, lifting Cathy out with ease and carrying her to the chair. He placed her in it triumphantly, as if to prove to the policeman that he was telling the truth.

'I will meet you here at one thirty, then we will go for lunch,' he announced as he slid back behind the driving wheel and started the car, forcing the policeman to step hurriedly back on to the pavement.

A torrent of Greek was directed at them and Cathy looked at Marion timidly. 'What is he saying?'

'I haven't the faintest idea.' Marion pointed to her chest. 'English. Do not understand.'

He continued to harangue them as Marion pushed the chair towards the museum entrance, then shrugged and turned back to directing the traffic, assisted by short blasts on his whistle.

The interior of the museum was cool after the intense heat of the sun and despite the press of people they moved easily from one display case to another, passing their guide book between them, sometimes listening to one of the professional guides as they explained the importance of particular artefacts.

'It must be so boring to have to say the same thing every day,' whispered Cathy.

'Maybe they don't. Most of the tourists who employ a guide don't bother to read the books so they can tell them anything they please. "Now this decorative piece of broken plate was part of the dinner service used by King Minos". Who's going to argue with that? Tomorrow it can become part of the Queen's breakfast set. We'll look through the guide book when we get back and see what suggestions we can make.'

'We could do it now,' suggested Cathy mischievously.

'We might offend them. So many speak English.'

Cathy shrugged. 'I've seen more than enough pottery. Do you think the lift is working and we could go up and see the frescoes?'

The small lift carried them smoothly to the upper floor and Cathy gave a gasp of pleasure.

'They're beautiful! I never expected to see such colours.' She wheeled herself slowly around the room admiring the frescoes from a distance and checking the guide book for more information. 'I wonder if the same person painted all those in the palace?'

'I expect a number of men worked on them.'

'To paint some of the unimportant pieces, maybe, but there must have been one who submitted drawings to the king and then had the intricate job of scaling them up.'

'They may have had different people for the different parts, you know, one for figures, another for flowers and a third for animals or birds,' suggested Marion. 'It would have taken years for one man to do it all.'

Cathy giggled. 'Think how long it would take if you decided to have your room redecorated. By the time it was finished the fashion would have changed. I wonder if they had a book of designs that you looked through, like choosing wallpaper today.'

'Which would you choose?'

Cathy shook her head. 'I don't know. They're all beautiful. At least they're beautiful over here. They'd look a bit silly in my bedroom at home.'

'I don't know,' Marion considered. 'You could have one. That could look quite effective.'

'You'd need white walls to show them off properly.'

'There you are, then. The next time you have your room decorated you don't have to worry about choosing wallpaper. Have the walls painted white and cover them with miniatures of the frescoes.'

'Somehow I don't think the effect would be quite the same.'

'It would be a talking point with your friends. You could say "come into my bedroom and see my frescoes". I'd love to see their faces.'

'I'd love to see my parents' faces if I dared to do it.'

'If you dared to do what?' Vasilis's voice in her ear made Cathy start with surprise.

'Cathy's planning to redecorate her bedroom,' explained Marion. 'She was trying to decide which frescoes to put where.'

Vasilis raised his eyebrows. 'To put them all in one room would be a mistake.'

'I wasn't serious,' protested Cathy. 'I think they're all beautiful, but they'd look wrong in an English house.'

'They were used only in the finest buildings. I do not think any of the ordinary people would have had a picture painted in the plaster.'

'I thought they decorated their walls?' Marion turned to him in surprise.

Vasilis nodded. 'With plaster which had been painted one colour, or sometimes with a pattern, but not a picture. They preferred to cover their walls with bright rugs.'

'How do you know?' asked Cathy.

'The frescoes have only been found in the palaces on Crete and in one or two very rich houses elsewhere. If you go to a village house today you will see rugs hanging from the walls in the winter,' he explained patiently.

'Why in the winter? Why not in the summer too?'

'They have them for warmth. A house of stone is cool in the summer, but very cold in the winter.'

'You don't expect Crete to be cold when you're here in the summer. Even in here it feels warm now.' Cathy's jacket still lay across her knees.

'I think it is time for fresher air. Do you enjoy fish to eat?'

'What kind of fish?'

Vasilis shrugged. 'Whichever kind you would like. I know a good fish restaurant. We could have some lunch, then visit the Venetian fortress. If there is any breeze it will come from across the sea.'

Marion relinquished the wheelchair to Vasilis and insisted on using the stairs to reach the ground floor. 'There's no room for a third person in the lift. I'll meet you down there.'

Before Cathy could protest she had left them and joined the slow moving throng who were making their way towards the lower level.

'So, you have had a good morning?' Vasilis raised his eyebrows at her quizzically.

'A lovely morning. I'm very grateful to you and so is Marion.'

'That is good. Whilst we have lunch we can make plans for another day.'

Cathy bit her lip. 'I don't think we should impose on your time. You have your work.'

Vasilis shrugged and pushed the chair into the lift at the same time. 'I can arrange my work. That is no problem, besides, your friend enjoys making the visits.'

'I know, but ...'

'Here we are, and Marion is waiting for us.' Vasilis turned the wheelchair skilfully to avoid an elderly couple who were waiting to use the lift. 'Now, follow me.'

Cathy looked at Marion and pulled a wry face. There was not going to be any escape for her that day from Vasilis's attention.

Marion sat on the side of her bed and removed her sandals. 'Did you enjoy yourself? I loved the museum and the fort was pretty impressive, wasn't it?'

Cathy smiled doubtfully. 'Yes, I did. I'm not sure about our arrangement to go out again tomorrow, though.'

'Why? Are you feeling tired?'

'Not particularly. I don't think we should become too dependent upon him.'

'I would make the most of it. Think how much easier it is for you to have him help you than some rough taxi man or bus driver.'

Cathy shuddered. The thought of some of the men she had seen having to lift her was not an appealing prospect. 'I suppose I should be grateful.'

'You certainly should. I'm going for a swim before supper if you don't mind.'

'No, you go and I'll shower when you get back. I still have some cards to write.'

'I won't be long. It's probably pretty cold by now.' Marion picked up her towel and draped it over her swimming costume. 'Shall I push you out onto the balcony before I go? The sun is still on it.'

Cathy nodded, collected her postcards and a book from beside her bed and wheeled herself to the door. 'I should be able to manage for myself.' She bumped against the door runner.

'Don't be silly. You could tip yourself out if you hit that just wrong.' Marion took the handles and tipped the chair back enough to clear the upstanding door runner. 'Anything else you want before I go?'

'I'm fine, thanks.' Cathy watched as Marion walked down the path towards the swimming pool, trying to stifle the envious thoughts she had. She shuffled through the cards, wondering if she should send one to Keith. Finally deciding it would be stupid of her, she began to write a few words of greeting on each. They could go to the staff at the hospital who had looked after her so well during her stay.

'You are very busy?'

Cathy looked up to see Vasilis standing before her, a bottle and glasses in his hand.

'I thought maybe you would like a glass of wine before your dinner?' Without waiting for her to agree he placed them on the table and removed the cork, pouring a generous measure for both of them. He raised his glass and saluted her.

'How did you know I would be here?'

'I saw Marion going to the pool alone. I did not think you would have ventured away from the chalet on your own.'

Cathy felt herself flush. 'I may have been taking a shower.'

'Then it would have been my pleasure to have helped you in and out.' Vasilis's dark eyes challenged her for a response.

'I am able to manage on my own,' replied Cathy stiffly.

'Really? It is much more pleasure when there is someone to wash your back.'

Cathy felt her blush deepening. 'I prefer to be independent when I can.'

'I was not talking of independence. I was talking of pleasure.' His dark eyes gleamed and Cathy wished her heart would stop beating so rapidly. He was flirting outrageously with her and she was enjoying it.

'I'm sure you have a great deal of pleasure,' she managed to answer.

Vasilis shrugged. 'Sometimes I have, sometimes I do not have. With you I could have great pleasure.'

'You hardly know me.' Cathy tried to be flippant.

Vasilis took the glass from her hand and placed it on the table beside his own. 'I know you are very beautiful. I think you could be very gentle. I, too, can be very gentle.' He leant forward and kissed her gently.

'Vasilis!' Cathy gasped.

'You do not like to be kissed?'

'Yes. No. I mean, I don't know you.'

Vasilis shrugged. 'I hope you will want to know me. I want to know you. Tell me, why are you unable to walk?'

'I was driving home and a pony ran across in front of me.'

'He had escaped?'

'No, they live in the forest quite close to my home. Usually they avoid the roads, but something must have frightened him. He came at me like a canon ball.'

'And you were badly hurt?'

Cathy nodded. 'Lots of broken bones and cuts and scrapes, now I'm just a hideous cripple.'

Vasilis shook his head. 'You are not hideous, Cathy, you are beautiful, and I do not believe you are a cripple.'

'I am not sitting in a wheelchair from choice,' Cathy replied bitterly. 'I just have to be grateful that I survived.'

'I am very grateful.' Vasilis leaned forward and kissed her again. Cathy did not resist. There was no harm in Vasilis kissing her and she had to admit that she was enjoying the attention of the man.

Cathy rose looking pale and tired. She had spent most of the night envisaging what could have happened had Marion's return from the swimming pool not been imminent. An inner voice told her not to be so foolish. The man probably charmed every unattached woman he came across. She had not taken the pill since her accident and she certainly did not want to return to England pregnant or carrying some horrible disease.

'What's wrong with you this morning?' asked Marion finally.

'Nothing at all,' snapped back Cathy. 'I just wish we weren't going out today.'

'Do you want me to tell Vasilis you're feeling too tired after yesterday?' suggested Marion.

'No, I'm not a bit tired.'

'You look it.'

'I just didn't sleep very well. It must be the heat.'

Marion shrugged. 'We could ask him to take us to the beach, then you could rest after a swim.'

'I could do that if I stayed here. I want to go to Malia.'

Marion turned away. Whatever was bothering her friend was not going to be confided to her so she might as well give up. 'Let me know when you're ready to go for breakfast.'

'I'm ready now.' Cathy slammed her hairbrush down on the dressing table.

Marion ignored the show of petulance. 'Fine.' She picked up her bag and cardigan, giving them to Cathy to hold whilst she opened the door. 'Right, then, breakfast here we come.'

Cathy's mood did not improve during the meal. Her eyes searched the dining room constantly for Vasilis, not sure if she wished to see him or hoped he had overslept. She toyed with her roll, finally accepting a second glass of fruit juice and pushing the bread to one side.

'Do you want to go back to the chalet or shall we go straight up to reception to meet Vasilis?' asked Marion.

'I really don't mind.'

Marion said no more but pushed Cathy from the dining room and up the long gravel path towards the road. 'He's waiting for us.'

Cathy did not answer. She had already seen the tall figure which had made her heart beat faster. He was talking to an elderly man and by the way they both turned and looked at her she knew she was the subject of their conversation. She felt herself flush and hoped she was too far away for either of them to notice. Before they reached the two men the older one had moved away and Vasilis came forward to greet them.

'Good morning, ladies.' His eyes lingered approvingly on Cathy who wore a pale lemon sundress. 'Today I see you wish to get a sun tan.'

'I was too warm yesterday,' answered Cathy tersely.

Vasilis smiled. 'I also was very warm. Today I do not have to wear a suit so I shall be more comfortable. Have you brought a towel for swimming?'

Marion looked at him in surprise. 'I thought we were going to Malia?'

'Yes, we will visit Malia, there is a good beach near there to swim.'

'I'll go back and get our things.' Marion thrust her bag and cardigan onto Cathy's lap and hurried back down to the chalet.

Vasilis lifted Cathy into the front seat of the car, bending to brush her hair with his lips as he did so. 'How is my Cathy this morning?'

Cathy felt her mouth go dry and was angry with herself; anyone would think she was a schoolgirl with a crush the way she was behaving. 'I'm fine.'

Vasilis leant over her and kissed her lips. 'I am better now I have seen you and touched you. It is only a small pleasure, but,' he shrugged eloquently. 'It is better than no pleasure, don't you agree?'

'What were you saying to that man about me?'

Vasilis drew back. 'Why should I say anything to him about you?'

'He turned and looked at me. I know you said something.'

'I told him I was taking you and your friend to Malia. That is all.'

'Why should he want to know?'

Vasilis laughed. 'This is his car. He would like to know where I propose to take it with two lovely young ladies.'

Cathy felt she had spoken foolishly. 'I just don't like to be talked about.'

'Cathy, you are very beautiful. Everywhere you go you will always be talked about. I asked my uncle if I could borrow his car when I took you out. Mine is not large enough to accommodate your chair. I told him I proposed to take you to Malia today, then I saw you coming and he turned to look at you and remarked on your beauty.'

'And probably asked why I was in a chair and you were wasting your time with a cripple.' Cathy spoke bitterly.

Vasilis gazed at her sadly. 'He did not look at your chair. He looked at you.'

'He may not have mentioned it, but I'm sure he noticed it.'

'Cathy, forget your chair. Do not spoil the day for your friend. Here she comes, hot and breathless because she made us wait for five minutes.'

Marion threw the beach bag into the boot of the car. 'You should have told us last night that we'd be swimming. I'd have had it all ready and not kept you waiting.'

Vasilis shrugged. 'We have all day to ourselves. To wait for a few minutes was no problem.'

Vasilis appeared to push Cathy in her wheelchair effortlessly over the rough ground of the site of Malia and Marion was more than grateful that he had accompanied them.

Marion looked at the ruins in disappointment. 'I had thought there would be much more to see here.'

'You need to know your Cretan history very well to appreciate some of the sites. It is good to see them, but you need help to understand them. It is different at Knossos. So much reconstruction has been done that you do not need to use so much of the imagination.'

'That sounds more like my kind of site.' Marion smiled at Vasilis.

'I will take you there next week,' promised Vasilis.

'It's quite close to Heraklion so maybe you could drop us there and meet us later, like you did when we went to the museum,' suggested Cathy.

Vasilis shook his head. 'Marion could not take you on her own. It is much steeper and rougher in places than here.'

'I'm sure she'd manage.'

'I will not let her manage. The chair could run away as you went down the hill and she would not have the strength to push you up. For some things you need a man, Cathy.' As he spoke his thumb stroked the back of her neck and she shivered at the hidden meaning behind his words.

Marion sat down on a low wall. 'I've seen enough. I'll sit here and wait for you if you want to walk around some more.'

Cathy's frown was lost on her friend as Vasilis began to wheel her towards the far end of the site, down two shallow steps and stopped behind the remains of a wall which screened them from view.

'Now I can kiss you properly,' he smiled, moving in front of her and holding out his hands in supplication.

Cathy turned her head away. 'Vasilis, this has got to stop.'

'Why?'

'We hardly know each other, and ...'

Vasilis placed his hands either side of her face. 'And this is a perfect way to get to know each other.' He leaned forward to kiss her.

Cathy moved away from him as he tilted her face towards his own. 'I shall be going home in a few weeks. This is just a holiday romance.'

Vasilis withdrew his hand and stood back from her. 'I will take you back to your friend.' Without another word Vasilis pushed the chair away from the wall, turning and dragging the chair effortlessly up the two steps.

Cathy bowed her head. Hot tears pressed behind her eyelids. She had behaved like an immature teenager. Why shouldn't she enjoy herself for a few weeks with this incredibly attractive man? She tried to speak, but the lump in her throat prevented any words coming out.

'We are back, Marion,' called Vasilis. 'Now we will find a beach for our swim.'

Marion rose lazily to her feet. 'Was there anything more to see?'

Cathy shook her head, not trusting herself to speak. She really must regain control of herself. Returning to the car Vasilis chatted easily with Marion and she felt his touch was impersonal as he lifted her onto her seat. A small frown had settled between his eyes and Cathy had a longing to stroke the tiny lines away with her fingers.

Vasilis carried Cathy's wheelchair down onto the beach before returning and carrying her in his arms. 'It is easier than trying to push the chair,' he explained. 'In the sand the wheels will not move.'

He settled them comfortably, placing an umbrella in the sand and their loungers in the shade it gave.

'Now, I will leave you to change whilst I swim. I will return for Cathy when she is ready.'

'I may not swim,' demurred Cathy.

Vasilis looked at her anxiously. 'You will become very hot if you do not swim. There are no trees here for shade. You could be ill.'

Cathy shrugged. 'I'll see. You and Marion enjoy yourselves.'

She sat back and watched as Marion joined Vasilis in the water and they swam out together. Vasilis began to forge ahead and Marion tried to keep up with him. It was hot. Already Cathy could feel the perspiration running down her neck, making rivulets of a darker colour on her costume as it travelled down to her waist and she began to long for Vasilis to return and carry her into the cool water. Marion returned first, running up the sand and jumping onto her towel.

'That sand is so hot! It was wonderful; far better than the pool. Maybe we could try the sea back at the hotel. I'll have a look and see if it's possible to get your chair down to the edge. I'm sure you could manage to get into the water with a bit of help.'

Cathy nodded. Her eyes were fixed on Vasilis who was swimming lazily towards the shore. Surely he would come out for her now. 'I wish he'd hurry up,' she sighed. 'No, don't call him.' She clutched at Marion's arm as she went to wave.

Marion looked at her friend critically. 'He could stay messing about in there for ages whilst you sit here cooking. I'll go down and tell him you're ready to cool down.'

Before Cathy could stop her Marion was running over the hot sand until she stood ankle deep in water. Vasilis allowed himself to float in on a small wave and lay on the sand looking at her.

'Cathy's getting very hot, Vasilis. Could you carry her down? I'll sit here with her if you want to continue swimming.'

Vasilis rose and ran his hands across his hair to remove the sea water. 'I can swim later.'

He strode up the beach, ignoring the heat of the sand beneath his feet and swept Cathy up into his arms. 'Marion says you wish to swim now.'

Cathy nodded. At his touch her heart seemed to stop beating and she locked her fingers tightly around his neck as he carried her carefully down to the water. He made to place her beside Marion and she shook her head.

'I want to go right in.'

Slowly he walked into the deeper water until he was up to his chest where he took his arm from beneath her legs and her feet floated downwards to contact the soft sand. Her hands still locked behind his head Cathy turned to face him.

'I'm sorry, Vasilis.'

'For what?'

'We seem to have misunderstood each other.'

'How?'

'At Malia; when I spoke about a holiday romance.'

'If that is what you think...' Vasilis shrugged.

Cathy swallowed hard. 'I don't mind if it is.'

Vasilis looked down into her eyes. 'I do not have holiday romances. Many girls come here for a holiday looking for a man to pass their time with. I am not interested in those girls.'

'I didn't come here looking for a man.'

'What did you come for, Cathy?'

'My parents and Marion thought the sunshine and a change would do me good. I was in hospital a long time; they thought it might help me to recover.'

'And has it?'

'Oh, I'll never walk again. I accept that.'

Vasilis shook his head. 'Poor Cathy. What is it that frightens you?'

'I'm not frightened of anything,' protested Cathy.

'You are frightened of walking again. Why? Because you will miss having a slave to wait on you?'

'Marion is not a slave – and I'm as independent as possible.' Cathy replied indignantly.

'And I frighten you. I offer to love you. At first you seem happy; then you become frightened. Why? I don't understand.'

Cathy dropped her eyes. 'I don't want to get hurt.'

'Why should I hurt you?'

Cathy shifted impatiently in his arms. 'You don't understand. I'm only on holiday. In a few weeks I shall fly back to England.'

'You do not have to leave.'

'Of course I do. I have my ticket. Marion has to ...'

'You could stay with me, Cathy. I would look after you.'

Cathy raised her eyes to his face. Slowly she shook her head. 'It's just not possible. You would very soon be tired of having a cripple around, being their slave,' she added bitterly.

'I am already your slave.' Vasilis's dark eyes seemed to bore into her as he unlocked her arms from around his neck. 'I am not free to follow you to England. You are free to stay in Crete.'

Cathy shivered. 'I'm getting cold. I ought to swim.'

Vasilis raised his eyebrows quizzically at her. 'I am not cold. Do you shiver from fear of me, maybe?'

'I've told you, I'm not frightened of you.'

'That is good.' He kissed her lightly on her forehead. 'You swim. I will be beside you if you need to rest.'

Marion was applying sun lotion liberally to her legs when Vasilis carried Cathy back up the beach. Gently he deposited her onto the lounger, picked up her towel and began to dry her back.

Marion removed a book from her beach bag, perched her sun glasses on her nose and turned on her side. 'I plan to read. If I fall asleep don't wake me up. I've smothered myself in sun tan lotion so I shouldn't burn.'

'I'll keep an eye on you. When you start to smoulder I'll let you know.'

Vasilis looked at Marion's golden back. 'I think some protection for your back and shoulders. Pass me your lotion and I will apply it.' He squeezed the cream into his hand and applied it with firm strokes. 'There is a little breeze and the sand will blow. It can make your skin sore very quickly, before you realise what is happening you would be burnt.'

He turned his attention back to Cathy. 'Where is your sun lotion?'

'In my bag.'

'Which way do you wish to lie?'

'On my back.'

'Then I will put the lotion on your front.' Vasilis knelt over her and tipped some of the oil into his hand. 'I will start with your feet. Feet can burn very easily.'

Cathy closed her eyes. It was like the massages she had been given at the hospital. Gradually Vasilis moved his hands up her legs, to her knees and thighs. The movements became less like a massage and more like foreplay with a definite end in mind. Her limbs were no longer relaxed, she felt her stomach constrict like a spring and wished they were not on a public beach but somewhere quite alone. With a deep sigh Vasilis moved his attention to her shoulders, bending and kissing her chin as he finished. The kiss sent an electric shock through Cathy and she opened her eyes with a start.

Vasilis ran a finger across her lips. 'Now you will not burn.'

During the afternoon Marion and Vasilis walked up to the beach cafe and purchased drinks, ham and salad rolls and fruit and Cathy was surprised to discover how hungry she was.

'You should have eaten more for breakfast,' observed Marion. 'All you did was crumble up that roll on your plate and drink juice.'

'I wasn't hungry then,' frowned Cathy.

'Why did you not tell me you were hungry?' asked Vasilis. 'I would have gone to the cafe earlier.'

'I could easily have waited until we had our meal this evening. What time do you plan to leave here?'

'You are in a hurry to return to the hotel?'

Cathy shook her head. 'Not at all. I will be quite happy to lay here to let my food go down, have another swim and then lay in the sun to get dry.'

'There is plenty of time for you to do that. Do you wish me to put more oil on you?'

Cathy shook her head. 'I'm not burning.' She did not feel she could bear to experience the sensations Vasilis's hands had aroused in her a second time.

The remainder of the afternoon passed lazily. Marion read and dozed alternately, going in to swim three more times before they decided to make a move. Cathy lay pretending to sleep, but thinking about Vasilis. She found him so attractive. Finally she allowed him to carry her back down to the sea for a last swim, feeling his erection as her legs slid into the water, his apologetic shrug amusing her.

He moved away, his hands still on her waist. 'I cannot help myself, Cathy.'

Cathy shrugged. 'I am sure that when I have gone home you will be standing here and saying the same thing to another girl.'

Vasilis looked at her sadly and shook his head. 'I do not usually spend my time on the beach with a beautiful young lady. I have to enjoy the pleasure whilst I can. Tomorrow I have to work and then I shall be away for the weekend.'

Cathy felt her heart sink. 'Where are you going?'

'I return to my house, to check all is in order.'

'Where's that?'

'At Hersonissos. Also I have to spend time with my relatives. They expect me to join them for a meal.'

Cathy nodded. Her mother had been insistent that she always joined them for Sunday lunch.

'I will be able to take you both out again next week. You will have to decide where you would like to visit.'

'I know Marion wants to go to Knossos.'

'Then that we will do. Also I could take you to Aghios Nikolaos. It is a very pretty town.'

'I really don't mind where we go. I'll ask Marion to have a look at the guide book. She's the expert.'

'I'm the expert on what?' asked Marion as she joined them with a splash in the sea.

'Places to visit,' smiled Cathy. 'Vasilis says he will take us to Knossos next week.'

'Wonderful.'

'He also said that Aghios Nikolaos is pretty.'

'Which way is that?' asked Marion.

Vasilis indicated with his arm, the other still around Cathy. 'It is a very pretty drive. We could visit the island and have lunch at Elounda before we visit the town.'

'What island?'

'Spinalonga.'

'How do we get there?'

'A small boat will take us over. It will be no problem.'

Marion smiled happily. 'I'd love to see every inch of Crete whilst we're here. You never know if you will have another opportunity.'

Vasilis looked at Cathy, his arm tightening around her waist. 'I hope you will have many opportunities. If you wish to drive with me I can take you to the places the tourists do not visit.'

Cathy felt herself blush, reading a different meaning behind his words.

'Really?' Marion smiled happily. 'I'll have a look at the map tonight and show you tomorrow. You can always tell me if it is too far.'

Vasilis shook his head. 'I have told Cathy. Tomorrow I have to work and then I shall be with my relatives at the weekend. I will be here again on Monday.'

'Oh, well, it will be no hardship for Cathy and me to spend time at the pool for a couple of days.'

'I think you would find the beach easier. I will ask Panayiotis to put down the matting to a lounger very close to the sea and make sure no one else sits there. You will be able to manage the chair across that.'

'You are very good to us, Vasilis. I do appreciate it.' Marion smiled at him gratefully.

Vasilis shrugged. 'Why should I not be good to you? I enjoy your company. Usually I spend my week alone.'

Marion pushed Cathy along the paved area that led to the beach, relieved when she saw the promised matting had been laid across the sand and down to the water. Two loungers were placed beneath an umbrella and an elderly man was sitting on one of them. Marion frowned in annoyance. If the man refused to move she would not be able to push the chair across the sand to another umbrella.

Carefully she manoeuvred the chair down the narrow strip of matting. It was only just wide enough to take the wheels. As she reached the loungers the man rose and indicated that it was for them, gave a toothless grin and walked back up the beach.

'I guess that's Panayiotis. I'm pleased he did as Vasilis asked. I'd never have managed to get you down here without that matting and we'd have been stuck at the back of the beach with no way to get to the sea.'

'We'd have been lucky to have a lounger even,' said Cathy looking around. 'Most of them seem to be already taken. I thought he had claimed ours at first and I wondered how we were going to ask him to move if he didn't speak English.'

Marion shrugged. 'Thank goodness the problem didn't arise. Do you want to go straight in for a swim? I'm roasted already.'

Cathy nodded, peeled off her sundress and bent to remove her sandals.

By mid afternoon Cathy was feeling bored. She missed having Vasilis there to carry her in and out of the sea and the feel of Marion's hands applying her sun oil did not arouse the same feelings in her. She tried to relax and rationalise her feelings, giving a deep sigh.

'What's wrong?'

'Nothing,' Cathy assured Marion. 'That was a contented sigh,' she lied. 'Have you decided where you will ask Vasilis to take us next week?'

'I thought we'd stick to Knossos and Aghios Nikolaos. It really depends how much free time he has. I'd like to go to Rethymnon and also up to Chania. How about you?"

'I'd quite like to go to go to his house. I'd love to see the inside of a proper Greek house.'

'I don't expect they're very different from ours. I'd like to know what work he does that he seems able to please himself what hours he keeps.' Marion looked at Cathy with a gleam in her eye. 'Do you think he's Greek Mafia?'

'Don't be silly,' Cathy suppressed a smile.

'You never know.' Marion put on a phoney accent. 'I am wiv de Grik Mafia. I am de big boss. Now you know my secret I 'ave to keep you pris'ner 'ere.'

Cathy giggled. 'He doesn't speak a bit like that.'

'Maybe your Dad was involved with them when he was out here? That could be why he never speaks about it. He probably had to swear never to give away their secrets on pain of death or having "traitor" etched into his forehead.'

'I'm sure it was nothing exciting like that.'

'Wouldn't you like to know exactly what he did?'

Cathy nodded. 'I'll have to ask him when we go home, see if he will tell me, although I'm sure it was nothing to do with the Mafia. It was probably something very mundane and boring. Dad's far too law abiding to be mixed up in anything devious or underhand. He never even exceeds the speed limit!' Cathy scrabbled in her beach bag and pulled out her purse. 'Can I be a nuisance and ask you to go up and buy me a drink?'

Marion sat up. 'What would you like?'

'Anything they have. I'm not fussy.'

'We ought to think about making a move.'

'Why?'

'We both need to shower and wash our hair. Then we could go and sit up in the lounge for an hour before dinner and share a bottle of wine. I feel that I've had enough sun for one day.'

Cathy looked at her friend anxiously. 'Have you had too much?'

'No, I've just had enough for today. It will be here again tomorrow. That's the wonderful thing about Greece. You can rely on the sunshine every day during the summer.'

Marion settled Cathy into her wheelchair and insisted she buckled the belt around her. 'This might be a bit rough and bumpy. I don't want to tip you out.'

With a series of jerks she pulled the chair a few feet and stopped to rest before repeating the procedure. Marion looked around the beach, hoping someone might come to offer her some assistance, but everyone appeared to be avoiding her eyes. Gritting her teeth she pulled again and covered a little more distance.

A brown hand was placed over hers and she turned to see Panayiotis giving her his toothless grin. He removed the bags from Cathy's lap and handed them to Marion to carry. With a torrent of indistinguishable Greek he waved Marion away and took the handles from her. Expertly he tipped the chair back and began to haul it up the matting relatively easily and smoothly. Finally he turned the chair on to the paved area, smiled again, raised his hand and walked away.

'Thank goodness he came when he did. I don't think I could have moved you much further. The wheels were just sinking despite the matting.'

'I have had more comfortable rides,' admitted Cathy. 'We won't try that again, Marion, unless that old man is around. You'll end up dislocating your back and you'll be in a chair too. A fine couple we'd make!'

WEEK TWO – JUNE 1973

'So, what shall we plan for today? We can try the beach again if you want.'

Cathy shook her head. 'I don't want to go to the beach for the whole day again.'

'What about going for a walk along the road? There's bound to be a taverna along there where we can have lunch.' Marion was relieved that Cathy did not want to go to the beach again. Her back ached and she knew she had strained her muscles trying to pull the chair and Cathy up the matting before Panayiotis had come to help her.

'Do you think Panayiotis will be expecting us on the beach? We can't leave him sitting there all day waiting for us.'

'I'll run down after breakfast and let him know we're not coming,' promised Marion. 'Do you think we should have given him a tip yesterday?'

'You could give him something today. Take it from my purse.'

'Maybe I'll wait and ask Vasilis,' Marion demurred. 'I wouldn't want to insult him. Who's first in the bathroom this morning?'

'You can be. I'll wait here and decide what to wear.'

'Include a sun hat in your wardrobe. It could be hot along the road and there may not be any shade.'

Marion found it considerably easier pushing Cathy along the narrow pavement, despite it frequently ending, forcing her to use the dusty, un-made road. They fingered the scarves and skirts that were hung outside, comparing prices from one store to the next; and admired the replicas of the pottery they had seen in the museum. The tiny supermarket yielded fresh peaches which they ate beneath a shop awning whilst pretending to admire the jewellery on display inside.

'It's pretty ostentatious,' remarked Cathy. 'It reminds me of some of the costume jewellery I wore. All glitter.'

Marion agreed. 'You don't actually see many of the locals wearing it. They seem to prefer a plain cross and chain.'

'Maybe they wear it in the evenings when they go out. Now I do like that.' Cathy pointed to a necklace which looked like clusters of gold leaves on a thin gold chain. 'I could wear that without feeling I was shouting "look at me".'

Marion peered closer. 'If that price is correct you'd still be shouting "look at me". I know my maths are not very good, but I reckon you've spotted the most expensive item in the shop. It's about one thousand five hundred pounds.'

'It can't be. Not in a little shop along here.'

'Work it out on the calculator, six hundred thousand drachmas.'

Cathy shook her head. 'I don't think I'll bother. It's somewhat beyond my pocket, but it is pretty.'

The shop keeper had seen them and before Marion had time to turn the wheelchair away he was under the awning with them. 'Come in, come in, please. I have many beautiful things for beautiful ladies.'

'At beautiful prices,' murmured Marion. 'No thank you. We were just looking.'

'You show me. I will bring outside for you. You wait.'

'We might as well let him show us. I might even find a pair of earrings for my mother.'

The shop keeper pointed to various items in the window and Cathy shook her head. 'She wouldn't wear anything as showy as those.' Finally he pointed to the necklace Cathy had admired earlier and she nodded.

'Why are you asking him to bring it out? You said you couldn't afford it,' protested Marion.

'I'd like a proper look at it. Maybe you misread the price tag.'

The man placed the velvet tray on Cathy's knee. 'Very beautiful. I show you.' He picked up the necklace and draped it around Cathy's neck, holding a mirror in the other hand.

'It certainly is. How much?' asked Cathy.

He squinted at the tag. 'Six hundred thousand drachmas.'

Cathy shook her head. 'I haven't nearly enough.'

'Five hundred and fifty thousand, special price for you.'

Again Cathy shook her head firmly.

'I take credit card.'

'I don't have one,' she lied. 'Thank you for showing us.'

Disappointed the man replaced the necklace on the velvet pad. 'Maybe I have something else you like? Something for less drachmas?'

'No, I really can't afford any jewellery.'

'Greek gold very good value.' He tried again.

'I'm sure it is, but we have to go now.' Marion began to edge the wheelchair forwards. 'Look, there are our friends waiting for us.' She pointed to a group of people further along the road. 'We really must go.'

'Who are these friends we are meeting?' asked Cathy once they had moved away from the shop.

'I've no idea, but we had to make some excuse to get away.'

'I feel quite sorry for him. He was trying so hard to make a sale.'

'At those prices he's not likely to make very many. If you really want to get some earrings for your mother I suggest you get them from a jeweller in the town.'

'I'll ask Vasilis. He's sure to know a reputable one.'

To their disappointment, once they had left the cluster of small shops behind there was nothing further to be seen. Wasteland, covered in a tangle of undergrowth that only a cat could have forced their way through, ran along one side and on the other side was a rocky beach.

'It looks deserted down here. We may as well go back. I'm sure we passed a taverna. Shall we stop there and have some lunch or do you want to return to the hotel?'

'Let's try the taverna. If we go back to the hotel all I can do is sit by the pool for the afternoon.'

'I'm sure I could find Panayiotis and he would help us down to the beach.'

Cathy shook her head. 'No, you can always have a swim when we get back and I'll sit in the shade and wait for you. I ought to write another card to my parents and tell them where we've been.'

Marion sighed with relief. She was hot and tired, having pushed Cathy a considerable distance. She wanted nothing more than a cool swim and to lie in the sun for the remainder of the afternoon.

Marion wheeled Cathy into the dining room. She had swum in the pool and lain in the sun reading her book before having a refreshing shower. She wondered what she could find to occupy Cathy with the following day. She could not expect her to sit beside the pool watching her swimming, but she did not relish having to struggle to get her down to the beach again. If she could rely on Panayiotis being there she would have been more willing, but as it was Sunday he would probably have the day off.

Their usual waiter greeted them and escorted them to their table in the window. He placed their napkins on their lap, poured their wine and offered them the menu.

'Sunday,' he said. 'You come for the barbecue and the Greek dance?'

Marion frowned. 'Where is it?'

'It is here. At twelve we start. I keep place for you?'

'What do you say, Cathy? Barbecue and Greek dancing afterwards.'

Cathy nodded. 'Provided no one is going to ask me to dance.'

Marion grinned. 'Don't worry. When you see it you'll see why they don't expect us to be able to join in.' She looked up at the waiter. 'Yes please. If you could save a space for us I'd be grateful.'

He nodded. He had his instructions from Mr Vasilis and he would make sure the two ladies were well looked after.

Marion sighed with relief. That was Sunday taken care of.

Vasilis approached their table as they were finishing breakfast on Monday morning. He swung a chair out and sat, signalling to the waiter that he would like some coffee.

'So,' he smiled, 'how was your weekend?'

Cathy nodded. 'It was fine. We went to the beach and took a walk along the main road on Saturday. We had lunch at a taverna along there and yesterday we enjoyed the barbecue and dancing.'

'I am pleased. There was no problem with the beach?'

'Well,' Marion hesitated. 'It was not too difficult getting down, but if Panayiotis had not come to help me bring Cathy back I think we would still be there. Should I have given him a tip for helping us? I wasn't sure and I didn't want to insult him.'

Vasilis raised his eyebrows. 'There is no need to tip him. If you wished you could give him a small gift before you return to England.'

'Could we give him enough for him to have some dental attention? I don't know how much dentistry is over here, but he could certainly do with some teeth.'

Vasilis shook his head. 'That is the last thing that Panayiotis would consider. He had his teeth extracted during the war, by the Germans. There was no pain killing injection for him. He will allow no one near his mouth.'

'What!' Cathy looked at him in horror, her hand going to her own mouth, remembering the pain she had suffered during her own dental treatment.

'Many people suffered. The Germans thought if they hurt someone enough they would give them the information they wanted.'

'What information would he have?'

'He was with the andartes. The Germans captured him and wanted to know where they were hiding.'

'Did he tell them?'

'Of course not,' replied Vasilis scornfully. 'Many men and women died withholding information to save their compatriots.'

Cathy shuddered. 'I really do not think I want to know the details. Are we going to Knossos today?'

Vasilis shook his head. 'Always on a Monday the sites are closed. We could make the trip I suggested to Aghios Nikolaos and have lunch at Elounda. I have some business there and I am sure Marion could manage your chair down by the pool shopping area until I am able to rejoin you. It is quite flat and there is no traffic.'

'After the beach I could manage anything,' announced Marion.

'Panayiotis was supposed to watch for when you were ready to return and help. I expect he had gone to sleep. The next time you must look for him and wake him up. You must not try to pull Cathy up alone. It is too difficult for you.'

'I think she's put on weight since we've been over here,' remarked Marion and winked at Vasilis.

'I have not,' replied Cathy indignantly. 'You know I can eat whatever I like and never put on an ounce.'

Marion grinned. 'Then the sun has sapped my strength. What time should we be ready, Vasilis?'

'Come up to reception in an hour. I will be waiting for you.'

When Cathy and Marion reached the reception area Vasilis was once again talking to the elderly man. He held a sheaf of papers in his hand and pointed to something on one of them before handing the paper back. He stuffed the others inside a satchel that he placed over his shoulder and walked over to the car. Before opening the door and helping Cathy inside he pushed the satchel beneath the driver's seat.

'Now, we are ready? You have your sun cream with you, your hats and sun glasses?'

'Yes, Mummy,' smiled Marion.

Vasilis raised his eyebrows.

'You sounded just like my mother used to before I left for school. She always checked I had everything I needed.'

'I am responsible for you whilst you are with me,' replied Vasilis seriously. 'I do not wish to return and you both have sun burn or a bad headache.'

Marion placed her hand on his arm. 'I'm sorry. I was joking. We do appreciate the care you give to us. I'm just not used to anyone asking me now. I'm expected to think for myself and remember everything I want. If I've forgotten it then it I have to do without.'

Once they had left Malia behind, they drove beside cultivated fields, both men and women working in them. Beneath an olive tree a donkey would be tethered and on waste ground a few goats could be seen rooting around for sustenance. Occasionally there was evidence of building work taking place.

'This is proper Greece,' smiled Marion contentedly.

'Not for very much longer, I am afraid,' said Vasilis over his shoulder.

'What do you mean?'

'There is little land left along this road that is not owned by large hotels. Each year they begin to build another. The nearest village begins to expand and very soon there will be no fields left for the farmers to cultivate.'

'Why don't the farmers refuse to sell their land?' asked Cathy.

'They are offered a good price. Since the war many of the young men prefer to find work in the bars and hotels. They think it gives them a better life. They will return to their family in the winter months and help with olive picking and preparing the ground, but as soon as they can they will return to a town. They are no longer content to spend their time in such isolated places. They wish to be with their friends and able to visit the cinema in the evening or sit in a bar with bright lights and music.'

Cathy remembered how she had fretted after spending some time in London and returning to the quiet suburbia where her parents lived. 'I can understand how they feel. I would hate it.'

'You like to live with the excitement every day?' asked Vasilis.

Cathy shook her head. 'No, but I like to know it is there if I want it. I know what it's like to be confined to one room for weeks on end. Even now I can't go out as I would like. I have to rely on someone to take me. It's very easy to become bored and miserable.'

Vasilis swung the car to the left and began a steep and winding descent, finally drawing into a parking space where there was a view over the sea, an island shimmering in the heat haze in the distance.

'Imagine how you would have felt if you had lived on that island. You were sick, you were not allowed to leave or have visits from your family. You would not have had the luxury of a wheelchair. Very quickly you would have been bored and miserable, Cathy.'

'I would have swum over to the shore. It's not that far.'

'Do you know what would have happened to you if you did that? The villagers would have thrown stones at you to drive you away. Even your family would have said they did not know you. If you tried to hide the authorities would search for you and you would be sent back to the island.'

'Why would they have done that?' asked Cathy puzzled.

'The people on the island suffered from leprosy. Everyone in Greece who had the disease was sent over there to live out their life.'

'Are they still there?' asked Marion.

'No, thank goodness. Those who survived the war were tested and most of them were found to be free from the disease. They returned to their families or to the hospital in Athens.'

'So there was a happy ending?'

Vasilis shrugged. 'For some, yes. If you would be interested to go over there I am sure we can find a boatman.'

'What is there to see?'

'I am told you can see their houses, the way they lived. Also there is the fortress. It is not as grand as the one in Heraklion as so much has fallen down now.'

Marion nodded. 'I'd certainly like to go. How about you, Cathy?'

'Have you not been there, Vasilis?' asked Cathy.

Vasilis shook his head. 'It will be something new for me also. Today we do not have the time, but we could arrange a visit at a later date.'

Cathy frowned. 'I'd like to see how accessible the boat is before I decide. You and Vasilis can go anyway. I can always sit at a taverna and wait for you.'

'I am sure we will all be able to make the journey.' Vasilis smiled confidently. 'Have you seen enough, ladies? Shall we continue to Elounda and have our lunch?'

Cathy eyed the fishing boats offering trips to Spinalonga that were moored at Elounda with trepidation. She would not feel confident travelling over the expanse of sea in such a small craft. She doubted that there would be space for her to sit in her wheelchair and she would be forced to sit on the wooden seats, squashed between the other tourists. Whilst waiting for their meal Vasilis wandered over to the man who was advertising boat trips to the island, shaking his head as he returned.

'I have spoken to the boatman. He would be willing to take us, but I do not think it is suitable for Cathy to travel with him. There are larger boats that go from Aghios Nikolaos.'

'Is there a guide book to the island?' asked Marion.

Vasilis smiled at her. 'I have no idea. There are some bookshops in Aghios Nikolaos. Whilst I complete my business there you could look.'

They ate their lunch leisurely, watching the boatman wait until he had a full complement of passengers before setting sail to the island. Finally Vasilis looked at his watch. 'It is time for us to move on, ladies. I will leave you down by the pool. There are shops and tavernas there and I will return as soon as I have completed my business.'

Cathy wanted to ask what business he had to complete in the town, but felt a reluctance to pry into his affairs. They drove over the hill, always within sight of the sea, until rounding a final bend they could see Aghios Nikolaos before them.

'It is pretty,' remarked Marion. 'I had expected it to look like Malia, just a cluster of buildings along the main road. It's actually quite large.'

Vasilis nodded. 'It has grown larger as it has become popular with the tourists. If you wish to buy anything make sure you do not pay the price they are asking. You must tell them it is cheaper to buy in Heraklion and eventually they will drop their price for you.'

'I shall only want a guide book,' Marion assured him.

Vasilis drew into the side of the road just before they reached the bridge. 'I will leave you here. When you have looked at this side you can cross the bridge and examine the other side. I will find somewhere to park my car and I will find you.'

Vasilis ignored the shouting and horns blaring at him for causing an obstruction whilst he removed Cathy's chair from the boot and settled her into it. A policeman strolled towards them, pulling a notebook from his pocket as he approached. Vasilis grinned and slipped behind the steering wheel, raising his hand to the policeman as he drew away.

Marion pushed Cathy along the paved area beside the pool, ignoring the calls from the taverna owners to stop and have a drink or a meal. The goods on display were very similar to those they had seen in Malia and displayed in the shops along the road from the hotel. Marion entered a bookshop and returned shaking her head.

'No guide book,' she announced. 'I'll try another.'

'Do you think the information centre could help?' suggested Cathy, pointing to the sign.

'Worth asking. Where is it?'

'The sign says further along.'

Taking their time they made their way to the far end of the paved walkway, gazing into the shop windows as they passed, halting to look more closely if something caught their attention.

'Look.' Cathy pointed to the jeweller's window. 'There's a necklace similar to the one I saw that was so expensive.'

Marion wheeled her closer and peered through the window at the price tag. 'Well, the one you were offered was a bargain compared with this one. It's seven hundred thousand drachmas and it's nowhere near as delicate looking or attractive. Vasilis was right when he said goods were more expensive here.'

'I'm not planning to buy it anyway,' said Cathy. 'I'd have no occasion to wear it. There's another bookshop. Do you want to ask for a guide book in there?'

Again Marion returned shaking her head. 'Plenty on Knossos. I even looked at one that claimed to have all the information a tourist would want, but it didn't mention that island.'

'They might sell them where the boats moor to take people over.'

'There's the information bureau. They should be able to tell us. I'll park you here and go in and see what they say.' Marion pushed at the door which did not yield. She looked at it in surprise, then the notice pinned to the door. It would not be open for another hour. She shrugged. 'So much for information! Shall we make our way back and see what's on the other side?'

They crossed the bridge, the pedestrian way only just wide enough to take Cathy's chair and Marion negotiated the two wide, shallow steps that led to the paved area around the pool. The shops on this side looked larger and there were a greater variety of goods on display. Marion spent time examining the leather handbags until the overpowering smell of so much leather began to make her feel sick. She shook her head at the owner and moved away. Two more bookshops were investigated in the hope of procuring a guide book, but each time Marion returned empty handed.

Reaching the end of the walkway the shops and tavernas petered out, giving way to cages where small animals and birds were penned. Cathy shuddered. 'I don't want to look at those. Can we go back into the sunshine and find a taverna where Vasilis will see us when he returns?'

Marion complied. She had been grateful for the shade afforded by the steep hillside, but realised that sitting still in her chair Cathy very quickly became chilled. Spotting some empty seats at a taverna that offered shade for herself and sun for Cathy she stopped by the table.

'What would you like?'

Cathy considered. 'An ice cream, I think. I'm not hungry or even particularly thirsty, but we can't expect to sit here without ordering.'

'We'll be ignorant tourists and sit here until they come to us,' Marion smiled. 'I have an idea we are supposed to go up to the window to order.'

It was only a few minutes before a young girl arrived. She looked at Cathy in her wheelchair and frowned. 'Do you wish me to bring your order?' she asked.

'Yes, please,' replied Marion firmly. 'We'd like two ice creams, one strawberry and the other vanilla.'

'They'll probably charge us double the price for bringing them over,' remarked Cathy.

'I shall protest if they do. They shouldn't have tables and chairs outside if they're not prepared to wait on the customers.' Marion looked across at the pool where a few boats bobbed lazily. 'It is very pretty here. I wonder what the town is actually like? We'll ask Vasilis when he returns.'

'You do like him, don't you?' asked Cathy.

Marion nodded. 'He's very pleasant and can't seem to do enough for us. I don't think he'd be as keen if I was here alone. He really has eyes only for you.'

Cathy blushed. 'I'm sure it's just a holiday romance to him.'

Marion raised her eyebrows. 'And what is it to you?'

Cathy shrugged. 'We're going home in a couple of weeks.'

'Meaning?'

'What's the point in letting it develop? I don't want to get hurt a second time.'

'You ought to find out a bit more about him. Ask about his family. I'm still not convinced he isn't married. Who was the family he had to spend the weekend with? I don't see how someone that good looking and charming can reach his age without some girl snaring him, unless he's gay?'

'He's not gay,' smiled Cathy, remembering the way he had held her and kissed her.

'He might be divorced,' suggested Marion.

'I wouldn't hold that against him. Marriage doesn't always work out.'

'That depends why he is divorced. He could be a wife beater.'

Cathy's eyes widened. 'You don't really think that, do you?'

Marion smiled at her. 'No, I can't really envisage him in that role, but you never know. See what you can find out about him the next time you have the opportunity. You ought to eat your ice cream, it's melting.'

Cathy pushed at the pink liquid that was forming in the glass bowl. 'I don't really want it.'

'Just pretend. We need an excuse to sit here until Vasilis

arrives. I forgot to tell you, when I was in the last bookshop I'm sure your Dad's books were on sale in there.'

'Really?' Cathy raised her eyebrows. 'What made you think they were his?'

'That symbol he always has on the spine.'

Cathy smiled. 'The fairy. I don't know if that's exclusive to him.'

'Well, I've never seen it on any others. Ask Vasilis when he comes.'

'How would he know? He's too old to have read them when he was a child. Dad began to write them when I was about three.'

Vasilis returned, his face wreathed in smiles. 'I have good news, ladies. I have spoken to a boatman. He will take us to the island tomorrow.'

'Tomorrow?' Marion's face fell. 'I thought we were going to Knossos tomorrow?'

'Knossos is there always. Some days it is not possible to visit Spinalonga; the weather, the currents. This week all the boatmen are happy to go across. If we delayed until next week Manolis may not be free or the weather could be against us.'

'I couldn't find a guide book anywhere,' complained Marion.

'That is no problem. Manolis knows the history of the island very well. He has agreed to come ashore and walk around with us. He will be better than any guide book, believe me.'

'How big is his boat?' asked Cathy dubiously.

Vasilis covered her hand with his own. 'Do not worry, Cathy. The boat is large enough to take your wheelchair. I will carry you aboard. You will be quite safe with me. I will look after you.'

Cathy smiled at him. She did feel confident that Vasilis would not stumble and drop her whenever he carried her.

'That is the reason I have kept you waiting. Would you like some more ice cream? You have only the liquid left where it has been sitting too long in the sun.'

Cathy shook her head. 'I don't really know why I wanted it in the first place. I'm not very fond of ice cream. Now I just have a dry mouth.'

'Then we will have a cold drink and then we move. Yes?'

'I'd like to have a look at the town if it's possible.'

'Of course, Marion. I can drive you through the main area. We can also go past the harbour and Cathy can see how large Manolis's boat is.' Vasilis signalled to the girl, who approached their table sulkily. The two women had been sitting there for over an hour and all for two ice creams.

Vasilis drove up the hill towards the square in Aghios Nikolaos. The traffic was heavy and they moved at a pedestrian pace, although there was little of interest to be seen. The shops were obscured by stalls pushed close to the road hung with embroidered goods, scarves, skirts and beach wear. Those that were visible seemed to be advertising speedy development for films, car hire or organised tours to the sites.

Slowly Vasilis drove around the square, pointing out the palm trees that surrounded it. 'You see the marks on the trees? They are from the German bullets. They brought the men from the local government up here and tied them to the trees before they shot them.'

'Why?' asked Cathy. 'What had they done?'

'They had done nothing. It was the German policy in all the large towns. They thought if they removed the government the people would be frightened of them and do as they were told.'

'And did they?'

'Of course not,' replied Vasilis scornfully. 'It made the people hate them. More men joined the resistance groups and fled to the mountains to live with the andartes.'

'What happened to the women?'

'Some went to the mountains, but many had no choice but to stay in their homes. They tried not to draw attention to themselves or their families. Life was very hard. They had little food, but they were expected to feed the soldiers who were billeted in their houses.'

'What a nerve,' exclaimed Marion. 'I'm surprised they didn't poison them all.'

'I am sure many of them considered the idea, but they had to think of their children or elderly parents. They knew how vicious the reprisals would be. Many men returned at the end of the war to find their family had disappeared.'

'Where had they gone?'

'Who knows? In some cases they had been shot and the neighbours had taken care of their bodies. Others were taken away, maybe to a prison, and did not return. Everyone on Crete could tell you a story about a missing relative.'

'Did you lose relatives, Vasilis?'

Vasilis nodded grimly. 'Of course. Now, do you wish to stop and visit the shops?'

Marion nodded. 'We've only looked at the shops along from the hotel and those down by the pool. They are very much for the tourists. I'd like to see proper shops that the locals use.'

Cathy agreed. 'I'd like to see if that necklace is being offered at a more reasonable price here.'

'You have seen some jewellery you like?'

Marion laughed. 'Cathy was tempted until she saw the price. A jeweller here was asking even more for a similar one that was not as pretty.'

Vasilis raised his eyebrows at Cathy. 'It was too expensive?'

'Much too expensive. It was very pretty, not like the usual tourist pieces. Like little leaves.'

'The man brought it out of the shop and tried it on her, he even dropped the price a little to encourage her to buy it,' added Marion.

'Oh, they will. Once they have your interest they're very loath to let you go before you have parted with your money.'

'Maybe if we went back every day he would drop the price even further until I could afford it.'

Vasilis laughed. 'They do have to make a living, you know.'

Cathy smiled. 'I was only joking. I think he genuinely offered me a bargain. What have you been doing?'

Vasilis shrugged. 'Nothing very interesting. I had to meet someone, do a little business.'

Leaving Aghios Nikolaos behind Vasilis took the main road back to Heraklion, despite the heavy traffic he was able to drive relatively quickly and they were back at the hotel by late afternoon.

'What do you wish to do now, ladies?' he asked as he placed Cathy in her chair.

'I shall go for a swim,' announced Marion. 'What about you, Cathy?'

'I ought to do my exercises.'

'You could do them in the pool,' suggested Marion and looked at Vasilis. 'Would you be able to come to help Cathy out?'

'Of course. I will be with you in half an hour. I do not think you will wish to stay there very much longer as the pool will soon be in the shade.'

Marion nodded. 'I shall be all right, but Cathy will get cold once she is out.'

'If you wish to stay I can take Cathy back up to the chalet. She can have a shower to become warm again.'

Cathy bit her lip. She remembered Vasilis saying it would be a pleasure to wash and dry her back.

Marion shook her head. 'I don't like her to shower with no one around. I'm always frightened she might fall.'

Vasilis placed his hand on Cathy's shoulder. 'If Cathy wishes to shower then I will wait with her whilst she does so. I can sit on the balcony and have a glass of wine until she is ready.'

Marion smiled happily. 'We'll see you in about half an hour then. Thank you for yet another interesting and enjoyable day.'

Vasilis lifted Cathy from the pool and wrapped a towel around her. 'I will carry you to the chalet. Marion can bring your chair when she returns. You have your key?'

Cathy showed it to him, looped around her finger.

'That is good. Marion will have to knock when she wishes to enter.'

Cathy laughed and shook her head. 'Marion has her own key.'

'Maybe we should have taken her key also.'

'Oh, Vasilis, that would be mean. She'd think she'd lost it.'

'I am joking, Cathy. I would not want to distress Marion.' He took the key from Cathy's finger and opened the door. 'We will go to the balcony,' he announced. 'We do not want to make the room too wet.' He placed Cathy onto the plastic chair and held the towel tightly around her. 'You are my prisoner, now.' He bent and kissed her, finally stepping back with a sigh. 'I have wanted to do that all day. Now what would you like to do?' He tucked a tendril of wet hair behind her ear.

Cathy did not dare tell him what she would like to do. 'I ought to have a shower and get dressed. What about you? You'll be cold.'

'I have my clothes.' Vasilis pointed to a bag sitting at the side of the balcony. 'I brought them here before I went to the pool.'

'Suppose I had waited for Marion?' asked Cathy.

Vasilis shrugged. 'Then I would have collected them when you returned. How do you get to the shower?'

'Oh! I haven't got my chair and my crutches are on the side of it.' Cathy looked around as if her wheelchair would appear. 'I use my crutches to get in there and Marion places one of the balcony chairs in the shower for me to sit on.'

'That is no problem.' Vasilis picked up the light plastic chair and placed it in the shower tray. 'I will dry the other chair and place it outside for you. Is there anything else you will need?'

'Just my wrap. Everything else is in there within my reach.'

'When you are ready you can call me. Maybe you would like to call me before you are ready to leave the shower and I can help you to dry yourself?'

'Vasilis.' Cathy wagged her finger at him. 'Remember Marion has a key.'

'I could lock the door,' he suggested, raising his eyebrows at her.

'I could lock the bathroom door,' she retorted.

Vasilis looked at her in horror. 'I promise I will not come in until you call me. Please do not lock the door. If you fell I would be unable to help you.'

Cathy giggled. 'I'm sure I shall be able to manage.'

Vasilis carried her into the bathroom and deposited her on the chair inside the shower tray. 'You need some help to remove your bathing costume?' he said hopefully, sliding the strap from her shoulder.

Cathy shook her head. 'You go and get dried and dressed. Make sure you close the door properly. I don't want to find that it mysteriously swings open whilst I'm showering.'

'You are too cruel, Cathy. You deny me the smallest of pleasures.' He gave her a last hopeful look and Cathy waved her hand at him. He shrugged and shut the bathroom door.

When Cathy finally called to Vasilis that she was ready he was dressed and waiting for her. As he carried her back out onto the balcony Marion could be heard noisily unlocking the door. Vasilis frowned. He had hoped to have some time alone with Cathy. He was sure she had nothing on beneath her wrap and hoped it was an invitation to him.

'Come in, Marion,' he called. 'Cathy has finished in the shower. I'll move the chairs out of your way.'

Marion threw her beach bag onto her bed. 'You're right about it suddenly getting cold when the sun moves round. I can't wait to get into the shower. I hope Cathy hasn't used all the hot water.'

'The tank is quite large,' Vasilis assured her. 'Take your time.' He pulled the curtain across the patio doors to give Marion her privacy.

He placed the chair on the balcony as close to Cathy as possible and dried it off with his towel before sitting down. 'It was a good shower?'

'Lovely. Just what I needed.'

Vasilis touched her hair. 'Your hair is still wet.' He picked up the damp towel and covered her head, squeezing the water from the ends of her hair before lifting it and kissing the nape of her neck.

'Your skin is so soft, like silk. I would like to know if it feels like silk all over.' He tilted her chin upwards and his lips began to caress the planes of her cheek, moving towards her ear and down her neck.

'Vasilis...'

'Shh.' He placed a finger on her lips and nibbled gently at her ear.

Cathy could feel every fibre of her body responding, she placed her own hand on his bare arm to try to steady herself, acutely conscious of his smooth skin. Vasilis drew back slightly and studied her flushed face and slightly parted lips. He leaned forward and placed his lips on hers. The kiss was long and deep, leaving Cathy breathless as he released her.

'Vasilis, please, stop touching me.'

He frowned. 'You do not like me to touch you?'

'Yes. No, you mustn't. Marion will be out of the shower any minute.'

'So?'

Cathy blushed furiously, at a loss for words.

'Your friend does not like you to enjoy yourself?'

'Of course she does, but...'

Vasilis kissed her again and Cathy shivered. His hand was still on her shoulder. 'You are cold?'

Cathy shook her head. 'No, just shivery.'

Dark, sympathetic eyes looked into hers. 'I also am shivery. What does it mean?'

Cathy was forced to laugh and Vasilis smiled in return. 'That is better. I do not like to see my Cathy sad. Tell me, what is shivery?'

'When you have a tingle up and down your spine.'

'Ah, I understand. I too have that. I have that the first time I see you, and when I touch you to lift you from the pool I have many tingles.'

He kissed the tip of her nose.

Cathy blushed, but did not move as he ran his hand down her neck and across her shoulder beneath her wrap. His hand travelled lower until he was cupping her breast in his hand, feeling her nipple harden with desire.

'Vasilis, please...'

'Yes, you want as much as I want.'

Vasilis kissed her throat whilst his fingers moved to loosen the belt on her wrap, pushing it apart. His lips moved downwards and Cathy caught her breath. Unable to control herself she placed her hand on the back of his neck and pushed his head further down towards her nipple which was craving attention from his mouth. He sucked at her like a greedy child before finally withdrawing and closing her wrap.

'You are right. Your friend will join us soon. To have our pleasure we need more time. We must stop now before it is too late.'

Cathy wished he had locked the door, leaving Marion to hammer on it to gain admittance.

'Well,' asked Marion as Cathy brushed her hair before they made their way over to the dining room. 'Did you ask him?'

'Ask him what?'

'About himself. I made my shower last for ages so that you had plenty of opportunity to talk.'

Cathy blushed. 'We just didn't seem to get round to the subject.'

'So what subjects did you get around to?'

'We just talked generally,' replied Cathy vaguely. 'What do you fancy to eat tonight? I thought I might go for the souvlaki.'

'What are you planning to wear today?' asked Marion.

'I thought a pair of trousers could be practical. If I'm being lifted in and out of a boat I don't want to display my underwear for all to see.'

'Trousers will be hot,' frowned Marion. 'I thought I'd go for shorts. Are we going to take our swimming gear? There must be somewhere there to swim.'

'We might as well take it, although Vasilis didn't mention swimming.'

'What did he mention when you were talking generally yesterday?' asked Marion mockingly.

Cathy blushed. 'Nothing of any consequence. Are you ready? We don't want to keep him waiting.'

The drive down to Aghios Nikolaos took longer than the previous day, despite Vasilis keeping to the main road. Tourists with hired cars drove slowly by comparison with the Cretans and Vasilis used his horn frequently.

'You see why I'm unwilling to drive over here,' remarked Marion. 'I would start to panic if drivers kept hooting me.'

Vasilis smiled. 'You do not use your horn in England?'

'Only when it is really necessary. Over here you also use it to acknowledge friends who are passing by.'

'What is wrong with that?'

'Nothing provided you're used to it. I would just think they were drawing my attention to a fault on the car or I had disobeyed a road sign.'

'You would like to drive the car? Cathy could sit in the back for a short while and I would sit beside you.'

Marion shook her head. 'I feel much safer with you as the driver. Maybe if we were on a really quiet road and there was hardly any traffic I'd take up your offer. I've never driven on the right.'

'One day we will do that. Very soon you will be confident and have no problem.'

They drove across the bridge and round to the small harbour which was almost deserted of boats.

'Where is everyone?' asked Cathy.

'The fishermen will have left early and also the larger tour boats. They visit the island then go to Elounda for lunch before they return for the coaches to take them back to their hotels. The tour guide will tell them about the island whilst they travel over.'

'If all the tour guides know the history why don't they have a guide book on sale,' grumbled Marion.

Vasilis smiled at her indignation. 'I am sure you will find Manolis is a good guide. He can answer your questions, a book cannot.'

'Does he speak English?' asked Cathy.

'A few words. I will be able to interpret for you.'

'Will we be expected to tip him?' asked Marion, not wishing to offend the boatman through ignorance.

Vasilis shook his head. 'That will not be necessary. I will invite him to lunch with us. That will be sufficient.'

'I must give you some money.' Marion began to dig into her purse. 'We put aside an amount to cover excursions and we haven't even paid you any petrol money yet.'

'That is not necessary. Put your money away, Marion. It is better that I pay. We get a better deal than the tourists.' Vasilis drew in towards the waterfront and raised his hand to a man sitting in a boat. 'First I will take Cathy's chair on board and then I will return for Cathy. You can manage the bags, Marion?'

Marion nodded. 'It's only our swimming gear. If we won't be swimming I can leave it behind.'

'I will ask Manolis. I do not know if there is a beach over there that is suitable.'

Vasilis lifted the wheelchair out of the boot and carried over to the boat, handing it to Manolis and explaining that Cathy would be more comfortable if she sat in it for the journey. He returned to the car and opened the boot again.

'We will take the swimming clothes. You can carry my towel also, Marion, or would you prefer to carry Cathy?'

'I'll take your towel rather than Cathy any day.' Marion draped it over her arm. 'Are you sure you will be safe to carry her on to the boat?' She eyed the narrow gang plank dubiously.

'Manolis will help me,' replied Vasilis confidently.

Marion watched as Vasilis strode up the gang plank to where Manolis was waiting for him. He held Vasilis's arm and steadied him as he stepped down into the boat. Cathy let out her breath. She had not enjoyed the short journey. Marion followed, Manolis helping her also, giving her a broad smile as she jumped down easily and took a seat on the hard wooden planking.

Manolis cast off and used the motor to clear the jetty. 'Do you want to motor all the way or sail?' he asked Vasilis.

'If we could sail you could tell us about the island. If you have the motor running I may not be able to hear you.'

Manolis nodded, cut the motor and hauled up the sail. Once satisfied that they were catching as much wind as possible he sat down at the tiller, jamming a disreputable old fisherman's hat with two large holes firmly on his head.

'Maybe he'd like a new hat,' whispered Marion to Cathy.

'They must have large moths over here,' replied Cathy smiling.

'So,' Manolis looked at Vasilis. 'What do you wish me to tell you?'

'Everything you know about the island. Go slowly. I will have to translate. The ladies do not speak Greek.'

He smiled lazily. 'I was born here. My father was a fisherman. When he died he left me his fishing boat. I was a young boy, not an experienced fisherman, and my aunt and uncle were poor. I paid to have a Government contract to take food out to the sufferers on the island. Each day I would sail out there, off load the containers, and fish as I sailed back. I was making a good living.'

'Did you go ashore and meet the people?' asked Vasilis.

A crafty look came over Manolis's face. 'I was not allowed to go ashore. Flora would wait on the jetty and let them know I had arrived. When I left they would then come down and move the food to their storage room.'

'So you never went on the island whilst they were living there?' Vasilis was disappointed. How could the man know all about the island if he had never set foot on it?

Manolis looked at him scornfully. 'Each day Flora would sit and wait for me. Each day she would ask me to take over some screws, nails, hammer and the like. The people were repairing their houses. I used to wander the streets in Aghios Nikolaos looking for anything they could use.'

'Why didn't the government send whatever they needed out to them?'

'They did not know what was needed. I ferried over a priest and his companion.' He explained how Father Minos had visited the island, eventually relinquishing his parish on the mainland to share a life of hardship and deprivation with the lepers. How he had insisted that a doctor should come over to examine them and they be given treatment and medication.

'Doctor Stavros was put in charge of the island. He went ashore, he spoke to the people, he examined them, each week he went over to treat them. I was his boatman. He was allowed ashore so why should I not be? The second time the priests visited I had to return for the doctor. That was the time the doctor amputated my wife's arm. I went ashore that day and every day after that unless it was too rough to make the journey.'

'I thought the Germans stopped anyone from going over?' frowned Vasilis.

Manolis held up his hand. 'That was later. I am talking about before the war. Father Minos had a sum of money at his disposal and he used it to purchase building materials for them. I was his boatman. He was a good man. He left his parish and came to live on the island. The people loved him.'

'So what happened then to the building supplies?'

'The young priest who had visited with him took over the parish that Father Minos left and also his commitment to the islanders. His cousin was on the island. I would post the letters Yannis wrote to Father Andreas. Eventually a government official came over and saw the situation for himself. It was agreed that each person should receive a pension. They would be able to purchase whatever they wished from the mainland.'

'How would they do that if they weren't allowed to go anywhere?'

'I became their bookkeeper,' announced Manolis proudly. 'They would tell me what they wanted. I would buy it and deduct the money from their account, then pay the bill. They were not allowed to touch the money.'

'Ingenious,' remarked Vasilis. 'You must have been kept busy. Official boatman for the government supplies and the doctor; bookkeeper for the islanders and doing all their shopping. Did you have any time left for fishing?'

'Sometimes I would drag my nets as I returned, but I no longer needed the money. When I had paid my aunt for my keep I would place my money in the bank unless I wished to buy a present for my wife. I was a very happy man and the islanders were happy also.'

'What happened when the Germans came?'

'They shot at me. They refused to let anyone take supplies to the island.'

'So you went back to just being a fisherman.'

Manolis shook his head. 'Father Dhakanalis asked me to take a message further down the coast. I expected to be gone a few days. I was gone for three years!'

'Three years?' Vasilis was not sure he had heard him correctly.

Manolis nodded. 'Each time I landed I was sent on to a different village. Finally I was asked to deliver an Englishman with a wireless to Toplou Monastery.' Manolis spread his hands. 'How could I refuse? He persuaded me to take him around the arm of land to Kato Zakros where he wished to meet someone. What choice did I have? From there we went down to the island of Koufonisi and collected a man who had only one leg. He needed to go to Matala.' Manolis chuckled. 'We had to make our escape quickly and leave him behind. Vasilis insisted we returned to look for him when it was safe. He had been taken to a nearby village. He had smothered his stump in goat dung and the Germans were told he had cut it off with a scythe. They believed the story! So it went on, we moved from place to place, until finally we took some injured men to Preveli. That was where I lost my boat,' Manolis said sadly.

'You were at Preveli?'

Manolis nodded. 'We stayed at Preveli for a considerable time.' He removed his hat from his head and pointed out the two holes to Vasilis, demonstrating with his hands how the bullet had travelled through it. 'The Germans made those holes. My English friend saved my life by pushing me to one side. I will keep it forever.' Manolis replaced his hat and continued. 'He saved many lives. The allies were sending in food to the monastery to help feed all the troops that had made their way to the area. I would deliver it to the villages nearby. The Germans made their way overland to the monastery and we tried to persuade the Abbot to escape. He agreed to come to a nearby village with us. We heard that the Germans were coming and hid. They did not find us, but the Abbot insisted on returning to Preveli. We went down to my boat and found the Germans had smashed it.' A tear ran down the side of Manolis's nose at the memory.

Vasilis waited whilst Manolis composed himself.

'My friend, the Englishman, his name was Vasilis, he said we would walk. We would walk to his home and stay there if he thought it was safe. We walked and we walked. I thought we would never get there. Never had I walked so far in my life. He lived on a farm a short distance from Chania. He was married to a Cretan girl and had a little boy.' Manolis shook his head. 'He would not stay. He knew if we were found there his family would suffer.'

'Where did you go to hide?'

'We did not *hide*,' Manolis answered indignantly. 'We walked back the way we had come, days and days of walking again, thinking we would return to Preveli. When we reached there we found it was in German hands. We made our way into the mountains and joined the andartes. We fought with them until the war was over. In the winter we suffered from the cold and in the summer we suffered from the heat.'

Vasilis had translated Manolis's story to Cathy and Marion and they had listened open mouthed.

'That's amazing,' said Cathy. 'We're in the presence of a real war hero.'

'I think you should tell your Dad the story. I'm sure he could make an exciting adventure story out of it.'

Cathy shook her head. 'I don't think so. It would be a bit traumatic for the age group he writes for. What did Manolis do when he returned? Buy another boat and become a fisherman again?'

Vasilis asked the boatman, who smiled contentedly. 'Father Andreas had this boat. It had belonged to his father. He had no use for it and he asked me to take it off his hands.'

'So you went back to delivering supplies to the island?'

Manolis shook his head. 'Very few islanders had survived. They were sick people and they had been starved. I was only needed to take out supplies once a week. After Yannis...'

Vasilis held up his hand. 'Who was Yannis?'

'Yannis was their leader. The islanders looked up to him, respected him. I am honoured to call him my friend. He wrote to the government and finally the islanders were given tests. Most of the people were free from leprosy and the island was closed. Some people went to Athens to live at the hospital, others returned to their families.'

A broad smile crossed Manolis's face. 'That was when my wife and I were truly married. She had survived. I was able to bring her over to the mainland to live openly with me.'

'Your wife has leprosy?'

Manolis nodded. 'She *had* leprosy. Her arm was so badly infected that the doctor had to amputate it. Gangrene had set in and she was close to losing her life. After that she was never ill.'

'You didn't know she had leprosy when you married her?'

'Of course I knew,' replied Manolis scornfully. 'She was on the island when I met her. When you love someone you do not look for excuses to leave them.'

A pained look crossed Vasilis's face. 'Would we be able to meet her?'

Manolis glanced at him keenly. 'From curiosity? What does a one armed leper look like? No.'

Vasilis shook his head. 'I am trying to convince the young lady in the wheelchair that being unable to walk does not matter to me.'

'Of course it does not matter. She is a beautiful young lady.'

'I think so,' smiled Vasilis. 'What happened to your English friend and his family?'

Manolis sighed deeply. 'So sad. He returned to his village and everything had been destroyed. All the villagers had been rounded up and shot by the Germans, then the village was fired. Everything destroyed. He was a man demented. He blamed himself for leaving them.'

'Where is he now?'

'I have no idea. He left for England. He said he could not stay here with his memories.'

'Understandable,' agreed Vasilis and as he translated Manolis's words to Cathy she felt as if someone was squeezing her heart and she realised she had tears dribbling down her face.

'He built a very big memorial to her and the other villagers,' continued Manolis. 'He placed her name at the top and beneath was their son's. After that he named the other villagers.'

'Where is it?'

Manolis shrugged. 'I cannot tell you the name of the village. It is close to Chania.'

Vasilis nodded. 'I think I know the one you mean. I've never stopped to read it.'

Manolis looked at him sadly. 'That is because you are too young to remember. You are fortunate. You do not know what it is like to be hungry, cold and frightened. Not knowing if you will be shot, or even worse, captured and beaten and left to die. Not to know if the ones you love are safe.'

Vasilis shifted uncomfortably in his seat. He felt guilty that he had never stopped to look properly at the memorial to the villagers and read their names. He would certainly do so the next time he drove that way.

Manolis hauled in the sail and folded it carefully before starting the motor and nosing his way carefully in towards a jetty. 'We will use this landing place. The bigger boats cannot come here. This is a good starting place. This is where I unloaded the goods and where I would stay and talk to Flora. When I sailed away the men would come down through that archway and collect the goods I had left.'

Vasilis made to get up and Manolis stayed him with his hand. 'Please, you will stay seated. I will place the lady from the chair on your knee whilst I take her chair ashore.'

As Cathy was placed on his knees Vasilis had no choice but remain seated. Manolis picked up the chair and placed it on the quay before arranging the gang plank and holding out his hand to Marion. He returned to the boat and lifted Cathy from Vasilis's arms.

'It is safer if I carry her ashore. I am used to the movement of the boat.' As sure footed as a cat Manolis stepped on the wooden seat and strode across the gang plank, placing Cathy carefully in her chair. 'Okay?' he asked.

Cathy smiled. 'Okay,' she replied. 'Thank you.'

'Will we need our swimming gear?' asked Marion.

Vasilis asked Manolis and at his reply he shook his head. 'Not yet. Do you both have some water with you? It can become very hot on the island and there is no fresh water.'

They nodded and Vasilis took up his position behind Cathy's chair. 'Lead on Manolis and please tell us everything you know about Spinalonga.'

It was more than two hours before they returned to Manolis's boat. He had taken them through the arch and up onto the main road leading down to the square. He stood on a block of stone and addressed them solemnly.

'It was like this when I first came here. Everything was neglected, falling to pieces. It was the same when Yannis came. People were sheltering wherever they could, many of them were in the church. Yannis insisted that some of the buildings could be repaired. With his bare hands he built a house to prove to them that it could be done. He threatened, persuaded, cajoled and finally they believed him. Gradually they succeeded in building a village and community to be proud of.'

'So what did they do with this pension they had been given?' asked Vasilis.

'They did many things. Some people bought some chickens, there were goats that gave milk, they had their gardens where they grew vegetables to supplement those that were sent over from the mainland. I will show you where they had their shops and tavernas. They lived like any other villager on Crete, despite being considered outcasts.'

He led them up the main path, remembering who had lived in

each house as he passed. He described the day he and Flora had been officially married by Father Minos and all the villagers had joined in the celebrations, many others coming over from the mainland.

Manolis pointed to the remains of the china fittings that had conducted the electricity to the houses, stating proudly that Spinalonga had electricity before the mainland. 'They were very crafty,' he chuckled. 'Doctor Stavros asked for medical equipment that needed electricity to power it. The government agreed,' Manolis spread his hands. 'The machines arrived and no power. What do they do? Do they take it back and break their promise to the people or do they install a generator? I will show you later where it was placed.'

They peered through the windows of both the churches, unable to see very much due to the grime on the windows and Manolis showed them the small graveyard, explaining that the bodies were exhumed to make room for new occupants.

'Ask him what they did with them,' said Marion.

'They were placed in the tower. Everyone was placed in the tower before Father Minos came. When they received a pension they could pay the carpenter to make a coffin and have a proper burial. They knew their resting place would not be permanent, but it was preferable to being thrown unceremoniously into the tower like a bag of rubbish. Do you wish to see it?'

Marion hesitated. She was quite curious, but felt she might offend if she declared herself interested. She shook her head. 'Are they still there?' She looked enquiringly at Vasilis who asked Manolis.

'Yes. One day they may be collected and taken for burial on the mainland, but now you do not know whose bones you are dealing with. Where did that person come from? He would not want to be buried in Plaka if he came from Sitia.'

Cathy frowned. 'Ask Manolis if their relatives ever come over to place flowers on their graves or in the tower.'

Vasilis translated her question and Manolis nodded. 'If they live locally they come, on a name day or day that is special to them. I am grateful that I do not have to come here for that reason.'

'Surely they could have a monument on the mainland, maybe at Heraklion, so the relatives could go there?'

Vasilis shook his head. 'These people came from all over Greece, not just Crete. Even if there was a monument in Heraklion it would not be available to a family from Volos. It would mean days of travelling for them. It is probably better if their remains stay here.'

Cathy gave a little shiver, despite the hot sunshine. 'Can we move on? No disrespect to the dead, but I don't really want to spend any more time looking at graves.'

'Do you wish to climb up to the fortress?' asked Manolis, looking dubiously at Cathy's chair.

'Tell him I'm not bothered,' said Marion. 'It's obviously in ruins so what is there to see?'

Manolis sighed with relief. It was more than twenty five years since he had spent time in the mountains and had not relished the idea of the short, steep climb.

'We will ask Manolis to take us over to Elounda and have some lunch. I'm sure he'll know somewhere good for swimming afterwards.'

'Why don't we go to the village over there to eat?' asked Marion pointing to Plaka.

Vasilis smiled at her. 'You don't remember it from when we drove through yesterday? It is in ruins. Just a few old people live there now. There would be nowhere for us to get lunch.'

Marion squinted into the sunshine. 'From here it looks perfectly all right.'

Vasilis nodded. 'If you stood on the shore over there and could see the houses on Spinalonga they, too, would look habitable.'

Vasilis repeated his remark to Manolis who nodded. 'When I first came to Spinalonga it was like this. All ruins, covered in weeds and rubbish. It was Yannis who made it into a beautiful island.' He sighed deeply. 'He would be so sad to see it now.'

They ate a simple lunch at a small taverna overlooking the picturesque harbour, Marion asking more questions about Spinalonga. 'I still want to see if I can find a guide book to the island. I've tried asking, but the shop keepers don't seem to understand. Could you come into the shops with me and explain what I want?' she asked Vasilis.

'That is no problem. I will tell Manolis what we plan.'

Manolis was only too happy to return to his boat. He had eaten well and hoped they would take their time before returning to him. He pushed a sack beneath his head and pulled his cap over his face. A sleep would not come amiss.

Marion and Vasilis entered a bookshop and Marion began to scan the shelves whilst Vasilis spoke to the owner. He came over to her and shook his head.

'They say there is no guide book that they know of.'

Marion picked up a book with a colourful, attractive cover. 'Who wrote these books?'

Vasilis raised his eyebrows. 'You want a fairy story?'

Marion smiled back. 'No, I just want to know the author.'

'They are written by the Englishman, Basil Hurst.'

Marion replaced the book on the shelf. 'I knew I was right. I'll tell Cathy. I don't think she believed me.'

'Why should Cathy want a fairy story?'

'I'm sure she already knows all of them,' smiled Marion. 'The author is her father. She says he used to tell her the stories before she went to bed.'

Vasilis picked up the book again and opened it. There was no photograph of the author and nothing inside about the man. He read the different titles listed inside. 'He writes many books,' he observed, 'but there is nothing about him.'

'When Cathy became too old for fairy stories he began to tell her adventure stories. He still writes them. They are very popular in England, but he keeps his own life very private.'

Cathy sat in the shade outside the bookshop that Marion and Vasilis had entered. She hoped they would not be very much longer. She could not read most of the titles on display in the window and she was unable to get the thought of the Englishman out of her mind.

Marion came out with a broad smile on her face.

'Have you found a guide book?' asked Cathy.

Marion shook her head. 'There isn't one apparently, but I was right about your father's books. They do have them over here.'

Cathy nodded without replying.

'What's wrong Cathy?' asked Marion.

'Nothing really. I just feel so sad for the Englishman who returned home to find his family had been killed.'

Vasilis shook his head. 'Not killed, massacred.'

'Why? What had they done?'

'Nothing at all. The Germans took out their revenge for their defeat on innocent villagers. You would like to see the memorial?'

'Yes, I would.'

'Very well. We will go there tomorrow. Is that all right with you, Marion?'

Marion shrugged. 'As you say, Knossos is always there. Mind you, so is the memorial.'

To Vasilis's amusement both girls fell asleep in the car on their return journey.

'It must have been the sea air out on the boat,' Cathy excused herself.

'I shall have a swim to wake myself up,' announced Marion. 'Are you joining me, Cathy?'

Cathy shook her head. 'No. I'm going to have a rest, then a shower.'

Vasilis smiled to himself. If Marion was swimming and Cathy was resting that would give him some time alone with her.

He placed Cathy on her bed and stood beside her, waiting until Marion had left for the pool. As soon as she had closed the door he bent over and kissed Cathy.

'I have been waiting to do that all day. I hope you have been waiting also.'

Cathy did not trust herself to answer and Vasilis sat on the bed beside her, slowly undoing the buttons on her blouse. She knew she should resist, but seemed totally unable to voice the words. He slid his hand under her back and undid her brassiere, pushing it up to expose her breasts. As they came into view he drew in his breath sharply and bent to kiss them.

Cathy's body arched involuntarily and she gave a groan. He flicked his tongue gently over and between her breasts, his fingers released the button on her trousers and slid downwards across her flat stomach.

'Please, Cathy,' he beseeched her.

The sound of his voice seemed to draw Cathy from her stupor. 'No,' she said harshly and tried to pull his hand away.

Vasilis sat up and looked at her sadly. 'What is wrong, Cathy? You enjoy me touching you, kissing you, then, suddenly, you do not want me.'

Cathy's eyes brimmed with tears. 'I don't want to become pregnant.'

'You do not want babies?'

'It wouldn't be very sensible of me to have children, would it? How would I look after them?'

'If you married me you could have babies and you could have someone to help you. Someone like Marion who could do what you were unable.' He slid one hand into her trousers again, and the other fondled her breast, feeling Cathy's immediate response.

'You want, Cathy. I want. I want you. I do not know how to contain myself when I touch you. I love you Cathy.'

Cathy placed her arm around his neck and pulled him down onto her. She could feel how desperate he was for her and she was longing for him to insist that he had his way. A noise outside made both of them stiffen. Vasilis sat up hurriedly and Cathy buttoned her blouse and trousers. Footsteps could be heard and carried on past the chalet.

'I thought it was Marion returning,' explained Cathy, not sure whether to be glad or sorry that the dangerous moment for both of them had passed.

'I did also.' Vasilis made to resume his position on the bed, but Cathy pushed him away.

'No, we must be sensible. Marion will be back quite soon now.'

'I cannot be sensible, Cathy. When I am with you I lose all my sense.' He looked at her seriously. 'Cathy, I want to marry you. I want you to stay in Crete with me and we will share a good life together.'

Cathy swallowed hard. She wanted to stay in Crete, married to this man who made her heart race and put her emotions into turmoil. 'I don't know, Vasilis.'

'You do not know what? You do not know if you love me? You do not know if you wish to spend the rest of your life in Crete?'

'It's a big decision,' she avoided the question.

'Do you love me?' persisted Vasilis.

'I – I – yes, Vasilis. I believe I am in love with you.'

Vasilis bent and kissed her. 'Then there is no big decision.'

Marion opened the door of the chalet. 'Oops! Sorry. I should have knocked. I didn't realise Vasilis had stayed here with you. Would you like me to come back later?'

Cathy blushed. 'No, of course not. This is your chalet too. You don't have to knock.'

Marion raised her eyebrows. 'I'm not so sure. I certainly will in future.'

'I am leaving now. I was only keeping Cathy company until you returned.' Vasilis took Cathy's hand and raised it to his lips. 'I will see you tomorrow, ladies. We are going to the memorial, yes?'

Marion waited until Vasilis had left the chalet and closed the door firmly behind him.

'So what did I interrupt?'

Cathy blushed and dropped her eyes. 'Nothing really. Vasilis has just asked me to marry him.'

'What?' Marion sat down on her bed and rose again rapidly. 'I can't sit there, I'm still wet. Say that again.'

'Vasilis has asked me to marry him.'

'And what have you said?'

'I haven't actually given him an answer.'

'No doubt you would have done had it not been for my untimely arrival.'

'I don't know, Marion.'

'What don't you know?'

'Whether it would be a wise decision.'

'Do you love him?'

Cathy smiled sheepishly. 'I'm crazy about him. I've never met a man who made me feel like this before.'

'Crazy about him doesn't mean you're in love with him,' observed Marion. 'You've only known him less than a fortnight.'

'It feels as if I've known him forever.'

Marion shrugged. 'It's not up to me to tell you what to do. All I can say is to be careful. Don't make any promises that you don't want to keep in a few weeks time.'

They joined the queue of traffic leaving Heraklion and continued along the coast road to Rethymnon, where they stopped for a late coffee. It was a far longer journey to the town than either girl had realised by looking at the map.

'It is almost the same distance again to Chania,' explained Vasilis.

'Will we be able to have a swim when we are there?' asked Marion.

'If there is time we will do so. We need to drive to the far side of Chania then we will turn down into the country roads. Fortunately we do not have to drive through the town. Today the traffic is particularly heavy. We do not want to return to Heraklion too late for your dinner.'

'I'm beginning to wish I hadn't asked to do this,' muttered Cathy.

'You want to turn back now?' asked Vasilis.

'Oh, no,' she assured him. 'I just hadn't realised how far it was for you to drive.'

'That is no problem. I enjoy driving, particularly if I am driving with you.'

Cathy dropped her eyes. She knew Vasilis was waiting for her to give him an answer and she had avoided being alone with him and ignored his beseeching looks.

'Well, if it's going to take us that long we shouldn't linger.' Marion pushed her empty cup away. 'I'm ready when you are.'

They returned to the hot car, winding down the windows, glad of the breeze that blew in and cooled them as they sped along. The traffic was still heavy, but it moved at a reasonable pace along the main coast road, Marion looking longingly at Chrysopigis Monastery as they passed.

'Down there is the house where Venzelos lived. If you wished we could make another trip up here and you could visit the sites in this area, Marion.'

'I would like that,' she agreed. 'I still have to see Knossos, though, and what about Aghia Triada and Phaestos?'

Vasilis smiled. 'Aghia Triada is not suitable for Cathy. It is very steep. Even I could not manage her chair up and down there. We could visit Phaestos; then go on to Aghia Triada and Cathy and I could sit in the cafe whilst you explored.'

Marion nodded enthusiastically. 'I still want to see Knossos first,' she insisted.

Vasilis slowed, waited for a gap in the traffic and turned left on to a well made, but much narrower road. After no more than a couple of hundred yards he pointed.

'There, you see, in the distance.'

Rising up from the barren earth was a large piece of white marble, from where they were the girls would have mistaken it for a rock.

'Can we go closer?' asked Cathy.

'We can go right up to it. You can get out and read the names inscribed on it.'

'Should we have brought some flowers or something?' asked Marion.

'There is no need. That is only done by the relatives.'

As they neared the memorial the size of it grew and they gasped in astonishment. An angel, twice life size, was depicted holding a child in her arms. 'It's amazing. It's bigger than many of the memorials in the villages in England and it's in the middle of nowhere.'

'There was a village here before the Germans came,' Vasilis reminded them.

He drew to a halt and helped Cathy from the car, handing her the crutches that enabled her to walk a short distance. He hovered beside her as she crossed the rough ground and stopped where they could see the names inscribed on the skirt of the angel.

'I can't read it,' she complained. 'What does it say?'

' "INNOCENT VICTIMS OF GERMAN SOLDIERS" ' read Vasilis.

'Are those their names?' asked Marion.

Vasilis nodded. 'Katerina Hurst, Vasilis Hurst, Yiorgo Iliopolakis, Elena Iliopolaki, Despina Iliopolaki, Maria Iliopolaki....'

Cathy held up her hand. 'What were those first two names?'

Vasilis looked again and traced the letters with his finger. 'Katerina Hurst, Vasilis Hurst, oh, the poor child, he was only four years old.'

Marion sucked in her breath. Cathy had turned as white as the marble. 'That's my name, Hurst.'

Vasilis nodded. 'If you were Greek you would be called Katerina.'

'What would your name be in English?'

'My name would be Basil.'

Cathy felt a shiver go down her spine. 'My father's name is Basil.'

'It is customary to call your child after their mother or father.'

Cathy frowned in concentration. 'I know so little about my father. I asked Mum where she and Dad had met. She said it was at the Red Cross Centre when he returned from Greece. He was in the army I think. I know he speaks Greek. Mum told me his first wife had died, but I have no idea if she was Greek. It can't just be a coincidence of name. It has to a memorial to my father's first wife. Why would he use a picture of the memorial as a symbol on his books otherwise?' Cathy turned distressed eyes towards Vasilis. 'How awful for him. To know that the woman you loved had been killed because the Germans wanted revenge for their defeat. No wonder he would never speak about the war.'

Vasilis nodded sombrely. He was trying to come to terms with his own discovery. His family name was Iliopolakis, his mother had been called Katerina and the family had lived in this area. He also knew his father had been an Englishman and he had been brought up by his aunt and uncle after the death of his mother. His chest hurt and his heart was thumping. Surely the woman he had fallen in love with could not be his sister?

They stopped for lunch in Chania, both Cathy and Vasilis picking at their food whilst Marion ate steadily. She could understand Cathy's distress, but why Vasilis should have taken the possible discovery so badly was beyond her comprehension. He seemed distracted when she spoke to him and his habitual smile had left him. He was obviously in a hurry to return to the hotel and was impatient with the traffic congestion they encountered, despite their journey taking less time than it had earlier in the day. He made no suggestion that they stopped at one of the beaches for a cooling swim.

He parked, placed Cathy in her wheelchair and left them with no more than a brief goodbye. He made no offer to wheel Cathy to the chalet or try to snatch a few moments alone with her. There was no promise to meet them later or see them the following day.

'What's wrong with him?' asked Marion.

'What do you mean?'

'He hardly said a word all the way back. Mind, neither did you.'

'I keep thinking about my father. If he did place that memorial there to his wife and child he must have loved them so much.'

'Meaning?'

'He must have suffered terribly. I just wish I knew.'

'Why don't you ask to use the telephone up in reception and call him?'

'I can't do that. It's just not the kind of thing you can ask over the 'phone. I'll have to wait until I get home.'

'Well, I'm going to shower and get ready for dinner. I feel really hot and dirty. It must have been the dust from the roads. I won't be long. You can decide what you're going to wear whilst I'm in there.'

Cathy nodded. Her feelings were in turmoil. If the memorial was to her father's first wife why had he never told her they had a son? Had she been called Catherine after the Katerina whose name was engraved at the top of the list of the dead? How did her mother feel about being a second wife? The questions went round and round in her brain unendingly and she had not given a thought to what she would wear to dinner when Marion emerged from the bathroom.

She sat down on the bed beside Cathy and took her hand. 'If we hadn't gone to Spinalonga that boatman couldn't have told us about the memorial and we wouldn't have seen it. You have no idea if it really is anything to do with your father and you refuse to try to find out until you get back home. Forget about it or you'll spoil the remainder of your holiday, besides, I thought you had something more important to think about.'

Cathy frowned at her. 'What?'

'I thought you said Vasilis had asked you to marry him.'

Cathy gave a deep sigh. 'He didn't mention it again today. I kept thinking he was going to ask me for an answer, but we were driving and after the memorial visit I couldn't think of anything else anyway. If we meet up with him after dinner he may ask me again.'

Marion raised her eyebrows. 'And do you have your answer ready?'

Cathy nodded firmly. 'Yes.'

'Yes, you have the answer ready or yes you will marry him?'

Cathy looked at her friend scornfully. 'Yes, I'll marry him, of course. I know I haven't known him very long, but we could always stay over here for a few more weeks.'

'You can, but I can't. I have to go back to work. Maybe your mother would come out?'

'Whatever.' Cathy shrugged. 'No doubt things will work themselves out. I'd better have my shower or you'll be sitting here half the evening waiting for me.'

Vasilis made his way through the reception area into the private room beyond. His uncle was sitting there concentrating on making out the various payments slips that he would ask Vasilis to take to the bank for him the following day.

'Uncle Elias, I need to talk to you.'

'What have you done to the car?' Elias sighed heavily.

'The car? Nothing. I need to know about my father. Who was he? What was his name?'

'Why this sudden interest in your father? I don't know who he was.'

'Please, Uncle, tell me exactly how you came to bring me up.'

Elias placed his pen on the table, picked up his cigarette from the ashtray and inhaled deeply. 'I've told you before. Your mother was the cousin of my wife. She had to go into hospital to have her wisdom teeth extracted. She had suffered with her teeth since she was a child. She asked us to look after you for the few days she would be in hospital.'

'Why you? Why not my grandparents?'

Elias shrugged. 'She and your aunt were cousins and close friends. She had fallen out with her mother. We already had Eleni so she thought another little one around would not make much difference to us.' He shook his head. 'It was very sad. A tragedy. She did not come round from the anaesthetic.'

'Did you know my father?'

'I met him a couple of times before you were born. I can't say I knew him. There was something strange about him. Katerina's family disapproved of him so he tended to disappear if visitors arrived. Maybe they disapproved because he was an Englishman. He did not return. He may not even have known about you. These things happened during the war.'

'So I may not have been killed by the Germans when they massacred the villagers?'

'How can you have been killed? You're standing in front of me.'

Vasilis ran his hand over his forehead. 'My mother was an Iliopolakis from the country area behind Chania. What was my father's name?'

'I've no idea. I'm not sure I ever knew. Your mother may not even have been married to this man. That was why you have always been known as Vasilis Iliopolakis.'

'Could my father be the Englishman Vasilis Hurst?'

Uncle Elias shrugged. 'Who knows?'

'Who would know?'

'Only this Vasilis Hurst I imagine. If he was over here at that time only he should know what he got up to with the local women.'

Vasilis winced. He had always assumed his father had been killed during the war and that was why he had not returned to claim him as his son. To think he might have been the result of a casual liaison was demeaning.

Elias stubbed out his cigarette. 'These are ready for you to take to the bank tomorrow, provided you're not too busy chasing around after that girl to do your work,' he added.

Vasilis shook his head. 'I'll not be taking them anywhere tomorrow,' he said sadly.

Vasilis entered the dining room just as Cathy and Marion were finishing a bunch of grapes. He looked pale and strained.

'I am sorry, ladies. I am unable to spend tomorrow with you. I regret I have to work. I will arrange for Panayiotis to help you up and down the beach.'

'Thank you,' smiled Marion gratefully. 'Are you going to join us for coffee?'

Vasilis shook his head. 'Not tonight. I have certain jobs that I have to complete. Goodnight.' He turned on his heel and walked out of the dining room.

Marion raised her eyebrows. 'Well! Someone has certainly upset him!'

'Do you think it's because I haven't agreed to marry him yet?' asked Cathy anxiously.

'If that's the reason make sure you say no. This is a side of him that you haven't seen until now. Spoilt little boy sulking because he hasn't got his own way.'

Vasilis tossed and turned, unable to sleep. If Cathy was his sister the feelings and desire he felt for her were disgusting. He could not go near Cathy again until he knew the truth about his father. He was pleased to have to go to the bank as it gave him an excuse to be away from the hotel. He wondered what else he could find to do that could delay his return, then he thought of Manolis. If he made the journey down to Aghios Nikolaos again he could speak to the boatman. It was possible the man would know more about Basil Hurst if he pressed him.

Vasilis waited in the queue at the bank. Despite being frustrated with the amount of time he spent in there he knew that in all likelihood Manolis would be either fishing or taking a group of people out to Spinalonga. He had told his uncle that after he had completed the banking he had business of his own to attend to and Uncle Elias waited for his nephew to request the use of his large car. When Vasilis made no mention of borrowing it he decided that Vasilis was speaking the truth when he said he was not escorting the two English ladies anywhere that day.

When Vasilis reached Aghios Nikolaos there was no sign of Manolis or his boat and he made his way morosely to the taverna that mostly served the fishermen. It smelled of fish and Vasilis wrinkled his nose, hoping he would not smell the same for the remainder of the day.

He took his coffee outside and sat on a seat facing the harbour. That way he would be sure to see the man when he returned. He did not want him to sail out again before he had a chance to speak to him. There were a number of boats out at sea, but from the distance he could not distinguish the one he was looking for. He walked up and down the waterfront and drank two more cups of indifferent coffee before he saw Manolis making his way towards the shore with a boatload of passengers. Long before he reached the jetty Vasilis was waiting for him.

Manolis recognised him and grinned. 'Another trip to the island? It's a bit late in the day, but we can go there and back. No stopping at Elounda.'

Vasilis shook his head. 'I need to talk to you. Can I come aboard?'

Manolis nodded. Was this man about to make him an offer to be a private boatman to the girl in a wheelchair? He could see no sign of her, but she and her companion could be in a taverna waiting for the man to make a deal with him.

'What can I do for you?'

'I'd like to ask you some questions.'

Manolis raised his eyebrows. 'My boat is registered, my harbour taxes paid.'

'I'm nothing to do with the port regulations,' Vasilis assured him. 'I want to ask you about the war, when you sailed with the English man.'

'That's a long time ago.'

'Do you remember his name?'

'Of course,' Manolis replied scornfully. 'It was Vasilis.'

'Vasilis what?'

Manolis frowned and finally shook his head. 'I don't remember. I'm not sure if I ever knew his family name.'

'But he was married to a Cretan woman?'

At this Manolis smiled, then his face dropped. 'A charming lady. Such a tragedy for him. I did not think he would survive. His heart was broken.'

'You met her?'

'On two occasions I walked to his farm and stayed there with him and his wife.'

'Did he have a child?'

'A small boy. He was so proud of him.' Manolis's face saddened further. 'He so wanted to be there with them to watch him grow up.'

'What happened to them?'

'I told you yesterday, the Germans shot them and burnt their village.'

'Are you certain they were amongst the ones who were massacred? Could they not have left the village earlier and escaped?'

'Vasilis was certain they had died. That was why he had the memorial erected. He trusted me to see that it was completed,' added Manolis proudly.

Vasilis frowned. 'If he trusted you to see it was completed he must have left a list of names to be engraved on it. Do you still have that?'

'Probably. Somewhere.'

'Do you remember any of the names?'

'Only the first two. He was most insistent that his wife's name was at the top followed by his son's.'

'What were they?'

'Katerina Hurst and Vasilis Hurst.'

'So you do know his family name,' said Vasilis triumphantly. 'It was Hurst.'

Manolis looked at him in surprise. He shook his head. 'I am becoming a foolish old man.' He spread his hands. 'I only ever knew him as Vasilis. When you asked me I did not think of the memorial. Of course his name would be the same as he had given to his wife and son.'

'If you met him now would you know him?'

Manolis considered the question and finally shook his head. 'I can't say. It's a long time ago. I think I'd know him if he stood before me. He'd look a bit older no doubt.' He ran his hand across his greying hair. 'We're none of us getting any younger.'

Vasilis swallowed hard. 'Do I look anything like him?'

'You?'

Vasilis nodded. 'Please look at me. Do I look anything like Vasilis Hurst when he was this age?'

'Stand up.'

Vasilis rose and held on to the mast to keep his balance. Manolis eyed him up and down, finally shrugging. 'You are about his build.'

'Nothing more?' Vasilis was not sure whether to be disappointed with the answer or relieved.

'He had dark hair and dark eyes.'

Vasilis sighed. Most Cretans had dark hair and dark eyes, bequeathed to them from the Dorian invasions and later from the incursions by the Turks.

'Where did he go when he left Crete?'

'Back to England.'

'Do you know where in England?'

Manolis shook his head. 'I don't think he knew where he was going. He did not care. Having fought hard to stay alive he now wished he was dead.'

Vasilis gritted his teeth with frustration. This man had told him nothing he did not already know. 'Can you remember anything else about him? Anything at all?'

'He knew the countryside well. He was a good shot with a revolver.' Manolis shrugged. 'What else do you need to know when you are fighting a war as we were?'

Vasilis sighed. His visit to the boatman had been a fruitless waste of a day. He handed Manolis a note. 'Thank you for your time. Buy yourself a drink when you go ashore.'

Manolis looked at the note in surprise, then pocketed it swiftly as Vasilis stepped back on to the jetty and raised his hand in farewell.

Manolis called after him. 'You could try Father Andreas. He might know more than I do.'

'Where will I find him?'

'At his church in Heraklion I expect. Ask around. He's well known."

Vasilis nodded. It was possible that the priest had some information that was never divulged to the boatman.

Cathy and Marion lay beneath an umbrella on the beach. Panayiotis had been waiting for them and helped Marion to wheel Cathy's chair down the matting. She thanked him profusely and he responded with a toothless grin.

'I do wish he wouldn't do that,' she said to Cathy. 'He's no oil painting and when he opens his mouth he reminds me of a gargoyle.'

'Don't be nasty,' replied Cathy. 'How would you feel if you had all your teeth pulled out without an anaesthetic?'

'Pretty awful, I'm sure, but I think I would also keep my mouth closed so people couldn't see. Do you want to swim now or wait until you get too hot and need to cool down?'

'I'll go in now,' decided Cathy. 'I'm not sorry to have a day on the beach. I was so hot yesterday in the car. I wonder if Vasilis will come down later when he has finished his work?'

'Probably. Come on. Lift yourself up and hang on to me.'

The morning passed lazily as they read, swam and sunbathed. Cathy found it difficult to get immersed in her book. Her thoughts kept returning to her father and the names on the memorial. She longed to know the truth, but wondered if she would dare to ask her father when she returned home. As he had never spoken about them before he might have decided to forget them entirely now he had a new family.

She wished Vasilis would come down to the beach, carry her into the water and swim with her. If he did so she would give him his answer. Thinking about being held in his arms made her body tingle and she sighed deeply.

'What's wrong?' asked Marion.

'Nothing.' Cathy did not open her eyes as she replied.

'Shall I go up and get something for us to eat? We won't be able to swim immediately afterwards, but we could go down and lay on the edge,' suggested Marion. 'If we get chilly we can move out of the water and when we get hot again we can go in up to our necks.'

'I won't be able to read if I'm lying in the sea.'

'You're not reading anyway. You've got your eyes closed.'

Cathy smiled. It was true; she had finally given up trying to concentrate on her novel. 'A sandwich would go down quite well.'

'What would you like?' asked Marion as she pulled her dress over her head. 'Cheese and salad or ham and salad?'

'Cheese,' replied Cathy firmly. 'I'm always a bit suspicious of the ham in case it has been in the sun.'

Vasilis drove rapidly back to Heraklion. He was tempted to try to search out the priest that evening, but realised the futility of such a task. He would have to wait until the following day. He just hoped the man was still in a parish in Heraklion and he would not have to travel to the other side of the island. It was so important for him to find out exactly who had fathered him.

He avoided the beach, unwilling to trust his self control when he saw Cathy. He knew he would want to take her in his arms and kiss her and he also knew that such pleasure was denied him until he was certain they were not closely related. He had been looking forward to the weekend. He had planned to spend it with Cathy, telling her about his family, preparing her to meet them and arranging for them to come and stay at the hotel the following week. He was sure that Cathy would understand and accept his situation. Now his plans and hopes were dashed and he realised he felt incredibly miserable.

He threw the satchel on the table. 'I've done the banking.'

'A long queue was it?' asked Elias sarcastically. 'Where have you been for the rest of the day?'

'I went down to Aghios Nikolaos. I wanted to speak to a boatman. He spent the war in the company of Vasilis Hurst.'

'So?'

Vasilis felt foolish. 'I wanted to know if I looked anything like him.'

'And do you?'

'He said I was about the same build and he had dark hair and eyes. That could cover half the men on Crete!'

'Depending upon what the man got up to he could be the father of half the men on Crete. Forget it, Vasilis. If we, your family, don't know the name of your father, how do you expect anyone else to know who he was?'

'I'm going in to Heraklion tomorrow. The boatman said the priest there might be able to help me. If he did have an affair with my mother and I was the result he may have gone to confession.'

Elias snorted. 'Highly unlikely. Besides, whatever he may have said to a priest in the Confessional would be confidential.'

'I'm going anyway,' said Vasilis stubbornly.

Elias shrugged. There was more to this than his nephew was telling him, but he was obviously determined to continue on his foolish search for the identity of his father.

Vasilis saw where Cathy and Marion were having coffee in the lounge. He deliberately stood next to Marion and hardly looked at Cathy.

'I regret I will be unable to take you anywhere tomorrow,' he spoke apologetically. 'There is some important business that I have to attend to.'

Marion smiled. 'We understand. We are very grateful to you for taking us out and about as you have. We could certainly not have visited Spinalonga or gone to the memorial without your help.'

'I hope I will be able to accompany you again next week.'

'Does that mean you will have to work over the weekend?' asked Cathy.

'Very likely,' replied Vasilis stiffly. 'Excuse me. Goodnight, ladies.'

Cathy looked after him longingly and sighed. She knew she could not expect Vasilis to spend all day every day with her, but surely he could have spared half an hour in the evening to join them for coffee?

Vasilis drove into Heraklion and stopped outside the first church he saw. He made his way inside and genuflected. The priest was replacing the candles at the altar and Vasilis waited patiently whilst he blessed each one before finally turning to him.

'How can I help you?'

'I am looking for directions, Father. I wish to speak with Father Andreas.'

The priest frowned. 'Which Father Andreas are you seeking? There are three priests with that name in this locale.'

Vasilis sighed. 'I don't know.'

The priest raised his eyebrows. 'Are you looking for a young man?'

'He would probably be in his fifties.'

'That narrows the choice down to two.' The priest smiled wryly. 'Can you give me any more help?'

Vasilis shook his head.

'Then I will direct you to both of them. Maybe when you meet them you will know which one it is you wish to speak with.'

'I would be very grateful,' replied Vasilis humbly.

Vasilis drove his car into the centre of Heraklion and parked in the public car park. It would be easier to find his way on foot. He left the centre of the town and turned down side streets until he reached the first church the priest had given him directions for. He went up the steps and tried the door of the church. It was locked. He stood looking at it impatiently. Maybe the priest was not in town, maybe he was ill. With a sigh he turned. He would have to go to the other location and hope that housed the priest for whom he was searching.

The second church was more difficult for him to find and he had to ask for further directions from a passerby. He walked down the steps and was gratified to see the door was open. It was far darker inside than the first one he had entered and he had to wait for his eyes to become accustomed to the dimness. The priest emerged from an alcove, hardly distinguishable in his black robes.

'Can I help you?'

'Are you Father Andreas?'

The priest inclined his head. 'I am.'

'Would you be able to spare some time to talk with me? I have a problem.'

'Of course. Do you wish to make a confession?'

Vasilis shook his head. 'No, I would like to ask you some questions.'

'If you are considering entering the church I am sure there are others better fitted to guide you.'

'These are personal questions. They relate to the war.'

'The war?' Father Andreas raised his eyebrows. 'Maybe we would be more comfortable if you came to my house.'

Father Andreas led the way across the courtyard and into his small house that stood at one side. He ushered Vasilis into a sparsely furnished room and offered him a seat. 'Can I offer you refreshment?'

'Thank you, Father, but no.'

'What is it you wish to ask me about the war? My church was a fortunate survivor along with myself as you can see.'

'It's about the memorial up by Chania.'

Father Andreas nodded.

'I took two ladies to visit it the other day. It was the first time I had stopped and looked closely at the names. Most of those commemorated are from the Iliopolakis family. I am from that family.'

Father Andreas crossed himself. 'I do not recall the names, but I remember the Germans massacred many villagers in their retreat to Chania.'

'There are two names, right at the top. Katerina Hurst and Vasilis Hurst. Can you be sure these people were amongst those who died?'

'I cannot. I do not know the area or the families involved. When Vasilis came to me he was convinced his wife and child were amongst their number.'

Vasilis felt hope surge through him and then die again. If Vasilis Hurst did not know that his wife had died in the hospital and their son was being cared for by relatives he would naturally assume they were amongst the slaughtered.

'Thank you, Father.' Vasilis rose to go.

Father Andreas frowned. 'I do not see how I have helped you, but there again, I do not know what you are searching for.'

Vasilis turned sad eyes on the priest. 'I am trying to find out the identity of my father.'

Cathy and Marion spent their time on the beach, Panayiotis waiting to help them each time for which Marion was truly grateful. He would greet them with his toothless smile and a torrent of unintelligible Greek. Despite Vasilis saying they did not need to give him a tip she would make sure she left an envelope with his name on it and trust Vasilis to pass it on to him. Marion was thankful that once again there was dancing after the Sunday lunch and Cathy seemed content to sit and watch them. On two occasions she insisted on going up to the reception area. Vasilis's car was missing from his usual parking place and of him there was no sign.

'I wish I knew what was wrong. It's almost as though he wants to avoid me.'

'Cold feet,' remarked Marion. 'He spoke in the heat of the moment and is now regretting it. He hasn't got the courage to say he made a mistake.'

'I do hope not.' Cathy's eyes filled with tears. 'I do love him, Marion.'

'His uncle may have forbidden him to associate with you. The Greeks are very family orientated and he wouldn't do anything if they disapproved.'

'He's a grown man. Surely he can make his own decisions about who he sees.'

'He would have to be very strong minded to go against their

wishes. If they forbid him to marry an English girl he either goes along with their decision or he loves you enough to cause a rift. Either way if he is genuinely fond of you it's a difficult decision for him.'

'He assured me he loved me. He told me so continuously.' Cathy frowned. 'Everything seemed fine until we visited the memorial. Do you think it had anything to do with that?'

'I don't see how it could. We're not here very much longer. Don't let him spoil things for you. Shall we go down for a late swim?'

Cathy agreed unenthusiastically, but short of being pushed along the road to look at the shops there was nothing else to occupy her.

There were more people on the beach than usual as most of the guests had stayed to watch the dancing. Having realised it was too late to go further afield they were taking advantage of the beach or the pool for the remainder of the afternoon. Cathy lay in the shallow water, her gaze travelling aimlessly across the beach. There were a couple of families, their children wearing swimming aids and being carefully supervised whenever they entered the shallow water and intermittent laughter from a group of teenagers at the far end came to her ears. A few single people lay soaking up the sun and Cathy looked in horror at the blonde man who was almost as red as the swimming trunks he was wearing. She suspected he was going to suffer that night and wondered if she should ask Marion to speak to him.

Nearest to them were a Greek woman and a small boy. He kept up a continuous stream of chatter as he moved from the woman to the edge of the water and back again, bringing shells and pebbles for her to examine, finally discovering a piece of driftwood. He sat in the water using the piece of wood as a boat, allowing it to float a short distance and then retrieving it. The wood floated out of his reach and bumped Cathy's side. He stood a short distance away, obviously wondering if he dared approach her and collect it. Cathy smiled and pushed it to him whereupon he pushed it back again.

'You've started something now,' observed Marion.

'I don't mind. I like children.'

'Mmm. It helps if you know what they're saying, though.'

The small boy had moved closer and was saying something to Cathy who shook her head. He tried again, then shrugged and moved away, glancing over his shoulder to see her response.

'Buy him some sweets next time you go up to the bar, Marion.'

'No.' Marion spoke firmly. 'For all you know he could be diabetic or on a special diet. You should never give sweets to unknown children.'

Cathy looked at the sturdy figure. 'I shouldn't think there's much wrong with him.'

'Nor would I, but I'm not taking a chance. Do you want me to help you out? We ought to think about getting showered and ready for dinner.'

Vasilis entered his uncle's house in Chania. The idea had come to him during the night. He would ask his uncle if he could borrow the family photographs. He knew there were some of him as a child; there was just a chance that there could be one of his father.

He opened the cupboard where the albums were kept and placed them on the table. There were more than he remembered. He opened each one quickly to see if there was any obvious chronological order and sighed. There were photographs of his grandparents and poked in beside them were ones of babies, children, and couples. He drew out the first one of a smiling man and woman and read the writing on the back. *'Makkis & Roula'*. There was no date or surname. He had no idea who the people were, probably cousins of his uncle or they could be just friends. He placed it to one side.

By the end of the afternoon he had a large pile of photographs that he sat and sorted into adults and children. He sorted them again, those with names and those that were blank on the reverse. If his uncle could pick out the man who had lived with his cousin he could show it to Cathy and if he was her father she would be bound to recognise him.

He felt guilty. He should have been waiting at the hotel to greet his family when they arrived, but this was more important. He was tempted to drive back to Heraklion immediately and confront his uncle with the photographs but realised that by the time he reached the town it would be late. In all probability everyone would be in bed. It made sense to stay the night in Chania and return the following morning.

Vasilis turned his attention back to the photographs. He had intended to ask his uncle to identify the people in them, but it could make more sense to take them straight to Manolis in Aghios Nikolaos. Elias admitted to only ever having met his father twice yet Manolis had spent three years in the company of Basil Hurst. He would be more likely to recognise a photograph of the man. He could then show that to his uncle and ask for confirmation that the man was his father.

Cathy looked hopefully around the dining room for Vasilis, but there was no sign of him. She lingered over her meal, hoping he would appear, then sat drinking coffee for a further half hour until Marion began to yawn openly.

'He's obviously not coming to the dining room for a meal tonight. If he has "important business" to deal with he may not even be here. I'm tired even if you're not and I'm sick of drinking coffee. We'll neither of us sleep tonight. If you'd told me you wanted to stay here for the evening we could have had a bottle of wine.'

'I'm sorry.' Cathy was immediately contrite. 'You should have said earlier. I tend to forget how tiring it must be to haul me around.' She wheeled herself back from the table and waited for Marion to take up her position behind her. 'It's silly sitting here any longer. As you said, he's probably terribly busy catching up on his work.'

Vasilis rose early, placed the photographs in the car and drove to the memorial. He studied it carefully, finally writing down the name of everyone who was listed on it. Maybe his uncle or Manolis would be able to link the names with the people in the photographs.

His journey to Heraklion was slow, due to the traffic, and he had only reached Rethymnon by lunch time. He stopped to eat and turned the problem of his parentage over in his mind yet again. He was being foolish. It was more practical to drive directly to Aghios Nikolaos and ask Manolis to look at the photos first. If he stopped at the hotel he would have to spend time with his family and there would be no opportunity to show the photos to his uncle until the evening.

Having made his decision to drive to Aghios Nikolaos he was now anxious to get on his way. If Manolis could identify a man as Vasilis Hurst and his uncle then denied that man was the one he had met when visiting his cousin, his problem would be solved. Convinced he had found the logical answer and hoping it would be the one he wanted to hear, he was even more frustrated with the slow crawl of the traffic.

At each delay he would lean out of the side window and try to see what was holding them up. He pounded his fists on the steering wheel as he entered the outskirts of Heraklion and had to wait behind a bus whilst the passengers alighted and then had to sit behind it at each subsequent bus stop. He wanted to reach Aghios Nikolaos and meet the boatman down at the harbour, not have to search for his address amongst the fishermen and then discover the location of his house.

He drove slowly along the harbour road, scanning the sea for Manolis's boat returning for the day. It was not until he nearly ran the boatman over that he realised how late in the day it was. He hooted violently and Manolis turned and waved his fist at him. He was entitled to cross the road at that junction. The traffic was supposed to give pedestrians priority.

Vasilis leaned out of the window. 'Manolis. Manolis, I need to speak to you.'

Manolis stepped back on the pavement and leaned through the window on the opposite side. 'You nearly ran me down. I had right of way.'

'That wasn't why I hooted. I wanted to attract your attention. I need to talk to you.'

'What about?'

'The man Vasilis Hurst.'

Manolis raised his eyebrows. 'What's so important about him all of a sudden?'

'It's very important to me to know if he could be my father. I've brought some photographs with me. Would you look through them and see if you can recognise him?'

Manolis looked at the pile of photograph albums and box on the back seat of the car. 'That lot!' Manolis shook his head. 'I can't do that now. My wife is expecting me. She'll think I'm drowned if I'm not back within the next half hour.'

Vasilis pulled a large denomination note out of his pocket and offered it to the boatman. 'Couldn't you go home so she knows you're safe and then come back to me? I could come with you if it's easier. Get in the car and I'll give you a lift. Just tell me which way to go.'

Manolis sighed deeply and slipped the note into his pocket. 'I only live one road over. It's quicker for me to walk than for you to follow the traffic diversions. I'll wait for you on the corner. You drive round and look for me.' Manolis withdrew his head and crossed the road in front of Vasilis's car. He did not know how Flora would feel about him bringing this unknown man into their home. She was still sensitive about the loss of her arm. The disability had never worried her whilst on the island, but she had been shunned by the people of Aghios Nikolaos for a considerable amount of time when she married Manolis and come to live in their in their midst.

Manolis opened the door of his house and called to her. As usual she was waiting to greet him, the house immaculate and savoury smells emanating from the kitchen. Manolis kissed her soundly, then held her away from him.

'I've had to ask a man to come back here.'

'Is he a friend of yours?'

Manolis shook his head. 'He's the one I told you about who came over to Spinalonga with the woman in the wheelchair. He seems to have some idea that he could be Vasilis Hurst's son and wants me to look at some photos.' He retrieved the note from his pocket and handed it to her. 'He's given me a good tip in advance.'

'Will he stay for a meal?'

'Judging by the amount of photographs he appeared to have with him, he'll probably need a bed for the night. I wanted to let you know he was coming so I said I'd meet him on the corner.'

Flora nodded. She knew it was Manolis's way of saying she did not have to stay with them if she felt uncomfortable. 'I'll get some glasses and a bottle of wine. For a tip that size we must be hospitable.'

Manolis stood and waited until Vasilis's car came into view, then he waved and indicated that there was enough space for him to park.

'If I've got to look through that lot you'd better bring them inside.'

Vasilis smiled in relief. Obviously the generous remuneration had worked. He had expected Manolis to sit in the car and give them a cursory glance. Now he would be able to make the man take his time and examine them closely. He passed the box to Manolis, loaded up his arms with the albums and followed the boatman into his house.

Flora greeted him with a shy smile and produced a bowl of olives whilst Manolis poured glasses of wine for them both. She then returned to the kitchen. Manolis would call her if he wanted her.

'Do I have to look at all of them?' asked Manolis as Vasilis began to place piles of photographs on the table.

Vasilis shook his head. 'I've sorted them roughly. If they have a name on the reverse I'm not interested. The same if they show old men and women or babies. I'd like you to look at the ones of the men and see if you recognise Vasilis Hurst amongst them.'

'What's so important about him being your father? Has he died and left you a fortune?'

Vasilis shook his head. 'I believe him to be alive and well. Remember the woman in the wheelchair?'

Manolis nodded.

'She's his daughter. I took her and her friend to the memorial you mentioned. She was very upset. She knew her father had been married before, but not the circumstances of his wife's death. Nor did she know about the child.'

Manolis looked at Vasilis dubiously. 'And you want to convince her that you are her long lost brother?'

Vasilis sighed deeply. 'I am hoping I am not. I was brought up by my aunt and uncle. My mother had died and my father disappeared. My uncle thinks he was an Englishman. My family name is Iliopolakis, the same name as most of the villagers on the memorial.'

Manolis frowned. 'If you do not want to claim her as your sister why is it so urgent for you to find out if Vasilis was your father?' Manolis looked at the man speculatively. He had never confessed to his own infidelity. Had Basil Hurst also been unfaithful to his wife?

Vasilis turned anguished eyes on the boatman. 'I love her. I've asked her to marry me. Now I cannot go near her until I know the truth.'

Manolis pursed his lips. 'Are you certain Vasilis is her father?'

Vasilis nodded. 'Her name is Catherine; she would be Katerina over here. He has become a writer and on the spine of his books there is a small picture. Until Cathy saw the memorial she always thought it was a picture of a fairy with a child. It is too much of a coincidence.'

Manolis pushed his chair back. 'Flora,' he called.

Flora looked out from the kitchen. 'Do you want to eat?' she asked.

Manolis shook his head. 'Go next door to Penelope. Ask if you can borrow one of her children's books. One by Vasilis Hurst. You can return it later this evening.'

Flora nodded, draped her shawl around her shoulders and left on her errand. Manolis began to pick up the photographs, some he discarded quickly, others he scrutinized more closely. He was half way through the pile when Flora returned and handed him the book. He placed it beside him and continued to look at the photographs, finally pushing them away from him.

'I don't recognise anyone at all in those,' he declared. 'You have to remember it was a long time ago.'

Vasilis nodded despondently. 'Look at the book. Does that remind you of the memorial?'

Manolis studied the spine carefully, running his thumb over the embossing. 'It does look like the memorial. Why should he put it on there?'

'I don't know. Maybe he wanted to be reminded of them whenever he saw one of his books. Maybe it was a symbol that they were not forgotten.' Vasilis placed some of the photographs back into the box and pushed the remainder towards Manolis. 'See if you can recognise anyone in these.'

Manolis poured another glass of wine, called Flora and asked her to return the book. He was tired of looking at photographs that meant nothing to him. He was hungry and if he was going to be expected to look through all through the albums also he would have to invite this man to stay and eat with them. He could not be expected to do it on an empty stomach.

It was late when Manolis closed the final album, stretched and yawned. 'I'm sorry. I can't help you. The last time I saw Vasilis Hurst he was thin, but clean shaven. No one in any of these photographs looks to me like the man I knew.'

Vasilis sighed deeply. 'What can I do? There must be some way I can find out.'

Manolis shrugged. It was not his problem. All he wanted now was this man to leave so he could go to bed. He rose from his chair and piled up the albums.

'I'll help you out to your car.'

'Thank you, and thank you also for my meal. I'm sorry I had to trouble you for so long.'

'No problem,' lied Manolis. 'I hope you are able to find the answer to your question.'

Vasilis placed the box back down on the table. 'I spoke to Father Andreas in Heraklion as you suggested, but he was unable to help me. Would anyone else have any information?'

Manolis shook his head and made for the door. He wanted this man to go before he asked him to look through the photographs a second time. 'I can't think of anyone else.' He balanced the albums on his arm, opened the door and looked expectantly at Vasilis.

Vasilis drove back to the hotel in Heraklion despondently. He had pinned his hopes on Manolis recognising one of the photographs as Vasilis Hurst. Now he would have to go through the same procedure with his uncle. He was surprised to find his uncle was waiting for him in the reception area.

'What's wrong?' he asked immediately.

'Where have you been? I tried to 'phone you in Chania.'

'I went down to Aghios Nikolaos. I thought Manolis might recognise Vasilis Hurst in one of the photographs.'

'And did he?'

Vasilis shook his head. 'If you look through them you might find one of my father. I could then show it to Cathy.'

'Not tonight. There are more important things to discuss.'

Vasilis was about to say that nothing was more important to him than finding out the identity of his father when he realised this was not the time to argue with his uncle.

'I had a telephone call from Athens. Old Stergios died last week. Obstinate old devil. He's left our land to his nephew.'

Vasilis shrugged. The land had been in dispute between the men for many years.

'At least he seems to be decent and reasonable. He says he has no use for the land. He's willing to pass half of it back to us. We won't be able to touch it. One half will be for his son and the other for yours when each become of age. You'll have to go into town and get the papers from the solicitor tomorrow.'

'What's the rush?'

'Christos lives in Australia. He's something in technology. He asked for some leave to visit Stergios and then extended it to deal with the funeral. He wants this settled before he returns. He wanted you to go over to Athens.'

'Athens!'

'I managed to talk him out of that. He's agreed to come over to Crete provided you meet him in Chania so he can have a look at the land he's relinquishing.'

'When?'

'He'll call again tomorrow when he has sorted out a flight. That's why I tried to contact you. I was going to tell you to stay in Chania.'

'Have Eleni and Vasi arrived?'

'This afternoon.'

Vasilis calculated rapidly. He would go to the solicitor in Heraklion first thing in the morning. He would then be able to spend the rest of the day explaining his problem to Eleni and asking her advice.

'So what would you like to do today?' asked Marion. 'I can offer you a choice of the beach, the beach or the beach.'

Cathy smiled. 'That makes it a difficult choice. I think I'll plump for the beach.'

'Wise decision.'

'Actually I'd quite like to go for a walk along the road again. We only went into the area where the shops are the other day. Why don't we go in the other direction? There were some shops along there too. One of them might have that necklace at a more reasonable price.'

Marion shrugged. 'There didn't look to be very much, but if that's what you fancy we can give it a go.'

'It will save having to rush back from the beach to shower before going to the barbecue. We can always go to the beach afterwards if we decide not to stop and watch the dancing.'

Marion pushed Cathy for over an hour, but they found little to interest them once they had passed the first few gift shops. They stopped and looked in the windows of each one, refusing to go inside, despite being offered drinks or pastries by the owners. Leaving the straggle of small business behind, Marion was forced to push Cathy's chair on the road. There was only a high grassy bank with wasteland stretching back as far as you could see or a wire fence giving access to a building site.

'I suggest we turn back,' said Marion at last.

Cathy nodded. 'There's absolutely nothing to see along here. You must be so hot pushing me.'

'I am. All I want now is to get back, have a long, cold drink and a shower.'

'You should have insisted we turned back earlier. I know I haven't done anything energetic but I really fancy a siesta.'

'It won't take long to get back. We don't have to stop at the gift shops and fend off the owners.'

'Maybe Vasilis will be back by this evening,' said Cathy hopefully. 'If he is we could ask him about taking us to Knossos on Tuesday.'

'It might be better to go on Wednesday.'

'Why?'

'If the site is closed on a Monday more people will be there on a Tuesday. Also the package holiday people come and go on a Wednesday, so they wouldn't be able to visit on that day.'

'I really don't mind which day we go. I'll leave you and Vasilis to decide. The day could depend how much work he has to do. We're here for the rest of the week.'

Cathy nodded. She was still considering Marion's suggestion that she asked her mother to come out to stay with her, but Vasilis's apparent avoidance of her had made her hesitate. If he had decided he had made a mistake in asking her to marry him it could be embarrassing for both of them if she extended her holiday.

Marion showered and put on a clean skirt and blouse. She looked at her watch. It was too early to go up for the barbecue and having just showered she was not inclined to go for a swim. She glanced over at Cathy who was obviously asleep. She would leave her to wake when she was ready.

Quietly Marion let herself out of the chalet. She would walk up to the kiosk and buy an ice cream. She could sit up there and eat it and by the time she returned Cathy would probably be awake. Marion walked leisurely up the path to the kiosk opposite the reception area. She lifted the lid of the fridge and selected her ice cream, sitting down beneath the trees to eat it before it began to drip over her fingers.

She heard a car arrive and she looked up to see Vasilis climbing out. He had hardly closed the door when a small figure hurled himself at him.

'Pappa! Pappa!'

Vasilis lifted the boy up above his head and hugged him to his chest as he lowered him. A woman walked out of reception and Vasilis kissed her cheek before placing an arm around her shoulders and the trio walked off in the direction of his chalet.

Marion sat as if she was turned to stone, the ice cream melting unheeded. Surely there must be a simple explanation, but they looked like a happy family and the little boy had called Vasilis his father. Had Vasilis really had the nerve to ask Cathy to marry him, thinking she would stay out in Crete indefinitely and become his mistress? The ice cream dropping in a soggy, sticky lump on her leg brought Marion out of her reverie. She would not mention the incident to Cathy yet, but she would be watching Vasilis very carefully in future.

Cathy awoke and looked across at Marion's empty bed. She felt aggrieved, then guilty. She could not always expect Marion to be there for her continually. No doubt Marion had fancied a little time on her own and gone for a walk. She lifted her legs over the side of the bed and pivoted round to sit in her wheelchair. If Marion had left the plastic chair in the shower she would be able to use the bathroom and leave it free for when Marion returned.

Before she emerged from the shower Marion returned, opening the door quietly in case Cathy was still asleep. Hearing the water running she called out.

'It's only me, Cathy.'

'I'll be out in a minute,' called back Cathy. 'Where've you been?'

'I went for a walk on the beach,' she lied

'Alone?' Cathy's head appeared round the door.

'Yes. I just fancied having a look at the sea. You were in a lovely sleep so it seemed a shame to disturb you.'

'Did you see if Vasilis was back?' asked Cathy eagerly.

'Does he usually park his car on the beach?' asked Marion as she removed her stained skirt and selected a clean one.

'No, you know what I mean.'

'You can't see reception from down there.' Marion evaded the question. 'I only walked a short way along.'

'Was there anyone else down there?'

'Only a couple of families. I expect everyone else is fighting for a place at the barbecue. Are you ready to go up?'

'The bathroom is all yours. I just need to brush my hair and put some lipstick on.'

The dancing had lost its novelty for both of the girls. Both of them were looking for Vasilis, but for differing reasons.

'I'm far too hot and I'm bored,' Marion finally declared. 'Do you want to stay here whilst I have a swim or would you rather we went to the beach?'

Cathy took a last look towards the reception area. 'We might as well both go to the beach,' she sighed. 'Vasilis will come and find me when he returns, no doubt.'

Vasilis sat with his uncle, handing him one photograph after another. Most of them Elias was able to name, but he could not recognise the man he thought was Vasilis's father amongst them. Vasilis tried to curb his impatience as his uncle reminisced, finally banging his fist on the table in frustration.

'How can I find out?'

'I'm certain none of these are of him,' declared Elias firmly.

'What about the men you couldn't name?'

'Just because I couldn't put a name to them didn't mean I didn't recognise them as family or friends. Many of them would have been friends of cousins. I probably never knew their names. Why don't you show them to the girl and see if she can pick out her father?'

'If Manolis couldn't recognise him how would she be able to?'

Elias shrugged. His nephew had always been a level headed business man. Now his common sense seemed to have deserted him and Elias wished heartily the girl had never come to stay at the hotel.

Vasilis packed the photographs away again. He would speak to Eleni again and see if she could help.

With trembling fingers Vasilis dialled the number and listened to the ringing tone, until a voice said 'Yes?'

Vasilis swallowed. 'Could I speak to Mr Hurst, please?'

'Speaking.'

'Mr Hurst, I am telephoning from Crete...'

'Cathy?' Vasilis could hear the alarm in the man's voice.

'There is nothing wrong with Cathy. She is fine.'

'Can I speak to her?'

'She is not here with me at the moment, but I do assure you there is nothing at all wrong with her.'

'Why are you calling then?'

Vasilis felt his throat go dry and the blood rushed to his face. 'I think it's just possible that you could be my father.'

'What! No, no, you can't be. My son was killed.'

'He may not have been. I could be him, Mr Hurst and it is terribly important for me to find out. For me and for Cathy.'

'What do you mean? She knows nothing about him.'

'I love Cathy. I have asked her to marry me and now,' Vasilis's voice broke, 'if I am her brother that cannot be. I need to know, we need to know. Please Mr Hurst come to Crete to see me, to visit my uncle. He knew the man who was my father. He will know if you are the same man. I will pay your expenses. That is no problem.'

Basil sat silently, trying hard to come to terms with the conversation.

'Mr Hurst, are you still there? Please, help us. Is there anything about me as a child that would carry through to adulthood that you would recognise? Did I need glasses, have a limp, any sort of disability?'

'No,' Basil's voice broke. 'My son was perfect.'

'Then please, I beg you, come to Crete and meet me and my

uncle. Telephone me back on this number when you have made the arrangements. We will meet you from the airport.'

'I don't know.' Basil hesitated. He had sworn never to set foot in Crete again.

'Please, Mr Hurst. For Cathy's sake. If you love your daughter and care about her happiness please come and see us.'

Basil sat with his head in his hands. It could not be true. Surely after all these years of believing his son to have been killed he could not have just held a conversation with him?

'What's wrong, Basil?'

'I don't know.'

'Are you ill?'

Basil shook his head slowly. 'That phone call. It was from a man in Crete.'

'Cathy?'

'He said there was nothing wrong with Cathy. I'm sure Marion would have telephoned if she had any cause for concern.'

'What is it then?'

'He thinks he may be my son. After all this time.' Basil's voice broke and he dropped his head into his hands.

'Basil, that's wonderful – if it's true,' Rebecca added.

'He wants me to go over there and meet him. To see his uncle.'

Rebecca frowned. 'Why his uncle?'

'Apparently the man knew this man's father.'

'You'll go, won't you?'

'I have to. This man who phoned said he and Cathy want to get married.'

'Married!' Rebecca gasped. 'But if he is your son...'

'Exactly. I have to go over.' Basil's face was grey. 'I would love to know my son was alive,' he shook his head, 'but for Cathy's sake I hope he is not.'

Cathy and Marion entered the dining room and Cathy's heart gave a lurch. Sitting at the far end was Vasilis. He and his uncle were engaged in an impassioned conversation, Vasilis continually shaking his head. He saw them enter and acknowledged them with his hand. Marion stopped at their usual table despite Cathy's protest.

'Let him come to you. He's talking with his uncle and it looks pretty serious. They might not like it if we interrupt them.'

They were half way through their meal when Vasilis walked up to their table. He looked at Cathy and Marion could not fathom the expression in his eyes. She wondered anew about his relationship with the woman and child.

'How are you ladies? How have you spent your time?'

'Mostly on the beach. We did go for a walk along the road this morning, but there was very little to see.' Cathy smiled up at him. 'What have you been doing?'

'I had to visit Chania on business.'

'Well, we're pleased to see you back. Marion wanted to ask if it would be possible for you to take us to Knossos on Wednesday.'

Vasilis frowned. 'I am not sure. I cannot commit myself at the moment. I may be busy on Wednesday. I have one or two urgent problems that I need to sort out, then I hope to be at your disposal again.'

Marion looked up, her eyes challenging him. 'I'm sure you have.'

Vasilis gave her a pained look and shrugged. 'Some events are beyond my control. Good evening, ladies.'

Cathy looked after him puzzled. 'What have I done? He seems so cold towards me.'

Marion debated whether she should tell Cathy about the scene she had witnessed earlier and decided to keep the incident to herself. There was no reason to distress Cathy unnecessarily. If Vasilis continued to behave in such an off-hand manner towards her she would probably be disillusioned by the time their holiday was over and pleased she had not agreed to marry him.

WEEK THREE – JUNE 1973

Monday

The day dawned hot and oppressive and Marion looked at the sky anxiously. 'I hope this weather isn't going to break.'

'I thought Greece always had wonderful weather in the summer.'

'It does,' Marion assured her. 'We ought to get to the beach and make the most of it just in case there is a freak storm. It doesn't usually last very long, but it can be pretty unpleasant until it has cleared.'

Cathy still sat on the edge of her bed. 'Marion, do you think Vasilis will be able to take us to Knossos?' she asked.

'How do I know? It probably depends how long it takes him to sort out these "urgent problems" he was talking about.'

'When we come back from the beach you could ask reception if we could hire a taxi to take us there and wait until we were ready to leave. I know Vasilis said it would be too difficult for you to push me around on the site and I wouldn't expect you to try.' Cathy frowned. 'There's sure to be somewhere I could sit and have a drink whilst you went off and explored. I know how much you want to see Knossos.'

'I suppose I could ask them,' replied Marion dubiously. 'I wouldn't have to decide there and then. We could wait and see, and if Vasilis still claims he's too busy by Wednesday we could arrange to go on our own. Now, are you going to get a move on or we'll be too late for breakfast.'

There was not a breath of wind on the beach. Despite cooling themselves at the edge of the sea both girls were hot and sticky within minutes of returning to their loungers beneath the umbrella.

'I really am not enjoying this,' complained Cathy. 'I think you're right there could be a storm coming. There are some terribly dark clouds out on the horizon.'

Marion lifted her sun glasses. 'They're not *that* dark. It does feel stormy, though.'

'I'd quite like to go,' said Cathy. 'I just can't get comfortable. My towel is damp and clammy and if I lay on the lounger I stick to it.'

'I'll see if Panayiotis is around.' Marion rose and tied her skirt around her waist. 'I could ask him to take you up to the pool and you could sit under the trees there whilst I go up to reception. If you were still feeling too hot or it did start to rain you could manage to get yourself back to the chalet from there, couldn't you?'

Panayiotis assured himself that Cathy's chair was safely positioned at the top of the bank overlooking the pool with the brake on. He gave his usual toothless grin to them and said something unintelligible.

'Are you sure you're safe there?' asked Marion anxiously.

Cathy rocked herself back and forth in her chair. 'Perfectly. Panayiotis really seems to know how to find a piece of flat ground. I'll sit and read until you come back. It shouldn't take me more than half an hour to finish it; then you can have it. I'm really enjoying this one.'

'Good. I finished mine this morning.'

'You read faster than I do.'

'It wasn't such a thick book. I've left a bottle of water in the pocket of the chair, don't get so engrossed in your book that you forget to drink.' Marion walked back down to the path that led up to reception.

Cathy opened her book and placed the marker a few pages on. She found it difficult to stay awake when she sat in the sunshine reading, however interesting the book. After reading no more than a page she could feel her eyes closing and she gave herself up to the sensation of drifting gently off to sleep. A noise disturbed her and she opened her eyes to see the small boy whom she had played with on the beach on a tricycle. He was pretending it was a motorbike and revving it noisily. Cathy sighed. She hoped he would soon go somewhere else to play.

He cast a look behind him and gave a final revving noise before pedalling rapidly down the path towards the pool, taking his feet off the pedals and free-wheeling until he reached the pool side where he stopped abruptly and began to pull the tricycle back up the path. Cathy watched him repeat the manoeuvre three times. As he free-wheeled on the fourth occasion he realised he was being watched and lifted his head to look at her. His concentration broken he ended up far too close to the edge of the pool and tried to make a swift turn without success.

There was a splash and a scream and Cathy froze in horror. From her position up on the bank she could see him flailing his arms helplessly. He tried to call out and swallowed water in the process and Cathy could hear him choking.

'Help,' she called, her voice sounding thin and reedy to her ears. 'Someone help.'

Silence answered her. Panic stricken, Cathy released the brake on her chair and began to let herself roll forwards. She had almost reached the path when the chair slewed violently to one side, stopped and almost toppled over. Frantically she applied the brake and looked down at the wheels. She was firmly stuck behind the root of a tree. Despite all her efforts she could not right the chair or get free from the root. Her crutches were wedged between the bank and the chair, there was no way she would be able to pull them out and use them. She looked across at the pool and could see the body of the boy floating just below the surface.

Cathy pushed her hands down hard on the arm rests and despite the precarious position of the chair managed to stand upright. Fixing her eyes on the motionless body she placed one foot in front of the other until she reached the side of the pool where she allowed herself to topple into the water.

The water where she had entered was not deep and she felt the glazed tiles against her legs. Thrashing wildly with her arms she began to make her way to the other side. It seemed to take an age before she was close enough to make a frantic grab for the boy's shirt and could pull him nearer and lift his head clear of the water. The limp body she had in her arms frightened her.

'Help! Help me!' she called again as she struck the boy a hard blow between the shoulder blades hoping to expel some of the water from his lungs. She reached the side and grabbed hold of the handrail with relief, looking round desperately in the hope that someone would come to her aid.

With one hand on the rail and her other arm around the motionless boy she managed to pull herself up to the second step, high enough to push him onto the side of the pool. She racked her brains to remember the first aid she had learnt when a Girl Guide as she felt for his pulse. She would need both hands if she was to help the boy at all and that meant she had to somehow get out of the pool.

Gritting her teeth she took her full weight on her arms and pulled herself up another step, the roughness of them scraping her knees. She moved her hands further upwards and pulled again, the water no longer helping to keep her buoyant. Somehow she managed to move up another step, there was only one more to negotiate and the blood was pounding in her ears as she summoned up the remains of her strength until she lay sprawled beside the child.

Sitting beside him she pumped his arms up and down until she was finally rewarded by a stream of pool water coming from his mouth and he coughed. Regardless of the rough paving scraping at her skin she pulled herself up closer and turned his head to the side as he vomited and coughed again.

'Help! Help! Help!' Her voice was shrill with panic and Panayiotis stirred in his chair at the top of the beach. That did not sound like children playing. The call came again and he moved rapidly up the half dozen steps to where he could see both the beach and the pool. The beach was deserted, the pool was empty – then he saw Cathy and realised the shrill sound was coming from her. As he ran closer he could see the boy and he crossed himself as he sent up a muttered prayer before placing his fingers in his mouth and sending out a piercing whistle.

He took the boy from Cathy and turned him deftly, massaging his chest to expel any remaining water, then holding him and rocking him gently as the colour began to return to his face. Cathy lay where she was, shaking with sobs as reaction set in with a vengeance and she finally lost consciousness.

Cathy opened her eyes and saw Marion sitting beside her. 'What's happened?'

'You pulled a little boy out of the swimming pool.'

'Is he all right?'

Marion nodded. 'Thanks to you he is. Now go back to sleep and we'll talk later.'

Cathy nodded drowsily and Marion relaxed back in her chair. There would be plenty of time for questions and explanations.

When Cathy awoke next she was conscious of the pains in her legs and arms. She flexed her limbs cautiously. Had she had another accident? She didn't remember driving anywhere. She had been sitting by the pool and... As the memory came back she screamed.

A woman who had been sitting on the far side of the room came over to her and took her hand, stroking it gently and speaking in a language Cathy did not understand. Cathy looked at her with wild eyes and tried to sit up. Firm hands pushed her back down and an irrational fear took hold of Cathy. She began to scream for help at the top of her voice, whilst the nurse pressed the call button on the panel above the bed.

A doctor rushed in, followed by Marion. The doctor took a hypodermic and squirted a few drops into the air.

'No, no, let me talk to her.' Marion pushed her way past him and clasped Cathy's hands. 'It's all right. Cathy. I'm here and everything is all right.'

Cathy stopped screaming and lay trembling in the bed. 'The little boy?'

'He's fine. They brought him to the hospital, just to be sure, but he'll be able to go home tomorrow. You lay there and rest. I'll stay here with you until you wake up again.'

'Why do my legs hurt so much?' whispered Cathy.

'You scraped them badly on the sides of the pool. You've probably got a good few bruises, but in a day or two you'll be as good as new and up and about. The doctor wants to give you another injection, to stop your legs hurting so much.'

Unresisting Cathy allowed the doctor to stick the needle into her arm and felt herself drifting off to sleep again.

Tuesday

Marion sat in the ante-room. She had lost count of how many cups of coffee she had drunk in the last twenty four hours. She had slept intermittently sitting in an uncomfortable chair and felt stiff and dirty. The doctor entered and Marion realised he was probably more tired than she was. She sat herself up straighter and tried to smile at him.

He leaned back against the table and regarded her seriously. 'Some questions, please. I have to ask you.'

Marion nodded. He no doubt wanted an explanation of Cathy's previous injuries.

'The lady. Why does she have a wheelchair?'

'She had a very bad car accident.'

'She is crippled?'

'The doctors say she could walk, but something is stopping her.'

'Something in the mind?' The doctor tapped his head. 'I understand she walked to the pool to save the child.'

'She must have done. Her chair was half way up the bank.'

The doctor nodded solemnly. 'So she can walk if the need is great. That need must be made for her.'

'I wish I knew how!'

'She is betrothed?'

'No.'

'That is sad. If she wished to walk on her wedding day, maybe she would overcome the obstacle she has placed in her way. Now, I want to keep her in hospital for the next couple of days to ensure there is no infection. Some of the cuts are deep, others superficial, but who knows what germs are lurking on the side of a swimming pool. When do you return to England?'

'A week tomorrow.'

'By then all should be well. You are nurse as well as her friend?'

'Yes.'

'Then you can look after her? My nurses are busy and they speak only a little English.'

Marion nodded. 'I'll be glad to do all I can.'

Marion returned to Cathy's room and looked down at the sleeping form. She looked better than she had a few hours before. She pulled the chair closer to the bed and sat down, leaning her head forwards onto the cover and closed her eyes. If she was expected to be a round-the-clock nurse she must snatch any sleep she could.

A woman entered the room and saw the two sleeping girls. She tiptoed to the table and placed a sheaf of red roses and an envelope down before crossing herself and exiting as noiselessly as she had entered.

Marion moved stiffly. She did not know how long she had slept in the uncomfortable position. Her neck and back felt ready to snap. She sat upright cautiously and looked at Cathy who was still sedated. She would just go to the ladies for a quick wash; then get another cup of coffee and a roll. As she left the room her eyes alighted on the roses and she frowned. No doubt the letter said who had sent them and if it was Vasilis they could go back at once. He had not even bothered to come in to enquire about Cathy.

On her return she pulled the sheet of paper from the envelope and looked at the signature. The name at the end of the note was unknown to her and the English was not good.

> *I pack case to use in hospital. Tell me you want other things.*

There was no mention of the roses and no sign of a case. Marion shrugged. Maybe they would be able to help her at the ward desk. She gathered up the roses and carried them along the corridor where she made herself understood to a nurse that she required a vase. She was just wondering how she would ask for a case when the nurse pulled one from under the desk.

'How did you guess,' murmured Marion. 'Thank you. Thank you very much.'

The case was light and Marion was able to manage both items back to the small room where Cathy lay. She pushed open the door and let it swing back behind her with a dull thud. Cathy opened her eyes and watched as Marion placed the vase of roses on the table.

'Are they from Vasilis?' asked Cathy eagerly.

'There was no message with them. I don't know who they're from. Someone has left a case for us.' She opened the lock and smiled when she saw the contents. 'Only a woman would have packed this. There are toiletries for both of us and a clean nightdress for you. There's even the book you were reading.'

Cathy shifted herself gingerly in the bed. Her legs were stinging and felt raw. 'Tell me exactly what happened.'

Marion sat down beside her. 'How much do you remember?'

Cathy wrinkled her forehead. 'The little boy was playing on his bike. He lost control and fell into the swimming pool and somehow I managed to get him out. I seem to remember Panayiotis being there and whistling.'

Marion nodded. 'He heard you calling for help and raised the alarm. How did you manage to get to the pool? Your chair was stuck half way up the bank.'

Cathy looked at Marion blankly for a minute. 'I must have walked.' She took hold of Marion's hand and gripped it tightly. 'I walked, Marion. Do you realise what that must mean? I can walk after all.'

'We always said you could. You just needed to believe it for yourself.' The lump she had in her throat made it difficult to speak.

'I can walk.' Cathy repeated the words as if they had a mystic quality. 'I remember now. I tried to get the wheelchair down the bank and it caught on a tree root. I couldn't get to my crutches. I suppose I hurt my legs when I fell into the pool.'

'Why did you fall in?'

'It was the only way. I remember feeling my legs on the bottom, then I used my arms to swim across to where he was. It was getting him out that was so difficult.'

'I think it's more likely that you hurt your legs as you climbed out. The side is rough to stop people from slipping on the edge. You must have pulled yourself along it. No wonder your poor legs are such a mess.'

'I thought at first I'd had another car accident.' Cathy smiled tremulously.

'I'm not surprised, waking up in here. How do your legs feel now? Any less sore?'

'A bit. I guess that means I've lost that lovely tan I had.'

'Very likely. Never mind, there's always next year.'

Wednesday

Basil paced up and down impatiently, continually looking at his watch. There were two more hours before the flight to Crete took off. He had insisted on leaving in plenty of time to allow for any delays on the road, despite Rebecca reminding him that once they reached the airport he would have to wait there.

Rebecca felt as tense as her husband. Suppose when they met this man he *was* Basil's son? They would be strangers after so long. Would Basil want to bring him to England to live with them? That could be an impossible situation for all of them. She clasped her hands tightly together, the knuckles showing white.

'Shall I buy a newspaper?' she asked Basil.

'If you want.'

Rebecca did not move. She knew neither of them would read it.

A bunch of camellias were delivered to Cathy with no message attached. Marion placed them in another vase on the table and wished she knew who had sent them, although she felt sure it was Vasilis. To her surprise throughout the morning more flowers arrived with get well messages, some in Greek and others in English, until the room was claustrophobic with their scent.

Cathy appeared to have little interest in the bouquets or in Marion's attempts to cheer her up. She lay listlessly in the bed, dozing and waking intermittently, whilst Marion tried in vain to encourage her to eat a little.

'I do wish Vasilis would come,' she said longingly.

'Maybe he doesn't know you're in here.'

Cathy looked at her sceptically. 'He must know I'm in hospital and he hasn't even bothered to put his head round the door to ask how I am. I really thought he loved me,' she said bitterly.

'Do you want to try getting up this afternoon?' asked Marion to try to divert Cathy's thoughts. 'The doctor said you could sit in a chair.'

Cathy shook her head. 'Why don't you go out for a while, Marion? This is supposed to be a holiday for you, remember. Just because I have to stay in here for a few days there's no need for you to stay with me the whole time.'

Marion looked at her doubtfully. 'I don't like to leave you on your own. The doctor said I was to be your nurse.'

'I don't need twenty four hour nursing,' replied Cathy irritably. 'Do go out, Marion, if only for half an hour.'

Reluctantly Marion agreed, although once outside the hospital grounds she did not dare to stray far as she had very little knowledge of the town and wanted to be able to find her way back. Spotting a small taverna she headed towards it. Despite feeling awash with hospital coffee she would treat herself to a sticky cake and a glass of orange juice. Maybe if she took a cake back for Cathy she would agree to eat it.

Sitting outside in the warm sunshine she realised just how tired she was. No doubt Cathy's apathy was due to shock, and her own weariness probably stemmed from the same cause. She must do something to keep herself awake. She looked around for something to hold her interest and saw a kiosk with an array of newspapers adorning its exterior. If they had an English one she could at least read about events which had taken place since they had been away.

She returned to her seat feeling quite pleased. The paper was dated the previous day so at least the news would be fairly recent. She looked at the front page idly. The love life of the royal family did not interest her, the second page had a selection of letters commenting on past articles that had been in the newspaper, most of which she knew nothing about. The third page made her catch her breath.

Staring at her was a photograph of Cathy modelling a swimsuit taken in the days before her accident. The caption beside it made her gasp.

HOTELIER'S SON SAVED BY MODEL

Four-year-old Vasilis Iliopolakis, was saved from drowning by the brave action of Miss Cathy Hurst, the well known model. Miss Hurst is holidaying at the hotel and was alone beside the pool when the child fell in. Despite being confined to a wheelchair since a serious car accident over a year ago, Miss Hurst managed to reach the pool, drag the boy to the side, climb out and give him first aid until further help arrived. Mr Iliopolakis, who won the lottery in 1969 and invested in a chain of hotels, is reputed to be a millionaire. He declared he would forever be in Miss Hurst's debt. Had it not been for her courage and presence of mind the boy would certainly have drowned.

Marion read the short article again. She felt quite weak at the knees. Was this the Vasilis they had come to know? The reporter was probably exaggerating when he said the man was a millionaire, but it could explain why Vasilis had been able to please himself when he worked and spend time with her and Cathy. It was not until she had read it through for a third time that Marion realised there was no mention of the boy's mother and wondered what to make of that. Not bothering to read any more of the newspaper, she finished her baklava and drained her glass of orange juice, tucked the paper under her arm and began to walk back to the hospital.

Cathy read the newspaper article without a great deal of interest. 'No doubt by the time we're home it will be yesterday's news.' She frowned. 'You don't think they'll try to interview me here, do you? Can you give instructions that no one is to be admitted to see me until they've asked my permission.'

'I'll try, but the nurse who's out there now doesn't seem to speak a lot of English. Maybe the doctor would be a better bet when he comes to see you tomorrow.'

'Give it a try at least. I certainly don't want a photograph of me looking like this to be in the newspapers. Thank goodness they chose one of my better ones to print.'

'I suppose you're in the Greek papers too. That would explain all the flowers you've been sent.'

Cathy wrinkled her nose. 'Couldn't we send some of them to the other wards? The scent really is becoming overpowering.'

'I'm sure I'll be able to manage that. Any preference about which ones you keep?'

Cathy shook her head. 'I don't plan to take any of them with me.'

'I'll send some of those that came this morning. I expect most of them are wired to make the displays and they won't last long anyway. Oh, I forgot, I'd planned to bring you back a baklava and seeing the newspaper article I forgot all about it. Would you like one? I can easily pop out again.'

'Not now. Maybe I'll feel a bit more like eating tomorrow. At the moment I just feel miserable and empty. I do wish Vasilis would visit me.' Tears glistened in Cathy's eyes.

Marion made six trips to other wards with the floral arrangements and was just about to make the last one when she saw Vasilis waiting at the nurse's desk. He came towards her, his hands outstretched.

Marion took a step backwards. 'What do you want?'

Vasilis dropped his arms to his sides. 'What's wrong, Marion?

Cathy – she's all right? They told me her legs were badly scraped.' He seized Marion by the arm. 'They told me the truth, didn't they?'

'There's no need for you to be concerned.' Marion's voice was icy. 'She'll soon recover from the incident.'

'Of course I am concerned. Cathy was so brave. She saved my son. I will never forget that.'

'Oh, so you are that Vasilis Iliopolakis. I'm sure you will remember Cathy saving your son as long as it's convenient for you.'

Vasilis looked at her, puzzled. 'What have I done, Marion? Please, I thought we were friends.'

'I thought we were friends too, but I don't like deceitful people.'

'Deceitful? I am not deceitful.'

'You're not exactly honest, either.'

'You mean because I did not tell Cathy that I owned the hotel? Do you remember the conversation about both of you looking for rich husbands? You both said you were joking, but she could think I was trying to impress her and I wanted her to love me for myself.'

'Really?' Marion raised her eyebrows. 'I don't think your money would have made much of an impression with her. She has plenty of her own from when she was modelling. To have told her about your wife and child would have impressed her more.'

'What do you mean, Marion?'

'I mean that a married man who plays with a susceptible young woman's feelings deserves all my contempt. Cathy doesn't want to see you ever again.'

'Marion, you don't understand.'

'Don't I? I've met your type before. Just because you have money you think that you can treat women how you please. What excuses do you give to your wife – or doesn't she know about your philandering with other women? Go away, Vasilis, and leave Cathy alone.' Marion turned to go and Vasilis caught her arm.

'Oh, no, Marion. You will come with me and listen to what I have to say.'

Marion tried to wrench her arm free. 'I'll not go anywhere with you. If you try to make me I'll scream.'

'I doubt that anyone will take any notice of you. You are in a hospital. They do have a ward for deranged patients. I am simply escorting you back there.' Vasilis said something in Greek to the nurse who nodded. Vasilis turned his attention back to Marion. 'Now I suggest you come along to a side room quietly with me and we get a few things straightened out.'

The grip on her arm tightened and Marion found herself being dragged along the hall way. She opened her mouth to scream; then thought better of it. She had no idea what Vasilis had just said to the nurse. They might just believe him and she would be shut up in a ward trying to prove it was all a mistake in a language she did not speak. He pushed open a door and thrust her inside.

'Please sit down.' He indicated a chair. Marion glared at him and he shrugged. 'Stand if you prefer, but I hope you will not mind if I sit.' He slumped down in the chair and Marion was struck by the haggard look to his face. He rubbed a hand across his forehead.

'Marion, I am not married. I would never have behaved towards Cathy the way I did had I still been married. I loved my wife. I never looked at another woman until Cathy.'

Marion looked at him suspiciously. 'So who is the woman at the hotel with your son?'

'She is my cousin. Marion, listen to me. I was married for seven years to a woman I thought I loved. We had little Vasilis and my world was complete. Often I had to travel about Crete, completing business deals. I was just beginning to make money in the hotel business. I had to check on building development, ensuring all was running smoothly, meet with contractors and suppliers; employ staff. My wife felt neglected. I had a friend, from my school days and he asked if she could attend a business dinner with him as he had no partner to accompany him. Why should I refuse? He was my oldest friend and thought I had no reason to mistrust my wife.'

Vasilis's face contorted with pain. 'For six months, without my knowing, they were in each other's company whenever I was away – and I suspected nothing. I arrived home a day earlier than expected and found them together. She had decided she preferred my friend.'

Marion gulped. 'Vasilis, I'm sorry.'

Vasilis shrugged. 'I divorced her. It is over now. I have my son.'

'How old was he when she left?'

'Six months.'

'How could she bear to leave him?'

'I gave her no choice. If she wanted a divorce I wanted my son.' Vasilis spoke grimly. 'I was not prepared to give him up.'

'And your cousin looks after him?'

'She is like a sister to me. We were brought up together. Vasi lives with her and her husband in Hersonissos whilst I am working. I go there every weekend to spend time with him. This weekend I had arranged for them to come to stay at the hotel. I wanted them to meet Cathy, to introduce her and see if she and my son would take to each other.'

'But you didn't introduce us.'

'Something happened to make me hesitate. The day we visited...' Vasilis broke off as there was a knock at the door.

'Your visitors are here, sir.'

Vasilis spread his hands. 'I thought when I met Cathy my suffering was over, but maybe it is to begin again.'

A puzzled frown on her face Marion followed him from the room.

Basil marched into the airport, Rebecca following in his wake, thankful they only had hand baggage with them and would not have to wait at the carousel for the luggage to arrive. Their passports were given a cursory glance and stamped before being handed back to them and they were waved through. Rebecca fumbled to replace them in her handbag, whilst Basil strode on regardless. As they reached the exit he rose on tiptoe to see above the heads of the other passengers and was relieved when he saw a placard bearing the name **HURST** printed on it in bold letters.

Basil took hold of Rebecca's elbow and steered her towards the man who greeted them with a smile.

'Are you the man who telephoned me?' asked Basil peremptorily in Greek.

'No, sir. I have been asked to meet you and take you to the hospital.'

'Hospital? There is something wrong with Cathy. What's happened to her?'

'A very slight mishap. The doctor wants to keep her under observation. He does not want an infection to develop.'

'What kind of infection?' Had someone dared to rape his beautiful daughter? Was the doctor concerned that she had contracted a venereal disease? If he found the man who had committed such an outrageous act he would kill him.

'I do not know, sir. I am not a doctor.'

Basil sat in the car inwardly fuming. Why had the man phoned him with the fictitious story that he might be his son? All he had needed to be told was that something had happened to Cathy and he would have chartered a private 'plane and been in the country within hours.

Rebecca allowed herself to look out of the window. Crete was not at all as she had imagined. They were driving along a main road, but everywhere looked poor and rundown, the houses seemed to be only half built with iron rods sticking up into the sky. She would have liked to ask Basil about them, but by the grim set of his mouth she thought it better to wait until a more propitious moment. The traffic grew heavier as they entered Heraklion and as the car crawled towards its destination Basil felt his frustration growing.

Eventually they drew up outside the hospital and Basil dug in his pocket for some drachma. The driver shook his head. 'I have been paid, sir.'

'Thank you,' said Rebecca automatically as the driver opened the door for her to alight.

'Yes, thank you,' called Basil over his shoulder as he strode towards the door.

He marched up to the reception desk. 'Where is my daughter?' he demanded. 'Cathy Hurst.'

The receptionist looked at him curiously. 'One moment, sir.' She walked down the hall way and knocked on a door.

A young man exited the room, looking nervous and ill at ease. 'Mr Hurst?'

Basil nodded. 'Where's my daughter? What's happened to her?'

'Mr Hurst! Mrs Hurst! What are you doing here?' Marion had followed Vasilis into the reception area and looked at Cathy's parents in amazement.

Basil whipped round. 'Marion, what's happened to Cathy? Why didn't you telephone us immediately?'

Marion quailed before his onslaught. 'There's really no need for alarm Mr Hurst. Her legs are badly scraped, nothing more serious than that.'

Basil turned towards the man. 'Are you the man who phoned me?'

'I am, sir.'

'Why didn't you just tell me my daughter had been hurt? I would have come immediately. You didn't need to concoct a story to get me out here.'

Vasilis looked at him with hurt eyes. 'I telephoned you before the accident.'

Basil swallowed. 'I want to see my daughter before I can speak to you.'

'Of course. Please, do not tell her the real reason for your visit until after we have spoken. I will be waiting here for you when you are ready.'

'Mr Hurst,' Marion spoke diffidently. 'You could have read the newspaper report and wished to come out to make sure she was perfectly all right.'

Basil nodded curtly and followed the receptionist down the hall until she stopped before a door marked 'PRIVATE 1'. She knocked gently and stood back to allow Cathy's parents to enter.

Marion looked at Vasilis. 'Did you send for her parents?'

'I had a good reason, Marion. I need to know if Mr Hurst is my father.'

'What!' Marion felt her legs buckling beneath her and Vasilis held her arm and steadied her. He guided her back to the room and helped her into the chair where he had sat earlier.

'Marion, remember when Manolis was talking about his days with the resistance? He was with an Englishman whom he called Vasilis. In English that would be Basil. I took little notice; it was just a coincidence of name. There are many men in Crete called Vasilis. We are called after our fathers or grandfathers; it is rare that we introduce a new name into the family.'

'So why should you think you had been named after Mr Hurst?'

'When we looked at the memorial Cathy immediately saw that it was the same as the symbol on her father's books. How could he know about the memorial? It was not erected until some years after the war. The first name is Katerina Hurst. Hurst is not a Greek surname. The woman had to be married to an Englishman and the four- year-old boy mentioned had to be their son.'

'But they were killed by the Germans, Vasilis,' protested Marion.

Vasilis nodded. 'That is what everyone believes, but is it true? My family name is Iliopolakis. They came from that area. My mother's name was Katerina. The name of my father is not known.'

Marion gave a gasp and her hand went to her mouth.

Vasilis turned anguished eyes on her. 'You understand my dilemma, Marion. I have to find out the name of my father. I cannot marry Cathy if she is my sister.'

'But surely...' Marion hesitated and shook her head. 'I still don't understand.'

'My mother died whilst she was having some dental treatment. Under the anaesthetic. I do not know the details. I was a small boy and she had left me in the care of my aunt and uncle, thinking it was to be just for a few days. They continued to care for me and I was brought up as a son by them. They gave me their name – Iliopolakis.'

Marion held up her hand. 'What about your birth certificate?'

'Everything from the villages was destroyed, remember. I have no birth certificate. I am not even sure if the day I call my birthday is correct.'

'So you are saying that Katerina Hurst and her son were not killed by the Germans?'

'I am saying I don't know. When Vasilis Hurst returned to the area and found out about the devastation he would naturally have assumed his wife and son were amongst the victims. But were they? His wife could be dead, but his son could be safe and well living in Chania. I went down to Aghios Nikolaos and asked Manolis to look at photographs of my family. He recognised no one.'

'Doesn't your uncle know?'

'My mother was his wife's cousin. Uncle Elias says he met my father twice. He also looked through the photographs and could not find a photograph of my father.'

'So this is the important business you have been doing in the last few days.' Marion let out her breath.

Vasilis nodded. 'For me it has become very important. I spoke to my cousin, Eleni. She said if I met Vasilis Hurst he might know if I was his son or my uncle might recognise him. I telephoned him.'

'What on earth did you say?'

'It was very difficult. I had to tell him I wanted to marry Cathy and ask him to come immediately to Crete to see if he could identify me. I think, if it had not been for Cathy, he would not have been interested in knowing if his son was alive after all this time,' Vasilis smiled sadly.

'Have you told Cathy?'

Vasilis shook his head. 'How can I go near Cathy until I know? I love her, Marion. I want to take her in my arms and smother her with kisses, to...' Vasilis shrugged. 'I cannot do that if I am her brother. Please, say nothing to her until I know the truth.'

Marion looked at the distressed man before her. 'I am sorry, Vasilis. I'm sorry about the situation and also about misjudging you.'

Cathy looked at her parents in amazement. 'What on earth are you doing here?'

'More to the point, what have you been up to?'

Cathy blushed. 'Nothing much. I just pulled a little boy out of the swimming pool.'

'Why are they keeping you in here?'

Cathy pulled back the sheet that was covering her legs and showed them swathed in bandages. 'I took the skin off when I was climbing out of the swimming pool.'

Basil picked up the newspaper that Marion had left folded to the short article and scanned it quickly.

Rebecca took Cathy's hand. 'Tell me about it.'

'There's really nothing to tell. I saw the boy fall in and I was the only person around.' Cathy shrugged. 'I couldn't leave him to drown.'

'So you wheeled your chair to the side and plunged in.'

Cathy shook her head. 'I was at the top of the bank. My chair got stuck on a tree root.' Cathy gripped her mother's hand tightly. 'I *walked*, Mum. It wasn't very far, but I actually walked.'

Rebecca's eyes filled with tears. 'Oh, Cathy.' She took her daughter in her arms, hugging her so hard that Cathy struggled to get free.

'I can't breathe, Mum.'

'Is the little boy all right?'

Cathy nodded.

'Have the parents been in to thank you?' asked Basil.

Cathy dropped her eyes. 'I left instructions that I was not to have any visitors without my permission. I didn't want any reporters,' Cathy explained. 'You know how intrusive they can be. I wouldn't want a photograph of me taken at the moment. My hair needs washing, I've a bump on my head and I'm wearing a hospital gown. Not exactly the glamorous image I used to project.'

Basil frowned. 'Where was Marion? She was supposed to be looking after you.'

'She'd gone up to the reception to see about us making a trip to Knossos. It wasn't her fault, Dad. If I hadn't tried to move my chair down the bank myself it wouldn't have tipped over.'

Basil ran his hand over his thinning hair. 'Are you quite sure there's nothing more wrong than a few grazes?'

'Quite sure. I'm still pretty sore, but I'm more upset about losing my sun tan. My scars had almost disappeared. Now I'll have to start again next year.' Cathy smiled ruefully.

Basil bent and kissed his daughter. He pointed to the newspaper. 'Now I've made sure I've been told the truth about you I'll go and see if I can have a word with the child's father.'

Cathy looked at him with alarm in her eyes. 'There's really no need, Dad. I don't even think he's around.'

Basil nodded grimly. 'We'll see. I'll leave your mother here to talk to you and come back later.' Basil walked down the hallway towards the reception. Now he must find this man and see if there was any possibility that he was his son.

Rebecca smiled at her daughter. 'Tell me about your holiday. What have you done and where have you been?'

A tear dribbled down Cathy's cheek. 'We met a lovely man. He took us to a number of places. We went to Malia and the museum in Heraklion. Then to an island called Spinalonga where lepers used to live. The boatman told us about his time with the resistance during the war.' Cathy looked at her mother warily. 'He spent three years with an Englishman called Vasilis Hurst.'

Rebecca nodded. 'I do know, Cathy.'

'He took us to a memorial this man had erected in memory of his wife and son. Do you know about that?'

'Of course. He placed a picture of it on the spine of his books. He said it was so they would be remembered for ever.'

'Didn't you mind?'

'I understood how he felt. I was engaged before I met your father. Charlie was shot down in a dog fight over the English Channel. Why should I forget what a fine man he was just because I had found someone else I could love just as much?'

Another tear dribbled down the side of Cathy's nose.

'What's wrong, Cathy?'

'I thought I had met someone.' Cathy looked at her mother miserably. 'He's married. It was his son I pulled out of the swimming pool.'

'Didn't you know he was married?'

Cathy shook her head. 'Marion tried to warn me that he could be hiding something. Whenever I asked him anything about himself he never gave me a straight answer. He just said he had "some business" or "work" that he needed to complete. At the weekends he said he went down to his house and visited family. He didn't say *his* family. I suppose I was stupid and gullible. I fell for his charm.' Cathy looked at her mother pleadingly. 'You won't say anything to Dad, will you?'

Rebecca chose her words carefully. 'I don't think there'll be any need for that.'

Basil eyed Vasilis up and down. There was no way he could confirm or deny parentage. He shook his head sadly. 'I don't know. The last time I saw my son he was four years old.'

'Would you look through the photographs? See if there's anyone you recognise?'

'It it helps, although I don't see what good it will do.'

'You might recognise yourself. I know my uncle thought he knew who everyone was, but he could have been mistaken. If you showed him a photograph of yourself at that time he might know if you were the man who my mother was living with.'

'If I am your father you are legitimate,' Basil assured him. 'Katerina and I had been officially married in the local church.'

Vasilis smiled thinly. 'At one time that would have been important to me. Now I am hoping I am a bastard from a casual liaison and no relation to you.' He held out his hand. 'Thank you for coming, Mr Hurst. I won't keep you from your daughter any longer. I wish I could join you. I am indebted to her. Let them know at the reception desk when you are ready to leave and I will send a car for you. Maybe after dinner we could look at the photographs?'

Basil nodded sombrely. He could not remember ever having his photograph taken whilst he was in Crete.

Basil returned to Cathy's room. She had dried her tears, but looked pale and wan, but gave him a smile.

'I'm pleased to see you, Dad. Come and sit down. I've been telling Mum all the places we've been.'

Rebecca relinquished the chair beside Cathy's bed. 'I'll leave you two to talk and see if I can find Marion. The poor girl looked quite exhausted. I'll try to persuade her to go back to the hotel and have a rest now we're here.'

Cathy waited until her mother had left the room. Cathy took her father's hand. 'Dad, I really want to ask you some questions. Why didn't you tell me you were over here during the war?'

Basil shrugged. 'There was no need for you to know. I talked to your mother before we were married and we decided that was the end of the matter.'

Cathy shook her head. 'I'm proud of you, Dad.'

'Whatever for?'

'I've heard a good deal about you working with the resistance and then spending time with the andartes.'

Basil frowned. 'You shouldn't believe all you hear.'

'I think I had the information from a reliable source. We went to Spinalonga. The boatman who took us over told us about you.'

'The boatman? What would he know about me?'

'His name was Manolis.' Cathy waited to see her father's reaction, surprised when she saw the smile that spread across his face, which was quickly replaced with a look of pain. She gripped her father's hand more tightly.

'I didn't know at the time that he was talking about you, just a man he called Vasilis. He showed us his hat with the bullet holes and said you had pushed him down and saved his life. That you saved the lives of a number of people.'

'Cathy...' Basil's voice was a growl.

'No, Dad,' continued Cathy. 'We have to talk about it. Manolis said after the war you returned to the village where you had lived with your Cretan family. They had been massacred.'

Cathy saw her father's eyes filling with tears.

'He said you had built a monument to them. We went to see it. It was my idea. I couldn't get it out of my mind that this brave man had lost everyone he loved whilst he was saving the lives of strangers.'

The tears began to run down Basil's face and he tried to brush them away with his free hand.

'It's the most beautiful monument I've ever seen.' Cathy spoke in a hushed voice. 'That was when I realised it was the same symbol as you used on your books. The first name engraved was Katerina Hurst and the second Vasilis Hurst, a boy of four years.' Tears began to flow down Cathy's cheeks. 'I'm so sorry, Dad.' Cathy began to sob in earnest.

Basil placed his arms around his daughter, his tears making a damp patch on the shoulder of her nightdress.

Rebecca settled herself in the small ante-room with Marion. 'I've left Cathy and her father to have a chat. I made the excuse that I needed to persuade you to go and have some rest. I do think you should go back to the hotel. You look completely washed out.'

'I've slept in a chair for a couple of nights. I'm fine, really.'

'Would you like to tell me what's going on?'

She looked at Cathy's mother warily. 'What did Cathy tell you?'

'She said she'd met someone over here and since found out that he was married. She's blaming herself for being taken in by a smooth-talking man, but deep down I can sense she's very hurt.'

Marion bit her lip. 'I was talking to Vasilis just before you arrived. His wife left him and he divorced her. He isn't married.'

'Does Cathy know that?'

'I haven't had a chance to tell her.'

'Do you know why Basil and I have flown out?'

Marion nodded. 'He told me that as well whilst you were both in with Cathy.'

'Marion,' Rebecca leaned forward, 'Tell me honestly, have they slept together?'

Marion shook her head. 'I'm sure they haven't had the opportunity. They've never been alone for very long.'

'Thank God for that.' Rebecca let out a sigh of relief.

'Do you really think he could be Mr Hurst's son?'

'It's possible, I suppose, but I don't know how we are going to find out for sure.'

Basil sat with Vasilis. He and Rebecca had shared a meal with him at the hotel, the atmosphere between them strained and uncertain. Vasilis still addressed him as "sir" or "Mr Hurst" and Basil was not sure how to react. To ask the man to call him by his first name did not seem appropriate. Basil studied the young man closely. He did not appear to have any of his own mannerisms, nor any he could have inherited from Katerina.

Elias had been introduced to him and Basil had undergone a close inspection from him until he had finally shaken his head.

'I don't recognise you as the Englishman Katerina called her husband. As I told Vasilis, I only met him twice. It was a long time ago. People change. You could be him. I just don't know.'

'Is there anything I could tell you that might help you to remember?' asked Basil wearily.

'If my wife were still alive she might know if you were Vasilis's father. She and Katerina were friends.' Elias shrugged. 'I can't say.'

Vasilis placed the photographs in front of Basil. Hesitantly Basil picked them up and began to scrutinise them carefully. He held one up to Vasilis. 'I think that was Dimitrakis.'

Vasilis wrote the name on the back. 'I'll check with my uncle, but it isn't important.'

Slowly Basil looked through the collection. Many of them had been taken from a distance, some were blurred or creased, some of them were of people he remembered dimly as neighbours, living half a mile down the road from the farm in the village, but most of them were unknown to him.

Basil shook his head sadly. 'I'm sorry. There isn't one of my wife. If there was I'm sure your uncle would be able to say if she was the Katerina who was his wife's friend.'

Vasilis sighed deeply. 'I will have to visit Cathy tomorrow and tell her. I need to thank her properly for saving Vasi and she has a right to know why I have been avoiding her.'

Thursday

Vasilis walked along the road from the hotel. He had spent a restless night, trying to decide how he could explain the impossible situation to Cathy and if there was anything he could do to make amends. The only thing that came to his mind was the necklace she had been so taken with. He would buy that for her and say it was a gift from Vasi for saving his life. Once he had talked to Cathy he would take his son along to visit her and he could thank her in person.

The shopkeeper placed the necklace in a padded box and wrapped it carefully. He had been forced to drop his price even more as the sale was to a local man and not a tourist, but he was still making a healthy profit. He showed Vasilis the matching earrings and Vasilis shook his head.

'If you have something else of quality and not so expensive I might be interested.'

Beaming with delight, the shop keeper brought out tray after tray of earrings and necklaces until Vasilis finally selected a pair of delicately made gold stars inset with a small emerald. They would be a present for Marion.

Disconsolately he walked back to the hotel. Much as he longed to see Cathy he knew he must resist the temptation to take her in his arms and smother her with kisses. He must accept the fact that when she left Crete he would probably never see her again.

He entered the reception area and walked into the private office. He would leave the earrings in the safe until he had visited Cathy and seek out Marion later.

Elias looked up. 'I'm glad you're back. The solicitor has just phoned. You're needed in Chania as soon as possible. Andreas has a flight and will be arriving early this afternoon.'

Vasilis groaned. 'Not now! I was just about to visit Cathy.'

'You have to go. She'll still be there when you return. You can see her this evening.'

Vasilis stood in the office hesitating, cursing old Stergios. Elias and Stergios had fallen out after the war due to the differences in their political opinions. Stergios had claimed the land as his out of spite, helped by the archaic laws that governed inheritance in

Greece. For years Elias had been fighting the family over the land he considered to be legitimately belonging to the Iliopolakis family. He knew how important this was for his uncle; and even more important for his son. It was true; Cathy would be there when he returned.

Elias handed him the papers. 'They're all there. I've checked them.'

Vasilis nodded and placed them inside the satchel. 'I'll be back as soon as I can.'

'You could take the photographs back with you as you're going that way.'

Vasilis shook his head. 'There'll be plenty of time for that on another occasion.' He took a last look at the two packages he had with him. 'I'll need to put these in the safe until I get back.'

Basil looked at his wife across the breakfast table. 'I'll arrange to hire a car; then we'll visit Cathy.'

'Is it worth hiring a car just to go to the hospital? It didn't seem to take very long to get back here yesterday.'

'I shall need it to drive to Chania.'

Rebecca raised her eyebrows. 'Do you want me to come with you or would you rather be alone?'

'You're welcome to come. It will give you a chance to have a look at more than a hospital and a hotel whilst you're on Crete. We can spend an hour with Cathy. Vasilis said he would visit her today. They need the time alone together; he has a lot of explaining to do.'

'She might need us after he leaves,' suggested Rebecca.

Basil shrugged. 'She has Marion. She's far more likely to confide in her than she is with us. I'm sure Marion would appreciate a morning to herself on the beach. She can go to the hospital after lunch and we'll call in when we return and spend the evening with Cathy. You can tell Marion whilst I arrange the car.'

Rebecca felt helpless. She had never known Basil this assertive. She felt she ought to protest over the arrangements he had made without consulting her feelings, but she knew he planned to visit the memorial and she wanted to be with him to offer her support when he did so.

Basil crumpled his napkin beside his plate. 'It will be quite a long drive. We ought to start as soon as possible.'

Rebecca nodded. She was not even sure if Marion was awake. There had been no sign of her in the dining room.

Basil drove up the main road towards Rethymnon, his mouth was set in a grim line as he remembered the last time he had made the journey and Rebecca sat silently by his side. She caught glimpses of the sea and hoped that before they returned to England she would have the opportunity to spend some time on the beach. Leaving Rethymnon behind them the traffic thinned for a while and Basil increased his speed until they reached the outskirts of Chania. He avoided the road into the town and drove more slowly, despite still being on the main road. Finally he took a turn to the left.

As the monument came into view both Basil and Rebecca drew in their breath. Rebecca had not been prepared for anything so large and magnificent and Basil had only ever seen the drawing he had made with the specifications. It had not prepared him for the size of the memorial. He drew the car in to the side of the road and rested his head on his hands. After nearly thirty years he still did not feel prepared for the moment of confrontation.

'Ready?' he said gruffly to Rebecca as he climbed out of the car.

Rebecca followed him, watching as Basil touched the smooth white marble and read the wording. He leaned his head against it and his shoulders heaved. Timidly Rebecca placed her arm around him and he gripped her hand.

Marion made her way down to the beach. She had not slept well the previous night, despite being in a comfortable bed again. The disclosure Vasilis had made to her kept going around in her head. She sincerely hoped that someone would be able to confirm

Vasilis's parentage, preferably so that he and Cathy could marry. The important thing was to know, rather than both of them have to live their lives apart and regretting what could have been.

She waved to Panayiotis and he gave her his usual toothless grin, miming pushing Cathy's chair and shielding his eyes looking for her. Marion shook her head, pointed to her legs and mimed sleep, hoping he would understand. He nodded and grinned again, leaving Marion to settle her belongings beside the lounger before she walked down to the edge of the sea and waded in.

Vasilis drew up outside the solicitor's office at mid-day, grabbed the satchel of papers and rushed through the door.

'I've an appointment with Mr Skoufakis.'

'What time is it, sir?' The receptionist ran her well manicured fingernail down the typewritten list.

'I was told to get here as soon as possible. I'm Mr Iliopolakis.'

'I'll let Mr Skoufakis know you are here.'

Vasilis stood and waited until the inner door finally opened and he was ushered in to the solicitor's office.

'I have all the papers with me,' he said eagerly as he opened the satchel.

Mr Skoufakis shook his head. 'They will not be necessary at the moment. Mr Christos has been delayed. I telephoned Heraklion only to be told you had already started your journey.'

Vasilis clapped his hand to his head. 'I don't believe it! What am I going to do?'

'I understand the delay should be no more than a couple of hours. I will examine the papers this afternoon and ensure all is in order for when he arrives.'

'What time shall I return?'

'Shall we say three thirty?'

Vasilis nodded his head miserably. 'I'll be here.'

He could have stayed in Heraklion and seen Cathy. What would Basil Hurst think of him now? He had assured him he would see Cathy today and explain his dilemma. If he was delayed too long in Chania it was possible Mr Hurst would decide to take his daughter back to England and he might never see her again.

'I need to call the hospital in Heraklion urgently. May I use your telephone?'

'If you ask my receptionist she will get the number for you.'

'I hoped to be able to make the call in private. It may take a while before I am able to speak to the right person and it's a rather delicate matter.'

Mr Skoufakis raised his eyebrows. 'Very well. You'll need to dial nine for an outside line. I'll get a cup of coffee. Let me know when you've finished.'

Vasilis spoke to the doctor at the hospital in Heraklion for some considerable time, finally persuading him that it would be to his advantage if he could find an excuse to detain Cathy in the hospital until his return. With a sigh of relief Vasilis telephoned the hotel and spoke to his uncle.

'Can you see Basil Hurst for me? Can you ask him to explain to Cathy that I have had to come here on business and been delayed. I hope I'll be able to see her tomorrow?'

'I will if I see him. He phoned Mikaelis and arranged to hire a car before they left for the hospital. They've not returned so I imagine they've gone out for the day.'

'Did they say where they were going?'

'Not to me. And what difference does it make?'

Vasilis sighed. 'You won't forget to tell him why I'm not there, will you?'

'I'll tell him if I see him. I've got to go to the "Imperial". Costas 'phoned to say there are a dozen guests complaining of sickness and diarrhoea. I need to get the local health authorities to do tests. I just hope they will be able to trace the outbreak to a taverna in the town. We don't want to be closed down or get a bad reputation. You concentrate on getting those papers signed and I'll deal with this.'

Vasilis wandered disconsolately around the town, continually looking at his watch and wishing the time would pass. He tried to eat his meal slowly, read the newspaper and still it was only three o'clock. With a sigh he paid his bill and walked back to the solicitor's office. He would no doubt now have a monotonous wait until Christos finally arrived, but there was just a chance that he could be early.

The hours sitting in the waiting room at the solicitor's office dragged. Three times Vasilis asked the receptionist if there was any news of Mr Christos Iliopolakis arriving shortly and she shook her head and he resumed his seat.

It was nearly six when Mr Skoufakis appeared. 'I'm sorry. He has just landed. He will pick up a hire car and then drive down,' Mr Skoufakis pursed his lips. 'He should be in Chania by nine this evening.'

'Nine! Why so late?'

'There was a problem at Athens airport. I do not know the details.'

'What am I supposed to do?'

Mr Skoufakis shrugged. 'You have the choice. You could return to Heraklion if you wished and drive up again early tomorrow. Personally I would think it more practical if you stayed overnight and I made an appointment for tomorrow morning, but the choice is yours, sir.'

Basil straightened his shoulders and tried to smile at his wife. Rebecca squeezed his hand.

'It's the most beautiful memorial I've ever seen,' she said sincerely. 'Thank you, Basil.'

'For what?'

'For allowing me to come with you and see it.'

'You have every right, Rebecca. I was a fool not to come back to Crete before. All these years I've been living with ghosts instead of forgetting the past and being truly thankful for you and Cathy. You saved me from myself. I would probably have ended up a derelict on the streets if I hadn't met you that day.'

Rebecca shrugged. 'I only gave you a cup of tea.'

Basil shook his head. 'No, you did much more than that. You made me realise I was not the only person to have suffered. You put up with my morose face and bad temper and never complained. I have never heard you complain throughout all the years we've been married.' Basil drew Rebecca to him and kissed her. 'Thank you, Rebecca.'

Marion left the beach reluctantly, had a snack at the beach bar and returned to the chalet for a shower before visiting Cathy. She hoped she would not find her friend too distraught after Vasilis's visit during the morning.

As she opened the door to Cathy's private room she was greeted by a smile. 'I'm glad you've come. I was getting quite fed up with my own company.'

Marion frowned. 'I thought Vasilis was coming to see you this morning.'

'That's what Dad said, but he hasn't appeared. Probably too busy spending his time with some other tourist who has taken his fancy.' Cathy spoke bitterly.

'I'm sure he isn't. Something important must have happened to delay him.'

Cathy shrugged. 'Let's face it. I just have to forget him.' Her face crumpled and her eyes filled with tears. 'Besides, I don't want to hear that his wife doesn't understand him and he is planning to divorce her. That's the man's usual excuse, isn't it?'

Marion could not meet Cathy's eyes. 'I think you ought to hear him out when he does visit you.'

'When! If he leaves it long enough we shall have gone home so he won't have to bother with explanations and excuses.'

'Has the doctor said when you can leave the hospital?'

Cathy shook her head. 'They removed my bandages this morning and everything looked fine. About an hour later the doctor came and said I have an infection in my right leg. They're changing my antibiotics and reckon it will clear up within a few days, but they don't want to let me out of here until they're sure it's healing properly.'

'Did they say you had to stay in bed?'

'No. Why?'

'I thought you might like to go out into the sunshine for a while. If you stay in here much longer the tan on your face and arms will start to fade. That would be a shame. There's quite a pleasant garden outside. I'm sure the hospital won't mind if I take you there for half an hour or so.'

'I haven't got my chair.'

'Cathy,' Marion smiled, 'this is a hospital. They're sure to have a chair you can borrow.'

'I haven't any clothes with me.'

'You don't need to get dressed to sit in the garden. I'll go and see what I can do.'

Before Cathy could raise any more objections Marion left the room. She hoped there would be a nurse around who spoke enough English for her to make her request for a wheelchair understood.

Marion found the doctor deep in discussion with a man and woman and she waited until they had shaken hands and walked away from him.

'Excuse me, Doctor. May I just have a quick word with you?'

The doctor nodded. People were always wanting a quick word with him and that usually meant half an hour of his time.

'What can I do for you?'

'Cathy Hurst – she says she has an infection in her leg and you don't want her to leave the hospital yet.'

'That is so.'

'Have you any idea how long she will have to stay? We are booked to return to England next week.'

'I do not think that would be a good idea until the infection is completely cleared. Airports and aeroplanes have millions of germs floating around in them. I would not like the lady to end up with gangrene.'

'Is that possible?' Marion frowned. She had known patients fly with far worse problems than an infection in their leg.

'Quite possible,' replied the doctor firmly. 'I suggest you delay your departure for another week. I can give you medical certificates so there should be no further charge from the airlines to you.'

'Thank you, Doctor. In the meantime may I borrow a wheelchair and take her outside, just to sit in the sun for a short while?'

'I'm sure that would be beneficial to her. Do not expose her legs to the sun. She will burn very easily until the new skin has healed completely.'

'I will make sure she keeps them covered,' Marion assured him.

Basil drove slowly through the streets of Chania. He felt lost in a town he had once known well. Landmarks had disappeared with new buildings taking their place. The streets were no longer narrow winding roads, but well made, wide thoroughfares flanked by busy shops. He drove beside Souda Bay to rejoin the main road leading back to Rethymnon, giving a deep sigh as he looked across the still, blue water.

'Here and at Maleme was where the worst carnage took place. It looks so peaceful and normal now.'

'Do you want to stop?'

Basil shook his head. 'No, we'll drive on and find a small taverna somewhere for some lunch. I've done what I needed to do. There's no point in driving around getting maudlin when I can't find the villages I was familiar with. I could hardly be sure that we were standing on the land I used to farm. Tomorrow we'll drive down to Aghios Nikolaos and I'll find Manolis and thank him for doing such a fine job. I owe him that much.'

Rebecca nodded. She was pleased to think that Basil was prepared to visit the man who had shared some of the most traumatic moments of his life. She wondered if she dared ask her husband to take her to Preveli and the other locations he had mentioned briefly to her. She would dearly love to see more of this island.

Basil and Rebecca went directly to the hospital upon their return to Heraklion and Marion greeted them with the news that Cathy had an infection and would have to stay in the hospital until it had cleared.

'How serious is the infection?' asked Rebecca.

'The doctor said it should go within a few days with a change of antibiotics, but he doesn't want her exposed to germs at the airport. He's going to give us medical certificates to enable us to change our flights with no extra charge.'

'So I should think! It's not your fault you've been delayed.'

'I'll have to telephone the hospital and explain to them. I'm not looking forward to that. Matron will not be happy for me to be away an extra week. It will upset her scheduling.'

Rebecca shrugged. 'If you were ill in England you would be unable to work. She'll just have to put up with it.'

'How did Cathy cope with meeting Vasilis?' asked Basil anxiously.

'He hasn't been near her.' Marion spoke grimly. 'Are you sure he said he'd come this morning?'

'Quite sure. That was why we arranged to go off for the day and asked you to come in this afternoon. I'll be having a few words with him when we get back to the hotel.'

'We must visit Cathy first. She still thinks we have come out to visit her because she is in hospital, remember.'

'I just wish that young man had had enough courage to come and tell her the real reason for our visit. He's probably disappeared somewhere and won't put in an appearance until after she's conveniently returned to England.'

There was no sign of Vasilis or his uncle when they returned to the hotel and Basil strode back to their chalet feeling furious.

'There's nothing you can do,' Rebecca tried to calm him. 'I'm sure there must be an explanation for his absence. Maybe his son has had a reaction to his accident or his uncle has been taken ill.'

'Then he should have been at the hospital with him. There was no sign of his car there and it isn't here either.'

'Maybe,' Rebecca spoke tentatively, 'it would be better if she didn't see him again. That way she would think he had just been toying with her affections and she would put him out of her mind.'

'Suppose he is my son?'

Rebecca shook her head sadly. 'Until the truth can be found out you are both in a terrible position. I wish I knew how to help you.'

Basil sat down on the side of the bed. 'I keep racking my brains. Someone must know.'

'Try to let it go and relax. Treat it the same way as you do with your books when you get stuck in the story line. Forget it and the solution will come to you.'

Basil smiled thinly. 'The trouble is, this is not a story. If I wrote it no one would believe it was true.'

Rebecca squeezed her husband's hand. 'I'm not trying to make light of the situation. I'm just trying to get you to relax. Are you going to come down for a swim with me?'

Basil shook his head. 'Not this late in the afternoon. If we visit Manolis tomorrow we could spend the following day on the beach if you wanted.'

Panayiotis tipped the loungers onto their side, closed and secured the umbrellas and began to collect the accumulation of rubbish that had been left behind on the beach. If the tourists arrived on the beach and found litter they complained but they did not bother to take their own cans and bottles up to the rubbish bin.

A splash drew his attention to the sea. A woman was swimming out strongly. He had not heard her come down as she had used the matting he had laid to enable Marion to move Cathy's wheelchair down to the loungers. He hoped she would be sensible and not swim out too far and get into difficulties. He had no wish to go into the sea and save her and no one would hear him whistle from the beach at this hour of the day. As he continued with his clearing he watched her as she cleaved through the water, relieved when she finally headed back to the shore and walked up the sand to where she had left her beach bag.

She wrapped her towel around her and wiped her face and hands before beginning to walk back up the beach. Panayiotis gave his usual toothless grimace as she passed and it was all Rebecca could do to stop herself from recoiling and smile back. He said something unintelligible to her and she smiled again, hastening up the beach before he could smile at her again.

'Good swim?' asked Basil.

'Lovely. Really refreshing. There was an awful old man on the beach, though.'

'What do you mean? Did he say anything to you?'

'Well, I suppose he works there. He was clearing the rubbish and he gave me this awful toothless grin and said something I didn't understand.'

'He was probably saying good evening to you.'

'He was only offensive when he smiled. It just gave me a shock.'

'If he worries you I'll have a word with him and ask him to keep to the other side of the beach.'

Rebecca shook her head. 'Certainly not, Basil. I'm sure he was just trying to be friendly. I'll be prepared if I see him again. I'm going for a shower. By the time I came out I was quite cold.'

Friday

Having arranged that Marion would spend the day with Cathy, Basil decided they would leave early for the drive down to Aghios

Nikolaos. 'It's a pretty little place. Once we've located Manolis you can always spend some time looking around. I'm sure you'll enjoy that more than listening to Manolis and me reminiscing.'

Rebecca nodded gratefully. She knew that she would not understand a word the men said and would have to rely on Basil to interpret for her. 'Don't you want to wait to see if Vasilis arrives?'

'No. He could be deliberately avoiding us. I've looked for his car and it's nowhere around. I'll leave a message with the receptionist.'

'I understand Mr Vasilis has gone to Chania on business and Mr Elias has been called to one of our other hotels to deal with a problem,' she explained.

'My wife and I are going out for the day. If Mr Vasilis returns before us please tell him that I insist that he waits here until we return.'

'Yes, sir.' The receptionist thought it very unlikely the hotelier would take any notice of the message. No one insisted that Mr Vasilis did anything.

Rebecca opened the map she had bought at the hotel. She spread it out on her lap. 'Show me where we are going today,' she said.

'Not whilst I'm driving. It was so much easier in the old days,' he sighed. 'Just an occasional bus or three-wheel cart; sometimes a herd of sheep blocked the way. Now it's cars and buses rushing everywhere.'

'Easier for the people to get around, though.'

Basil shrugged. 'No one bothered to go anywhere. There was no need. You sold your surplus produce in one of the villages and only made a trip up to the nearest town if you needed medical treatment. The peddler used to come through once a month and he could be quite useful.'

'A peddler?'

Basil nodded. 'He had a cart with a donkey and it would be piled high with just about everything you could think of. Even the poor old donkey had panniers stuffed full of goods. If he didn't have it with him you would ask him to bring it for you the next time he came by. The system worked well.'

'You told me you had a cart with a motor. Why did you have one?'

'I'd bought it when I first decided to stay over here. It was much easier to get to the archaeological sites. So many of them were off the beaten track and it would have taken half the day to walk there and back. I saw no reason to get rid of it and I was certainly glad I had it when I went off to Heraklion and Aghios Nikolaos. I realised later just how long it took to walk to the various places. They look quite close on the map, but if you're walking the terrain has to be taken into account. Unless there's some sort of road or cart track you spend all your time pushing through the undergrowth or climbing up and down the hills.'

'So why didn't you walk down the tracks that were there?' asked Rebecca reasonably.

Basil smiled grimly. 'Not when you had Germans sniping at you. At least if you were away from the roads you had a chance to avoid them or some cover to hide in if they were in the vicinity. Do you want to stop in Malia for coffee?'

Rebecca nodded. 'I'd like that. Have we time for me to have a quick look at the shops?'

'That shouldn't take you very long unless things have changed drastically. You'll find more to look at in Aghios Nikolaos.'

'I'd still like to have a quick look.'

Basil did not reply. There was really no great rush to reach Aghios Nikolaos. Manolis had probably taken a party of tourists out to Spinalonga or had gone fishing.

As they walked down the main street of Malia Rebecca realised her husband was right. There was very little to look at. All the shops seemed to be selling the same cheap cotton beachwear or jewellery. One had inflatable animals to ride in the water and beach towels, whilst another promised fast developing of camera films.

Rebecca walked towards the taverna and Basil caught her elbow. 'Not in there,' he smiled.

'Why not?'

'It's men only.'

'What?'

'Only the men go there. The women are not welcome.'

'That's archaic! Would they throw me out or just refuse to serve me?'

'They'd try to explain and if you didn't understand they would probably serve you. You'd find every man just sat and looked at you and there would be no conversation between them. You'd feel most uncomfortable.'

'So where do the women go?' Rebecca looked at the collection of men, mostly elderly, sitting in the taverna, either playing cards or just sitting swinging their worry beads.

'They stay at their homes. I suppose it's like the gentlemen's clubs in London.'

Rebecca raised her eyebrows. 'Not quite as salubrious.'

'You're in Crete, remember.' Basil steered her towards the table and chairs that were placed outside a small taverna. 'You'll be welcome here,' he assured her.

Vasilis was waiting on the step of Mr Skoufakis's office when it opened. He had spent a sleepless night and felt dirty and unkempt not having brought a change of clothing with him. Now all he wanted to do was meet the nephew, sign the final papers and return to Heraklion.

He sat in the waiting room, looking up each time the door opened, expecting the arrival to be Christos Iliopolakis. Each time Mr Skoufakis dealt with the client and ushered him out until Vasilis felt his patience evaporate.

'How much longer before this nephew arrives?' he demanded.

Mr Skoufakis frowned. 'I was expecting him to be here earlier. I will telephone his solicitor and see if he knows.'

Mr Skoufakis returned a short time later. 'I have spoken to Mr Gennakis. Mr Iliopolakis is with him now. He is verifying the legality of the papers. He says they will definitely be here this afternoon.'

'So there's not much point in me sitting around!'

'I suggest you return here about three. We should certainly be able to complete the formalities then.' Mr Skoufakis tried to placate the frustrated man.

Marion entered Cathy's room smiling brightly. 'How are your legs today?'

'Actually they feel very much better.'

'Has the doctor been to see you?'

'Not yet.'

'Why don't we give him a surprise?'

'What? Let him find the room empty where I've discharged myself?'

Marion shook her head. 'That would be a bit unfair. He'd have to spend time looking for you and I'm sure he's busy. I was thinking of you walking a few steps.'

'I can't walk,' replied Cathy mutinously.

Marion sat down in the chair beside Cathy's bed. 'Do you remember when you first came round from the sedation? You told me you had walked. You were so pleased you had finally managed more than a couple of steps. Why don't you try whilst we're here alone? If you could do it then you could do it again now.'

Cathy shook her head stubbornly. 'There's no point in trying. I know I couldn't manage it.'

'How do you know if you don't try? You're such a defeatist, Cathy. You have an accident and instead of fighting back you're prepared to be an invalid for the rest of your life. What will happen when your mother is too old to look after you? You'll end up in a home where you sit and look at four walls every day.'

'But you'll be with me, Marion.' Cathy sounded shocked and hurt.

'Will I? How do you know that? I might want to get married and have a home and family of my own, not spend my life being a nurse to you or anyone else.'

'You wouldn't leave me, Marion? Promise you'll never leave me,' Cathy pleaded desperately.

Marion shook her head. 'I can't promise. I'll always be your friend, but I may want a life of my own. If you had married Vasilis you would not have wanted me around any longer.'

'I would have asked him if you could stay and be my nurse.'

Marion stood up and folded her arms. 'Cathy, you do not need a nurse. You *can* walk. Get that idea into your head. Just a few steps at a time. From your bed to the door. What's that – four steps? I'll move the wheelchair over there ready for you; then we'll go out into the garden. I'm not taking you out unless you walk to your chair.'

Cathy stared at her friend mutinously. 'You're mean,' she said, her lip trembling.

'No,' said Marion firmly. 'You are the one that's mean. You won't make the effort. Do you think I want to sit inside your room making small talk when I could be outside sunning myself?'

'Then go and do so.' Cathy turned her face away from Marion.

'Very well. I will.' Marion rose and walked out of the room.

Cathy stared after her. She had never fallen out with Marion before and she had a dull, miserable feeling inside herself. She felt the tears dribbling down the side of her nose. If only Marion would come back she would try to make the effort to walk to the door.

Basil drove slowly along the harbour road at Aghios Nikolaos. At regular intervals there were signs saying that a boat trip to Spinalonga would depart at a certain hour and return three hours later, but Basil had no idea which sign belonged to Manolis. He finally drew up beside an elderly man who was sitting on a bollard.

'Do you know where I could find Manolis, please?'

The old man looked at him and pointed out to the sea. 'Left about half an hour ago.' He pointed to a board on the quayside. 'Says he'll be back at four. Dimitris will be going to the island in an hour. You can always go out with him.'

Basil shook his head. 'I need to speak to Manolis. I'll come back later.'

Basil returned to the car. 'He left for Spinalonga about half an hour ago.'

'I'm sorry, Basil. I shouldn't have asked to look at the shops in Malia.'

Basil shrugged. 'I haven't seen him for so long that a few hours will make little difference. We'll go and have some lunch, then we can walk around the town. I doubt if I shall know my way here any better than I did in Chania. It means you'll probably have to spend a rather boring couple of hours with us whilst we talk.'

'I'll fit in with whatever you think is best,' said Rebecca.

Basil parked the car and led the way to the taverna on the quayside. Rebecca stopped and wrinkled her nose.

'No, Basil. I don't think that would be the best place to eat.'

Basil looked at her in surprise. 'The food was good in there when I was here last.'

'I'm sure after the way you'd all suffered from hunger any food would have been good. It obviously caters mainly for the fishermen, and I'm afraid it smells rather strongly of fish. There must be other places.'

Basil took her elbow and they walked past the taverna, Basil having to admit that when they were close he too could smell fish. He led her along the waterfront until they reached the bridge, where they crossed the road and began to walk along by the side of the pool. Rebecca immediately began to look in the shops, but was disappointed to find the goods they were offering for sale were no different than those she had seen in Malia.

'Where do the locals shop?' she asked. 'You don't see them wearing all these beach clothes so they must have to buy their skirts and blouses from somewhere else.'

Basil shrugged. 'I don't know. When I was here last there weren't any gift shops. Some of them specialised in embroidered goods and tourists would buy tablecloths and shawls to take home, but the clothes they sold were quite ordinary. When we've had lunch we can go off into some of the side streets. You might find the kind of shops you're thinking of there. What do you want to buy?'

'Nothing particularly. I'm just curious. There seem to be hardly any shops selling ordinary food. Everything seems to be aimed at the tourist.'

'Tourism is their main industry now. They will stock anything that a tourist will buy.'

'I wouldn't think so many shops selling the same goods would make much of a living.'

'You have to remember that they usually employ family members. You just give them their board and lodging and some pocket money. That way you save on your overheads. Haven't you noticed how young some of the shop-keepers are? They've probably finished school for the day and they would be expected to come down and work in the shop.'

'That's slave labour,' protested Rebecca.

'It's called "helping the family",' smiled Basil. 'They've probably done odd jobs around the shop since they were toddlers. It's second nature to them now.'

'Does that mean you approve of the system?'

'It doesn't seem to do them any harm. It instils a sense of responsibility into them from a young age. That can't be a bad thing.'

Rebecca mulled over her husband's words. She began to notice just how many young people there were in the shops, some of them did not look more than about twelve and were obviously doing their homework, only looking up when someone entered.

Basil led her to a taverna where the table and chairs were placed close to the pool. 'Are you happy to sit here?'

Rebecca nodded. 'Do you think they'll have that pork thing on a skewer with peppers and onions?'

'Souvlaki? Bound to have. Do you want chips or rice with it?'

'Chips,' replied Rebecca decisively and Basil made his way up to the counter to give their order.

Basil looked at his watch. 'There's still an hour and a half until Manolis is expected back. Do you want to walk around the other side of the pool?'

Rebecca nodded. 'I doubt if there's anything different there, but we can't sit here for another hour without eating or drinking and I'm full.'

The pedestrian area the other side of the pool was no less congested and had more photographic shops and jewellers but many were selling the same clothes and sandals. Rebecca quickly lost interest in looking at them.

'Why don't we go up that road there?' she suggested.

'What for?'

'Just to see if there is anything up there. We can always come back down.'

'The museum is up there if you're interested.'

'Why not? At least it will make a change from looking at gaudy jewellery and all these clothes.'

Basil found the museum frustrating. The lighting was dim, the labels faded and either unreadable or incorrect. He sighed heavily and Rebecca quickened her step. She was quite enjoying looking at the items that had been found locally and she had no idea if the information given on the labels was correct.

'Have you seen enough?' she asked Basil and he nodded.

'I hope when we manage to get to Heraklion museum the displays will be better than here.'

'Marion was telling me about their visit. She thought it was excellent. Cathy was particularly taken with the frescoes. Do you think we could manage to go to Knossos one day and take Marion with us? She was so looking forward to seeing it. That young man had promised to take them, then when he seemed to be too busy she was going to see if they could hire a taxi to take them there.' Rebecca looked at her husband eagerly.

'I don't see why not. We'll take Cathy as well once she's out of hospital. It will be something to occupy her. Stop her from brooding.'

They stood on the pavement outside the museum waiting for their eyes to become accustomed to the sun again.

'Let's have a look in that shop,' said Rebecca.

'What's it selling?'

'I don't know. There's a beautiful cat in the window.'

'Could be the butcher,' said Basil wickedly.

'Basil!' Rebecca was shocked. 'They wouldn't!'

Basil smiled. 'I'm not saying they wouldn't, but I don't think they'd be quite that blatant about it. I ate a couple of cats during the war. They were a bit tough and stringy, but better than nothing.'

'I don't want to hear.' Rebecca tossed her head and looked in the window. The cat stared back at her challengingly. 'Look, there are some lovely things in here. Can we go in?'

'Don't expect to come out empty handed,' Basil warned her.

'You could buy something for Manolis's wife,' she suggested. 'What do you think she would like?'

'I've no idea. I've never met her.'

'Well, I'm sure she'd be pleased to have anything from here. This is much nicer than those other gift shops. What a shame they're not amongst the others. They'd do a roaring trade.'

'Not at these prices,' observed Basil as he turned a label over in his hand.

'Goodness!' Rebecca could hardly believe the price tag. 'I'm not suggesting you spend that much on a present for Manolis's wife. I just thought she might like something and everything seems to be far better quality here.'

'So it should be,' muttered Basil. He looked over to the counter where a woman sat leafing through a magazine whilst she watched them carefully.

Ourania was surprised when the couple approached her counter and the man spoke to her in almost fluent Greek. 'Excuse me; I'm looking for a gift for a lady. Nothing too expensive.'

Ourania raised her eyebrows. 'A wedding gift, maybe?'

'No, just a present.'

'For a young lady?'

Basil looked at Rebecca. 'About the age of my wife, I think.'

'What kind of thing does this lady like?'

'I have no idea. I've never met her.'

Ourania frowned. 'Please, have a look. When you see something that you think is suitable let me know.'

Rebecca wandered slowly around the shop. She immediately discounted the leather goods, silver picture frames and the sketches that hung on the wall. She hesitated when she came to the display of ornamental glass wear.

'What about that, Basil? I've not seen anything like that in any of the other shops.' She pointed to the model of a swan in clear glass. The body had a perforated glass inset, obviously meant to hold flowers, attached to each side and behind the swan was a smaller one of the same design.

Basil looked at the price tag. It was expensive. He shook his head. 'No, it could be embarrassing for Manolis if we took something of that value.'

Rebecca looked again. 'What about a paperweight? They're so pretty.'

'What would she use it for?'

'She doesn't have to use it. It would just be an ornament. Don't be so practical, Basil.'

'Choose whichever one you like, then.'

Rebecca hesitated, changing her mind frequently until she finally settled on one that had flowers beneath the glass dome.

'Pay for it quickly, Basil, or I'll decide I like another one better. They're all so lovely.' She placed the paper weight on the counter, smiled at the woman and wandered back to look at the sketches more closely.

Ourania removed the price, but left the sticker with the name and address of her shop before gift wrapping the weight carefully and smiled at him. 'Where are you from?

'England,' replied Basil. 'We are on holiday.'

'Would you like me to send this to your English address? It is heavy to add to your luggage.'

'There's no need. It's a present for someone who lives locally.'

Ourania raised her eyebrows. She was longing to ask why they would wish to give someone unknown such an expensive gift.

'You are staying locally? In Aghios Nikolaos?'

'No, we're only visiting here for the day.'

'How did you know about my shop?'

'We found it by accident. You should advertise your goods.'

Ourania smiled. 'I have advertisements in the hotels. If someone wants to buy something of quality they usually end up with me. Is there anything else I can interest you in?' She had noticed that Rebecca was looking at the framed pictures hanging on the wall. 'The sketches are all of local scenes and people. They were drawn by a member of my family. On the wall are the originals, but we have reproductions of every one in stock.'

Basil shook his head. 'I'm not into art, I'm afraid.' He walked over to where Rebecca was and she pointed to a man in a fishing boat, raising his hand in farewell to someone. He appeared again lifting boxes onto a jetty.

Basil took his glasses from his pocket and looked more closely. 'That's Manolis,' he declared. 'I'm sure it is.' He turned back to Ourania. 'When were these pictures drawn?'

'Many years ago now. Before the war.'

'Do you know the people in them?'

'Some of them.' Ourania walked over and stood beside him.

'Who's that?' asked Basil pointing to the fisherman.

'Manolis. Anna often drew him.'

Basil shook his head in disbelief. 'Do you know his wife?'

A cautious look came over Ourania's face. 'I do not know her well.'

'Do you think the present we have chosen would be suitable for her?'

'I am sure she will appreciate it. It is a very beautiful item, well crafted.' Ourania did not want to lose a sale and now she knew who they wanted the gift for.

Basil looked again at the sketch. 'Does Manolis still look like that?'

Ourania shrugged. 'I have not seen him recently. I understand he is busy taking tourists to the island.' She was not going to admit that she had not seen the man for some years.

Rebecca checked the time on her watch and picked up the parcel from the counter. She was beginning to realise how long a conversation could take when people realised Basil spoke the language. 'We ought to go, Basil. We've only another ten minutes before Manolis should return.'

'Of course.' Basil turned back to Ourania. 'It has been a pleasure to meet you.'

Ourania smiled. 'The pleasure was mine. Please come again if you are in the area and do not forget to tell your friends that we have the best stock of high quality decorative items in the whole of Crete.'

Vasilis paced up and down the waiting room at the solicitor's office. He had arrived just after two, expecting Christos Iliopolakis to arrive shortly afterwards and there was no sign of him. Mr Skoufakis had telephoned Mr Gennakis and confirmed that the man was with him. As soon as he had finished reading the papers and agreed that all was in order for him to sign they would be over and the deal could be completed.

Vasilis looked at his watch. It was gone four. If the man did not arrive soon the solicitor would be closing for the day. No doubt the solicitor and Christos Iliopolakis had gone somewhere for a leisurely meal, whilst he was left kicking his heels, desperate to return to Heraklion.

Mr Skoufakis came out from his office. 'I am sorry Mr Iliopolakis. Mr Gernnakis has just telephoned. There is a small problem. It is the dimensions of the land. Someone has had to be sent out to take the measurements again.'

'What! How much longer is this fiasco going to last? I need to get back to Heraklion.'

Mr Skoufakis shrugged. 'It is outside my control, you understand.'

'Telephone the solicitor again and tell him it is essential he and Mr Iliopolakis are here within the hour. I've been hanging around up here for days.'

Mr Skoufakis looked doubtfully at his client. 'I will do my best, sir.'

Mr Skoufakis returned shaking his head. 'The solicitor says it will not be possible to come over here today. A new land certificate has to be registered. His secretary has gone to the Town Hall but he has no idea how long she will be. There is no point in having an appointment here until all is in order. Both you and Mr Iliopolakis have to sign all the papers before both solicitors. It has to be at the same time. It is called an exchange of contracts.'

'I know what it is called,' snapped back Vasilis. 'I am prepared to wait until ten tomorrow. If the papers are not ready for signing then I shall be leaving.'

'It is Saturday tomorrow, sir. We do not usually open on a Saturday.'

'Then you will have to make an exception. Now get back on the 'phone and tell the other solicitor the deadline I have stipulated. If there is any problem with him and Mr Iliopolakis being here by ten tomorrow morning I shall return to Heraklion tonight.' Vasilis glared at the solicitor.

'I am sure the other Mr Iliopolakis is equally anxious to complete and return to Athens.' Mr Skoufakis tried to placate his irate client.

Marion bought a drink from the taverna across the road and sat under a tree whilst she drank it. She felt guilty about the way she had spoken to Cathy and leaving her room. She would have to go back and make amends.

Cathy appeared to be asleep when she entered, but turned her head as Marion closed the door.

'I'm sorry, Cathy.'

Cathy looked at her friend, her eyes were red and swollen where she had been crying. 'I wish we'd never come here.'

Marion took her hand. 'I shouldn't have spoken to you like that this morning.' She sighed heavily. 'I thought it might encourage you to try. You seemed so excited when you told me you'd walked.'

'I think it was just a reaction thing. My legs feel lifeless again.'

'Would you try, just once, to please me?' begged Marion.

Cathy looked at her dubiously.

'Think how pleased your parents would be if when they visited tonight you were able to walk over to the door when they left,' persisted Marion.

'Suppose I fall?'

'I'll be right beside you. I'll put your chair over by the door. I'll even hold your elbow if you think that would give you confidence.'

'I don't know. I just feel so miserable.'

'Of course you do. You're lying in here when you should be on the beach. You're pumped full of antibiotics and they always give people depression.'

'I just wish I'd never met Vasilis. I suppose I'm one of those stupid females who always fall for the wrong man.'

Marion chewed at her lip. She wished she had not given her word that she would not disclose the terrible dilemma that confronted Vasilis, but she did not think Cathy would be any happier if she understood the situation.

'Forget him for now. I'm sure he has a good reason for not coming to see you.'

'So am I! His wife realised what he was up to and put a stop to his philandering. He's worthless.' Despite her harsh words Cathy's eyes filled with tears.

Marion pulled back the light sheet that covered Cathy's legs. 'Has the doctor been in yet to look at your leg?'

'No. Why? Does it look worse?'

Marion shook her head. 'I can't see under the dressing, but there's no redness or swelling. You must be responding well to the new antibiotics. Now, do you want to put your slippers on or would you prefer to be barefoot?'

'You're determined, aren't you?'

'I want you to try. That's all I ask. Please, Cathy.'

Reluctantly Cathy lifted her legs over the side of the bed and sat with her feet resting on the cold marble floor. Tentatively she pushed herself upright and stood uncertainly. 'Maybe if I had my crutches.'

Marion shook her head. 'You don't walk properly with those. You just swing yourself forwards and take the weight on your arms. That's not walking.' She pushed the wheelchair over by the door and took Cathy's elbow. 'Come on. You can lean on me. Four steps, that's all.'

'I feel dizzy.' Cathy sat back on her bed again.

'Rubbish.' Marion spoke briskly. 'You've no reason to feel dizzy. You're just making excuses. If you can manage to walk to the chair I'll see if I can get you some sticks. You won't have the same support from them as you have from crutches and you'll have to move your legs.'

'Why don't you get some now?'

'Because I want to see you walk first. Once you've proved to yourself that you can do it once you'll want to do it again, believe me.'

'Because you're a nurse.' Cathy smiled wryly.

'Exactly. Now, up you get.'

Cautiously Cathy stood again, this time letting Marion take her elbow. 'I can't,' she said lamely.

'Yes, you can. Don't think about it. Just lift one foot and put it slightly in front of the other.'

Wobbling precariously Cathy finally moved her right foot forward.

'Now the left one. That's good. Do it again.'

With small, halting, steps Cathy finally reached her chair and sank into it. Beads of perspiration were standing out on her forehead. Marion smiled triumphantly.

'You see. You *can* walk.'

Cathy shook her head. 'That's not walking.'

'It's a start. All you need is to get your confidence back and practise. When you've got your breath back you can walk back to the bed.'

'Not again now. I'll wheel myself back.'

'No you won't. I've put the brake on. You either walk or sit here for the rest of the afternoon.'

'Marion!'

'I mean it, Cathy. You walked over here so there's no reason why you can't walk back.'

Cathy looked at her friend's obstinate face and sighed. 'Come on then.'

'I'm not holding you this time.'

'You must.'

Marion shook her head. 'I'll keep my hand just under your arm. If there's a problem I'm there, but you don't need to lean on me.'

'I don't want to fall and hurt my legs.'

'You won't, believe me.'

Marion waited until Cathy had taken a deep breath and pushed herself into a standing position. She moved alongside, her hand hovering just below Cathy's elbow, but not touching her.

'That's fabulous,' she announced when Cathy regained the bed. 'Ten minutes rest and then we'll do it again.'

Basil began to hurry Rebecca along the road to the waterfront. 'It's too hot to walk at this speed,' complained Rebecca. 'There's at least twenty minutes before Manolis is due back.'

'You said ten when we were in the shop.'

'I only said ten because I knew how long you would stay there talking if I didn't make you move. Besides, from here you can see when a boat is approaching. Why don't we sit there and wait?'

Basil shook his head. 'I want to make sure I'm where he moors. I don't want to miss him.'

Rebecca shrugged. Where she had suggested sitting there was no shade so she would be no worse off sitting on a bollard on the quay. Her feet were swelling from the heat and she would really like to dip them in the sea.

Basil scanned the bay where a number of small boats could be seen making their way back to the shore. As they neared their berths he walked forward and stood to one side whilst the passengers climbed back onto the shore, a boy on the quay helping them to keep their balance as they left the rocking boat.

Basil walked forward. 'Are you going to Spinalonga?'

'No. That was the last trip for today. Ten tomorrow I shall be going again. You can book a ticket in advance if you want.' Manolis did not even look up at him as he secured the mooring.

'You don't fancy a trip to Preveli I suppose?'

This time Manolis did look up. 'Vasilis? I don't believe it.' He jumped ashore and clasped Basil in his arms. 'My friend. Is it really you? After all this time? You've come back.'

Their arms around each other Basil began to lead Manolis over to where Rebecca was sitting. 'You must meet my wife.'

'Your wife?' Manolis stopped and looked at Rebecca from the distance.' You have married again? That is good news.'

'You saved my life and she saved my sanity.'

'No, no. You saved my life, remember.' Manolis took off his old fisherman's cap and showed Basil the holes.

Basil shook his head. 'When I came to you after the war I was suicidal. You understood. You looked after me as if I was a helpless child. Without your care I would not have survived.'

Manolis squirmed uncomfortably. 'So, we are equal. Let me meet your wife. Does she speak Greek?'

'No. She is English.'

'You did not teach her?'

'There was no need. I did not plan to return to Crete.'

'But you are here now. That is all that matters. You have come for a holiday? To show her where you fought the war? That is why you wish to go to Preveli?'

'I don't want to go to Preveli,' laughed Basil. 'That was just to get your attention and see if you recognised me.'

'You look the same. The hair, it is a little grey, but...' Manolis shrugged and spread his hands, 'we are all a little older.' Basil did not mention the amount of weight the man had accumulated had made him almost unrecognisable as the young fisherman he had known thirty years before.

Manolis held out his gnarled hand to Rebecca. 'I am pleased to meet you, Vasilis's wife.'

'Her name is Rebecca. How is your wife?'

Manolis beamed. 'She is still the joy of my life.' He crossed himself. 'May she be with me forever.'

Basil crossed himself also and a stricken look came across Manolis's face. 'Forgive me. I was forgetting.'

'I went to the memorial,' said Basil. 'I've come to say thank you.'

'Thank you? There is no need for thanks. You had trusted me to have it erected. I would not betray your trust in me.'

'It's very beautiful. Have you seen it?'

Manolis nodded. 'I went up there, when Flora went to Athens, but come, why are we talking here? We must go back to the house. Your wife must meet my wife. We have much to talk about.'

Rebecca looked around the small room of Manolis's cottage curiously. The furniture was plain and cheap and the walls whitewashed, adorned only by a single portrait of a man; a television set took up most of one wall with a settee placed far too close to the large screen. On every available surface there was a potted plant which gave colour to the otherwise drab room. She handed the present to Flora and watched whilst the woman undid the wrapping deftly with her right hand. Flora drew out the paper weight and gasped. She turned it around in her hand, watching as the light reflected from the different coloured surfaces. Basil smiled at Rebecca. She had chosen wisely.

'It is so beautiful. The most beautiful thing I have except my cross.' She fingered the ornate cross that hung round her neck. 'Look Manolis.'

Manolis smiled at her. 'We will find a special place to show it off.'

Flora looked around the room. 'There,' she said. 'If you put a small shelf beneath Yannis's portrait it can sit there.'

Manolis nodded. It would be a fitting place to display the paper weight, mementoes of the two most influential men in his life. He opened the cupboard in the corner and brought out a bottle of raki, whilst Flora hurried into the kitchen and returned with small glasses.

'You may not like this,' Basil warned Rebecca. 'It is pure spirit.'

'Don't drink too much, Basil. You have to drive back to Heraklion, remember.'

Basil nodded. He had not touched raki for years and remembered how strong the liquor was. 'No more than two,' he promised.

Rebecca sat there and Flora sensed the woman was thoroughly bored, whilst the men talked non-stop, reminiscing, laughing and, raising their glasses to each other. Flora stood up and beckoned to Rebecca to follow her. She took her out through the kitchen and into the small garden at the back of the house.

Rebecca caught her breath. The garden was a riot of colour. Everywhere flowers grew in profusion, dominated by geraniums. Flora smiled proudly. She loved her house, but had never considered adding colour to the interior. The garden, with its multitude of colours was her passion. Rebecca wished she was able to ask how she accomplished so much with only one arm. She blushed as she realised the question would be indelicate and was quite pleased she did not speak Greek and had been unable to embarrass both of them.

Flora pointed to a flower and said the name in Greek. Rebecca smiled delightedly and told her the English name, until it became almost a competition between them to name the flowers in the others language. Basil heard the two women laughing together in the garden and smiled at Manolis.

'I wish they could talk properly to each other. I think they would become friends. They have both been very patient with us, but we must leave you. I have to drive back to Heraklion and also call at the hospital to visit my daughter.'

'Your daughter is ill?'

Basil shook his head and explained how she had saved a child from drowning, but hurt her legs whilst doing so.

'Of course. The beautiful lady in the wheelchair. I was forgetting she was your daughter.' Manolis leaned forward confidentially. 'Is the young man your son?'

Basil sighed deeply. 'I wish I knew. He is the reason I have come to Crete. He telephoned me in England and asked me to come over to see if I could identify him. He was no more than a baby the last time I saw him.' Basil spread his hands.

'There is no way you can find out?'

'The Germans didn't keep records of the villagers they shot,' he said bitterly. 'If I had thought he had survived I would never have returned to England. I would have searched for him until I found him and stayed here to be a father to him.'

Manolis nodded soberly. He had never bothered to return to Skinaria to see if his affair with Eleni had resulted in a child being born. Once back in Aghios Nikolaos and finding Flora still alive he had put the girl out of his mind. He lifted the bottle to refill their glasses and Basil placed his hand across his own.

'I told Rebecca I would only have two glasses and I've already had more. If we stay longer I am likely to drink two bottles.'

'You will come to visit us again before you leave?'

Basil hesitated. 'I cannot promise.'

'Please, you will try to come again. I will catch some fish and Flora will cook for you. We will spend the whole night drinking and talking.'

Saturday

Christos Iliopolakis was most apologetic for the delay Vasilis had experienced and the pressure that had been put upon him to sign immediately.

'I returned from Australia to see Uncle Stergios before he died,' he said. 'I was his closest relative and felt it was my duty to see him one more time. When I found he had left the disputed land to me I was not happy. What would I do with it? I asked the solicitor if I could sign it over to your uncle and he said that was impossible. The Will said I could do as I wished with the land provided it did not go to Elias Iliopolakis. He pointed out that my son might need it at a future date, or want to sell it to you. By then the government would probably have stepped in and claimed it as derelict land. I suggested that the land was split between your son and mine and they will inherit when they become of age. How they sort it out will be between them.' He looked at Vasilis earnestly through the thick lens of his glasses.

'I do hope they will be more sensible than their uncles. The other problem, of course, is that both boys are too young to sign in their own right. We have to sign on their behalf and the land has to be legally transferred within six months of Uncle Stergios's death. I need to return to Australia as soon as possible. The firm have been very good extending my leave, but there is a limit to their patience. I have no idea when I would be able to return to Greece again. You do understand, don't you? I wasn't trying to be difficult.' He gave a thin smile. 'It was certainly not my idea to sit in the plane on the runway for a couple of hours.'

Vasilis shook his relative's hand and wished him well. He felt guilty that he had not offered to spend time with the man and get to know him, but with the papers finally signed and safely stowed beneath his seat all he wanted was to return to Heraklion as speedily as possible.

He would take the necklace with him when he visited Cathy and it would be a farewell gift. After his request to the doctor he was at least secure in the knowledge that she would still be in the hospital and had not been taken back to England by her family.

Basil followed Rebecca down the matting towards the edge of the sea. He had delayed going out into the sunshine until he had drunk numerous cups of black coffee. His head felt like cotton wool after drinking a considerable quantity of the raw spirit the previous evening.

'Where do you want to sit?'

'As close as possible,' she replied. 'There are couple of loungers free down here.'

Rebecca placed her bag on the sand, sat on the lounger and shook her mules from her feet. 'Shall we swim before we get too hot?'

Basil nodded and pulled his shirt over his head.

Panayiotis saw them making themselves comfortable and shook his head. They could not sit there. He had strict instructions from Vasilis to keep those loungers free for whenever the girl in the wheelchair came down to the beach with her friend. He knew it was unlikely that she would be coming down today but he was not prepared to take the chance. He hurried across, waving his hands.

'No, no,' he called shaking his head.

'That's the man I was telling you about,' said Rebecca.

'I'll see what he's on about.'

Basil turned to Panayiotis and smiled, speaking in Greek. 'Good morning, what's the problem?'

'This space is reserved. It is for the girl who has to use a wheelchair.'

'Well she won't be coming down today.'

Panayiotis stood there uncertainly. 'I cannot allow you to sit there. Mr Vasilis's orders.'

'Really. Well Mr Vasilis can come and speak to me himself if he objects to me sitting here.'

Panayiotis looked at the grim faced man before him. He had not seen him at the hotel before, but he was definitely familiar. He shrugged and turned away. He could not force them to move. He began to walk back up the matting to the patch of shade where he would spend most of his day, keeping an eye on the beach and walking up to the swimming pool occasionally to ensure there were no problems there.

He had almost reached his seat when he turned and looked back at the couple. He drew in his breath sharply and began to run back down the matting.

'Mr Vasilis. Mr Vasilis.'

Basil looked up; expecting to see Vasilis walking down the beach, instead Panayiotis almost threw himself into his arms.

'You're Mr Vasilis, the Englishman who lived here, aren't you?

Basil took a step backwards and frowned.

'You *are* Mr Vasilis. Don't you remember me? I'm Panayiotis. I used to visit you in the village.'

'Panayiotis?' Basil looked at the man in amazement. 'You're Panayiotis? I thought you were dead.'

Panayiotis held out his hand. Basil ignored it and opened his arms, clasping the man to him. 'Sit down, man and tell me what happened to you.'

Panayiotis perched on the end of the lounger. He shook his head dolefully. 'Bad things. The Germans thought I had some information that would be useful to them. They tried to make me tell them.'

'What information did they want?'

'They wanted to know where you had gone. Who you were meeting. Had you joined the resistance.' He gave a chuckle. 'I could not tell them what I did not know.'

Basil looked at the man keenly. He bore no resemblance to the young man he had known when he had lived on the island previously. 'What did they do to you?'

Panayiotis grimaced. 'They pulled my teeth, one by one.'

Basil shuddered. He could imagine the agonies the man had endured. He laid his hand on the man's arm. 'How long did they hold you?'

'I don't remember. Probably a week. It seemed like eternity at the time.'

'What did you do when they released you?'

'I crawled back to my home. My mother tended me as best she could, but I was in so much pain. My gums were bleeding, I could not eat. I had jagged stumps left in my mouth, the nerves exposed. I could not eat, even to drink was painful. She was convinced I was going to die. Finally I went to the hospital and the dentist there treated me.' He shook his head. 'I never want to see a dentist again.'

'Didn't he give you anaesthetic?'

Panayiotis nodded. 'It was afterwards. I can still remember how my mouth throbbed. For weeks on end I did nothing but sit with my head in my hands. I had infections in the gums and there were no pain killers.' He gave his ugly grimace that was supposed to be a smile. 'Enough about me. What happened to you? Were you captured?'

Rebecca touched her husband's arm. 'I'm getting hot. I'm going in for a swim. You stay and talk.'

Basil nodded. 'I'll explain to you later. Panayiotis and I know each other from before the war.' He turned back to Panayiotis and began to tell him how he had spent the war years, first sailing half way around Crete with Manolis, then walking to the mountains and living with the andartes. 'I finally returned and found what they had done to my village, to my wife, my child.' Basil's voice broke and tears filled his eyes. 'I said I would never return to Crete.'

'But you are here now?'

'I had to come. My daughter, the girl in the wheelchair, she met this man Vasilis. He wants to marry her.'

A broad grin spread across Panayiotis's face, showing his toothless gums. 'That is good. She will make him happy again.'

Basil shook his head. 'It can't be. He could be my son.'

'Your son? But you said your son was shot by the Germans at the village.'

Basil sighed deeply. 'That is what I always believed. This man telephoned me and said he came from that area. His mother was Katerina and she had died before the end of the war. He had been brought up by his relatives in Chania. He does not know who his father was; he only knows he was an English man.'

Panayiotis looked at Basil in amazement. 'You think he is your son?'

Basil nodded sombrely. 'He could be.'

Panayiotis shook his head. 'It is not possible.'

Basil shrugged. 'It could be. How can we prove one way or another? All the records were destroyed.'

Panayiotis shook his head again. 'No, he is not your son. I know he is not your son.'

Basil gripped his arm. 'You know? How do you know?'

'I was at the hospital when his mother arrived for her dental treatment. Her name was Katerina, but she was not your wife. She had married an Englishman and her family disapproved. They did not like him. Although she lived only a few doors from her mother they did not speak. Most of the village did not speak to her.' Panayiotis stopped and thought. 'It was sad, really. There was nothing wrong with Barry, except his eyes. One was brown and the other was blue. You didn't notice this until you were close to him, but the villagers thought he had been touched by the devil and shunned him, so they avoided her as well. If anyone did visit his wife he would leave the house and wait outside until they had left.'

'What happened to him?'

Panayiotis shrugged. 'The Germans shot him.'

Basil stared at him aghast. 'Just because he had odd eyes?'

'Probably being English had something to do with it as well.'

'Are you sure he was Vasilis's father?'

'Quite sure. Vasilis was with his mother at the hospital. She was waiting for Penelope, Elias's wife, who was a relative. Penelope was going to take the boy back to stay with them in Chania whilst Katerina was in hospital. It was only to be for three or four days. She was not worried about having the anaesthetic. She had been having dental treatment since she was a child. She told me it was simple, I would feel no pain, I had nothing to worry about.' Panayiotis shook his head. 'Poor lady. I heard afterwards that she had not recovered.'

Basil sat immobile. 'Tell me if I am understanding you properly. My Greek is rusty after so many years. You were at the hospital for your treatment at the same time as a woman called Katerina from another village. She was also married to an Englishman and had a son, Vasilis.'

Panayiotis nodded vigorously. 'The Katerina I met at the hospital was definitely not your wife. I knew your wife and your son. Your Katerina had curly hair and a beautiful smile. This lady had straight hair and her teeth were crooked when she smiled.'

Basil hugged the man to him. 'Thank you, Panayiotis. I am indebted to you.' Basil's voice broke. 'I wanted to think I had found my son; then I would think of my daughter. She suffers enough being unable to walk.'

Panayiotis frowned. 'She cannot walk?'

Basil shook his head. 'A couple of steps, no more.'

'But she walked from her chair to the pool to save Mr Vasilis's son.'

'I don't know how she reached the pool, but I do know she cannot walk.' Basil stood up and cupped his hands to his mouth. 'Rebecca,' he called, 'Rebecca.' He waved wildly to her indicating that she should return to the beach. 'You must meet my wife. She does not speak Greek, of course.'

Rebecca swam languidly back to the shore and walked the few yards to the lounger. 'It is beautiful in there. Why did you call me out, Basil?'

'I want you to meet Panayiotis. He has given me some wonderful news. Vasilis is not my son.'

Rebecca dried her hands on her towel and held one out to Panayiotis. He ignored it, held her shoulders gently and kissed her on both cheeks. Blushing with embarrassment, Rebecca sat down on the lounger. She took Basil's hand. 'Tell me,' she said.

Vasilis took a deep breath and entered Cathy's room. He had thrust the papers at his uncle, removed the necklace from the safe and rushed from the hotel to the hospital, stopping only to purchase a large bunch of roses. He stopped in amazement, Cathy was standing beside her bed, Marion at her side and she was taking a tentative step towards the door.

'Cathy!'

'How dare you enter my room without knocking?' Cathy glared at him.

Vasilis stopped, nonplussed. 'I'm sorry,' he stuttered. 'I didn't think. I wanted to see you.'

Cathy felt behind her for her bed and sank back onto the mattress. 'I have no wish to see you. Not now or ever again.'

'Cathy, please, I have to talk to you. I have to explain.'

'There's nothing to talk about. I don't want to hear your excuses.'

Vasilis shook his head. 'I have no excuses for you, but you need to understand why I cannot marry you.'

'I know exactly why you can't marry me. Go back to your wife. I feel sorry for her, married to a man like you.'

Vasilis looked at Marion appealingly. 'Please, Marion, ask Cathy to listen to me. You understand what has happened.'

Cathy turned to Marion. 'What do you know? Why haven't you told me?'

'I promised Vasilis and your father that I would say nothing.'

'My father? What has he got to do with this? He has no right to interfere with my life. Go away, go away both of you and leave me alone.' Cathy lifted her legs back up on the bed and pulled the pillow up around her ears.

Vasilis clenched his fists. He wanted to pull the pillow away from her face and cover her in kisses, to hold her to him and comfort her.

Marion touched his arm. 'I think we should leave her for a while and I'd like to know why you've been avoiding us for the last few days. I understood you were coming to see Cathy on Thursday. Today is Saturday,' she added grimly.

Vasilis's shoulders slumped and he followed Marion meekly out into the corridor. 'I had to go to Chania on Thursday. It was an important legal matter that could not wait. I expected to be back by the evening and I was delayed until this morning. I telephoned the hospital and insisted the doctor kept Cathy here until I returned. I could not risk her parents taking her back to England before I had spoken to her again.'

'You asked the doctor to keep her in hospital?'

'There is no infection in her leg. It was an excuse. Please persuade Cathy to listen to me. You know how important it is that she understands.'

Marion frowned. 'I'll try. I don't know how successful I'll be.'

'I'll wait here until you call me. I'll wait all day and all night if necessary.' He thrust the bouquet of flowers into Marion's hands. 'At least give her these from me. I feel foolish standing here clutching them.'

Basil pulled his shirt and shorts back on, thrusting his feet into his sandals. 'Hurry up,' he said to Rebecca. 'We have to find Vasilis.'

'We don't know where he is. He's gone to Chania, remember.'

'Someone must know where we can contact him. His uncle may be back by now. He's sure to know.'

'You go up to reception and see what you can find out whilst I get dried and dressed. I'll meet you up there.' Rebecca draped the towel around herself and began to remove her costume.

Basil hurried up the path, his head forgotten, and pushed open the door to the reception. 'I need to see Mr Vasilis urgently,' he told the young woman behind the desk.

'You have just missed him, sir.'

'Missed him? Where has he gone?'

'I don't know. He did not tell me. Maybe Mr Elias could help you?'

'Where is he? Let me speak to him.'

'I will see if he is free,' she answered frostily and walked to the door marked "private" before knocking discreetly and entering. Elias frowned at the interruption. He was busy studying the papers Vasilis had left with him; so far all seemed to be in order.

'What does he want?'

'He asked for Mr Vasilis. I told him he had just missed him so he asked for you.'

'Tell him I'm busy and Mr Vasilis has gone to the hospital.'

With trepidation the receptionist relayed the message to Basil, expecting him to insist on seeing Elias. To her surprise he turned on his heel and she saw him beckoning urgently to his wife as she walked up the path.

'He's at the hospital,' called Basil and Rebecca increased her pace.

Basil burst through the door of the hospital, Rebecca following him, thankful they had finally arrived. Basil had driven recklessly, ignoring the speed limit and her frequent requests to slow down. Vasilis stood there, deep in conversation with Marion and they both looked up at his arrival.

'Vasilis,' Basil approached him with outstretched arms. 'You are not my son. I know you are not my Vasilis.'

'You know?' Vasilis looked at him in disbelief. 'How do you know?'

'Panayiotis. He knew your parents.' Basil felt the energy draining from him and his pounding head returning.

'Is that true?'

'Quite true. I would not lie about something so important.'

A look of tremendous relief crossed Vasilis's face; then he gave a delighted smile. 'So I can marry Cathy?'

'Legally there is no reason why you should not.'

Vasilis turned to Marion. 'Did you understand?'

Marion shook her head. 'Not a word.'

'I can marry Cathy. Please, make her see me, make her listen to me. I will explain the problems to her and then she will understand.'

Marion sighed. 'I'll do my best.'

Marion entered Cathy's room. She had turned on her side and her shoulders heaved with sobs. Marion placed her arms around her.

'Cathy, please, stop crying and listen to me.'

'It's no good you trying to persuade me to see him. I won't,' she muttered between her tears.

'You have to see him, Cathy. He has a right to explain what happened.'

'I won't believe his explanations,' declared Cathy stubbornly.

'You must at least listen. You could regret it for the rest of your life if you refuse. Come on, dry your eyes and wash your face. You don't want him to see you like that.'

'I don't want to see him,' repeated Cathy.

'I'm insisting,' Marion spoke firmly. 'If you refuse to see him in here I shall ask the nurses to get you into your chair and wheel you out into the hallway. Do you really want your private business discussed where everyone can hear?'

'They wouldn't understand.'

'I think most of them would. I've found they speak quite good English.'

Marion handed Cathy a tissue and waited whilst she scrubbed at her face. She straightened Cathy's sheet over her legs and passed her hair brush. 'I want you to be looking your usual beautiful self,' she explained.

Cathy looked at her suspiciously. 'What's going on?'

'You'll see.' Marion squeezed her shoulders and gave a broad smile. 'I'll tell him to come in and I'll be back later.'

'I'd rather you stayed here with me.'

Marion shook her head. 'I'll be back in about an hour.'

Marion walked with Cathy's parents out into the hospital garden. 'Have you really found out that Vasilis is not your son?' she asked Basil.

Basil passed his hand over his throbbing head. 'Panayiotis knew his parents. Is there somewhere I can get some coffee? I was drinking raki last night and I'm suffering today.'

'Let's go to the taverna.' Marion smiled mischievously. 'I have some pretty effective headache tablets with me. One of the benefits of being a nurse. I'll give you a couple provided you promise to tell me the whole story.'

Vasilis stood at the foot of Cathy's bed. He felt suddenly at a loss for words. 'May I sit down?' he asked eventually and Cathy nodded.

'I want to thank you first for saving the life of my son.' Vasilis gazed at her earnestly.

'Someone should have been with him,' replied Cathy accusingly.

'Of course. Eleni had to telephone to the garage about her car and she thought Uncle Elias was looking after him. He thought the receptionist was watching him but she became involved with some visitors.'

'Why didn't you tell me you were married?' she asked, challenging him with her eyes.

'I'm not married, Cathy. I divorced my wife. I planned to tell you last weekend. I had arranged for my son to come up to the hotel so you could meet him. I hoped you would accept each other.'

'So who is the woman who was with your son on the beach?'

'I call her my sister. We were brought up together. She looks after him during the week and at the weekends I spend my time with them. He must not forget his father. I do not remember mine.' Vasilis lifted Cathy's limp hand to his lips. 'I love you, Cathy. I want to marry you, and now it is possible.'

Cathy frowned. 'If you are divorced why wasn't it possible before?'

'You remember the memorial? You realised the man who had erected it in memory of his family was your father. My family name is Iliopolakis, the same as many of the villagers mentioned. A terrible thought occurred to me. Suppose I was really your brother?'

'What?' Cathy opened her eyes wide and sat up straighter. 'You can't be. The name of my father's son was on the memorial.'

'My father was an Englishman. I do not know what happened to him. My mother's name was Katerina and I knew she had died in the hospital. Relatives brought me up and I was known by their name. Until then I had never been interested in finding out about my parents. Suddenly it became very important for me to know.' Vasilis smiled at her. 'Was it possible that your father's wife and son had not been shot?'

'Why didn't you tell me?'

'I could not trust myself to be alone with you and behave as a brother should. I went up to Chania and brought back all the family photographs and showed them to my uncle. He could not recognise my father in any of them. I visited Manolis again and asked him if I looked like my father. He could not say. In desperation I telephoned your father in England and asked him to come over immediately. I hoped he would know by looking at me, but he did not.'

'I thought they had come because I was in hospital.'

'I asked them to let you think that. I talked to Marion, told her the problem, and asked her not to tell you either. I had to know the truth before I spoke to you.'

'And now you know?' Cathy could feel her heart beating faster.

Vasilis nodded. 'Panayiotis knew both my parents. My father was definitely not your father.'

'Panayiotis – the old man on the beach? Why didn't he tell you before?'

'I had never asked. He recognised your father as the Vasilis who had lived in one of the villages behind Chania. Your father told him why he was here and Panayiotis immediately confirmed that I was not his son. He arrived here to tell me just after you had thrown me out of your room. You will not throw me out again, will you, Cathy?' He looked at her beseechingly.

Cathy withdrew her hand from Vasilis's and placed it around

his neck, pulling his head down towards her. 'I really do love you, Vasilis.'

Basil looked at his watch. The tablets Marion had given him had certainly helped his head or else the effects of the raki had had time to wear off.

'I can't sit here any longer. I need to know what has happened with Cathy and Vasilis. There could be arrangements to make.'

'What arrangements?'

'We may have to stay here longer than we originally planned. I shall want to get to know this man considerably better if I'm going to agree to him marrying my daughter.'

Rebecca looked at her husband in disbelief. 'Basil, you have never denied Cathy anything she wanted in her whole life. You are not going to start forbidding her to get married! This is an excuse so we can stay here.'

Basil smiled sheepishly. 'Would you mind?'

'Of course not. I'd like to finally spend a day on the beach.'

WEEK FOUR – JUNE 1973

Sunday

Vasilis drove to Hersonissos with Cathy and Marion, Basil and Rebecca following in the car behind. Cathy drew in her breath as he stopped before a large house set in its own grounds just outside the town.

'This is your house?'

'No,' he smiled. 'This is Eleni's house. Either I stay here or I am at the hotel. I gave her my house in return for looking after Vasi. She and her husband had only a small apartment. It was not suitable.'

Cathy swallowed. She now felt incredibly nervous about meeting Vasilis's son.

Vasilis lifted Cathy's chair from the boot of the car, bending to open it and ensure it was safe before Cathy sat in it. Marion raised her eyebrows at her friend. 'Now?' she asked and Cathy nodded.

Cathy placed her feet firmly on the ground and Marion took her elbow. She pulled herself upright and walked haltingly towards Vasilis. He looked up at her in disbelief.

'You can walk! You do not need your chair?'

'I will do. I can't walk very far yet.' Cathy smiled. 'I wanted it to be a surprise for you.'

Vasilis wheeled Cathy past the side of the house to the garden. 'We will have some refreshment in the garden and you will meet my sister and her husband. Vasi is waiting to say thank you for saving his life.'

'Oh, Vasilis, please. He doesn't have to say anything. Anyone would have jumped into a pool to pull a child out.'

'Anyone who could walk and jump would do so. Not someone who was sitting in a wheelchair. Besides, Eleni tells me he was up at five this morning. He wanted to see the lady without legs.' He positioned Cathy's chair beneath an umbrella and called Vasi over to him. He put his hand in his pocket and withdrew a package that he handed to his son and nodded.

Vasi walked over to Cathy, holding his father's hand. 'Pappa says I have to say thank you. I am sorry I was a naughty boy.'

Cathy looked at him and stretched out her arms. He regarded her doubtfully for a moment then allowed her to give him a brief hug before dropping the package in her lap and retreating. 'He didn't have to give me anything. What is it, Vasilis?'

'You will have to open it to find out.'

Carefully Cathy removed the wrapping to expose a jeweller's case. She opened it curiously and gasped in surprise. 'Vasilis! The necklace. You cannot give me that. It cost a fortune.'

Vasilis shrugged. 'My son is worth more than a necklace. Besides, you remember you suggested if you went back every day the jeweller would lower his price? I decided to take your advice.'

Cathy fingered the necklace carefully. 'It is beautiful. Thank you, Vasilis. Thank you, Vasi.' She held it up so he would understand she was thanking him for his present.

'You're going to have to learn Greek, Cathy,' smiled Marion.

Cathy pulled a face. 'It might be easier if I helped Vasi to learn English.'

'Marion, Vasi also wants to thank you.'

'Me? Whatever for?'

'You brought Cathy to Crete. You have been a good friend to both of us.'

Again Vasi was handed a small parcel and pushed towards Marion. He smiled shyly at her as she took it from him and she said thank you to him in Greek. He replied and she shook her head. 'Please tell him that my Greek is limited to please and thank you.'

Marion opened her own gift and exclaimed in delight over the small gold earrings. 'They're perfect, Vasilis. Thank you. I wish we had brought presents for Vasi.'

'Another time, besides, he needs nothing. I try not to spoil him, but it is difficult for me. Now, we will have a drink, yes? We will have many toasts. The first one is to Cathy.'

Vasilis lifted a glass from the tray Eleni was handing round and held it aloft.

Basil touched Rebecca's arm. 'Careful. This could go on for hours. Each time your glass is empty it will be refilled.'

Rebecca nodded. She understood how easy it would be to have far too much to drink in a short space of time. 'I hope Cathy knows.'

'I'll tell her if I can prise Vasilis away from her side for a moment.'

'You like him, Basil?'

Basil nodded. 'I respect him. Many men would have ignored the possibility that they could be closely related to the woman they loved. Others would have let her go away without any explanation, but he was determined to find out the truth, whatever the cost.'

'So you still want to stay here a bit longer to get to know him?'

Basil looked at Rebecca seriously. 'I'd forgotten how much I love this country.'

'What you are trying to say is that you want to come back?'

'We would be close to Cathy.'

Rebecca closed her eyes and took a deep breath. 'I'm not sure, Basil. It's all very unfamiliar to me at the moment.'

'I'm not suggesting that we live here permanently. We could get a little place of our own and have long holidays.'

Rebecca smiled. She knew her husband well enough by now to know that one holiday would merge into another. 'I'm willing to give a long holiday a try,' she said and Basil squeezed her arm.

As the sun dipped in the sky Eleni led the way into the lounge. She had provided small morsels of food that could be eaten easily in the fingers during the afternoon and now Rebecca saw there was a table set for a full meal.

'I will take Vasi up to bed and then we will eat,' she said to Vasilis.

Vasi shook his head. 'I don't want to go to bed.'

'It is time, Vasi. Look at the clock. The big hand is on twelve and the little one is on eight.'

'No,' repeated Vasi stubbornly. 'I want to stay up.'

Basil looked at his watch and realised Eleni had turned the clock on an hour. He listened to the interchange, sensing the small boy was on the verge of a tantrum due to tiredness from his early rise and the excitement of the day.

'Vasi,' said Basil in Greek. 'If I tell you a story will you go to bed then like a good boy?'

The child looked at him solemnly with large brown eyes, finally nodding his head.

'Come and sit on my knee.' Basil stretched out his hand and Vasi wriggled up onto Basil's leg. He gazed up expectantly at the man.

As Basil placed his arm around Vasi and looked down at him he felt a lump coming into his throat and tears filled his eyes. 'Once upon a time there was a little boy and his name just happened to be Vasilis,' he began.

It was a long time since a small boy had sat on his knee whilst he told him a story.

The saga begins with the compelling story of Yannis, who comes from the village of Plaka on the island of Crete. He attends school in the town of Aghios Nikolaos and gains a scholarship to the Gymnasium in Heraklion.

Whilst in Heraklion, he is diagnosed with leprosy, shattering his dreams of becoming an archaeologist. He is admitted to the local hospital for treatment and subsequently transferred to the hospital in Athens. The conditions in the hospital are appalling and the inmates finally rebel, resulting in their exile to Spinalonga, a leper colony just across the water from Yannis's home village.

The book tells the heart-rending account of his life on the small island, his struggle for survival, his loves and losses, along with that of his family on the mainland from 1918 to 1979.

The saga continues with Anna and goes on to relate stories based around other characters in his family.